ALL THE DAYS
OF THEIR LIVES

ALL THE DAYS OF THEIR LIVES

Betty McInnes

This first world edition published in Great Britain 2002 by
SEVERN HOUSE PUBLISHERS LTD of
9–15 High Street, Sutton, Surrey SM1 1DF.
This first world edition published in the USA 2002 by
SEVERN HOUSE PUBLISHERS INC of
595 Madison Avenue, New York, N.Y. 10022.

British Library Cataloguing in Publication Data

McInnes, Betty, 1928-
    All the days of their lives
    1. Domestic fiction
    I. Title
    823.9'14 [F]

    ISBN 0-7278-5858-0

Typeset by Palimpsest Book Production Ltd.,
Polmont, Stirlingshire, Scotland.
Printed and bound in Great Britain by
MPG Books Ltd., Bodmin, Cornwall.

One

'It'll be a miracle if the baby survives, Nurse,' the doctor said. He had discarded his frock coat and starched collar, but still he sweated in the stifling nursery.

The nurse looked into the cradle, an ornate affair that had held generations of well-off Rutherford babies, but the heavy woodwork only served to highlight the frailty of this tiny infant. 'It's a miracle she's survived a week! I've never seen a smaller wean. You could hold her in the palm o' your hand, the motherless mite!' She sighed. 'What a start to 1900! A Sabbath Hogmanay bodes ill for a'body, and sure enough, news from South Africa is terrible, there's sickness in the parish, and now tragedy in Angus House, with the laird's wife dead and this baby born before its time.' She touched the tiny mouth with a finger and felt a feeble pressure on the fingertip. 'At least she can suckle, Doctor!'

'The mother died two days ago. I wouldn't raise the bereaved husband's hopes if I were you,' he warned.

It was sad. The nurse wiped her eyes. 'Poor Mistress Rutherford! I'm glad the Colonel has two sons as comfort. This lass might have brought solace to the widower, but I'm afraid she'll follow her mother to the kirkyard.'

The infant's eyes opened. A tiny hand stretched upwards, searching vainly for a mother's love . . .

Less than half a mile away, down a rough track leading to the meal mill, Agnes Murdoch sang as she cleaned the brush braid of her Sunday skirt with fuller's earth, ammonia and benzine. She'd been kirked last Sunday after the birth of her baby, and the mucky weather had muddied her best skirt. She hung the

1

pungent-smelling garment on the scullery pulley and returned to the living room.

The Gowrie burn was in spate and her husband Dougal Murdoch was hard at work in the adjoining mill. Agnes smiled. She was happy when the mill was working full blast. Every turn of the water wheel meant money to the Murdochs. The wheat harvest had been good in 1899, but oats had suffered in an August drought and were dearer this winter. That meant more profit for her husband the miller. But one must always remember that oats are the mainstay of man and beast in Dundee, and have sympathy for the poor, she reminded herself.

The thick wall dividing the living quarters from the mill proper resounded to the thunderous rumble of the wheel. Faintly from within came the metallic clanking of cogs, gears, pulleys and chains as grindstones ground the grain.

'Mam, how d'you make an "H"?' Jamie Murdoch, Agnes's four-year-old son, was seated at the table writing on a school slate with a squeaky slate pencil. Patiently, she showed him. He was a bright lad who like herself had no bother with reading and writing. She was proud of his achievement. Jamie had a good grasp of the alphabet and could count, though the wee lad was not yet old enough to go to Gowrie School.

'How d'you spell Hannah, Mam?'

'Are you writing your baby sister's name, lovie?'

'Do you think she'd like me to write it?'

Agnes laughed. 'She's not a fortnight old and a bit young for reading, but yes, I think she would.' She was quietly pleased. Jamie had been disappointed when she gave birth to a girl on New Year's Day. He had hoped for a brother to share his endless games of marbles. But Jamie was a good-natured lad and was soon showing affection for the baby. He was proud as Punch last week when Hannah tipped the mill scales at a bouncing eight pounds two ounces.

With his mother's guiding hand Jamie printed the name, then remembered he was hungry. 'Is it stovies tonight, Mam?'

'Aye. You know it's always stovies, on a Monday.' She made lovely mashed potato mixed with roast beef gravy, tender scraps of meat left over from the Sunday joint and onions from plaited strings hanging in the storeroom. Tatties in the pit remained firm despite December frosts and were their mainstay. They were lucky at the Milton. The greater part of Angus estate lay on higher, hilly ground to the north, but soil on the lower level beside the Gowrie burn was rich river silt deposited over the years by the river Tay on its long journey through Perthshire to the sea.

'With ingins, Mam?'

'Of course, dear, plenty of onions!' Agnes took a quick peep into the top drawer of the dresser, where the baby lay asleep. The open drawer was the safest place, too high for dogs to lick the baby's face and too restricted for a cat to creep into unobserved. They said cats can draw the breath out of a newborn infant. Better safe than sorry! There was a cluster of snoozing cats in the ingle by the kitchen range, but they were doing useful service keeping warm a motherless lamb the shepherd had brought in last night. The first few days of 1900 had been mild, and though mild weather was a welcome break in a long winter, it brought beasts on, giving birth before their time. This reminded Agnes of poor Mrs Rutherford at the big house, who had lost her life last week after premature childbirth. The tragedy had shocked everyone, for Anne Rutherford was well liked in the short time she and her husband Charles had been living in Angus House. The shepherd said the laird was inconsolable. The Angus House servants were keeping mum on the condition of the baby, which was ominous, since they were the biggest blethers in the Carse.

The connecting door to the mill swung open and a blast of mechanical sound escaped as her husband Dougal Murdoch came through the doorway in a white haze of mill dust. He closed the door and dropped a quick kiss on her cheek.

'I've left Eck in charge of the bagging off. He might as well earn his corn and I'm starving. Is that stovies, love?'

3

Jamie answered. 'With ingins, Dad!'

Agnes laughed. Her husband's arm was round her waist. He leaned across and lifted the pot lid. Skin, hair and dungarees were powdered with floury dust and the clean smell of fresh-crushed grain clung to him.

She slapped his hand away playfully. 'Stop it, you big loon! I'll dish up while you wash.'

When they were seated she glanced proudly round the nicely set table. Dougal was saying grace, but her thoughts were wandering. I'll shear Jamie's curls before he goes to school when he's five, lest the boys call him names, she thought, but I'll mourn every snip of the scissors.

Baby Hannah wakened with a demanding cry just as they were finishing the meal. Dougal glanced towards the dresser. 'That one's impatient for the good things in life. I don't remember Jamie making such a fuss.'

Agnes picked up the crying baby. 'Och, baby cries are soon forgot!' She carried the infant through to the wash-house and changed her napkin in the warmth. The fire under the boiler was kept stoked night and day. Agnes took pride in a line of snow-white nappies flapping daily on the green. There wasn't a whiter wash to be found anywhere in the Carse of Gowrie. She kissed the indignant infant, who hadn't stopped bawling for an instant. 'There, my lambkin. All done.'

Returning to the living room, Agnes seated herself in the nursing chair, modestly draping her shoulders with a shawl before unbuttoning her bodice. Fortunately, she had more than enough milk to satisfy the hungry wean and there was immediate silence.

Dougal Murdoch allowed himself a pipe before returning to the mill. He sat smoking contentedly at the table watching his bonnie wife feed their lusty bairn. I'm a lucky man, he thought. Which brought their landlord's great loss to mind. He was hearty sorry for the man, though Colonel Rutherford's curt, military manner had tended to put Dougal's back up right from the start. Charles Rutherford was a career soldier forced to leave the army last year to run the family estate after the sudden death of his elder brother. He didn't know a thing about farming.

Jamie tugged his father's sleeve. 'Tell me the story about the steam engine, Dad!'

He sighed good naturedly. 'Well, it's a scunner when there's not enough water in the burn to turn the wheel, as you know, son. If we'd a steam engine to drive the mill we could work every day, no matter the weather. We could install new machinery, have rollers instead of grindstones, make refined white flour that refined folk want, instead of coarse-ground country stuff. We could make a fortune.'

'Why don't we, Dad?'

'Because we don't have a fairy godmother, and besides our landlord the laird—'

He broke off with a start as the front door was flung open. An icy draught flared the oil lamps, the rumbling splash of the wheel outside invaded the room and the dogs barked and growled. The tall man who had burst suddenly into their midst appeared so wild and mad, that Jamie had slid quietly beneath the table.

Dougal half-rose, then sank back as he recognized the visitor. Speak of the devil, Colonel Rutherford!

Charles Rutherford was bareheaded for once, an army greatcoat slung across his shoulders. He clutched the thick folds tightly to his chest. Dougal and Agnes stared. Their landlord was usually spruce and immaculate, but today he was dishevelled and out of breath as if he'd come running along the rutted track. He reached behind him with one mud-spattered boot and kicked the door shut. The lamplight steadied, the dogs stopped barking and silence fell. The Colonel stumbled towards Agnes, and stood staring down at the mother and child.

Dougal was outraged. 'For shame, sir! Kindly state your business and get out!'

'No, Dougal, wait!' Agnes said. Covering herself, she looked up at the anguished man. 'Is it your wee lass, Colonel? Is she—?'

'No, she's not dead, but the doctor says there's little hope.'

He was reputed to be a cold man, but she saw the shine of tears.

'Where there's life there's hope, sir,' she said.

'You think so? Look at her!' He drew aside a corner of the greatcoat to show the baby in the crook of his arm. All that could be seen was a tiny, wizened face swaddled in shawls.

Agnes was shocked. 'She's so small!'

'Almost too small to live.' He took a step closer. 'The midwife tells me you've milk and to spare, Mrs Murdoch. You could save her.'

'I . . . ?' But what if I can't? Agnes thought in panic. It would break my heart as well as the laird's. 'No, sir, I couldn't!'

'Please. You must!'

She looked at him. Fighting spirit was fierce in this soldier. What if his daughter had inherited it? Hadn't she already survived against all the odds? she thought. 'Very well, Colonel, I'll try.'

Dougal objected. 'Wait a minute, Agnes! This isn't a motherless lamb you're taking on; it's a premature baby. You'll get the blame if the worst happens.'

The Colonel swung round angrily. 'I swear she won't! I'll pay you handsomely, Murdoch.'

Dougal flushed. 'Keep your filthy money, it's mother's milk your bairn needs.'

Agnes gave her husband a warning glance. 'I'll nurse your child gladly, sir. Any money you give us will be used only for the bairn's comfort.'

She settled her own sleepy infant back in the drawer. Charles Rutherford grasped Agnes's hand and pressed it to his lips. 'Bless you, ma'am!' It was a gesture so out of character it took them all by surprise.

Agnes held the weightless bundle. 'You haven't told us her name.'

'She's christened Kirsty. It was her mother's wish.'

'Kirsty? That's a hardy name.'

'Yes. Maybe.' With a sad glance at his tiny daughter, he left as abruptly as he'd arrived.

'Well I'll be damned!' Dougal exploded. 'What a cheek! I thought you'd more pride than take his money.'

'His pride needed saving more than ours, Dougal. Would you rather he was indebted to us?'

He looked sheepish. 'Maybe you're right. Best keep this sad affair on a business footing.' Apprehensively, Dougal eyed the small bundle in Agnes's arms. He had a premonition that this fragile scrap of humanity meant serious trouble.

The tiny baby was a far greater challenge than a newborn lamb. Agnes was driven to despair many times, sure the battle for its life was lost. Kirsty sucked feebly and refused to put on weight. It seemed impossible she could survive, but somehow she did.

The weather was no help. January 1900 was unhealthily mild. Clammy fogs and mists rising from the river caused an epidemic of influenza. Agnes's huge washings hung damp and limp on the line and she was in constant terror the delicate baby would catch a fatal cold. Inside the Milton, fires blazed day and night to keep the little one warm and to dry steaming nappies. Dougal and Jamie complained. Agnes had endless patience for her fosterling, and no patience whatsoever with complaints.

Baby Hannah sensed a rival and was fractious and girny. Jamie also felt neglected. He had been the centre of attention before the arrival of two demanding babies, and now found his nose put out of joint. When he wasn't occupied writing his alphabet or playing lonely games of 'chuckie-stones', Jamie trailed miserably after Agnes and drove her wild with 'Why this?' and 'Why that?' Wisely, Dougal retreated to the mill, out of harm's way.

Kirsty Rutherford was still clinging to life when February arrived. Skies cleared and hard frost set in, the most severe since 1895. A thick crust of ice formed on the lade and the mill wheel ground to a halt. The cold intensified and the sky turned leaden-grey. Everyone in the Carse laid in stocks of oatmeal and potatoes and prepared for the worst.

Mountain ranges and hills to the north and west protect

Dundee from the ferocity of inland blizzards. Sometimes the coastal city escapes with light snowfalls when Perth, Strathmore and Glamis lie buried deep. But when easterly gales come howling unchecked across the North Sea bearing blizzards bred on Siberian steppes, the city cowers beneath a furious onslaught.

A violent easterly flung stinging drifts against the Milton windowpanes on the night of the fifteenth of February 1900. Agnes was so exhausted she would have slept through a bombardment of cannon, but she wakened instantly at Kirsty's first whimper. Fortunately, Hannah slept on as Agnes stumbled out of bed and crouched over one of the cradles beside the fire. 'Hush, my wee lamb!'

The baby stopped whimpering. She was wide awake, eyes bright in the firelight as she lay staring up at her foster-mother. It's not possible those eyes can focus properly yet, Agnes thought in surprise, yet I could swear the baby smiled at me! A grimace of colic, a trick of the light? Trembling, she reached into the cradle and lifted her out. Why had she not noticed there was more weight and substance to the little body? Agnes clasped the baby to her breast. All her prayers were answered on that wild, stormy night.

'Kirsty, you'll live!'

By the time she was four, Kirsty had worked out who was who. She had two brothers called George and Samuel Rutherford who lived in the big house. George was fourteen and Samuel eleven, and they were big schoolboys who attended boarding school. She met them so infrequently they were strangers. On the other hand, she saw Jamie Murdoch every day, but he was not her brother, he was Hannah's. He was a schoolboy too, eight years old and top of the class at Invergowrie school. Hannah Murdoch was four on New Year's Day just like Kirsty, but was not her twin, though Kirsty wished she was. She and Hannah loved one another, fought, yelled and shared secrets just as if they were sisters. Hannah was taller and had beautiful curly chestnut hair and sparkling hazel eyes. Kirsty's reflection, studied anxiously in the looking-glass, paled by comparison. A wee elfin face, large smokey-blue eyes with surprisingly long, dark lashes and silken silver-fair hair that refused to curl despite Agnes's efforts with curling tongs and rags. The latter were so lumpy that they caused much discomfort, which Kirsty endured, hoping that in the morning her hair would curl like Hannah's. It never did.

Still, not many little girls could boast two fathers. Kirsty had Dad Dougal – who by now was a devoted slave – and she also had a wonderful, godlike father who visited regularly.

Papa Rutherford was very tall and handsome. When he came to the Milton just to see her, Kirsty's chest would swell with such love and pride she was rendered speechless. Papa Rutherford's visits drove Hannah daft with jealousy. She would turn somersaults and show off her knickers, throw tantrums, rattle downstairs on the tin tray, all in an effort to attract his attention. It never worked. Papa Rutherford would sit Kirsty quietly on his knee and tell her stories, while Mam grimly removed a bruised and yelling Hannah from the scene.

Mam Murdoch, of course, was Kirsty's best-loved person, although Hannah insisted Mam belonged exclusively to Hannah and Jamie and had absolutely nothing whatsoever to do with Kirsty.

One beautiful summer's day in 1905, when the little girls were five, Kirsty's maternal grandmother came all the way from Edinburgh to see her. The visit was memorable because afterwards Kirsty's life changed.

As Lizzie Robb's carriage sped along the road to Agnes House, Kirsty's grandmother caught sight of three dusty children squatting in the ditch. She adjusted her spectacles to see them better. 'Who are those urchins, Charles?' she asked her son-in-law.

Charles glanced out and was surprised to see the children by the side of the busy road. The rascals had obviously escaped Agnes's vigilance to wave to the carriage. 'The smallest, dirtiest one rolling in the ditch is your granddaughter, ma'am, the other two are her foster-mother's bairns.'

'Indeed!' Lizzie Robb said grimly.

Charles hid a grin as the carriage turned in through the lodge gates. His mother-in-law was a brigadier's widow and seldom let him forget it. He quite welcomed the chance to take her down a gentle peg. The elderly lady said no more, but was not pleased. Fancy her granddaughter rolling about with ragamuffins in a dangerous ditch! She considered such behaviour an affront to her beloved daughter's memory.

Lizzie removed the viewing spectacles and dabbed her eyes with a scrap of lace. The carriage had left the road and travelled along the estate driveway, which she noted was rutted and ill-tended. Charles was obviously letting standards slip with no wife to keep him up to scratch. She must do something about this sad state of affairs. She decided to make a start with her granddaughter.

Agnes went into labour that night. It was a prolonged labour that had Dougal pacing the floor anxiously, his children sent hastily to the shepherd's wife. The foster-child, Kirsty, was despatched to the big house to become acquainted with her grandmother.

That afternoon, Agnes gave birth to another little girl. Later, she smiled contentedly as she and her husband examined the new arrival. 'This lass has such a bright wee face and the cornfields are bright with poppies today, I'm tempted to call her Poppy. What d'you think, Dougal?'

He laughed and kissed them both. 'Poppy? Well, it's unusual, love. Not a name you'd forget.'

So Poppy it was.

Agnes was resting in bed a few days after the birth when Dougal ushered in an unexpected visitor.

'Colonel Rutherford!' she exclaimed. 'Oh, it's kind of you to call!'

He came to the edge of the bed. 'I trust you're well, Mrs Murdoch, and the baby?'

'We're both grand, sir, thanks. I'm just a big fraud lying here, but Dougal insists I take this chance of a rest.'

Dougal laughed. 'It's a rest for us, Colonel. There's nobody to keep us in order.'

Agnes ignored him. 'How's Kirsty, sir?'

'Splendid!' He tried not to dwell upon the pathetic picture his little daughter had made seated beside her grandmother at dinner in the huge dining room. He tried not to remember the child struggling manfully with cutlery too heavy to handle, to eat food she did not want, and how scared, lost and lonely the wee girl looked in the huge lonely bed when he kissed her goodnight. His respected mother-in-law had returned to Edinburgh, rather to his relief, but Charles had made the elderly lady a promise which he intended to keep. He knew that it was for the best, but Agnes Murdoch would take it hard.

'I wanted to talk to you and Dougal about Kirsty, Mrs Murdoch. You've done wonders for my daughter, but the time's come for her to return home.'

'No!' Agnes cried.

Dougal took her hand. He knew what a blow this would be. She loved Kirsty like her own. She was the bairn's mother in all but birth.

The Colonel was sympathetic. 'I know it's a wrench, but you'll have your hands full with the new baby. You've made my little lass independent, able to look after herself. She only needs a housemaid to fasten buttons and suchlike and I've engaged a governess for her education.'

Agnes was nearly in tears. 'A governess! I thought she'd go to Invergowrie school with Hannah. How lonely she'll be!'

'That did worry me, but there's a way round that problem, if you'll agree. Would you let Hannah share Kirsty's education? It could be beneficial to both girls to have company and competition. This governess has first-class references, and seems a kind, sensible woman.'

The suggestion took the Murdochs by surprise. It was a wonderful chance for Hannah but didn't it smack of charity? 'Sir, we couldn't possibly let you—' Agnes began.

Dougal interrupted. 'Hold on, Agnes. Hannah's future is what matters here. The Colonel offers our lass a golden opportunity to better hersel'. For Hannah's sake we should accept.'

Agnes wasn't convinced. She had lost Kirsty, and they would take her own daughter from her during the day and educate her above her station in life. It didn't seem right.

The Colonel looked at her. The same look that had swayed her five years ago. 'Mrs Murdoch, Kirsty and I owe you a debt we can never repay, not in a hundred years. Please let me do this for Hannah.'

She sighed. 'When put that way, Colonel, how could I refuse?' But even so, she thought, it doesn't seem right.

Kirsty Rutherford remembered the Edwardian era as the learning years, mainly because she learned surprising facts about herself and others during elderly King Edward VII's nine-year reign.

Charles Rutherford had been fortunate in the choice of governess. Miss Mildred Holland was a daughter of the rural Manse and by her own admission an old maid of thirty, plain as rice pudding without the raisins. She had taken eager advantage of an excellent education from her scholarly father and possessed brains which far outshone her six brainy brothers. It was unfortunate she'd been born a woman.

Kirsty learned from Miss Holland that she would never keep the wolf from the door writing essays, but nobody would beat her at maths.

'Which is a pity, dear,' Mildred frowned. 'Mathematics at your high standard are considered positively blue stocking and no use to a lady. The best I can do is give you a good grounding in accountancy, then nobody can fiddle your books and get away with it.'

Hannah was just as bright, but had no patience with mathematics. She loved books, history, geography, general knowledge and anything at all to do with fashion, etiquette and good manners.

'You're lucky,' Hannah told Kirsty one summer's day in

12

1914, when they were fourteen, almost old enough to put their hair up. 'You were born with a silver spoon in your mouth.'

'I was not! I was so wee I nearly went to heaven with my mother.'

'I meant you'll marry someone rich. You live in a big house and have a rich granny who'll make sure you're presented to King George and Queen Mary. Poppy and I never will be.'

Kirsty giggled. 'Poppy wouldn't want to be presented to the King and Queen, and their majesties wouldn't want to be presented with Poppy. She's either sticky or muddy.'

Hannah tossed her chestnut curls. 'Go ahead and laugh! You were born a lady. I've to work hard at it.'

Hannah's envy was a revelation. Kirsty hugged her. 'Never mind, love. You're prettier than I am.'

'Well, yes,' she conceded. 'But Jamie thinks you're pretty. He told me so.'

'Did he?' Kirsty was startled.

Jamie Murdoch had worked in his father's mill since he'd left school four years ago at the age of fourteen. His teacher had declared it was a criminal waste of a very fine brain, but it wasn't really. Since Jamie left school he and his father had improved the mill beyond recognition. They'd obtained Kirsty's father's permission to install new machinery and enlarge the building. The mill was doing so well that a percentage of milling profits plus rent to the estate had boosted her father's finances; previously always shaky.

Kirsty had admired Jamie from afar since she'd left the Milton for Angus House almost ten years ago, but he'd never let her see that he admired her. In fact, his behaviour when they met reminded Kirsty of Annie the housemaid's romance with the seemingly disinterested second ploughman, which had been simmering hot and cold on the back-boiler for years.

Next day, Kirsty just happened to drop in to the Milton to see Agnes, bearing a pot of honey from the store-cupboard. Nine-year-old Poppy pounced on it.

'Is Jamie around?' Kirsty asked casually.

Agnes gave her a sidelong look. 'Not at the moment. Why?'

'Oh, nothing.' She watched Poppy dribble honey on to a buttered scone, the table and her front. 'Papa and Samuel are looking at the Powgavie pasture. They're planning to put oats in next season and I thought Jamie might be interested.'

'Your brother Samuel seems to have taken to farming. Your father will be pleased.'

'He's better pleased with brother George. He's been promoted to first lieutenant in the Black Watch.'

Agnes made a face. 'I can't be doing with fighting! If you want a word with Jamie, he should be coming home down the Errol road.' She watched the slight, bonny young girl head off eagerly to meet her son. The sight troubled her.

Jamie was riding his bike, daydreaming it was a motor car, and was surprised when he saw the girl standing at the roadside, sun lighting her silvery hair like a halo. He caught his breath and stopped. 'What are you doing here?'

'Waiting for you.' She wished she hadn't been so bold. He didn't seem pleased.

'Why, what's happened?'

'Nothing!' He was making her feel foolish, and she was annoyed. 'I'm not a wee girl, Jamie, I'm allowed on the road. Samuel and Papa are at the Powgavie pasture wondering if they should grow oats next season. I thought you might be interested.'

He was. He had studied all aspects of growing and milling grain at night-school classes and the subject was dear to his heart. 'They shouldn't,' he said. 'That land's more suited to wheat or vegetables, it's so rich. Oats'll flourish better higher up, where they catch more sun to ripen.'

She smiled. 'You'd better tell them right away, or Samuel will have the land ploughed and seed ordered. He really knows nothing at all about farming, poor dear.'

'Sit on the crossbar then, Kirsty. I'll take you there.'

How small and slender she was, perched in front of him as he rode with an arm encircling her waist to steady her. Just an innocent wee lass, leaning against him laughing as they freewheeled downhill. To her it was just a game, but he was eighteen and knew better.

'My love is but a lassie yet—' the words sang in his head. How long must I wait? He thought.

There was a cyclist coming towards them from the Dundee direction, bent over the handlebars, beetroot red with exertion. The man dismounted and motioned them to stop. Jamie braked and let Kirsty slide from the bar, still in the crook of his arm. 'What's wrong?' he called.

The middle-aged cyclist seemed extremely agitated. 'Have you seen Colonel Rutherford? I've an important message for him. They told me he was working hereabouts.'

'Turn back the way you came and take the first road to the left. We're going there too, as it happens.'

The man prepared to speed off again. Jamie called after him. 'What is it? Has there been an accident?'

He looked back, shaking his head. 'Worse than that, son! It's war, and the Colonel has to be told.' He paused for a moment, staring up at the cloudless August sky. 'So peaceful! Difficult to believe the first shots have already been fired.'

They watched him cycle away again, fast.

'War?' Kirsty said. Miss Holland had kept track of recent events in 1914, assassinations in Bosnia, disturbances in Russia and France, but these had seemed distant, nothing to do with life in the Carse. She couldn't imagine what war would be like, and she was suddenly afraid, not for herself but for the young men. Her brothers and Jamie.

She clutched his arm. 'Will you have to go?'

There was an excited gleam in his eye. 'I hope so. What a lark. I wouldn't miss it for anything!'

He glanced at her. She looked very young and a little tearful. If she'd been older he might have pulled her into his arms with considerable passion and kissed away her fears, but he restrained himself. He respected her youth and innocence and would not rob her of that.

'Don't worry about the war, Kirsty. It'll be over by Christmas,' he predicted.

Two

War. Such a wee word with power to change lives forever! Though for a time, life on the Angus estate went on as usual. Kirsty had begun to hope that common sense had prevailed and the emergency was over, but one day a troop of Fife and Forfar yeomanry trotted into the estate and made its way towards the stables.

Kirsty was working in one of the stalls, combing her stallion's mane and tail, grooming its glossy black hide and generally fussing around the handsome animal as he munched hay in the rack.

The stable door opened, a shaft of sunlight pierced the stall's coolness and a soldier appeared in the doorway.

'This 'un to go too, sir?' he called.

Her father's voice answered. 'That's right. All the three-year-olds.'

The soldier seemed surprised to find Kirsty there, but smiled politely. 'If you'll just stand aside, miss, I'll take the beast out.'

'Where are you taking him?'

He tugged at the halter. 'To the cattle trucks. He'll go to Barry Buddon for training first before being shipped to France.'

'France?' She was bewildered.

'Horses are sore needed for the war. The Colonel's giving us the pick o' his stable.'

She nearly fainted with horror. Estate workers had volunteered in droves and left, but it had never entered her head that horses would go. She grabbed the man's wrist. 'No! You can't have him.'

Young Lochinvar, the stallion she had helped to bring into this world, shifted restlessly, threatening to trample the pair of them. The soldier struggled with horse and child. 'If you've a grievance, away and annoy your father, you daft wee besom!' he growled.

'Don't worry, I will!'

Kirsty ran outside. She would never forget the nightmare scene that met her in the yard. The stable doors were wide open. There was dust and shouting soldiers struggling with frightened horses. She recognized brave hunters that had never refused a fence, alongside the two matched bays that had pulled the Rutherford coach for as long as she could remember. Josh the coachman stood by, tears coursing down his sad, old cheeks. In the midst of these heart-rending sights stood her father, quite unmoved.

She ran to him. 'Papa, you must stop them!'

He glanced down in surprise. 'What are you doing here?'

'Papa, they're taking Lochinvar. Don't let them, please!'

'Dear, it's wartime. We must make sacrifices.'

'But not horses!'

'We must all serve, Kirsty, even dumb animals. Now remember you're a soldier's daughter and dry your eyes.'

'Don't worry, I won't forget!' She stepped back, hating him, then turned and ran.

Cunningham, the grieve, stood behind his master. 'I think you should've listened to your lass, sir. She had plans for the stallion.'

'When I want your advice, Cunningham, I'll ask for it!' the Colonel snapped.

Kirsty ran to the house and burst into the schoolroom. Hannah and the governess looked up. They'd had their heads together studying a map of Europe pinned to the wall. Mildred Holland and Hannah followed each twist and turn in the war and the map's surface was covered with pins threaded with coloured wool. Since yesterday the Kaiser's army had retreated across the river Aisne after the battle of the Marne, and the map was split into two obstinate lines facing one another.

'They're taking Lochinvar and all the other horses and sending them to France!' she cried.

'Oh no!' Hannah was just as upset. She rode too, but side-saddle. That morning she'd been poring over the *Lady's Home Companion* dealing with proper behaviour in a crisis. A ladylike alternative to a manly stiff upper lip should be cultivated. She swallowed anguish. 'Men have to go, so why shouldn't horses?'

'It's not their war and they don't understand it. It's not fair!'

The governess intervened. 'Life is seldom fair, Kirsty.' Mildred loved these girls as if they were her own, although she would never tell them so. She wagged a finger in their faces. 'Now listen, you two. I was not a suffragette because I draw the line at setting fire to postboxes, though I would welcome a vote if I had one. When the Colonel took you with him to Dundee last week, you must have noticed queues outside the recruiting offices?'

Hannah smiled. 'I was too busy looking at the gorgeous gowns in G.L. Wilson's window.'

'I saw the poor men,' Kirsty said.

Yes, thought Mildred, you would. You are all heart, my dear. She went on briskly. 'Well, it's a great shame about the horses, and there's little we can do about it, but who will do the work when the men have gone? Women will! What a marvellous chance to show them what we're capable of!'

The idea appealed to Hannah, with reservations. 'But how can we? Dad and Jamie are short-handed, but I wouldn't want to work in a meal mill.

'Then look around till you find something useful you *can* do, dear.'

'I'll stay home,' Kirsty decided.

'You were always chicken-hearted!' Hannah laughed.

'I'd rather be chicken-hearted than heartless!' Kirsty shouted furiously, then whirled round and ran out of the room.

Her foster-sister's genteel upper lip trembled. 'I'm not heartless, Holly! I just want to act proper, like a lady.'

'Of course you do, my dear,' Mildred said comfortingly. She reached for a fresh strand of coloured wool. 'Give me a

18

hand to mark the British lines, Hannah. No, dear, not yellow! That's for the Kaiser's mob.'

Kirsty headed for the fields and her brother's help. Samuel greeted his young sister with pleasure. He felt closer to Kirsty than to brother George or their father. He had tried to please the Colonel by taking on the running of the estate, but he knew he was a disappointment to his father, whose pride in George's successful army career was quite evident.

Kirsty was in tears. 'Oh Sam, Papa's soldiers are taking the horses. They've taken Lochinvar away from me!'

'What? They can't do that!' Samuel cried, angrily. Taking the other horses was bad, but he was damned if he'd let them take Lochinvar as well and break Kirsty's heart. He flung down the scythe. 'Where are they, Kirsty?'

'They're heading for the main road. We could be too late.'

'Come on!'

Poppy, who had been watching Samuel working in the field, clung to Kirsty's hand. She wouldn't miss this for anything.

The soldiers had almost reached the lodge gates when the youngsters crashed through the shrubbery and blocked their path. The sergeant in charge swore under his breath as his troop struggled to control a startled column of horses. He glared at the three. 'D'you want to get yoursels killed?'

'Hand over the black stallion!' Samuel ordered.

'Can't be done. Colonel's orders!' the sergeant snapped.

'My father has no right to give it to you. It isn't his.'

Before the sergeant could respond there was a commotion at the rear of the column and the Colonel came riding through, mounted upon Thrawn Janet. 'Samuel! What the devil's going on?'

Samuel faced him angrily. 'You'd no right to give them Kirsty's horse. It'll break her heart to lose him, or don't you care?'

Lochinvar let out a plaintive whinny at the sight of Thrawn Janet, his dam. The Colonel's mare had been put on edge all morning by strange goings-on and that was the final straw. She put her head down and began bucking and kicking madly.

Only superb horsemanship saved Charles Rutherford from

a tumble. He struggled desperately to control the mare, but though Kirsty had pushed Poppy aside out of danger, she herself was within range of the mare's flailing hooves. Samuel flung himself forward and hung on grimly to Thrawn Janet's bridle. He was battered and bruised but refused to let go till the frantic horse calmed down and stood still. Charles Rutherford was shaking. Not because of his horse's antics, which were predictable, but because his son and daughter could easily have been killed.

'Thanks, Samuel,' he said gruffly. He looked at Kirsty and his heart lurched painfully. He stared at the ground, ashamed. 'Forgive me, Kirsty. I forgot the horse was yours.'

Charles turned in the saddle and shouted. 'Take the black stallion back to the stable. He's not mine to give.'

The harvest was excellent in September 1914, Nature making up for man's folly. Yields of oats and wheat on the Angus estate were phenomenal, but men were scarce. Every able-bodied man, woman and child rallied round to bring in the harvest, but not the Colonel, who was organizing defences and a guard upon the Tay bridge, which was a prime target for Zeppelin raids.

The harvesting squad included the Murdochs. Dougal had closed the mill till harvest was in, since grain was his livelihood. Mildred Holland volunteered for harvest duty, but Hannah wriggled out of it. The *Lady's Home Companion* warned against exposing skin to sunlight and encouraging a working person's tan. Hannah looked around anxiously for a way out of the dilemma. By a stroke of luck she heard that the Invergowrie branch of the Red Cross was seeking volunteers, and lost no time in enrolling. Hannah set off to cycle to the village every morning, a Red Cross badge pinned to her lapel and a virtuous glow hiding relief as she rode past sun-kissed fieldworkers.

Cunningham was keeping an eye on the inexperienced squad. 'The barley's hangin' its heid and the grain's hard to the teeth and ripe. Oats are a wee bit green yet,' he said.

Few bothered to listen as they gathered the sheaves. Once

the binder had done its work there were eight sheaves to be set into stooks angled across the field to dry in the sun and wind. They found it was far more difficult than they'd bargained for. The first eight sheaves Kirsty's team tried to stack collapsed in a heap. Jamie came to the rescue. He'd been waiting for the chance. Kirsty was dressed in mannish overalls and wore boots, which somehow only served to accentuate a feminine charm. You couldn't hide generations of good breeding, he thought, and the thought was depressing.

He had brains, though. He had helped to transform his father's business since leaving school, and in his spare time he'd gained a first-class certificate in engineering at Dundee Technical College. During the carter's strike in 1913 Jamie had driven the mill cart into the city, passing the beautiful mansions owned by jute barons. That was where he intended to live, one day.

'Thanks, Jamie!' Kirsty smiled and wiped her brow. With his help, they were getting the hang of it, which was more than could be said for Samuel, working not far away.

Poppy had been helping him. She came dancing over. 'Samuel swore. He said bad words.'

Jamie frowned. 'Where's your sunbonnet, you wee tyke? You're as brown as a berry.'

'I like berries.'

'So I see. Look at the state o' your pinny!'

Privately, Kirsty thought the child looked beautiful. She was envious of their easy banter. Jamie made Kirsty shy. She trembled when their hands touched and when their eyes met her heart fluttered. She wished she could recapture the easy friendship they'd enjoyed when they were children.

'Oh blast! Here's Mam!' Poppy had a lost sunbonnet on her conscience, not to mention a stained pinafore. She jouked smartly behind a corn stook.

'Your own team's looking for help, Jamie,' Agnes called.

'I was only showing Kirsty how to lay the sheaves, Mam.'

'You're taking long enough about it!'

Her tone was so biting Jamie stopped and stared. She knows I'm in love with Kirsty! he thought. 'I was only telling her—'

'It's not your place to tell the Colonel's daughter anything. Come away,' she ordered.

Jamie turned on his heel and trudged tight-lipped up the field by her side. 'There was no call for that,' he said. 'I'm a grown man, not a wee boy.'

'You think I don't know about you and her?' she said. 'She's only a wee lassie, more like a sister to you. It's a wonder you're not ashamed.'

'I've done nothing to be ashamed of, dammit!'

'Well that's a blessing anyway,' Agnes retorted. 'Go wash out your mouth wi' soap and stop swearing at your mother.'

Hannah Murdoch had not intended Red Cross training to be a permanent feature in her life, but after gaining a First Aid Certificate qualifying her to dress cuts and bandage broken limbs, she was encouraged to go on. By October Hannah also possessed a Home Nursing Certificate which entitled her to soothe fevered brows, make beds with hospital corners and brew beef tea for invalids. It was at this juncture that Marjory Pitleavie, commandant of the local Voluntary Aid Detachment, suggested that Hannah had the makings of a VAD. The Honourable Marjory Pitleavie, mind you! Hannah almost fainted with delight.

'You never saw such a fine lady, Kirsty!' she enthused while the two girls were enjoying a cosy chat curled up on the sofa. Mildred Holland had gone off to assist her elderly parents with a flitting and lessons were disrupted. 'Marjory's uncle is Lord Pitleavie. All her relatives are Sirs, Ladies and Honourables,' Hannah went on. 'She lives in a great barn of a place in the Carse with servants waiting on her hand and foot, yet she speaks to me as chummy as you like.'

Hannah was rubbing shoulders with the rich and titled in the Red Cross. Some lady members had even assumed that she was Colonel Rutherford's daughter, and she had not corrected them.

'You're really keen on this VAD lark, aren't you?' Kirsty said.

Hannah thought about it. 'Yes, I am.'

'It's all very well being chums with the Honourable Marjory, Hannah, but will you faint at the sight of blood?'

'I don't know. I haven't seen any,' she confessed.

Brave smiles were the order of the day on the thirtieth of October as wives, mothers, sisters and sweethearts assembled at Dundee's Tay Bridge station to watch the 5th Battalion Black Watch depart on active service to France. There was still a desperate shortage of men despite thousands of patriots who had enlisted in the first rush. Measles, mumps and influenza in epidemic proportions had swept through crowded barracks even before the men reached the battlefields. VADs in those areas had already been tested to the limit.

It was the turn of the Angus Red Cross on November the third, when the first trainload of wounded steamed slowly home across the bridge. The most serious cases would go straight to the Royal Infirmary, but Marjory Pitleavie's detachment had spent a hectic few days making Pitleavie House ready to receive others. Waiting nervously on the platform, Hannah didn't know what to expect. Strictly speaking, she was too young to be wearing VAD uniform, but Hannah was tall for her age and the Hon Marjory was not one to bother about regulations. Hannah had carefully bleached the newness out of the red cross on the bib of her apron so that she looked experienced, but her stomach was in knots as the train steamed in.

They had been warned about bandaged Tommies cracking jokes and giving nurses the glad eye, but nothing had prepared the girls for the harrowing sights that greeted them when the doors opened. Hannah felt her senses reel, but hastily pulled herself together.

Marjory Pitleavie was not one to waste time on sympathy. 'Come along, girls, the ambulances are waiting. Look lively,' she commanded, ushering her VADs inside.

Hannah knelt beside a badly wounded Tommy. He smiled. 'Look lively, the wifie ses, and here's us, half deid!'

She couldn't help laughing, though laughter seemed out of place. The men seemed to appreciate it though, so Hannah kept smiling. She smiled and laughed till her chest ached almost as painfully as her heart. I must remember to tell Kirsty that I didn't faint at the sight of blood either, she thought.

The war showed no sign of being over by Christmas. Dundee's weather that winter was depressing. Torrential rain in early December was followed by the coldest day of the year on Christmas Day.

At New Year Kirsty and Hannah shared a fifteenth birthday party in Angus House, and Agnes made a dumpling to celebrate. Some of the younger servants had given notice, eager to escape the drudgery of domestic service for war work, and Agnes was helping out in the big house when she could.

Fifteen! The girls were still officially children, but war had given them adult status. Hannah had grown taller. Agnes was forced to lengthen her daughter's skirts yet again. With her hair up, Hannah could easily pass for eighteen.

Kirsty would never be tall, but was tall enough to show off an ethereal beauty that was striking. Not that she gave her looks a second thought. She was tougher than she looked and worked with Samuel in the fields. She thought nothing of helping her friend Cunningham to calf a cow if the calving was proving difficult.

Samuel did his best to run the estate, but Kirsty could see his heart wasn't in it. Still, farming was a reserved occupation, and she hoped Sam wouldn't be called up. It was worrying enough with brother George already at the front.

Charles Rutherford was fully occupied with military defences. He had given Samuel control of the estate and asked Kirsty to help with the accounts. 'You're a dab hand at bookkeeping Miss Holland says, my dear. This will be a grand experience for you.' He kissed Kirsty's cheek, mounted Thrawn Janet and trotted off to attend to defences at Broughty Castle, leaving his daughter to sort out the estate's muddled affairs.

Mildred Holland became anxious about the future as the girls sixteenth birthday approached and demands placed upon them by the war left little time for lessons. With a heavy heart, she decided to do the decent thing and resign gracefully. Choosing her moment, she tapped on Colonel Rutherford's study door and was told to enter.

Charles raised his brows when he saw her. Teachers and brainy women made him nervous, and he avoided them when possible. 'Well, Miss Holland, what can I do for you?' he asked, jovially.

'I've come to tender my resignation, Colonel.'

That gave him an unexpected jolt. The woman was part of the fittings, wasn't she? 'Why? Aren't you happy here?'

Trust him to make her feel bad! 'Of course I am, but I've taught the girls all they can learn from books. They must learn about life now they're young women.'

'Bunkum! They're only bairns.'

'I suggest you take off the rose-tinted spectacles, Colonel.'

'That's impertinent, Miss Holland!'

'But true!'

Charles couldn't understand why he and the governess were suddenly engaged in an argument he seemed to be losing. He sulked. 'If you're determined to leave us in the lurch I can't stop you. I suppose you've something more lucrative lined up?'

'I have something in mind, yes, but there's no hurry. This has been a long association and it's only fair to give three months' notice.'

'How considerate!'

The sarcasm was not lost on her. 'My concern is for the girls.'

'Of course. I only pay your blasted wages.'

'Just till the end of February, Colonel. After that you can save your blasted money.'

Charles wished he had asked her to sit down at the beginning of this interview. Seated behind his desk he was forced to look up at her. She seemed to tower over him and he was reminded of an angry female teacher he'd crossed swords with as a small boy.

'Very well, Miss Holland, that will be all for now,' he said coldly, dismissing her with his stiffest military manner.

The girls were distraught when they heard. 'But why, Holly?'

'You've grown up and gone your separate ways,' she said. 'You don't need me.'

'We do! We do!'

She hugged them. 'You only think you do. You'll be fine.'

'Where will you go?' Kirsty asked, tearfully.

'Do my bit for the war effort maybe.'

'You could do it here!' Hannah cried. 'Marjory Pitleavie is on the lookout for VADs.'

Mildred laughed. 'No, my dear, I'd be no use soothing fevered brows. I'm much too plain!'

By January 1916 the British Expeditionary Force had fought so many battles, faced so many setbacks and suffered such devastating losses that many more volunteers were needed. As fighting became bogged down in trench warfare a Military Service Act was passed by Parliament in desperation, and call-up papers issued to those young men on the register who were not in essential occupations.

Kirsty was confident that Samuel would not be called up. German U-boats were sinking merchant ships and food was growing scarce, so farmworkers were badly needed at home. She was curled up with a book in front of a blazing log fire when one of the servants appeared in the doorway with the mail.

Her father didn't bother to look up. Probably more bills, he thought. Samuel took the letters from the maid and flipped through them casually, then paused. He slit open an official-looking envelope and scanned the contents.

Kirsty noticed her brother's expression. 'What is it, Sam?'

'I've been called up.'

She felt chilled. 'You can't be!'

The Colonel frowned. 'I thought this might happen, Sam. You're classified only as a farmer's son. You'll have to go.'

Samuel folded the official document and replaced it in the envelope. 'Not if I refuse.'

Charles stared. 'Refuse? Have you gone mad? You can't refuse!'

'I've thought this over ever since war was declared, Father. I won't fight. What's the use? I could never take anyone's life. My conscience wouldn't let me.'

His father was pacing the floor angrily. 'Your life will be made a misery. Don't you realize that one man's conscience is another man's cowardice?'

Samuel watched sadly. 'I know what they'll say. I won't change my mind.'

The Colonel sat down and sank his head in his hands. 'Then God help you, my boy, because I can't!'

The maid, whose ear had been clapped to the keyhole, scuttled to the kitchen. Fancy the laird's son being a cowardly conchie! She could hardly wait to tell the others.

The news reached the Milton next day. 'I can't say I'm surprised,' Agnes remarked. 'That lad wouldn't harm a mouse if he found it in a meal poke. He has a heart of gold.'

'That's the trouble,' her husband said scornfully. 'Gold's a soft metal easy melted,'

'But it endures,' Jamie added.

Poppy said nothing. The child hung her head so that a lock of hair hid her eyes. She loved Samuel.

Jamie pushed back the chair and stood up. The news had unsettled him. He wondered how Kirsty would take it. 'I'll go feed the hens, Mam.'

Agnes handed over a pan of warm bran to him and watched her son go out into the freezing morning.

Jamie had taken his mother's words to heart and had decided it was daft to imagine he loved the Colonel's young lass. He had kept Kirsty at a distance ever since and had gone courting Bella Macpherson, a farmer's daughter. But somehow Bella seemed large and clumsy in his arms, her kisses shamefully bold and eager. Morosely, he fed the hens.

'Jamie?'

He hadn't seen Kirsty coming and didn't know she was there till he'd set down the mash and the rooster and his

27

flock were pecking round his feet. Startled, he looked at her and his heart gave a great lurch. He knew then why the affair with Bella Macpherson was doomed.

Kirsty had matured while he'd dallied with buxom Bella. At sixteen she was every inch a woman, silver-fair and neat. He suspected that she had been crying.

'Have you been called up?' she asked.

'No. And I won't be. I'm in a reserved occupation in my father's mill.'

'How convenient!'

That was despicable, but it was only a measure of her distress. She was just beginning to realise the terrible consequences of Samuel's decision.

Unfortunately, the sarcasm had annoyed Jamie. 'If my call-up papers should come I'll go willingly. I'm not a coward like someone I could name.'

She turned pale. 'You've heard about my brother.'

'Aye,' he said brusquely, already regretting the remark.

So the news is all over the estate! she thought. Jamie's taunt was merely a foretaste of worse to come. She came close to hating him. 'You're a fine one to talk,' she cried, beside herself with rage. 'You know you're safe.' Stooping swiftly, she snatched up a white hen's feather that had caught her eye and waved it in his face. 'You're the coward, Jamie Murdoch!'

'Stop it!' He caught her wrist, twisting his head away.

'Go fight for your country then!' she yelled, jabbing the feather in his face. 'Go and fight, coward!'

'Stop it, Kirsty!' He grabbed her by the shoulders, driven wild by her taunts and the white feather waving in his face.

'Sam's not a coward,' she cried tearfully. 'He has strong principles. You have none! Oh, why don't you go and fight?'

He released her suddenly. They stood, both their hearts beating furiously in anger. She let the loathsome white feather float to the ground. 'Very well, Kirsty, if that's what you want, I *will* go,' Jamie said quietly.

Three

'I'll volunteer,' Jamie said. 'Will that satisfy you?'

Kirsty shivered in the chilly haar drifting inland from the river. 'I just wanted you to tell me my brother's not a coward,' she said wretchedly.

'How can I? I don't know what's cowardly and what isn't. Samuel could be a braver man than I'll ever be. I can't tell. Maybe I have to join up to find out.'

'Oh, all right. Go if you must!' she said, close to tears.

'Right, I will.'

There was no need for him to go, and now he could be killed and she'd be responsible because she'd deliberately goaded him to fight. All because Sam had stuck to his principles. What made her feel bad was the fact she knew her brother wasn't a coward. She didn't need Jamie to convince her of that. The day the soldiers had come to take the horses away Jamie wouldn't help, but Samuel hadn't hesitated. He'd saved Young Lochinvar and probably saved Kirsty's life at the risk of his own when Thrawn Janet went mental.

'Well anyway, I suppose my father will be pleased to hear of your decision,' she said bleakly.

'Tell the Colonel it'll be a relief to be out of this place!'

'Jamie, you don't mean that!'

'Don't I?'

'But it means you want rid of me, too!'

'Maybe I do.'

The damp air felt icy. She backed away from him. 'I'd better go.'

'Aye, you'd better.'

She gave him a stricken look then hunched her shoulders

and hurried off without a word, scattering the hens that had been crowding round the feeder.

He gazed after her, watching till she crossed the burn and disappeared into the misty haze. He sighed heavily. He'd sent away the lass he loved, but it was for the best. Jamie was not vain, but his mirror told him he was good-looking, and the light in lasses' eyes said he could take his pick. Maybe I could make Kirsty Rutherford love me, he thought, but can you see the Colonel welcoming the miller's son to court his only daughter when it's a wealthy husband that's needed? The man would have the horsewhip out! She'd have to choose between her father and me, and that would break her heart. Aye, it'll be a relief to get away!

But to leave home and face the unknown horrors of war? That was a different story! Soberly, Jamie picked up the empty pail and trudged homewards to the warmth of his mother's kitchen . . .

Although Dundee's trolleybuses had been abandoned in 1914 after a short trial, by early 1916 the streets were so cluttered with carts, tramcars and motor vehicles that Charles Rutherford's progress into town riding Thrawn Janet became hazardous. The mare loathed mechanical vehicles and reacted violently. It took all Charles's skill to stay in the saddle sometimes. The daily journey to the Territorial Army headquarters was fraught with such danger something had to be done. The carriage horses had gone, the old coachman retired and the coach sold, so that was not an option. Trouble was, Charles was a horseman and always would be. The thought of him driving a motor seemed sacrilege.

His jaw was grimly set and hands firmly on the reins as he trotted down the driveway a few days after Samuel had delivered his bombshell. Gossip had ensured that the news that the Colonel's son was a conchie had spread through the Carse faster than burning straw, but fortunately there had been no official repercussions just yet. There was a breathing space before Samuel was due to report to the barracks, and the young man might have a change of heart. Charles was working on it.

Immersed in thought, the first indication of a motor car's presence was Thrawn Janet's predictable reaction when the two met head on at a corner. She reared and pawed the air, catching her rider by surprise. Charles slid off backwards and landed in the bushes as the mare bolted for the stables. He crawled out of the greenery, fuming but unhurt.

The driver had pulled up. 'I say, Father, are you all right?'

'George, my boy! What a surprise,' Charles cried joyfully, recognizing his soldier son despite driving goggles.

'Here, let me give you a hand.' George jumped down and helped his father to his feet.

Charles beamed. 'This is quite unexpected, George.'

'I have a spot of sick leave. The CO fixed it. He diagnosed battle fatigue.'

'There was none of that in my day!'

'Things are different now, Father,' George said.

'They should have sent the cavalry in, my boy. There's nothing like a cavalry charge to put the wind up the enemy.'

A shadow crossed the young man's face. 'It's been tried.'

Charles glowered at the motor car. 'I'm surprised you've fallen for one of those!'

'It belongs . . . belonged to a good friend of mine. I bought it from his widow. She was glad of the cash, and has two wee boys to bring up on her own now.'

'Charity's all very well, but what the blazes will we do with a motor car?'

'Drive it, Father. It's more predictable than Thrawn Janet. It may run out of petrol, but won't toss you in the bushes. Come on, hop in!'

Charles was not converted by the time they reached the stables and checked on the mare, who had homed safely to her stall. 'Smelly, noisy thing!' Charles snorted as he eyed the motor car.

'You mean the horse?' George had a twinkle in his eye.

31

Charles gave him a look. He had more serious matters on his mind. He hadn't told George about Samuel yet.

'Oh, Jamie!' Agnes Murdoch sat down, an unusual occurrence on washing day. 'Whatever possessed you to volunteer?'

Her husband frowned worriedly. 'You might have had more consideration for your parents, son. There was no call for you to go; you were doing vital work here.'

'Well, it's done now,' Jamie said.

'How the devil d'you expect me to manage with only old Eck and a raw lad?' Dougal cried with a rare show of anger.

'The new machinery's in place, Dad. You'll find it easy to operate without me.'

Agnes's expression hardened. 'It's that lass. She's done this! I saw you two arguing the other day.'

Dougal agreed. 'You're right, Agnes. I'll bet she persuaded our lad to join up to draw attention away from her brother, that damned conchie.'

Poppy began sobbing quietly. The child had been sitting on the rug in front of the kitchen range, hugging her favourite sheepdog for comfort. Poppy's world was tottering around her.

'Now, see what you've done, upset your wee sister!' Agnes cried.

'We'll never know a moment's peace from this day forward, Jamie Murdoch, and that's the truth,' she wailed.

Samuel Rutherford set off for Dundee market as usual the next day, even though on the short railway journey from Invergowrie to Dundee he imagined the train's occupants staring and whispering, and he felt sick at heart.

He'd been delighted to see George come home yesterday apparently unscathed. Yet, though his brother seemed sound in wind and limb, Samuel couldn't shake off the impression that somehow he'd been seriously wounded. It had first crossed his mind when he had looked into George's eyes yesterday.

At first Samuel had guiltily assumed it was because he'd refused to fight. He'd presumed George had been told, but if not he must have guessed something was up, judging by the strained atmosphere round the dinner table last night. There had been dark smudges beneath Kirsty's blue eyes as she stared sorrowfully at her brothers.

Only their father had been in fine fettle. 'I just heard young Murdoch has volunteered. Good show, what?'

The remark had been greeted by a deafening silence.

Samuel soon regretted attending market that day. The purpose was to select a fine ram to improve the stock of the hill sheep. The flock had been Samuel's only real success. He had been deeply interested in breeding, lambing and the diseases the hardy animals were prone to. Cunningham recognized this ability and quietly encouraged it. He had been content to leave the choice of a vigorous young tup to Samuel's keen eye.

There was a fair crowd in Market Street that day, despite the chilly weather. Farmers stood in groups beneath tall gateposts decorated with fine stone animal sculptures. One or two wives and daughters had resisted the pull of D.M. Brown's and G.L. Wilson's and lingered with the men. A buxom young woman suddenly planted herself in front of Samuel. He raised his bowler hat politely, recognising Bella Macpherson, the farmer's daughter Jamie Murdoch had courted in a desultory fashion.

'It's a wonder you have the cheek to show your face, Mr Rutherford!' she cried in carrying tones. Heads turned, encouraging Bella to louder efforts. 'Everyone knows it's your cowardice that's prompted Jamie to join up when there's no need.'

A hushed silence had fallen. Somebody booed softly. Samuel pushed past his tormentor, but she shouted after him. 'You can't run away from us that easy. Everybody hates conchies!'

The heart had gone out of him and he couldn't concentrate on the sheep on offer. He imagined accusing eyes fastened on him and contemptuous murmurs every time he turned his back. He broke out in a sweat and dared not bid lest he drew attention to himself. At last he abandoned the attempt and left the pens. He was trudging despondently along Dock Street when a car pulled up and his brother leaned out.

'I hoped I might see you, Sam. Get in! There's a coat in the back. Put it on. You'll need it,' George said.

The coat smelled of leather and tobacco and Samuel found its warmth comforting. George didn't say much until he had negotiated city traffic and they were heading into open country. The early afternoon light was fading already, and the landscape was grey, all colour bleached by the cold.

'It's not easy being a social outcast, is it, old chap?' George said.

Samuel gave him a quick glance. 'You know?'

He nodded. 'The old man told me.'

'I expect you despise me.'

He changed gear. 'No, I don't. I wish I had your guts. What you're doing takes courage.'

Samuel was silent for a moment. 'George, what should I do?'

'Do you believe Britain shouldn't go to war? Are you a pacifist?'

'No, this is purely personal. I couldn't take a life. What use would I be on a battlefield?'

George smiled thinly. 'That's for us all to find out, old chap. I do sympathize, but you must obey the call-up, you know. The alternative is prison. If you turn up at the barracks and state your case, you could be classified as C3, unfit for active service. You won't be expected to carry a weapon. Mind you, you'll be highly unpopular and will get the filthiest jobs nobody else will take. Can you face drudgery for the duration?'

'Maybe,' Samuel said thoughtfully. 'I'll think about it, George. Thanks for clarifying the situation.'

They had reached the gates of Angus estate. George stuck a gloved hand out the window and twirled the steering wheel. 'Don't thank me, old bean. As I said, it takes all kinds.'

* * *

George's arrival dug everyone out of a rut. Mildred Holland in particular was glad to see him. Her departure from Angus House loomed large, and despite putting on a brave face Mildred had no job and nowhere to go to. She could impose upon her elderly parents, and the dear souls would welcome her gladly, but she knew she wasn't needed in their charming cottage close to a village church where her eldest brother preached. The active old couple were happily occupied with grandchildren and a large, productive garden. Her other brothers occupied university and teaching posts scattered throughout the land. Although the Hollands were a close and affectionate family, Mildred's services were not required. She was not the stuff of which nurses are made, nor did she fancy teaching dull students after the stimulation of educating two bright girls. Middle age had bred restlessness and a panicky feeling that life was slipping away without much to show for it.

Kirsty was glad of a diversion. George's car was a novelty and she wished she could drive it, but he was emphatic. 'Not till you're seventeen, Kirsty. I'm concentrating on Father. He's agreed to take some instruction from me today.'

'Can I come? I might pick up a few tips.'

'Oh, very well,' he agreed, and was pleased to see her smile. Kirsty's smile had been lacking recently. 'Put on something warm, though.'

She raced upstairs, almost knocking Mildred over in her eagerness. 'Where's the fire?' the governess said. Kirsty explained the reason for haste. 'Why don't you come too, Holly?' she said, trying to persuade her by using her nickname.

Mildred hesitated. She had examined the car with interest in the stable yard, but had never ridden in one. 'Won't the gentlemen object?'

'Of course not! The more the merrier. We'll sit in the back and they won't even know we're there. Driving looks easy. I expect Father will pick it up in no time.'

Charles almost rebelled when he clambered into the car

35

and found two muffled figures seated in the back. Kirsty he could put up with, but the governess was a different matter. Before he could voice a strong protest, George had swung the starting handle and the engine roared to life. Charles clung to the steering wheel, the monster's power trembling through his limbs. He had been afraid many times in his army career, but never had he felt so helpless.

George scrambled in beside him. 'Remember what I said. Double de-clutch, accelerator, hold the gearstick and push it through the gate.'

'Gate? Where is the damn gate?' Charles cried, peering ahead.

George explained and there was subdued laughter from the back. It was perhaps inevitable that from then on the driving lesson went from bad to worse.

He got the wretched vehicle moving. It had a convulsion and leaped forward. George came to his aid and as they crawled in a decorous straight line a corner came in view. Charles swung the wheel anxiously. Too far. The car swerved crazily, clipping the bushes to a chorus of screams till George corrected the swerve and braked. Charles was trembling. He was incapable of controlling the powerful beast. It was like a bolting horse, and not one horse, mind you, but a whole handful! Beads of sweat stood on his brow.

'I can't do this, George. I'm sorry.' He was so ashamed of failure it almost drove him to tears.

George's hand covered his. 'It's all right, Father. It doesn't matter.'

But humiliation matters to a proud man. Charles mumbled some excuse and clambered out. Head down, he walked to the stables, went into Thrawn Janet's stall and leaned against the mare's warm flank. Thrawn Janet could be gentle when it suited her. She turned her head and gently nuzzled away her master's salty tears.

The two women sat silently in the back seat. Mildred pitied the poor man. She had always thought her employer a stiff-necked military type with no imagination and therefore incapable of emotion, but this incident had revealed a more vulnerable side. She wished she hadn't witnessed his humiliation.

Mildred had also sensed the vehicle's power, though far from terrifying her, the sensation had been thrilling. 'George, might I have a go?' she ventured.

Seated in the driving seat, she listened intently to the young man's instructions, breathless with anticipation. Fancy being able to go where I please at speeds never dreamed of! she thought. She released the brake and the car surged forward. She felt in tune with the engine as she grasped the steering wheel. The gear change was difficult, but she managed it with only a grating sound which could be improved upon. Mildred laughed delightedly as the car picked up speed.

'Jolly good, Holly dear!' George said admiringly. 'You're a natural.' Mildred felt a twinge of remorse. The poor Colonel would feel even worse when he heard of her success.

The Hon Marjory Pitleavie had fixed it for Hannah to have three months' nursing training at Dundee Royal Infirmary. Pitleavie House was bursting at the seams with wounded Tommies, but sadly lacking in trained nurses to deal with them. Of all Marjory's VADs Hannah showed most promise and extra training was an obvious next step. Three months seemed a short time, but Hannah was sure she'd aged three years by the end. She was lodging in the nurses' quarters, but with one month left to go was permitted a weekend at home. Hannah made a beeline for Angus House to report to Kirsty.

Curled up in their favourite spot on the schoolroom sofa, she regaled her with tales of hospital life. 'You wouldn't believe how strict the discipline is! Sister's word is law, but you wouldn't dream of arguing with a staff nurse. As for Matron! Everyone stands to rigid attention when she's on her rounds.'

'But you're learning a lot?'

'Oh yes, apart from our wounded Tommies, jute workers

suffer from all sorts of injuries and ailments. I'd no idea infant mortality was so high in Dundee, especially in the Hawkhill slums. It's really sad, Kirsty.' Then she giggled. 'I had a severe talking-to from Sister because of my bosom. VADs aren't supposed to have one. I've been issued with an apron two sizes too big, and look an absolute fright.'

Their laughter attracted George, who happened to be passing. He looked in and was surprised to see his sister in conversation with a stunning young stranger. George had attended local balls and functions on many occasions and had met most of the eligible young ladies in the district. Not this one, though. He smiled. 'Won't you introduce me, Kirsty?'

'But you know her, George. It's Hannah!'

Of course! he thought. She had grown taller and looked older with her hair up. George laughed. 'Hannah Murdoch, and I thought it was a lady!'

She stood up with dignity. 'I was not born a lady, Master George, but that has never mattered except to a snob like you!' She pushed past him and slammed the door behind her.

George winced. 'I could kick myself, Kirsty. How thoughtless of me. I didn't mean to offend.'

Kirsty sighed. 'I'm afraid you chose the worst possible insult. Hannah is more of a lady than I'll ever be, and proud of it.'

'Should I chase after her and apologize?'

'No. Leave it to me, I'll go.'

Kirsty dawdled on the path to the Milton to give Hannah time to cool down. This time she did not barge in to her foster-mother's house, but knocked gently.

Agnes flung the door open. 'Oh, it's you!'

It was unfortunate for Kirsty that Agnes's world was teetering on the verge of collapse that afternoon. Her only, dearly beloved son had just received orders to report to Maryhill Barracks in Glasgow for basic training. The agony in Agnes's breast was not soothed when Hannah had burst into the house not five minutes ago in floods of tears, with a tale of humiliation and insult. Her anger knew no bounds when

Kirsty turned up on the doorstep. She glared at the beautiful girl she had once loved like her own. Today she hated all she stood for.

'It's a wonder you dare show your face after what you've done to this family, Kirsty Rutherford!'

Kirsty was shocked. 'Mam, I don't understand. I haven't done anything.'

'Haven't you, indeed?' Agnes's voice rose. 'You've sent my son to the war when there's no call for him to go. Not content with that, your brother insulted Hannah. She's inside breaking her heart. You folk are all the same, cruel and heartless, never sparing a thought for decent folk.'

'That's not true!'

'Isn't it?' She came close. Her hot, furious face only inches from the girl. 'I wish your father hadn't come to my door that night sixteen years ago. I wish I'd never—' she stopped short, but the meaning was clear and the damage done.

'Oh, Mam . . . Mam!' Kirsty whispered brokenly.

The older woman was suddenly pushed aside and Jamie stood in the doorway. 'That's enough, Mother. Get inside!' Agnes looked like someone waking from a bad dream. She turned and went into the house with halting steps like an old woman. 'Don't mind her, Kirsty,' Jamie said. 'She's off her head with worry. She doesn't mean it.'

'I think she does.'

He put an arm round her. She was obviously very shocked. 'Come on, I'll see you home.'

Ancient beech trees made a cathedral roof of branches over their heads on the lovers' path. He kept an arm round her waist and she leaned against him. He dreamed they were walking as lovers. A bitter-sweet pleasure, for soon he would be far away. The same thought was in Kirsty's mind.

'Jamie, I'm sorry.'

'What for?'

'It's my fault you're leaving.'

He pulled her round to face him. 'Listen, I would've volunteered sooner or later. It was only a matter of time. You just helped to make up my mind.'

'I'll never forgive myself!'

He drew her close and kissed her gently at first, then more thoroughly. His senses were reeling when they drew apart. He tried to make light of it. 'I'm sorry I took the liberty, Miss Rutherford.'

She smiled. 'I'm not.'

'Kirsty, you'll not forget me when I'm gone, will you?' he demanded, seriously.

She reached up and kissed him shyly. 'Never!' she promised, and meant it.

Samuel Rutherford had reached a decision. His father and George were seated before a dour, smoking log fire occasioned by the coal shortage and he decided the time was right to make an announcement. 'Father, I've made up my mind to report to Perth barracks.'

Charles roused himself. He'd been pensive since Mildred Holland had taken to driving like a horse to a water trough. Since his own failure to master the motor car, Charles had found he could view Samuel's dilemma with clearer understanding. He smiled warmly. 'Then I'm proud of you, Sam, for I know what that decision cost.'

'I'll obey the call-up, Father, but I'll make it plain I refuse to carry weapons.'

'Well, my boy, there are plenty other ways you can help. The main thing is to serve your country,' Charles said leniently.

Samuel smiled his relief. 'That's what George said.' He glanced at his brother. 'I can't hope to match your fine army record, of course, George. I couldn't kill anyone.'

George shot to his feet. 'Don't say that, Sam. For pity's sake, don't!' he yelled, before rushing from the room.

His father half-rose. 'Something's wrong. I'll go to him.'

'No, I started this. Let me,' Samuel said, worriedly.

George was lying on his bed staring at the ceiling when Samuel tapped on the bedroom door and entered. He sat on the edge of the bed.

'What's up, George?'

'Sorry, Sam. Nothing anyone can fix.'

'Care to talk about it?'

'I can't. But Sammy, I wish to God I had your courage!' He smiled in disbelief. 'Nonsense! I'm a disappointment to all, while you're—'

George cut him short. 'I'm a murderer. That's what I am, a cold-blooded murderer.' Samuel couldn't ever recall seeing George cry, but now he saw tears run down his cheeks. 'Go away, Sam. Please. I know you mean well, but you can't help me. Nobody can,' he said, turning his head away.

Sorely troubled, Samuel left his brother alone to face his demons.

War brought such changes, Kirsty thought tearfully. Mildred Holland was packing. She had only been persuaded to stay till she finished a course of driving lessons George was giving her during sick leave. That was another puzzling thing. George looked the picture of health, yet Samuel insisted to her that George was gravely ill. Sick in the mind. It was alarming.

Hannah had not reappeared, which meant George's insult was not forgiven. Kirsty did not dare approach the Milton in case she came face to face with Agnes. She longed to see Jamie before he left, but decided she had caused him enough trouble. It was only from kitchen staff gossip that she heard he was leaving for Maryhill Barracks in Glasgow the next day at ten o'clock.

She spent that night tossing and turning restlessly. By morning she was in such a state that she waylaid George and begged him to drive her into town.

'Certainly. Where to?' he said obligingly.

'The West station.'

'Oh?' He gave her a keen glance.

'Jamie Murdoch is leaving today to join the army and I must wish him luck,' she explained. 'It's the least I can do, George. We've known one another since we were bairns.'

'Of course, Kirsty.' His expression was thoughtful as he watched his young sister hurry off to get ready.

Getting ready meant donning her best costume, a lacy

41

blouse and stylish bonnet. She would freeze to death on this cold morning, but that was the least she could do for the man she loved. Yes, I love him, she thought. I knew it the moment he kissed me, and now it's too late to tell him. Her only concession to weather was a pink chiffon scarf tied over the bonnet to keep it anchored in a gusty March wind. George cast an eye over his sister, but made no comment as he helped her into the car. Jamie Murdoch was obviously favoured, but perhaps it was well that the poor fellow was off to serve king and country. This was not a match that would meet with their father's approval.

There was unrest in Dundee; many of the mills were standing idle as the jute workers were on strike. There were groups of workers marching down Union Street when George and Kirsty arrived. A crowd was congregating outside the red sandstone railway station, hoping to lobby the local MP, due on the next train.

George looked anxious. 'Shouldn't I come with you?'

'No. I'll be all right.' She kissed his cheek. 'Thanks, George.'

Moodily, he watched her thread her way through the crowd. They drew aside, glowering. She was so neat and pretty in that lovely outfit she could have arrived in their midst from another planet, he thought.

Kirsty's thoughts were centred on Jamie as she made her way through the crowd. She reached the platform where the Glasgow train was standing, and looked around. Her heart gave a lurch as she saw Jamie some distance away, leaning out of a carriage window.

The maids had told Kirsty that his mother was too distressed and ill to see him off, but to her dismay all the Murdochs were there, gathered round him. He reached down, held his mother's hand and said some comforting words as Agnes smiled wanly.

Kirsty stood hidden in a nearby doorway. She didn't know what to do. She couldn't barge forward and risk an unpleasant scene, but she longed to let him know she was there. Time

42

was running out. The guard was unfurling the green flag and there was a sudden flurry of goodbyes in the heightened bustle of departure. In desperation, Kirsty stepped out of the doorway. Some instinct may have alerted Jamie for he glanced up suddenly and saw her. He dropped his mother's hand. At a distance, they stared at one another.

He had been desolate because she had not come. Now his love for her was so strong he didn't hear his mother cry out as the train started moving.

Kirsty kissed her fingertips and blew a kiss to him. She saw him smile, touch fingers to his lips; then he was gone.

Four

S amuel Rutherford had decided to answer the call to serve king and country. The evening before his departure, he and Kirsty walked around the estate he had struggled hard to maintain. Samuel surveyed the scene ruefully. He'd done his best, but there was still much evidence of neglect.

He sighed. 'I don't know what's to become of this place, Kirsty. Father's too preoccupied with military affairs to be bothered. You've seen the books. There's no capital to invest in machinery to make up for the loss of men and horses.'

But Kirsty refused to share her brother's pessimism, she loved the old house and its surroundings too much to contemplate defeat. 'Mr Cunningham won't be called up. He'll keep the estate going till the others come back.'

'Cunningham can't fix years of neglect on his own.'

'You forget I'm here, Sam.'

Glancing down at the little beauty walking by his side he was tempted to laugh, but didn't. 'Yes, of course,' he agreed seriously. 'You'll be in charge once George rejoins his regiment, but you can't change things without money.'

'Don't worry. I'll think of something.'

He smiled. 'Maybe you will.' He couldn't believe a slip of a girl could reverse the family's flagging fortunes, but was too kind-hearted to say so. Unless she married a rich husband, of course! Samuel breathed in deeply the pure, cold air. It was a beautiful evening, a nip of frost brought a tinge of red to a misty sunset beyond the Fife hills. I can't honestly say I've been happy here, he thought emotionally, but I'll miss it.

They paused for a moment to lean on the dyke and watch

44

the ewes graze. The shepherd and his dogs had brought them down from the hills before lambing.

'I'd hoped to be here for the lambing,' Samuel said wistfully. The shepherd had been experimenting with new breeds, and Samuel had been anxious to see results.

Kirsty had marvelled at her brother's skill and patience with sick or injured animals. It was one aspect of farming he enjoyed. She hugged him. 'Don't worry, Sam. I'll write and tell you how it goes.'

But lambing did not go well.

'The lambs are puny, Miss Kirsty, and we've lost quite a few,' Cunningham said. 'Samuel warned us this might happen. He said we needed to improve the original hardy blackface stock, no' bring in untried breeds that were soft in harsh conditions. Pity he didnae buy the blackface tup he had his eye on at the market.'

She looked puzzled. 'What's a tup?'

'It's a young ram, Miss Kirsty.'

'If that's what's needed, let's go to market and buy one, Mr Cunningham.'

He grinned. 'Och, miss, there's no call for a lady to set foot in thon rough place! I'll go mysel'.'

'No, we'll both go. You can keep me right.'

'Don't say I didnae warn ye, then!' Cunningham said ominously. She was only a wee bit lassie and he knew the boisterous ways of farmers round the sale ring. They'd have great fun at the novice lassie's expense. She wouldn't last five minutes bidding, but you had to take your bonnet aff to her, for pluck.

Kirsty was keen to go. She had been brooding over Jamie's departure and was eager to take her mind off her part in it. He had written a hurried note to her describing basic training with the Highland Light Infantry in Glasgow. 'Square-bashing' most of the time. Maryhill Barracks was not the most comfortable of billets and Jamie, a fastidious man, was sharing one cold tap between thirty recruits.

Samuel had left home without fuss. Hannah's amusing

45

accounts of hospital life would have helped raise Kirsty's spirits, but Hannah was in the huff and refused to visit Angus House while George was there. Worst of all, Kirsty's beloved foster-mother had cut her dead in the kirk, and Dougal Murdoch, who'd been like a father to her once, had refused to catch her eye. It was small wonder Dundee cattle market held no terrors for her after that.

George drove them to the sale, but declined his sister's invitation to participate. 'No thanks, Kirsty dear. All sheep look alike to me. I shall drive to Broughty Ferry, take a breath of bracing sea air on the beach and pick you up later. Minus a blackface ram in the back seat, I trust!'

That day, there was to be an important sale of rams and gimmers. Cunningham explained that gimmers were one- and two-year-old ewes that had not yet borne a lamb. There was a large crowd of farmers around the sale ring already and Kirsty's arrival caused a stir.

'That's a bonnie wee gimmer you've brought tae the ring, Cunningham!' somebody shouted, to the accompaniment of laughter.

Kirsty fortunately did not catch the remark and Cunningham grimly ignored it. He ushered her towards a solid wall of farmers' backs wedged round the rails. There were also tiers of grandstand seats which gave an excellent view of proceedings, but these were tightly packed. Above the sea of bowlers and bonnets Cunningham could just see the auctioneer's dais. Kirsty could see nothing. She attempted to burrow through, but nobody budged.

'It's no use you shovin', Miss Kirsty,' Cunningham muttered. 'They'll no' shift for ye. Business is business, and good manners flee out the window.'

There was a sudden commotion at the top of the grandstand. Heads turned, and Kirsty was surprised to see an elderly lady prodding a burly farmer to his feet. 'Get aff your backside, Wullie Baird. Where's your manners, man? Can ye no' see there's a lady standing?'

The farmer gave way and offered Kirsty his vantage

point. She thanked him prettily and climbed up beside her benefactress. Now she had a fine view of proceedings, drovers were hustling sheep through the weighing gate from the pens and the auctioneer had begun a sing-song litany of facts and figures at such speed Kirsty couldn't catch a word. Separated from Cunningham, Kirsty had no idea what was going on or what to do. Prices seemed higher than she'd expected. She clutched her slender purse and despaired.

Her companion had been studying her shrewdly. 'New to the game?'

'I'm afraid so.'

'What are ye after and what's your price?'

Kirsty told her, recklessly disclosing every penny she possessed. What did it matter? She had not a hope.

The elderly lady winked. 'Now then, that's a braw tup they've brought in, see?'

'What should I do, ma'am?'

She fingered her chin. 'Och, nothing.'

'Shouldn't I attract the auctioneer's attention?'

She rubbed her nose thoughtfully. 'Not yet. Wait'll I tell ye.'

'But . . . it's no use! Maybe I should go home.'

'In a minute,' she nodded, then dug Kirsty in the ribs. 'Wave your hankie at the auctioneer, lass. Smile and make the man's day.'

Kirsty obeyed. An expectant hush fell over the sale ring. All eyes were fixed upon the elderly lady. She slowly shook her head and the auctioneer glanced round a ring of impassive faces.

'All done?' There wasn't a murmur. He banged down the gavel. 'Sold to the bonnie young lady at the back!'

'Me?' gasped Kirsty. 'But I wasn't bidding!'

The elderly lady chuckled. 'Aye, you were. It was between me and Jockie Gibb, but you stepped in at the last with your hanky. Haven't you heard o' a nod an' a wink, Miss Rutherford? That's all you need in the sale ring. It's a braw blackface tup, and you beat me fair an' square after that scunner Jockie Gibb dropped out. There's no' many dares bid

47

against Betsy Macpherson! It's a good price. You'll maybe find you've a pound or two spare in your purse,' she added generously.

'I don't know how to thank you, ma'am!'

She patted her arm. 'No need, dear! I'm Bella Macpherson's auntie, and I was affronted when Bella accosted your poor brother at the last tup sale. It wasn't mannerly to shame the lad in public, so now I've set the record straight. You can write an' tell Samuel Rutherford he has a fine young tup, with old Betsy Macpherson's compliments.'

What a time for departures! Kirsty thought, as the month of April wore on. George was next to go, recalled to his unit after news that the French were struggling to hold the line at Verdun, which Holly said was the gateway to France.

George insisted he was recovered and raring to go. 'Home leave has done me the world of good,' he told his father and sister. 'No need to worry. The regiment is in reserve beside the river Somme, in lovely countryside beyond the northern industrial part of France. It's a quiet sector. They send blokes there for a rest.'

Kirsty watched as her brother's trembling fingers lit yet another cigarette. He smoothly changed the subject, going on to what should be done with his beloved motor car in his absence.

'I've told Holly she can drive the car as often as she likes in order to keep the engine tuned. I've explained how the combustion engine works and shown her how to do minor repairs. She's very quick on the uptake, I must say.'

'Bossy females usually are,' his father said. 'I don't know why you bothered. She's determined to leave. Damned inconvenient!'

Charles had been subdued since his failure with the motor car. They were all behaving oddly these days, Kirsty thought. War heightened emotions to such a pitch that tensions became unbearable. Kirsty's solution was to gallop young Lochinvar to the hills, where pockets of snow still lingered and icy winds whipped colour to her cheeks. There she would rein in and sit looking out over the silver ribbon of the river, planning a fine stable of horses and imagining how beautiful the house and grounds would look when restored to their former glory. It was a dream to cling to in the gloom of war.

Kirsty struggled with tears as she stood beside her father on the railway platform the next day. She was sad to see George go, because she was sure he wasn't fit. He seemed his usual cheery self, but she knew better. Sometimes she had surprised him when he was alone, slumped in a melancholy depression. He bucked up immediately, but something was wrong. Samuel had told her sickness in the mind was hard to diagnose and very difficult to cure.

After the train had left the station and was rumbling across the Tay bridge, her father sighed. 'Just the two of us now, Kirsty.' He glanced at his pocket watch. 'And we've missed the last train home, drat it! We'll have to hire a motor cab.' A prospect he heartily detested.

The next day, when Mildred tapped on Colonel Rutherford's door, he had been expecting her. In fact, the governess's future had been nagging at the back of Charles's mind.

'Come in, Miss Holland. Take a seat,' he invited cordially.

She sat down, hands folded meekly. 'I've come to bid you goodbye, Colonel.'

'May I ask if you've found another job?'

'No, not yet.'

'Tell me, are you looking for another teaching post?'

'Not necessarily. I'll go to my parents till something turns up, then find lodgings.'

Charles drummed a tattoo on the blotting pad. 'My son was impressed with your driving.'

'George is a patient instructor.'

'Some take readily to the infernal machine. I do not.'

'Maybe if you were to try again, Colonel?'

'I've neither the time nor the inclination, Miss Holland, but all the same, I have to turn up at the Territorial Army headquarters most days. The journey to Dundee is becoming impossible on horseback, because the mare is terrified by motor vehicles. Meanwhile, George's car is lying idle in the shed, so—' Charles paused awkwardly.

'You need a driver! Are you offering me the job, Colonel?'

'If you want it,' he said, trying not to sound eager. "You would stay on, of course, and be on hand to drive me to various destinations. We can come to an agreement about pay. Cunningham could help you with maintenance and repairs. What about it?' To his astonishment he found himself waiting breathlessly for an answer.

To Mildred the future suddenly promised excitement. However, she was not one to rush into any situation. 'Driving you would be no problem, Colonel, but if we're seen together every day there will be talk.'

'What d'you mean, talk?'

'Of a scandalous nature.'

He flushed. 'Oh, I see. Don't worry, your uniform will take care of that.'

'Uniform?'

'An army driver can't wear civilian clothes. You would enrol in a territorial unit on a voluntary basis and be issued with uniform worn by females on active service.' Charles was beginning to enjoy himself. 'There would be no talk of scandal, Miss Holland,' he went on, 'because as your superior officer I'll sit in the back seat.' Her shoulders started shaking. For a moment he thought she was having a seizure, then realized she was laughing. He frowned. 'What's so funny?'

She brought out a handkerchief and wiped her eyes. 'Oh, I'm sorry, it's such a hilarious prospect!'

'Will you or will you not take the job?' he demanded, enraged.

She smiled serenely. 'I'll think about it.'

The two new recruits in Kitchener's New Army had fared very differently. Samuel Rutherford stated his case upon arrival at Perth Barracks and had stuck to his guns, or rather to his refusal to carry any. He had survived icy disapproval, rudeness, thinly disguised contempt and considerable pressure to persuade him to change his mind. All to no avail.

He was finally marched at the double-quick in front of the CO who studied him with ill-concealed disgust.

'This is a sad day, soldier. Heaven knows what your father must feel! Colonel Rutherford is a legend to us regulars who remember his bravery in the South African campaign.'

Samuel stood rigidly to attention, eyes fixed on a point one inch beyond the officer's left ear. No comment was necessary or expected. The CO tapped the desk in frustration as he eyed the fine-looking young chap standing before him, obviously a man of high calibre, good officer material but sadly flawed. Such a waste! What the devil am I to do with this fellow? he wondered.

'I see you've been classified C3, physically fit but mentally unstable, is that so?'

'Yessir.'

'I could assign you to cookhouse fatigues, but that's an easy option for slackers like you.' He studied the man's broad shoulders and glanced thoughtfully through the report lying on the desk. 'I see you're accustomed to work on the land?'

'Yessir.'

'Very well then, you'll work on the land. No Man's Land. You can begin training as a stretcher bearer.'

He scribbled a memo to that effect and dismissed the soldier. He was quietly pleased to have found a solution that would bring one shirker face to face with reality. Besides, one did not wish to upset the illustrious Colonel by having his son dig latrines for the duration.

In Glasgow, Jamie Murdoch had fared better than Samuel. He was now a name and number. It was stencilled on his kitbag, 1428 1382 Murdoch James, a rookie attached to the Highland Light Infantry. He was known as 'Jock' to his mates in Maryhill Barracks, or more familiarly, 'hey you, Jimmy!' Jamie answered to either, pleased to be one of the lads. He had taken kindly to army discipline. He had an organized mind which helped him to master complicated drill manoeuvres with ease and an excellent memory which simplified laying

51

out kit for inspection. Other recruits were not so lucky, and suffered grief at the hands of the sergeant.

Jamie had been fitter from the start than many undernourished wee runts from the Glasgow slums, and route marches across the Campsie Fells greatly increased his fitness and stamina. It wasn't long before Private Murdoch had caught the sergeant's eye. By the end of six weeks, Jamie was in line for a stripe, a spot of embarkation leave, and shipment to France.

Jamie sent a telegram to announce his arrival, which gave Agnes a few hours grace for a frantic baking session and airing of bedding before her son came home.

She hugged him tearfully. 'Jamie, love!'

'Aw, Mam, don't cry!' he said, embarrassed. He'd forgotten the heartbreak of seeing women cry. He was used to cheery, rough humour which successfully disguised fear, apprehension and homesickness. A friendly hand on the shoulder was enough to buck up a pal.

His young sister Poppy appeared in the doorway. 'Heavens, Poppy, you've grown!' he cried. He'd only been gone six weeks, but the eleven-year-old lass had stretched. Learned decorum, too, he thought with amusement, as she crossed the room gracefully and pecked his cheek.

'The teacher says Poppy's talented,' Agnes told him proudly. 'And that's without the *lah-di-dah* education Hannah and thon other one had up at the house.'

'How is Hannah?'

'Och, she's at Pitleavie House nursing wounded officers and speaking with a plum in her mouth like her gentry friends.'

He longed to ask for news of Kirsty, but could see by the glint in his mother's eye that she anticipated the question. It would be wise not to ask.

The connecting door was flung open, and his father came hurrying in from the mill liberally dusted with flour, as usual. A wave of nostalgia overcame Jamie, and father and son hugged one another in an unusual display of emotion.

Dougal held him at arm's length. 'My, but you look grand, Jamie! And they've given you a stripe already!'

'They must be hard up for lance corporals, Dad!' Jamie joked, but it was a sober truth. He'd been told there was a serious shortage of lance corporals in the trenches. The single stripe on the arm was an accurate target for snipers. Luckily, innocent civilians didn't realize promotion could spell danger.

'I knew you'd get on in the army, son,' Agnes said proudly. She bustled off to prepare the fatted calf. There was a wonderful aroma of roasting meat that made Jamie's mouth water.

'Come away into the mill till your tea's ready,' Dougal said. 'I'll show you what's been done since you left us.'

Dougal was no mean engineer, and small adjustments made to new steam engines had speeded production and improved the quality and texture of the grain. He explained there were enough orders in hand to take on three or four lads invalided out of the army, and the mill was doing very nicely, supplying fine flour for Dundee bakers. 'I'm angling for a contract to supply oats for the army horses,' Dougal said. 'The Colonel's put in a good word. I've a steady order from the co-op for pearl barley and the bakers take as much flour as I can mill and beg for more. The U-boat blockade is stopping wheat imports, you see. We could do with larger premises, Jamie.'

'So you aim to expand, Dad?'

'Aye, but the Colonel blows hot and cold. The man's strapped for cash and won't spend a penny on new building.'

'Never mind. Looks like you'll be rich before the war ends.' Dougal looked grim. 'I won't deny I'm well off, but it's for you I'm making all this money, son. It's for your future.'

Here's hoping I have one! thought Jamie dryly.

He sneaked out of the Milton the next day while his mother was pegging out washing on the green. She'd washed everything washable in the kitbag. Oh, but it was grand to fill your lungs with clean air after the smoke and smogs of Glasgow! he thought as he strode eagerly towards the big house. The June weather smiled for him. The early sun was dispelling river haze and it would be a beautiful day. He was casually dressed, a white shirt unbuttoned at the neck. He felt uncluttered and free. Just fancy, I'm only twenty! he marvelled. The past six weeks he'd felt old beyond his years. Now he was young and in love and hadn't a care in the world. But when Jamie reached Angus house the housemaid greeted him with giggles and told him Miss Kirsty was out.

He guessed where she'd be and hailed Cunningham in the stable yard. The grieve fingered his chin doubtfully. 'Last I saw of the lass, she was heading the stallion across the lower pasture at a dangerous lick. A sure sign she's troubled.'

Jamie frowned. 'What's troubling her?'

'Take your pick!' Cunningham shrugged. He indicated all the jobs needing doing. The place was falling to bits!

Jamie headed down the driveway soberly. If the little rascal hadn't taken a nasty tumble by now, she must return this way. He remembered an incident in the past that had almost claimed the lives of two wee girls and possibly his own, and quickened his pace. Kirsty came round the corner riding the weary horse at walking pace. Her expression was preoccupied; young Lochinvar lathered with sweat.

Kirsty's face lit up and she slid recklessly from the horse's back into his arms. 'Jamie! I didn't know you were home.'

In the cheerless light of the barrackroom he'd thought it would be enough for him to see her again, but now she was in his arms it was not enough. He wanted to kiss her, to make love, but resisted temptation and hugged her instead.

'I've missed you! You didn't write very often,' she said, accusingly. She studied him, head to one side. He looked lean and fit. He'd been in the army nearly two months, and nothing dreadful had happened to him. Maybe the war will end soon and I can forgive myself at last for sending him away, she thought.

He laughed. 'There's no time to write letters in Maryhill! You're bonnier than ever, you know. I bet the lads come courting!'

She laughed. 'Silly ass! I promised I'd wait for you, and I'll wait forever!'

A chill ran down his spine. 'Forever's a long time, Kirsty!' he said uneasily.

'No, it's only till you come home for good.' She stood on tiptoe and kissed him.

The Colonel's car rounded the corner at that very moment. His driver braked sharply, nearly tipping Charles off the back seat. Colonel Rutherford and Private Mildred Holland were on their way to the city in a tearing hurry. That morning an urgent message had arrived from HQ informing the colonel that the *Hampshire* was reported torpedoed and sunk off Orkney with no survivors. General Kitchener had been aboard, bound for talks in Russia to boost the allies' morale.

'Well, well!' said Mildred, smartly dressed in khaki uniform.

'What d'you mean, "Well, well"?' Charles snapped.

'Young love is wonderful, don't you think, Colonel?'

'No, I don't,' he answered, glaring at the embracing couple. 'Kirsty was fostered by the Murdoch clan and regards young Murdoch as a brother, that's all. My daughter is still a child. She's only sixteen, dammit!'

'You know what they say about sweet sixteen.'

'Drive on, driver. We'll be late,' he ordered.

The two young people had moved the horse out of the way and Mildred gave them a broad grin as she drove past. Charles looked the other way.

He was more rattled than he cared to admit. His daughter kissing James Murdoch! He had nothing against the young man, and he and Kirsty owed Agnes Murdoch a debt they could never repay, but he didn't want her son for his daughter. Not to put too fine a point on it, Kirsty could do better for herself.

Charles decided it was time he paid attention to his pretty daughter's future. Children grow up so fast! She would soon be seventeen. Rather young to be launched in society, but these were unusual times. He would write and explain the situation to his Edinburgh mother-in-law. Matchmaking is right up Lizzie Robb's street, he thought. She's sure to have a list of eligible young bachelors, preferably with wealthy parents.

Kirsty stared after the car. 'Do you think my father saw?' 'Oh yes, he saw. If looks could kill I'd drop dead!' Jamie said. Why must life be so complicated? he wondered. He glanced at her worried face. 'Does it bother you?'

'I want him to be happy. He's had years of loneliness, Jamie. That's why he spends so much time with the army.'

This was what Jamie had feared. Kirsty needed her father, and the man needed his daughter's love and support. He couldn't cause bad feeling between them. He turned away and patted Young Lochinvar's sweat-streaked flanks. 'Let's take this lad back to the stable before the poor beast gets chilled, Kirsty.' As they set off, an awkward silence fell. It seemed to both young lovers that all the brightness had faded from the lovely morning.

The nation was shocked by Lord Horatio Herbert Kitchener's sudden death. The General had been part of British military history for the past fifty years and it was hard to imagine war could be waged without him. His face was the best-known in Britain, a commanding image staring out of hundreds of thousands of recruiting posters, although it was rumoured that in real life the General had never allowed his gaze to rest upon any rank below that of sergeant.

Hannah Murdoch had been given leave of absence from nursing duties in Pitleavie House to spend the last few days of her brother's leave with him. Now that George Rutherford had returned to France, Hannah made a beeline for Angus House to catch up with Kirsty's news. Curled up on the old sofa in the schoolroom, the two young women settled down with a bowl of strawberries between them for a long, delicious chat.

It was a hazy, dreamy afternoon, and very warm. The view from the open window was sunlit and peaceful and war seemed a million miles away. But they could not forget. They were too emotionally involved.

'Any word from Samuel?' Hannah asked.

'We had a letter last week. He's finished training as a stretcher bearer.'

Hannah yawned, not quite recovered from a spell of night duty. 'Does one require training to carry stretchers? It seems a simple operation.'

'There's more to it than you might imagine, he says. They're sending him to France immediately and have refused home leave. They've been absolutely beastly to him, but he'll never give in.'

'Takes courage,' Hannah said, biting into a strawberry.

'Yes, talking about courage, what about our Holly?' Kirsty laughed.

'Papa ordered her to keep her ankles covered and she refused. She said long skirts interfered with the driving pedals and hoisted the hem another six inches.'

'Jolly good for her! She has awfully neat ankles.'

'I think he's noticed, too. I saw him looking.'

Hannah gave her a speculative glance. 'Talking of admiration, I've noticed Jamie's very smitten.'

'Is he?' She carefully selected another berry.

'You know he is.' She clasped her hands. 'Oh, Kirsty, how wonderful if you married Jamie! We'd be real sisters then!'

'Your mam would have something to say!'

Hannah dismissed that obstacle with a wave of the hand. 'Och, Mam's at that funny age. She'll grow out of it.'

Kirsty changed an awkward subject. 'How's your Honourable Marjory?'

Hannah sat up. 'I was going to tell you, but promise not to tell a soul! Marjory is joining Lady Sewell's nursing unit at Etaples in France early next year. She's arranging for me to have a further six months' training at the Infirmary, then she wants me to go with her.'

'But Hannah, you can't!' Kirsty protested. 'You're too young. VADs have to be twenty-three before they go abroad.'

'I'll be seventeen by then and quite old enough. Marjory says I can easily pass for twenty-three and she'll back me up.'

'What if you're found out?'

'I won't be. Marjory says Lady Sewell's a brick and won't ask awkward questions.'

'Remember what Holly taught us? "Oh, what a tangled web we weave, When first we practise to deceive!"' Kirsty warned.

'If I am deceiving anyone, it's in a good cause. Lady Sewell has assembled a dedicated team of titled ladies like herself. What wonderful nurses our boys will have!'

'I hope they enjoy mixing with the gentry as much as you do,' Kirsty remarked caustically.

Hannah flushed. 'You sound like your wretched brother, George!'

The door opened quietly and the Colonel entered. Hannah shut up guiltily, sure he must have overheard. Charles clutched a slip of paper in one hand, and rested the other on the back of the sofa as if he needed its support before he spoke. He was very pale.

Kirsty's heart lurched. 'Papa, what is it?'

He held out the crumpled sheet of paper for his daughter to read. 'It's bad news, I'm afraid, Kirsty dear . . .

Five

'**B**ad news?' Hannah stood up. 'I'd better go.'
'No! Stay,' the Colonel commanded sharply. 'It concerns my son, George.'

George! Hannah sank back. She'd just insulted the man, now this.

Kirsty was on her feet. 'What's happened?'

'There was a poison gas attack at Verdun while George was visiting the French lines as an observer. His CO has written to tell me it's possible George may have been blinded.'

His voice broke. Hannah gave a cry of distress, but Kirsty couldn't utter a sound. She remembered her brother's smile, his twinkling blue eyes . . . But she wouldn't break down and make things worse. To be blind was better than dying, of course, but what a prospect for an active young man! She felt suddenly angry. It shouldn't have happened. There was something preying on George's mind that had made him ill and he should never have been on active service.

She took the letter her father handed to her and read it. It ended on an optimistic note:

> *Of course, it will be some time before we can tell if George's blindness is temporary or more permanent, but I felt it my duty as George's commanding officer to warn you and your family of the possible outcome. In the meantime, I assure you that your son will have the best of care.*

She glanced up. 'There's still hope, Papa!'

He looked grim. 'I've seen battlefields and casualty clearing stations, Kirsty. Most likely George was subjected to dirt flies and infection before they got him to hospital.'

'Medical care has improved since the Boer war, Colonel,' Hannah ventured. 'There's a serum to match blood groups and they're experimenting with blood transfusions. I've seen it done. Donor and patient lie side by side with a flask containing sodium citrate solution between them. The results are amazing.'

'But can the medical profession save a man's sight?' he asked.

Hannah hesitated. She'd nursed blinded men and knew the outlook was bleak. 'No sir, not . . . not always.'

'I thought so.' He turned and quietly left the room.

Hannah groaned. 'I wanted to comfort him, and all I did was make it worse.'

Kirsty hugged her. 'My dear, you couldn't comfort my father. Nobody could.'

But there was someone who did help the colonel, merely by causing a welcome diversion. Charles had business to attend to in the small hamlet of Barry, the site of a well-established army training camp on the coast not far from Dundee. A batch of raw recruits were living under canvas while undergoing rifle training in the sand dunes. There was a buzz of excitement and much coming and going of military brasshats at Dundee HQ that summer with rumours of a 'Big Push'. In other words, an offensive planned to break the stagnation of trench warfare. One massive effort could push through German lines into the poorly defended open countryside beyond, and might even end the war. Everyone seemed to know about it, including the Dutch press, which had published speculation about a possible date that summer. Charles hoped nobody had told the Germans.

Sitting in the motor's rear seat as they drove into Dundee, Charles studied the back of his driver's head. Today, everything about the vehicle reminded him achingly of George, including Mildred Holland, his driver. Mildred had made good progress from Angus House into the city, but now they were caught in a jam of tramcars and jute carts advancing from Dock Street at a snail's pace. Cart wheels fitted snugly into tram rails and made good progress for horses hauling heavy loads of jute bales.

Charles fumed. 'Good heavens, woman, can't you hurry up? Thrawn Janet could trot faster than this!'

'Oh, I agree!' snapped Mildred. 'Janet would've battered her way past two trams and made half a dozen cart horses bolt by now.' Mildred was just as frustrated, and extremely upset to hear about George. She hauled on the brake and rested her arms on the steering wheel to let the muddle sort itself out. 'Any more news?' she asked.

'Another letter from George's CO this morning. He'll be sent to an English hospital for treatment if . . . er . . . when his condition improves.'

Mildred noted the hesitation. Driving the colonel every day, she had glimpsed some emotions Charles Rutherford kept hidden under a stiff upper lip. It was odd, but the emotions he imagined were weakness, she considered his greatest strength. She was beginning to admire and like the man, and that bothered her. She glared at the rear of a crawling tramcar, willing it to move. She'd always liked Dundee's green and cream trams, which had a home-made look that was endearing, but today she'd had enough of them. Mildred honked the horn and received an uncouth gesture from the tram conductor in reply. Irritation gave her courage to broach a subject that was certain to cause strife.

'By the way, sir, General Wilson has asked me to drive him.' She was glad she couldn't see the colonel's expression. She could bet it was thunderous.

'You refused, of course?'

'No, sir, I begged leave to consult you first. After all, the General's request was practically an order.'

'Don't pull rank on me, my girl! This is what comes of wearing scandalously short skirts. General Wilson has an eye for neat ankles.'

61

'I was hoping he admired my driving, but thanks for the compliment. I didn't know you'd noticed my ankles.'

The jute carts turned aside to trundle uphill towards mills which were working overtime on sackcloth for sandbags. The jute strike was over and there was promise of a two-shilling rise in September. She took the chance to overtake. They had reached Broughty Ferry Road and were passing mansions of the rich and well-to-do before he broke the heavy silence.

'So, what will you do?'

'If you are agreeable, sir, I shall tell the general I'm willing to drive him when he visits HQ, providing you accompany him as his aide.'

Charles considered this. He was not averse to hobnobbing with influential generals. 'I don't see any objection to that,' he said. He studied the back of his driver's head with respect. Maybe it was handy having a brainy woman at his beck and call, after all. On a more personal note, it was pleasant to sit back and contemplate a slender neck and glossy dark hair neatly coiled beneath a smart khaki hat, instead of a glengarry and whiskers. For the first time since he'd had the devastating news about George, Charles's upper lip relaxed in a smile.

Kirsty wakened with a start. She'd been dreaming about Jamie Murdoch, such a vivid dream she'd almost expected to find Jamie standing beside her, but of course the room was empty. She threw back the bedclothes and climbed out of bed. It was still barely 5.30, but she knew she couldn't hope to sleep and anyway this morning she planned a thorough audit of her father's affairs. The estate's finances had been worrying her for some time, and before the hard work of harvesting began she intended to have the financial situation quite clear.

Her father had taken even less interest in the running of the estate recently. It was as if he could not contemplate the future now his son and heir could be blind. He spent long hours at Territorial HQ and Mildred brought him home late. Kirsty suspected it was the colonel's way of coping with an impossible situation, so she took the entire burden of the estate upon herself, making decisions as she thought fit and praying for the best.

Kirsty's detailed study of the finances covered several days, and depressing weather kept pace with plunging spirits. Sunshine gave way to showers, gentle rain became a downpour and soon the Gowrie burn was a raging torrent. The lower fields flooded, the ripening grain mildewed and turned black. By her reckoning, the estate was almost running at a loss anyway and something must be done quickly to tide them over till the sheep and cattle were ready for market. She sat in her father's study going over the books, hoping she'd made a mistake, but the figures did not lie.

She could see one solution, not a welcome one, but there was no choice. She pulled on her macintosh and wellingtons and plodded through the rain to the Milton. But she did not knock at Agnes's door, she crossed the bridge over the roaring torrent and made her way into the stoury, noisy confines of the mill.

The mill was working at full stretch. Dougal Murdoch employed quite a large staff now, mostly wounded ex-servicemen, but he himself still wore dungarees and worked harder than most. He was surprised to see her. 'What brings you here, lass?'

'Could we talk privately, Mr Murdoch?'

His smile faded at the formality. 'Come into my office, Miss Rutherford.'

When they were settled, Dougal leaned forward. 'What's this about, Kirsty?'

She told him the state of the finances, holding nothing back, and his expression grew grim. 'I know your father takes little interest, but what do you propose, Kirsty?'

'You could buy the mill.'

He raised his brows. 'I'm doing fine, but I'm not made o' money!'

'I know,' she said. 'We could agree an asking price and instead of rent you could pay larger monthly instalments to include interest. At the end of an agreed period the mill would be yours. In the meantime the extra cash will help us over a bad harvest.'

Dougal considered the proposal while Kirsty waited in trepidation. She didn't know where to turn if he wouldn't co-operate. 'Please!' she begged. 'It's only right the mill should belong to you. It'll be waiting for Jamie when he comes home.'

Murdoch and Son? Dougal thought. He could see the name in gold letters above the door. If it was theirs, he and Jamie could go ahead with plans their landlord would never approve. It would be an investment and a future for Jamie, a hope for them all to cling to. He looked at the clever lass with respect. 'It's a sound idea to our mutual benefit and I'll agree to it, Miss Rutherford. I could buy all the grain the estate can grow in a good year.'

She could have danced a jig, but this was a business deal. She knew that in the eyes of the law she was still a child. 'It would be better to let my father think this is his idea,' she smiled. 'You must promise not to tell him, while I prepare the ground.'

He laughed, amused. 'I won't let on, Kirsty. Cross my heart!' And the two of them shook hands delightedly on the deal.

Nothing that passed Agnes Murdoch's window escaped her notice. She held her breath when she saw Kirsty coming and was intrigued when she walked by and disappeared into the mill. Wetting a finger and testing the heat of a flat iron with a sizzle, Agnes frowned. What's that wee madam after? she wondered uneasily.

Time passed, and, with one eye on the mill and the other on Poppy's dress, Agnes became impatient. Months ago she'd watched Kirsty Rutherford exchange words with her son. That had led to disaster, and now Dougal was threatened. Men were like putty in the wee minx's hands.

Kirsty reappeared and hesitated for a moment outside her door while Agnes held her breath, then the lass hurried on.

Agnes waited. She knew Dougal's routine and he'd be

through any minute. Sure enough, the connecting door swung open and in he came. 'What was Mistress Rutherford after?' she demanded, fists on hips.

Dougal gave her a quick glance. In this mood he'd get no peace. 'I'll tell you over a cup o' tea, love. I'm parched.'

Later on, Agnes sipped tea and considered the scheme Dougal had outlined. 'So where's the catch?'

'I can't see one. That lass has a sound head on her shoulders.'

'I don't trust her after what she did to Jamie!' Agnes said.

He held her hand. She was weepy these days, not like the laughing lass he'd married, but then you could hardly blame her. Jamie was the light of her life. 'You mustn't blame Kirsty for Jamie leaving, Agnes, love,' he said gently. 'There's terrible pressure put upon young men to go and maybe our lad was just seeking an excuse. You know the Colonel leaves the running of the estate to that poor young lass. Her only aim is to save us all from ruin. If I can pay the higher instalments I'll be my own master in time, and what's more important, so will our son.'

Agnes began to see the advantages. It's a step up the ladder, she thought. If Dougal owned the Milton and the surrounding ground, the Murdochs would be landowners with a fine future for Jamie to look forward to. 'Maybe you're right, love.' She smiled and pushed a slice of freshly baked cake towards her husband. Dougal accepted the peace offering with relief.

Poppy Murdoch could hardly wait for school to reopen after the summer holidays. Miss Lansdowne, the art teacher, had promised to teach Poppy how to use watercolours. Only gifted artists could master the technique, Miss Lansdowne said. Poppy's fingers itched to try, but she didn't own a paintbox and brushes. The box she had her eye on, in a shop in Invergowrie, cost a whole shilling and sixpence, which was expensive, but her birthday was coming and she'd been hinting. Poppy had grown impatient with the pencil drawings which Miss Lansdowne insisted must be mastered. She was tired of drawing endless Greek mouldings and plaster casts and pencil sketches of bored classmates. Arrangements of jugs, books, flowers and fruit had taught her perspective and composition, but Poppy longed to run riot with thick black pencil, scribbling wildly and smudging shadows with a fingertip. Miss Lansdowne wouldn't allow it. Not yet.

'Discipline and draughtsmanship first, Poppy dear!' she'd scold. 'When perspective, composition and anatomy are second nature, then you can begin to show us what you can do.'

Poppy lay on the bed in the room she shared with Hannah and admired a pattern of evening sunlight playing on the walls. She should have been helping her mother with domestic tasks, but there was a blazing row going on downstairs and Poppy had escaped without anyone noticing.

She could hear Hannah yelling.

'I'm going, Mam! You can't stop me!'

Their mother's voice sounded shrill with desperation. 'Oh, can't I? You need your parent's permission to leave home, my girl.'

Hannah's voice rose to a scream. 'For heaven's sake! Haven't you read about the Somme? So many casualties hospitals can't cope. The War Office needs nurses urgently and they're turning a blind eye to rules. Anyway, the VADs going to London from Pitleavie House will be under Marjory Pitleavie's care and she's very strict.'

'You should keep away from gentry folk, Hannah! They've brought nothing but trouble to this house!' Mam yelled.

'Too late. I've signed a contract. My bag's packed and we leave for London tomorrow. It's all settled. You can't stop me.'

Poppy sat up. Gosh! She'd wondered why Hannah had emptied the chest of drawers.

'If you leave this house you'll be sorry for it, Hannah!' Mam's voice sounded hopeless now and muffled with tears. Her only answer was the door slamming. Rushing to the window, Poppy pressed her nose to the glass and watched her sister head towards the main road to catch the bus.

66

It gave her a horrid feeling, watching Hannah go away from home in anger. It was as if she might never see her again.

Jamie Murdoch picked a carrot out of the mess tin and examined it with wonder. He hadn't seen a carrot all the weeks – or was it months? – that the Glasgow Highlanders had fought and died on the banks of the River Somme.

'Meat an' veg!' his pal Lofty said in awe. 'King George ought to give the heroes in the cookhouse the VC.'

Jamie agreed. It took guts to struggle through knee-deep mud to bring a steaming pot of meat and veg to lads crouched in dugouts in the front line. It happened rarely, and no wonder. Funny, he thought, savouring the carrot and licking gravy from his fingers, but it's small pleasures you remember. The horrors you live with every day are best forgot.

'What month is it?' he asked Lofty, who kept a tally of the days Jamie preferred to forget.

'End o' November, Jimmy.'

A whizzbang went screaming over their heads and exploded somewhere to the rear. Neither man turned a hair. Jamie carefully picked a dollop of mud out of the mess tin. There was steamed pud to follow. Those cookhouse lads deserved a medal!

'The good thing about November, the mud is so damn deep nothing can move,' he said.

''Cept us. Corporal says our section's on patrol over the top tonight.'

There were few currants in the pudding and it tasted of onion, but it was memorable, Jamie thought, chasing crumbs round the tin with a fingertip. Lofty was a good mate. By a stroke of incredible luck, they'd both survived the offensive unharmed. So far so good. Nobody dwelt on tomorrow. Lofty had escaped the 15th Bantams by half an inch. The Bantams were formed specially for the tiny and tough. Jamie doubted if he would have survived the last few weeks without his wee Glasgow pal.

'Have we advanced any, d'you think?' he asked.

Lofty shrugged. 'I seen thon mangled tree stump two month ago. We've gained two hundred yards.'

'We did capture High Wood, though.'

'Oh, michty, aye!'

They both fell silent. High Wood was a horror you wiped hastily from your mind. Lofty squinted at the evening sky. 'Nearly time to go roamin' in the gloamin'.'

'Wi' a lassie by your side,' finished Jamie unwisely. He mustn't think about Kirsty. Beauty and innocence did not belong in this ugliness. Her image refused to leave him. 'I'll wait forever,' she'd whispered.

'Forever's a long time,' he said aloud.

'You can say that again, mate!' Lofty laughed. He picked up his rifle and bayonet and examined the weapons scrupulously. He polished them with a ragged piece of knitting someone's mother had sent, then stood up. 'Here's the Corp, dead on time.'

Eight men had assembled soundlessly in the gathering gloom. There was an uneasy silence at the unfortunate choice of words, but nobody said anything.

'Right then. Give's a leg up, Jimmy,' Lofty said.

Jamie obliged, then wriggled out of the trench after his chum, into the weird, chaotic half-light of no-man's-land.

Kirsty's scheme worked perfectly. Her father believed it was his own idea to sell the mill to Dougal Murdoch by instalments.

'It's fortunate I landed an order to supply fodder for army horses, Kirsty. Murdoch won't be short of funds to pay instalments,' he said.

Kirsty kissed his cheek. 'You *are* clever, Daddy!'

'The trained military mind, my dear. Always ready to grasp an opportunity,' Charles agreed complacently.

Charles had more than one reason to feel grateful that November morning. The post had brought two letters, one from George's CO to tell him George would be transferred to hospital in England, and the other in response to a plan concocted with his mother-in-law Lizzie Robb some weeks ago. This contained an invitation:

My dear granddaughter (of whom I have seen not enough over the years, Charles!) is invited to come spend a winter season with me in Edinburgh. Of course, even in the capital wartime is dreary and tiresome, but there are still pleasant soirées and parties worth attending. Although Kirsty is rather young to be introduced to society functions, I am sure my granddaughter would be an asset to any gathering. Besides, without a mother's tender care, the poor child's wardrobe must suffer, and I shudder to think what her social skills can be like, marooned in the uncouth countryside!

'What a blasted cheek!' Kirsty cried after she'd read the letter.

Charles smiled. 'Oh, I don't know. You haven't seen much of the old dear, and reading between the lines she's lonely. It would be only civil to accept the offer and spend some time with your grandmother. After all, Kirsty, you are her only granddaughter and I daresay the poor old soul would love some young company.' He played shamelessly upon his daughter's kind heart, but couldn't hide a grin as he imagined Lizzie's fury if she heard herself referred to as a 'poor old soul'.

Kirsty looked guilty. 'You're right, Father, I have neglected her. It's sweet of Grandma to want to see me, and it's thoughtful of her to worry about entertaining me. Of course, I don't mind about dresses and parties, I shall be quite content to read to her in the evening. I expect her eyesight is failing.'

'I expect so,' Charles agreed blithely. When he'd met his mother-in-law in Edinburgh to approve a list of suitable candidates for his daughter's hand, Mistress Robb's piercing blue eyes had struck him as remarkably keen.

Royal Terrace, Edinburgh is as imposing as the name suggests. The terrace of magnificent dwellings was once the

69

traditional home of wealthy city merchants, who from impressive windows could keep an eye on the comings and goings of cargo ships berthed at Leith Docks. Years ago, the terrace had been dubbed Whisky Row by local wags, and the nickname stuck.

Edward Merrilees, a merchant himself, actually preferred the nickname. Present day merchants inhabiting Royal Terrace were, like Edward, self-made men who owed some of their sizeable income to the export of Scotland's national drink. Apart from Mrs Lizzie Robb, of course, who occupied a neighbouring suite of apartments to his. That lady was a brigadier's widow and aggressively teetotal.

It seemed colder than usual, even for the middle of January, and Edward shivered as he walked along the terrace. Or is it because I'm wearing thin evening togs? he wondered. He envied his twin daughters, one hanging on each arm, cosily wrapped in expensive furs.

Pearl grimaced. 'This evening will be a frightful bore, Daddy.'

'Utterly, completely boring,' Ruby agreed.

'When Mistress Robb issues an invitation, one does not refuse. One goes and grins and bears it,' he said mildly.

'I hope this bunch of officers is more interesting than the lot Lettie Parsons had at her do. I never met such dreeps, Dad,' Ruby remarked.

Her twin nodded. 'They were infantry, Daddy. We like cavalry,'

Edward sighed. His daughters were well-built sixteen-year-olds passionately in love with horses. Unfortunately, they had taken after their poor dead mother, whose passion for galloping horses full tilt at fences had ended in one final, fatal accident. He'd hated horses ever since and preferred to stick to his Rolls Royce.

'I gather the object of the exercise is to introduce Mrs Robb's granddaughter to eligible husbands,' he said. 'I'm attending as a strong-arm chaperone in case any young gentleman steps out of line. Your presence is not required in the marriage stakes, girls. As you know I'm absolutely

70

against youthful marriages.' Edward had married at 18, been a father a year later, and a widower at 30. Since the tragedy six years ago he feared he had given his beloved twins a somewhat unorthodox upbringing, but he'd done his best.

Pearl wrinkled her nose. 'I don't mind the officers so much, but do we have to endure the silly old granddaughter?'

'Not old, my dears. Seventeen, I believe.'

They mounted steps towards a brass-bound bell-pull. 'Bound to be silly, though,' Ruby muttered glumly.

Lizzie Robb greeted Edward graciously and steered him towards an alcove which gave a fine view of the ballroom where Scottish reels were in full swing. Ridiculously young officers were dancing with girls or drinking fruit cup and nibbling sandwiches at tables round the walls. Apart from the khaki uniforms, one could hardly tell there was a war on. A frisson of interest ran round the female chaperones as Edward took his seat. He was handed an orange drink and a plate of bite-sized sandwiches and obviously not expected to participate in dancing.

Disappointing, he thought. He was not yet in his dotage and enjoyed an energetic eightsome reel. Well, at least the crowded room was beautifully warm. He settled down to keep an eye on the proceedings, though his manly presence seemed superfluous. Mrs Robb had the young officers thoroughly cowed. Anyway, Edward pitied any fresh young man who attempted anything improper with his well-built daughters. He noticed the twins were talking animatedly to a girl in a shimmering, silvery-blue gown.

The nearest mama leaned across and whispered, 'That's Mistress Robb's granddaughter, Mr Merrilees. Isn't she lovely?'

Edward gazed and felt his whole body – indeed his heart – shimmer and shiver as if he'd had a silvery-blue electric shock.

'Yes. Yes, she is,' he agreed weakly.

Kirsty took thankfully to the Merrilees twins the moment they appeared. The two were a great relief after giggling females

71

and stupid, ogling young men. Kirsty had seen right away that the men were poor immature creatures and felt quite maternal in her pity for them. The twins had immediately recognized a kindred spirit and ranged themselves protectively either side, banishing Kirsty's admirers with ferocious glares. The three young women drank jugs of orange juice, demolished plates of sandwiches and exchanged laughing confidences while seated at one of the tables.

'Do you have horses on your father's estate?' Pearl asked Kirsty enviously once her lifestyle had been established.

'Oh, yes!' Kirsty told them about Young Lochinvar and eagerly outlined plans for brood mares and riding stables. 'I could teach riding as well maybe. It's amazing how many people ride like a sack of potatoes.'

The twins exchanged a telepathic glance. 'I say, Kirsty, if you're looking for a mate for Lochinvar, our mare Guinevere comes from good hunter stock. She's three years old and takes fences like a dream,' Pearl said.

'She sounds like the answer to my prayers. Would your father agree, though?' Kirsty demanded delightedly.

They laughed. 'Daddy agrees to everything. He didn't bat an eyelid when we told him we wanted to be vets when we leave school.'

Kirsty was startled. 'Can women be vets?'

'Dad says women can be anything they want to be.'

Kirsty glanced curiously towards this paragon of fatherhood. He was younger than she'd expected and was watching them. Caught out staring, Kirsty hurriedly looked the other way.

Since his wife's untimely death, Edward Merrilees had concentrated on turning his late father's business into a global enterprise with interests in tea, coffee, spirits and rubber. The war had put that on hold, but meantime he had secured lucrative contracts to supply local goods to the War Office. Apart from his daughters, women had had no part in Edward's busy life. So why should his heart hammer like a gong when he saw a beautiful girl who seemed to shine like a star? Edward took a quick sip of orange juice and found his hands were shaking. A girl not much older than my own daughters? I must be mad! he thought.

After a winter season spent with her energetic grandmother, Kirsty was glad to return to the peace and quiet of the countryside. Quite early on she had seen through Lizzie's attempts at matchmaking, and her grandmother's efforts in that direction had merely amused her. None of the young officers made any impression. How could they, when her heart belonged to Jamie?

Although her grandmother's hopes of a match were dashed, at least Kirsty had made friends with the Merrilees twins, who were great fun. She couldn't say the same for their father. Mr Merrilees had been brusque to the point of rudeness with her. She suspected he'd even gone far out of his way to avoid her. Thinking about the man once she was back home, she tossed her head with annoyance. So, he didn't like her, well, so what! She didn't like him!

She went to the stables and told Young Lochinvar she'd found a mate for him. The twins had urged her to ride Guinevere at the East Lothian farm where the mare was stabled and Kirsty had been impressed. She was everything Kirsty had hoped for.

'Sweet, docile and beautiful, Lochinvar,' she told the stallion. 'You'll meet when the time is right, I promise.'

Kirsty left the stables, preoccupied with plans for the future, and was dismayed when she almost fell over Agnes Murdoch, who was gathering kindling by the edge of the wood. Agnes had already collected an armful of dry twigs and that made escape awkward. For a moment neither knew what to say, then Agnes made up her mind to speak out. She'd had time to reconsider. To be honest, she'd missed seeing Kirsty around the estate. The place had seemed quite dull without her.

'Kirsty love, I'm sorry,' she said. 'I don't know what got into me, but I'd no right to blame you for Jamie leaving. Can we be friends?'

'We can be more than friends, Mam! I've never stopped loving you!' Kirsty cried.

'Aye well,' Agnes smiled. 'Come to the Milton and we'll celebrate with a cup of tea.'

On the way, Kirsty regaled her foster-mother with an account of life in Edinburgh.

Agnes couldn't believe it. 'Afternoon tea served on a silver tray with plates of tiny wee sandwiches and scones that wouldn't feed a mouse, Kirsty? What a carry on!'

They were laughing when they reached the Milton, but laughter faded when they saw the red bicycle propped beside the door and a uniformed lad holding the dreaded brown telegram. The sight was every woman's worst nightmare these days. Agnes dropped the twigs and clutched Kirsty's arm. They supported one another as Agnes tore the envelope open. She held the War Office telegram so that Kirsty could read the words:

Regret to inform you that Lance Corporal James Murdoch 1st Div. Glasgow Highlanders is reported missing presumed killed on active service.

Agnes let out a moaning wail.

Kirsty hugged her desperately. 'Mam, Mam! They don't know for sure. Don't give up hope! Please don't—!'

But the older woman stared at her as if she were a stranger, then shoved her aside and ran into the house.

Six

K irsty stood shivering outside the Milton in the chill February morning.

'Will there be a reply, miss?' the telegram boy asked. There rarely was, but he was duty bound to ask.

She shook her head and he swung a leg thankfully over the bike's crossbar and escaped. Kirsty gathered the scattered kindling Agnes had dropped. It would be needed. Arms full, she put a shoulder to the door and went inside. The twigs scraped against the door panel as Kirsty closed it, but the sound made no impression upon Agnes Murdoch. She sat at the table staring into space, hands resting on the flimsy telegram that had shattered her life.

Kirsty crossed to the wicker basket where the kindling was kept. A long piece wouldn't fit, so she broke it across her knee with a resounding crack which echoed through the room like a rifle shot.

Agnes winced. 'Don't!'

'Mam, there's still hope.'

'Precious little!'

'You mustn't give up hope!' There was no answer. Kirsty's eyes blurred with tears. Maybe there was only a slender chance that Jamie was alive, but she loved him and daren't stop hoping. If she did, she'd have nothing. If only she didn't feel so guilty! If I'd held my tongue that day, would he be with us now? she agonized. She picked up the bellows and roused the fire, blowing on the dull embers till they glowed red and flamed up. Even so, she felt cold.

From his office window Dougal Murdoch had seen the red bike coming. He'd watched the telegraph boy disappear round the side of the mill and seen Agnes and the young lass reach the Milton at the same moment. For the life of him he couldn't move a muscle. It had to be Jamie. Who else could it be?

The floor shook beneath Dougal's feet. The building always resounded to the beating heart of the mill, but he'd never heard it sounding so loud. He waited in trepidation for the sound of women weeping, but all he heard was the clamour of machinery. Dougal stumbled from the office. His men glanced up and exchanged a startled look as he passed without a word and pushed open the connecting door.

His wife sat at the table and the young lass crouched beside the hearth. He had never known the room so quiet. He put an arm around Agnes and read the telegram spread between her hands.

'Missing!' he cried. Dougal was suddenly weak with relief. 'I thought he was dead. There's hope yet, love!'

'Hope makes the heart sick. I'll not live in hope and sicken, Dougal. I'd rather face the worst now,' his wife said.

Dougal was dismayed. 'But you mustn't give up hope, love! Tell her she mustn't, Kirsty.' He turned to the lass. She had a wise head on young shoulders. Surely she'd know what to say to help Agnes?

'I tried. She wouldn't listen.' Kirsty buried her face in her hands and sobbed.

Dougal had expected more spunk from her. He waved her away impatiently. 'Och, run away home to your pa. Agnes and I have enough on our plate!'

Shamed, Kirsty crept away. Agnes watched her go. 'You were hard on the girl, Dougal.'

'I can't be scunnered with wailing women at a time like this.'

'Woman? She's only seventeen.' Agnes felt strangely calm. The worst brings out the best in me, she thought with surprise. Already she was making plans. 'Hannah should be told, Dougal. I don't know how, since she went off in the huff and left no address.'

'I'll cycle over to Pitleavie House. They'll know where she is and send word.' He put an arm round his wife and kissed her cold cheek. 'Will you be all right on your own, my dear?'

'I'm fine. Away you go.' She'd been a weepy wet blanket for weeks, but she could feel strength flooding back. She'd report to the Red Cross tomorrow, though some bossy women in charge were enough to put your back up. She'd volunteer to roll bandages, make bog-moss dressings, anything to help wounded soldiers. But first she'd scrub the floor before Poppy came home from school and had to be told. Aye. Down upon my knees. That's where I ought to be, Agnes thought . . .

Hannah Murdoch had not expected London streets to be paved with gold, but even so she found the city disappointing. The Hon Marjory Pitleavie and her group of VADs arrived at King's Cross station tired and travel-stained in a train packed with troops and civilians. They were met by an off-duty orderly who pointed them towards a crowded bus heading for Edgeware Road and their lodgings. Hannah's first impressions were not favourable. War-weary crowds thronged pavements lined with sooty buildings, a jumble of traffic congested streets that were narrower than she'd imagined. Here and there she caught glimpses of destruction caused by Gotha bombers and Zeppelin raids. Surreptitiously, Hannah wiped away a tear, homesick for the pure clean air of home.

It wasn't so bad once they'd had a good night's sleep and were introduced to the wards at the London War Hospital. Marjory Pitleavie had arranged for her squad to receive three months' training with cases they might expect to find once they went to France.

Hannah and a jolly, roly-poly member of the aristocracy named Beatrice Fellowes were placed in Sister Frances's ward. She was a formidable woman who certainly didn't intend to be lenient with these new recruits.

'Follow me!' she ordered.

They had reached the closed door of the ward, and Sister paused. 'You will start in a ward which treats abdominals and chests, next month you will move on to limbs and lungs, and end the course with facial injuries and eyes. After three months I trust you will have learned respect for your seniors if nothing else. These patients are officers and gentlemen and only trained nurses will attend them. You will keep your eyes lowered, mouths shut and fetch and carry when told.'

'Bed pans and bottles!' muttered Beatrice.

'Exactly,' said Sister Frances.

So began the busiest weeks of Hannah's life. She could hardly take time to shed tears when the news came that her brother Jamie was missing.

They were on night duty and Beatrice hugged her. 'Buck up, old thing. He'll turn up. My brother went missing for a spell too, but he'd only got himself lost behind enemy lines and came back leading half a dozen prisoners. They promoted him to captain. What rank is your brother, by the way?'

'Captain.' The lie came out pat.

'Jolly good, just like mine.'

To keep her end up, Hannah had adopted Kirsty's identity with one or two embellishments, such as a wealthy father and a remote Scottish castle and estate. She'd created the illusion by smiling knowingly when the subject of land or parentage was mentioned, and her first-class education had helped bolster it. She hadn't told a downright lie till this moment, and the lie was a serious jolt to the system. Marjory Pitleavie knew all about Hannah's background, of course, but Marjory didn't care tuppence whether one's father was duke or dustman.

'I expect they'll promote your brother when they find him,' Beatrice said kindly.

'I expect they will.'

Which was more nonsense, but strangely comforting. Hannah dried her eyes and prepared to face the rigours of night duty a little more cheerfully.

Kirsty was expecting visitors and had a busy schedule ahead. The guest bedrooms had to be dusted and aired, beds made and shabby old furniture polished.

Kirsty's friends Pearl and Ruby Merrilees had kept the postie busy lately concerning the mare Guinevere, chosen to be Young Lochinvar's mate. Kirsty had welcomed the diversion as time passed with no word of Jamie. She had found it difficult to keep hope alive when his mother had so patently abandoned it.

Fierce frosts and snowfalls in March had thawed and the east coast was enjoying a spell of mild spring weather that April. Kirsty and the twins had arranged a meeting. They would bring Guinevere to Angus estate, and had agreed the mare would remain in Cunningham and Kirsty's care until a foal was born.

She had written asking how the horse was to be transported, but the twins had dismissed that airily. *Don't worry*, they'd replied, *Daddy will fix it.* Kirsty had raised her brows. She'd gathered that Daddy couldn't abide horses. Maybe that was why he was so keen to be rid of this one.

I must be mad! Edward Merrilees thought. He was inching a cattle float containing one precious mare on to the Forth ferry, his excited daughters prancing around on deck yelling encouragement. He disliked dealing with horses at any time, but this was the most hazardous manoeuvre yet. He edged the lorry across the ramp to the deck. The vessel heaved at a crucial moment and there was a loud rasp of damaged metal. The captain glowered from the bridge.

The twins cheered. Well done, Daddy! You only took a lick of paint off the ferry and the dent in the lorry hardly shows. Darling Guinevere is fine.'

I must be mad! he thought again as the busy little ferry plied across the river. He should have put his foot down when this expedition was suggested. He should have told the twins that Jock the warehouseman would transport the wretched animal to its destination.

But who could withstand concentrated hugs, kisses and cajolings? Who could resist tearful pleas that the bridal mare could not be deprived of loving support en route to the nuptials?

So, he had given in. He had ignored his wise head and followed his heart, which even now was beating faster than was good for him at the thought of seeing Kirsty Rutherford. He prayed this trip would end the infatuation. He would see her as she really was and not in flattering settings engineered by her cunning grandma. He would meet a country girl on her home ground – very nearly bankrupt ground, if rumours could be believed.

Still, he had to admit the countryside grew prettier as they drove on. They stopped once at the twins' insistence to let the mare graze in an obliging farmer's field, then stopped once more in Perth to attend to the lorry's needs. Edward's insides were tied in nervous knots as they approached Kirsty's home. They turned aside in clear air just before reaching the smoky yellow haze that obliterated Dundee, and proceeded along a driveway that was in a dangerously potholed condition.

Glimpsing a large house ahead, Edward took a right turn which he rightly guessed would lead to outbuildings and stopped the lorry in a yard. Nearby stood a motor containing two individuals arguing so fiercely that the lorry's arrival completely escaped their notice.

'I saw the wretched man kiss you with my own eyes!' the officer in the back seat was accusing the lady driver.

'A friendly peck on the cheek. Besides, it's none of your business, Colonel! I am a volunteer. I've a good mind to resign.'

'You can't, you'd never find another job.'

'Oh, wouldn't I?'

The Colonel discovered he had an audience and his face turned a deeper shade of beetroot. 'Oh, ah . . . there you are! Sorry I can't stay, but Kirsty will be back in a tick. I have a meeting and I'm late already . . .' He glared at the lady driver, who angrily let in the clutch and accelerated so fast it caught her passenger unawares and he fell backwards in an untidy heap on the back seat.

The car had barely gone before the cobbles resounded to the thunder of hooves, and a magnificent stallion came cantering into the yard. Kirsty slid from the saddle, boots and skirt mud-spattered. Her face lit up as she called out a greeting.

Past memories of a terrible tragedy came flooding back and left Edward frozen in his seat. He had a crazy impulse to gather her in his arms, take her away from the danger lurking in the hooves of the great black beast. He cursed the chance that had brought her to meet him looking like this, small and vulnerable, oblivious of the dangerous power of the horse, and her power as a woman.

Edward leaned his arms glumly on the steering wheel while his twins spilled out with girlish squeals, hugging Kirsty, patting the big horse that could easily crush them beneath its massive weight. He closed his eyes against the horrors of imagination, and when he opened them she was looking up at him.

'I'd no idea you'd intended driving the lorry yourself, Mr Merrilees!'

'The lorry driver couldn't be spared, but don't worry, I'll arrange to stay in a hotel till the girls are ready to go home.'

'Nonsense! You'll stay here, of course!' she smiled. 'There are more bedrooms in Angus House than we know what to do with.' She seemed mature beyond her years in the confident role of hostess, and Edward mumbled a weak acceptance, mentally kicking himself.

After dinner that evening it took only an hour or so to gauge the situation in Angus estate. Conversation over a glass of port in the colonel's study confirmed Edward's suspicions. His host's talk was of war, weapons and defensive tactics, yet it was obvious house and land needed their owner's undivided attention. When Edward guided the conversation gently in that direction, Charles Rutherford grew impatient.

'Oh, Kirsty sees to that! Now, sir, you may recall that during the Boer War . . .'

Poor Kirsty! Edward thought as the colonel rambled on. He could see the whole crumbling edifice rested on her slender young shoulders.

Next morning, while her father went off to attend rifle drill, Kirsty gave her guests a guided tour. Her pride in what had been achieved and her frustration over what still needed doing were evident, but the twins only saw the romantic side.

'You *are* lucky to live in such a big, beautiful place, Kirsty!' Pearl sighed enviously.

'You wouldn't think so if you had to make it pay. Give me Royal Terrace any day.'

Ruby wrinkled her nose. 'It's only a boring old terrace.'

Ungrateful hussy! Edward thought, mildly.

'It's a breeding ground for wealthy husbands, according to Grandmama Robb!' Kirsty laughed.

The twins giggled. 'You didn't fancy the chinless wonders!'

'Ah, but I'm spoken for!'

Edward paused. This was news to him. His daughters were immediately agog. 'Who's the lucky man? Come on, Kirsty, tell us!'

'His name is James Murdoch . . . but I'd rather not talk about it if you don't mind.'

Now, is she shy, or is there perhaps parental disapproval? Edward wondered.

The twins opted for romantic shyness. 'Of course, Kirsty. We understand,' they nodded, worldly-wise.

Cunningham came hurrying towards them at that moment. He looked worried. 'I'm having trouble calving a heifer, Miss Kirsty. I'll need help. We'll maybe need to call in the vet.'

'It's ten shillings before he'll cross the threshold, Mr Cunningham!'

'Aye, that's so.'

'We'll see what we can do ourselves first.' She turned apologetically to her guests. 'I'm sorry, I must leave you to your own devices for a bit.'

'Can we come?' begged Pearl eagerly.

She hesitated. 'It could be messy. I'm not sure if you—'

'They want to be vets,' Edward said. 'That includes cows in labour as well as pussy cats.'

'Oh, very well. Come on.'

Edward followed her to the byre. This experience would either confirm his daughters' career or scupper it. The poor animal was obviously deeply distressed. It was sad to see. One felt helpless.

But not Kirsty. She had rolled up her sleeves and tied a sacking apron round her waist and was examining the cow.

'It's a big calf for a heifer to carry, Mr Cunningham, but the calf's alive and quite well presented. Don't you think we should end this quickly before the mother is too exhausted to help and the calf suffocates?'

'Aye, we should, but it'll tak' more strength than yours to help me with the ropes.' He eyed Edward doubtfully. 'This gentleman has the muscle, if he has the guts.'

'Tell me what to do,' Edward said.

In the end, it was the desperate efforts of all present that brought a living, breathing calf slipping into the world. Kirsty cleared the tiny animal's nostrils with a twist of straw as it lay beside the mother.

'Wonderful!' Edward breathed. His jacket lay somewhere in the straw and his shirt was torn and filthy. His daughters were in no better state, but the Merrilees family had come through the ordeal with flying colours.

He had no words to express his admiration for Kirsty. He had seen her radiant in a shimmering gown and fallen in love with a vision. Now he saw her in a stained overall, gently tending a newborn calf, and knew he would love her till he died.

Soon the mother had recovered sufficiently to lick her calf and nudge it on to shaky, spindly legs. Kirsty laughed. 'Look, see how wise she is! She knows the wee one needs colostrum, the first milk after birth, if it's to grow big and strong.'

Pearl tugged Edward's sleeve. 'Dad, did you notice? We didn't faint!'

'And neither did you, Daddy,' Ruby added.

The last day of the visit arrived too soon. Edward had a meeting to attend in Edinburgh. He had hardly spoken more than a few words to Kirsty and never been alone with her, but she filled his thoughts to the exclusion of all else. He tossed and turned fitfully, and rose restlessly after dawn. The house was dark and sleeping, only a yawning maid carrying a coal scuttle greeted him with startled surprise as he made his way outside.

Despite the dilapidation, it was a beautiful place and

Edward could understand why Kirsty loved it so. The love of house and land showed in her eyes as she looked across the ill-tended acres, he could see it in her small hands, red and rough with hard work. To be honest, he could not imagine where he, a middle-aged man, might fit into the picture. He wondered about James Murdoch, the young man – he would be young! – who had won her heart. Did he share her dreams for the place?

To Edward's amazement, he came out of a darkness of overgrown trees to find her leaning on the paddock fence, feeding sugar lumps to the mare. Heart thumping foolishly, he walked over and leaned his elbows on the fence beside her. 'You're up very early!'

'I wanted peace to think, Mr Merrilees, and this is the best time.'

'I apologize for my rowdy daughters. I know coherent thought is impossible.'

'Oh, I don't mind them! They're my friends.' She gave him an earnest glance. 'You've no idea how much I've enjoyed your visit. It's helped me over a very bad time.'

Some intuition of sadness made him say gently, 'Tell me about James Murdoch.'

'There's nothing to tell, Mr Merrilees. That's what's so awful. Nobody knows where he is or what's happened to him. He's been posted missing.'

'I'm so sorry, Kirsty.' He meant it. If this young man could make her happy, then he prayed with all his heart that James Murdoch was alive.

The mare nuzzled Kirsty and she offered the horse the last sugar lump. 'It's been months now. You'll think I'm daft to keep on hoping.'

'No. It's what I would expect of you.'

'But you hardly know me!'

'I know enough to wish my harum-scarum daughters could be like you when they grow up.'

'I'm only a few months older than they are, Mr Merrilees!'

'I know. But they're children, and you're a very beautiful, mature young woman.' He knew at once he'd allowed emotion to run away with him, and his heart sank as he noted her embarrassment.

Kirsty didn't know where to look. The twins' father had stayed in the background for most of the visit, making no secret of the fact he hated horses. He had hardly addressed a word to her, but had talked endlessly with her father. She'd decided he disapproved of her preoccupation with animals. Now came this emotional compliment out of the blue.

Kirsty collected her wits. 'Oh, I'm afraid you flatter me!' she said lightly. She could smell coalsmoke. Cook had roused the kitchen range. She adopted the safe role of hostess. 'The kettle will be boiling. Would you prefer tea or coffee, Mr Merrilees?'

Edward's spirits sank even lower. 'Thank you, a cup of tea would be fine.'

They walked to the house in silence in the grey, colourless dawn.

Hannah Murdoch had almost completed three months' training in the London War Hospital. It had proved invaluable, and the pretty VAD was popular with her officer patients. She did not always heed Sister Frances's advice: keep your eyes down and remember they have womenfolk of their own! In fact, when Sister wasn't around, Hannah flirted shamelessly. It amused her to have high-ranking officers mooning over her. She wondered if they would be so keen if they knew she was an ordinary country girl. It was fun to lead them on, and her aristocratic friend Beatrice backed up the illusion.

Unfortunately, illusions can be shattered.

Over the weeks, Hannah and Beatrice had worked their way through a range of injuries which culminated in ears, noses, throats and eyes. There were only two more weeks to go when Hannah walked briskly into the ward one morning and found herself face to face with a new admission. She turned cold with shock. It was George Rutherford.

True, his eyes were bandaged, but a quick peek at his records revealed that damage caused by phosgene gas had healed and bandages and dressings from a recent operation

85

on scar tissue were to be removed any day. George's arrival could end the story of Hannah's noble birth. She'd be a laughing stock!

'Don't stand gawping, Nurse. Help me settle this soldier,' Sister Frances ordered. It was fortunate Sister was on duty at the time, because VADs were not permitted to speak, and it was on the cards George would recognize her voice instantly.

Just my luck! she thought as she helped Sister make him comfortable. When the bandages were removed George would recognize her and the game would be up.

'Maybe I should go on night duty, Sister,' Hannah suggested later. If George were asleep there would be less chance of recognition.

'Take the easy option? Oh, no, you don't! You'll report to the ward at 7.30 tomorrow morning. The eye specialist is doing the rounds and I want the ward gleaming.'

Next morning Hannah stood trembling by the door, listening to the quick tramp of specialist and acolytes approaching. She planned to nip outside as they barged in, but Sister foiled the attempt, shoving a metal dish containing syringe and thermometer into her hands.

'Follow me, Nurse!'

They joined a circle around George's bed, Hannah to the fore where George could not miss her.

'Now then, Captain Rutherford, we shall see what we can see,' said the specialist.

Hannah watched breathlessly as George's bandages and dressings were removed. He lay at first with eyes shut, then blinked them cautiously open and looked around. He seemed puzzled.

'Well?' the specialist demanded.

'I thought it was morning, but it's pitch black. Are the blinds drawn?' Nobody spoke. The metal dish rattled in Hannah's hands. She would gladly have been branded a fraud, if only George Rutherford could see. His records showed the operation had been a last attempt to save his sight. Alas, it had failed.

Seven

A woman's quiet voice said 'Goodnight, *Engländer*.' The soldier stirred restlessly. 'No! Scottish.' 'There is difference?' 'Of course there's a difference!' James Murdoch opened his eyes and saw a shadowy face beneath a white cap. She was smiling. 'You are angry. This is better.' She could be right, he thought hazily. It was months since Jamie had felt any emotion at all and even mild irritation was welcome. He remembered that after the shell exploded he had been totally deaf. It had been a bewildering experience. His captors had shouted commands he couldn't hear, and kicked him when he didn't respond. They had marched him to a prison camp behind the lines, stripped him of the ragged tatters of his uniform, sloshed blood off his shivering body with a bucket of icy water and given him workman's clothing and a pair of old boots that never fitted. Then they'd put him to work with a gang of refugees and displaced persons, repairing roads and relaying damaged railway tracks.

Hearing had returned eventually, but then he had been isolated from his companions by the barrier of language. His fellow prisoners were mostly Russians, French, Belgians and Italians. He gathered that having been found wandering behind enemy lines he was lucky to be alive. Others had been shot as spies.

It was obvious that the German army in that sector was short of manpower and glad of any help it could muster to restore communications. For weeks during that deplorable winter the prisoners toiled like navvies. However, navvies require good food, and a diet of weak vegetable broth and rye bread was not enough for hard-worked prisoners. Jamie fell sick. He struggled on till one day he fainted by the side of the track. With the ever present fear of typhoid and cholera, the camp guards hastily loaded the sick man on to a passing trainload of prisoners of war, bound for Germany. As the secure cattle-trucks rattled onwards Jamie recovered consciousness, and when the train stopped in the early hours at a junction called Trier, his groans attracted the attention of a German MO who happened to be checking on the sick and dying.

Jamie was carried from the train to a nearby German army barracks, a grim stronghold doing duty as a hospital for prisoners of war. There he was treated kindly by German medical staff, stripped, bathed and tucked into bed. They did not know what to make of the new arrival, who had no identification and muttered deliriously in a garbled version of English. He very nearly died with pneumonia, but after weeks of nursing Jamie Murdoch had survived. Slowly, painfully and cautiously, he was returning to life.

'*Wasser trinken*?' The Sister held out a large jug of water. She carefully poured a glass, then supported him while he drank. The water was cold and refreshing and her arm was warm. Small comforts indeed, but gratitude brought tears to his eyes.

'Thank you, Sister.'

She plumped the pillows and settled him down. She was not a bonnie woman, but beauty was not important to James Murdoch at that moment. His eyes followed her as she continued the round of the ward. She had a warm smile and a kind word for every man.

'*Bon nuit, Français . . . Buona sera, Italiano . . . Pokoynoy nochee, Russki . . .*' She had bothered to learn those few words to comfort sick captives far from home. It was so kind!

Her face hovered close to his for a moment, a twinkle in her eye. 'Good night, Scottish!'

'*Güte nacht, Schwester Elise,*' he managed carefully, smiling.

Sister Elise stood still for a moment. It was the first time this *Engländer* – no! this Scottish – had smiled since he had arrived. And such a smile!

A smile to capture your heart.

Dougal Murdoch held the buff envelope in shaking hands.

'I can't open it, Agnes. I haven't the nerve!'

'Give it here!' She took it from him. 'It's best to face the worst.' Resolutely, Agnes ripped open the envelope and read the contents. She gave a shout. 'Jamie's alive! The Red Cross traced him. He's a prisoner in Germany.'

'Thank God! Oh, Agnes, thank God!'

Agnes had never seen her husband cry. He was dressed in overalls as he'd come hurrying in from the mill, and his tears made clean tracks down his floury cheeks. It would have been comical if it hadn't been so moving. He sobbed helplessly, and she hugged him to her breast. 'Hush, my dearie, it's over now. Our boy's safe.'

He wiped his eyes. 'It was difficult to keep hoping, Agnes. Weeks went by. It was difficult.'

'Yes, love, I know.'

He looked shamefaced. 'You've been wonderful. A tower of strength.'

'No. I gave him up for dead. I'm not sure I can look Jamie in the face when he comes back.'

'We could maybe write to him now. Does it say where?'

She examined the official note. 'It just says they located him in hospital.'

'What's wrong with him?'

'It doesn't say, only that he's recovering and they'll keep us informed.'

'More worry! It's been three years! When'll it end?'

'Worry'll not speed the end, dear,' she said. So calm, yet it's me that should be crying, Agnes thought. She'd lost the ability when she'd abandoned hope and now her only emotion – if you could call it that – was a warmth spreading outward from the heart. Still, though emotionally dead she'd worked tirelessly for the Red Cross, and they'd rewarded her by finding her boy. She'd be grateful to them all the days of her life.

'Kirsty Rutherford should be told, Dougal.'

'Must we? She hasn't been near us for weeks.'

'It was you that sent her away,' she reminded him. 'It would be a kind gesture if you were to tell her the good news yourself. It's more than a passing affection wee Kirsty has for Jamie, and it's my belief Jamie was biding his time till the girl was grown.'

Dougal was startled. 'The Colonel's daughter and our son? That could never be.'

'Could it not? Consider, my dear. You're making money hand over fist and well on the way to owning the mill while the Colonel hasn't two ha'pennies to rub together. It would be the saving of the man if his lass and our clever lad were to marry. The way those two were carrying on before Jamie went to France, it's on the cards.'

'What d'you mean, carrying on?'

She smiled. 'There's a grand view from this window down the lovers' path through the wood. The kissing and cuddling I've seen over the years would amaze you, Dougal . . . and mortify many!'

He frowned. 'I thought you were dead set against her?'

'I've come to my senses. If you'll just run up to the big house and tell Kirsty, I'll scrub the floor.'

'You scrubbed it yesterday!'

'I know, but I need to get down on my knees and scrub it, today.'

When Poppy Murdoch heard the news she decided to paint a picture. It would be a painting of green fields, sunshine and blue skies. She was sad Jamie was still a prisoner, because that meant her brother wasn't free to come home, so she would paint a few grey clouds, but with silver linings.

Last birthday Mam and Dad had taken heed of broad hints and bought her a paintbox. This paintbox hadn't come from Jenny A'things though, it was a much grander affair out of a Dundee shop. There was a dazzling array of paints, a wee

90

dish on which to mix them, and two bristle brushes, one thick and one thin.

Poppy cried when she saw it. She had sobbed into her porridge and Mam thought she was sickening for something and dosed her with Syrup of Figs before Poppy could explain the trouble was only extreme happiness. She'd gone off to school that morning convinced that at last she could let her imagination rip.

Miss Lansdowne had approved of the paints. 'Splendid, Poppy dear! Now you can learn new techniques.'

First she'd been taught how to lay washes of pale colour over white paper without making blots and streaks. Then came a tedious course of theory, all about the colour spectrum and making patterns, followed by never-ending arrangements of leaves and flowers, groups of vases, bottles, fruit, and various schoolfriend models who refused to keep still. It was a demanding discipline, but by the end of it she could portray a pale snowdrop in a crystal vase, the glowing texture of fine silk, patterned brocade or the delicate folds of intricate lace. She could paint the bloom on black grapes, the luscious shine on ripe apples and catch a glint of mischief in a schoolmate's eyes.

One fine day Miss Lansdowne pinned all Poppy's paintings on the wall and stared at them for a long time. Miss Lansdowne was given to theatrical gestures, and at last she wiped her eyes and flung open the artroom door. 'Go out into the world and paint, my dear Poppy, for I've taught you everything I know.'

And so, on the day she heard about Jamie, Poppy vowed she would remember all that dear Miss Lansdowne had taught her, add a few discoveries of her own, and paint the best picture she'd ever painted. She would paint the mill, the beech trees, white sheep dotted in green fields with misty hills beyond. She would choose a day when clouds were dark with a hint of silver, just like the song every message boy was whistling. It would be specially for Jamie, who was a prisoner, and for Samuel Rutherford her friend, who was a hero.

*   *   *

Hannah Murdoch had spent the last two weeks at London War Hospital in a state of nerves trying to avoid George Rutherford. Not that the poor man could recognize her, more's the pity. The eye specialist had established that George could make out hazy shapes in his darkness, but otherwise the loss of vision was permanent. It was a common enough tragedy these days.

She suspected George's hearing was sharper as a result of his affliction. That was often the case with the blind. She'd watched him listen carefully when someone spoke and as often as not name the voice. As a precaution Hannah followed Sister Frances around the ward like a shadow and stuck rigidly to the rule of silence.

She was just beginning to feel safe when unfortunately George Rutherford showed signs of depression. His low spirits worried Sister Frances, and one evening she paused at his bedside with Hannah in tow. 'There are no Scottish patients apart from yourself in the ward at the moment, Captain Rutherford, but Murdoch my probationer is Scottish, and you might welcome a chat with her,' she suggested.

He roused himself. 'Funnily enough, Sister, the miller on my father's estate is called Murdoch and his daughter's a VAD.'

'I doubt if they're related. Hannah's father is a titled gentleman who lives in a Highland castle.' Sister Frances turned to Hannah, who was standing petrified. 'You may chat to the Captain for five minutes, Hannah. I'll relax the rules this once.'

'Thank you, Sister.'

Sister Frances left them alone together. George was looking thoughtful and Hannah knew the game was up. 'Hannah, did she say? Now that *is* a coincidence!' he said.

'I'm afraid it's no coincidence, George.'

'By Jove, it really *is* you, Hannah Murdoch! What's this about a titled father in a Highland castle? Has Sister got it wrong?'

'No, she hasn't. You see, the other VADs in my group are the daughters of aristocrats and landed gentry, and they assume I am, too. I had a governess and a first class education thanks to dear Holly, you see.'

'You've been living a lie!' he said accusingly.

'It's their fault, jumping to conclusions. I just never denied it, and the story sort of snowballed, George. I've only lied once.'

'It'll happen again, you know. Lies multiply.'

'I don't care!' she said defiantly. 'I only intended to keep up the pretence till the war ended. Now you've come along to spoil everything and make me a laughing stock.' She was on the verge of tears.

'I'm sorry, Hannah.'

'Oh, it doesn't matter. I've learned something. I'm as good as them.'

'Possibly a dashed sight better,' George smiled, the first time for days.

She looked at him. It was strange looking into eyes that couldn't see. It made it difficult to guess what thoughts lay behind. 'I suppose you think it's a joke, me acting the lady. I expect you'll tell everyone.'

'No, I won't disillusion your friends. It's a pity about the lie, but you must live with your conscience. There's enough on mine.'

Impulsively, she said, 'George, I'm sorry about your eyes.'

He lay quiet for a moment. 'You know, it just occurred to me, maybe this has happened to me because I did something terrible to an innocent human being. Maybe justice has been done, Hannah. A tooth for a tooth, an eye for an eye.'

'Och, away! The Invergowrie minister preached forgiveness.'

'Now there's a thought! You'll make a fine nurse, Hannah Murdoch,' he yawned.

She sighed. 'But maybe not a fine lady, Master George.'

'Keep climbing, my dear. You'll reach the top drawer yet.'

Heartened, Hannah gently rearranged the bedclothes over George's shoulders and left him sleeping peacefully.

* * *

93

Kirsty Rutherford had never been happier, despite the horrors of 1917: food shortages, butter queues, meatless days and fierce battles on the Western Front. Jamie was safe!

She waited impatiently for a letter that never came, but even so she was happy. Her beloved was not fighting in the trenches and when the war was over he would come home. She begged a photograph from Agnes, and his smiling image sat by her bedside. She kissed it every night after saying a prayer for his safety.

It's true what they say, she thought. Absence *does* make the heart grow fonder. She had promised to wait patiently for him, but now she counted the days till she could marry Jamie Murdoch and be his wife.

That November Dundee was badly shaken by news of the Russian revolution and civil war. Many exile Dundonians lived and worked in Russia and were caught up in the ensuing power struggle. It was an anxious time affecting the jute and linen trade and caused short time in the mills. In charge of Dundee's defences, Charles Rutherford and his staff were kept on their toes with rumours of Bolsheviks and agitators let loose on Dundee streets.

Although American troops had arrived in France in large numbers, they were untried in battle and there was still a growing demand for British conscripts. General Wilson was a constant visitor to the Drill Hall to organize training for older men who were called up. Charles disliked his superior officer and made no attempt to hide it, which made their shared journeys awkward. It was a huge relief to their lady driver when a fierce blizzard brought traffic to a standstill early in 1918, soon after Kirsty's eighteenth birthday.

The snowstorm gave Mildred a welcome break. When the blizzard blew itself out after a day or so and the sun appeared, the snow was as fine and powdery as pre-war flour and Mildred and Kirsty volunteered to help Cunningham clear snowdrifts from the driveway. As the two women worked side by side, Mildred was in a confidential mood.

'I don't know what's got into your father, Kirsty,' she said.

'He was rude to General Wilson last week when the poor man held my hands for a few minutes. I was frozen, and the general was only trying to restore circulation. I can't think why your father was so angry.'

Kirsty smiled knowingly. 'I can. He's jealous!'

Mildred stopped shovelling. 'No. You must be wrong.'

'I'm not. He's displaying classic symptoms.'

'But this is terrible!'

'Don't be so shocked. You're a fine-looking woman with shapely legs and a beautiful bosom.'

'Kirsty!'

She gave a peal of laughter. 'Holly, if you go any redder you'll start a thaw. I'm willing to bet those two are rivals for your affection. My father is green with jealousy. I think it's wonderful.'

'Well, I don't.' Mildred snapped, thrusting the shovel angrily into the snow.

Now that Kirsty had put the possibility into her head, Mildred had no peace of mind. How could she go on driving the colonel every day, knowing the man was admiring her legs, or worse still, her bosom? Even the thought of it made her heart flutter – if Kirsty's suspicions were correct, that is! It was possible a young woman whose head was filled with romantic nonsense was wrong. There was only one way to be sure. The direct approach.

The thaw began on January the twenty-sixth and roads were soon passable again. Charles had agreed to turn up at the Drill Hall to watch a batch of forty-year-old recruits start training. Mildred drove carefully. Hazardous road conditions did not bother her, but the question she was framing in her mind certainly did.

'Colonel, are you jealous of General Wilson because he has shown an interest in me?'

'Jealous?'

'Yes. You're rude and horrid whenever I drive the General. I'm told those are classic symptoms.'

In deep shock, assailed by other emotions he did not care to go into, Charles stared at the back of her head.

The impudence! 'Miss Holland, General Wilson's ogling has gone to your head!' he said in cutting tones. 'Your attractions leave me cold. I tolerate being driven by a woman in order to release an able-bodied man for more important duties, that's all.'

'I see.' She made a grating gear change. 'Thanks for setting the record straight . . . sir.'

The remainder of the trip was accomplished in silence as cold and unpleasant as muddy slush.

That night, Mildred Holland packed her few belongings. She stole out of the house very early the next morning and hitched a lift on a milk cart heading to Dundee. Later that day, she arrived at Territorial HQ and formally tendered her resignation as volunteer driver. Hours after, when a furious Charles Rutherford reached HQ after much inconvenience, nobody knew where she'd gone.

Word came that George was to be invalided out of the army and sent home. He returned to Angus House in March 1918 just as Ludendorff's German battalions launched an offensive which punched a huge hole in British and French lines and drove the Allies back for many miles. The situation was grave.

Hospital attendants brought George home in an ambulance, helped him stumble up the steps and left him standing facing his father in the hallway. Charles had come rushing out of the study, alerted by the sound of voices. He stopped dead. The poor blind man took a few faltering steps towards him. 'Father, is that you?'

Charles wanted to weep. What have they done to my handsome boy, my pride and joy? He hardly recognized this gaunt stranger with the dead eyes and uncertain step. George was about to blunder into a small table. Charles grabbed him. 'Careful, son!' Son! he thought emotionally. Still my son, always my son. Tears flowed silently as he hugged him. 'Welcome home, George.'

'I forgot about that damn table!'

'I'll have it shifted.'

'No, Dad. Leave it. No concessions. I want to live a normal life.'

'Of course,' Charles said heartily. But he didn't believe it. Normality wasn't possible now.

Samuel Rutherford was granted seven days' leave from the front to see his brother. There was an emotional family gathering round the fire the evening he arrived. Kirsty sat on the hearthrug at George's feet, ready to anticipate her brother's needs. She had given the maids orders that nothing in the house must be moved out of place, but even so George stumbled and tumbled. Tactfully, she pushed a glass of port closer on the little table, so that the tips of his searching fingers would find it. Proud George flew into a fury if he thought he was being helped.

'I miss Holly, Dad,' he was saying. 'She was a good sport and a dashed fine driver. I'm surprised you let her go.'

'I didn't. The wretched woman walked out on me.' It was a sore point with Charles because he found that he missed her. He discovered he had an affection for brainy women after all. She was witty. She made him smile quietly in the back seat with some of her observations. Besides, she was more pleasant to look at than the burly rednecked corporal who drove him these days.

He'd searched everywhere, but there wasn't a clue to her whereabouts. He worried about her more than he cared to admit. Charles took a quick sip of port to settle his thoughts. 'So, Sam, it looks as if Ludendorff's offensive has run out of steam. It was touch and go, eh?'

'Yes, but I think it was Kaiser Bill's last attempt to win the war. They have nothing left to fall back on while we have the American battalions and plenty of tanks for a counter-attack. Besides, the medics at the clearing stations tell me German prisoners come in with flu-like symptoms and some die within hours. That's disturbing.'

'Maybe there could be an end to the war at last. Maybe this time next year you'll be back on the land, my boy!'

Samuel looked uncomfortable. 'I won't be coming back, Father. I'm going to train as a doctor.'

'What about the estate?' Charles demanded. His younger son could always be trusted to do the unexpected!

'Once your war duties are over you could handle it, and Kirsty will help you.'

Charles's expression darkened. 'I've no interest in farming, Sam, and Kirsty will marry and leave home one day with a wealthy husband, I hope!'

Kirsty was horrified to hear it. Jamie was the only man she would marry. She had planned to make Angus House their home and in time the estate would thrive in Jamie's clever hands.

George spoke up eagerly. 'I could run the estate, Dad. It'll give me a purpose in life.' The silence that greeted this offer was so eloquent the blind man could hardly mistake its meaning. He stood up angrily, sending the drink flying. 'You don't think I can do it! You think I'm done for, no use for anything now I'm blind.' He paused, perhaps hoping for some protest. There was none. 'Damn you all!' he cried bitterly. Hands outstretched, George groped and stumbled to the doorway and went out.

His father sighed and shook his head. 'Poor boy, but what could I say? It's capital we need to buy machinery, Sam. I saw the Tank Bank when it came to Dundee last February selling war bonds. It was a real tank, you understand, I watched it climb easily over the obstacle we'd created in Albert Square. Imagine if we could buy a tractor like that to plough the lower hill ground. We could double the acreage of grain.'

'That's the way ahead,' Samuel nodded. 'But you'd need capital.'

'Yes, and the bank won't lend me a bean,' Charles said. 'There's another option though. My friend Edward Merrilees said he was interested in buying land as a long-term investment, though he didn't want to work the land himself. He has enough on his plate with his shipping interests. I was thinking of offering Edward a share in Angus estate.'

'No, you mustn't!' Kirsty cried.

Her father raised his eyebrows. 'I thought you'd be delighted. His daughters are keen to raise horses and he indulges their every whim. He'd pour cash into the project.'

'No, he wouldn't. The man hates horses.'

'No wonder. His wife was killed in a riding accident.'

'I . . . I didn't know.' That explained a great deal that had puzzled her about the man's behaviour. Did it also explain the heavy-handed compliment, and the look in his eyes in the cold dawn light? Kirsty wondered uneasily.

Influenza! That October Hannah Murdoch was sent to a hospital in Le Havre to nurse soldiers dying like flies in a flu epidemic. Most of the men were exhausted and undernourished when brought to the small hospital perched above the old transatlantic liner berth. Despite airy wards bathed in sunshine, they could not fight the flu virus. Men who had survived bullets, shells and dreadful conditions in Flanders for years, were brought in as walking wounded, or 'hoppers', and died within days in the clean, white sheets.

Their deaths seemed ironic with victory in the air. Many times Hannah broke down and cried over tragic cases when alone in her bare little cubicle. But she presented a smiling face to patients. Hannah was SMP now, Special Military Probationer, because of her training in British hospitals. At eighteen, she was officially too young to be in France, but she looked older and nobody had questioned her age. Good nurses were more valuable than gold, and Hannah was a good nurse.

She cared enough to write letters in her spare time for men who were too ill to write to their loved ones. She took time to pause in her busy schedule to read aloud to a sick man the letter just arrived from a wife or mother. Sometimes that gave the strength needed to recover, sometimes not, but always it gave comfort.

One day in late October when the flu epidemic was at its height, Hannah and the other nurses braced themselves for another grey trainload of sick and wounded. The wards had been cleared to accommodate them, Hannah's patients labelled with the prized 'Blighty' label attached to pyjama buttons and shipped off home.

When the Tommies arrived, officers were brought to Hannah's ward. The arrangement did not please her, for she was more at ease with rank and file. All the men were in the usual filthy state, uniforms smelling of rank decay. The nurses immediately set to work with hot water and carbolic. The officer allocated to Hannah had been wounded in the arm. It was a flesh wound, but he had lost blood and was semi-conscious. The wound looked clean, but time would tell, she thought.

He was asleep when she reached the ward the next morning, but his eyes opened as she bent over him. 'I must've died and gone to heaven. You're an angel.'

She smiled. 'Hardly. I'm a nurse.'

'Just my luck. I must be destined for the "Other Place".'

'Time for repentence, Captain.'

'I don't look beyond tomorrow.'

She'd heard that said often by sick, exhausted men, and it always saddened her. 'Cheer up. You have a Blighty wound that'll keep you out of mischief for a while. The war could be over by then.'

'And I may be missing my right arm.'

'Not if I can help it!'

He studied her with dark, weary eyes. 'Forgive the impertinence, Nurse, but I would like to know your name.'

'It's Hannah Murdoch.' She felt shy, an unusual occurrence for Hannah, but she had just realized, now he was washed and shaved, that he was a very attractive gentleman.

'Are you related to the Wedderburn-Murdochs?' he asked. 'They're good friends of ours. My father, Sir Henry Winslow, fished on their estate in the Borders before the war.'

'No, I'm afraid not. My father is laird of a Highland estate. The castle has been in our family for generations, but is quite remote.' The lies tripped off her tongue so confidently she almost believed them herself. Till she looked into his honest eyes and saw he was impressed.

'Really? Where . . .'

She reached hastily for a thermometer in sterile solution and popped it under his tongue to stop further questioning.

100

Hannah remembered George Rutherford's warning. Lies can multiply. How true!

At the eleventh hour of the eleventh day of the eleventh month, 1918, silence fell across the battlefields. The war was over, Germany was on the brink of starvation and Kaiser Bill had made a judicious retreat to exile in Holland. There were celebrations in Dundee, but these were muted. A large crowd gathered in front of the Pillars, Dundee's much-loved Town House, but the mood was relief rather than exuberance. Most households had lost relatives and friends and there were sore hearts in the crowd. Charles Rutherford's plan to mechanise the estate must go ahead. Many farmhands would never return to till the soil. Kirsty mourned for the men, most of whom she'd known since childhood, but could not hide her relief and happiness because one young man had been spared. It was rumoured that prisoners of war had been quickly released and would be home soon. She could hardly wait.

One bright day in early December, she came across Poppy Murdoch painting in the paddock, well-muffled against the cold. Poppy was often to be seen with sketchbook and paints and Kirsty hailed her.

'I thought you'd finished that painting ages ago.'

'This is a different view. I wanted to get it exactly right, and the cloud formation's perfect today.' She glanced up from the watercolour.

'A shipload of prisoners of war berthed in Leith yesterday, Kirsty, and Jamie was on it. Mam had a postcard this morning. He'll be home tomorrow afternoon.'

'Oh, Poppy, how wonderful!'

'Aye, it is.' She put in one or two careful brushstrokes. 'He writes that we're not to be too shocked when he arrives.'

'Poor dear, he must have suffered terribly!'

'Mam says he'll be half-starved. It's a good job it's not a meatless day, you should see the joint she wheedled out of the butcher. I left her on her knees scrubbing the floor. Again!'

Next day, Kirsty was too excited to eat lunch. She hurried

upstairs and brushed her hair, then pinned it up in a fashionable style which made her look taller and older. Dressed in her smartest costume and blouse, she studied the effect critically in the mirror. Satisfied, she applied powder to her glowing face and lipstick to her lips. Only a trace, mind, for they would kiss. Oh, how they would kiss!

Her legs were trembling as she made her way along the woodland path to the Milton. When she reached the house she did not barge in, but knocked and held her breath. Agnes answered.

'Oh, Mam, is Jamie home?'

'Aye, he is.' Agnes looked strained, but Kirsty was too happy and excited to notice. She took a step forward, but Agnes barred the way. There were stars in the girl's eyes, and she looked so sweet and bonny that the sight made Agnes want to weep. 'Kirsty love, I must warn you—'

Kirsty hugged her. 'Mam, I know he's suffered. I don't expect him to look the same. I'm ready for anything!'

'Are you?' muttered Agnes.

Kirsty clasped her foster-mother's hand, and together they went into the living room. There were folk there already, Dougal of course, and a neighbour or two come to welcome Jamie home. Jamie rose abruptly when he saw her, and she could see at once that his ordeal had marked him. He was so thin her heart contracted with love and pity.

'Kirsty . . . !' he cried in a choked voice.

He would have said more, but she didn't wait. She flew across the room, flung her arms around his neck and kissed him. For one glorious moment she felt his response. He held her close, then pushed her away. She stared bewildered. It was only then that she noticed the tall, plain woman standing behind him.

Jamie drew the stranger forward, an arm round her waist. He looked at Kirsty with no expression at all. 'Kirsty, this is Elise, my wife. I hope you two will be good friends.'

Eight

Jamie's wife? Kirsty could hardly believe it. This was the boy who had loved her, the man who had waited for her to grow, kissed her as they walked on the lovers' path. That kiss had meant a serious commitment to her but not, alas, to him.

'You're married?' she said blankly.

'Elise and I were married three weeks ago, Kirsty. The hospital chaplain performed the ceremony.'

She looked at the woman who had stolen her man. She was no beauty. Kirsty had never hated anyone in her life, but she came close to hating this lanky woman.

'Elise nursed me in the prison hospital,' Jamie was explaining to family and friends who had gathered to welcome him. 'Conditions were grim and I nearly died, but Elise saved my life. She's the kindest person I ever met.' Turning to his wife, he smiled tenderly. 'The poor lass lost two brothers in the war and her parents in the Berlin flu epidemic. She has no relatives left in Germany now.'

'You mean she's German?' Kirsty cried in disbelief.

Jamie's eyes were cold. 'Yes, Elise speaks very little English, but she'll learn.'

'We'll soon teach her the good Scots tongue, son,' Dougal said heartily. He sensed hate and prejudice and they'd had enough of that these past four years. His son was safely home. He'd taken a German wife. Good luck to him!

'Scots wi' a German accent is a queer mix after what we've been through,' Mrs Ryan remarked, eyeing the enemy woman. Her man had returned from the war without a left arm, a constant reminder of war for the rest of their lives.

Elise stood beside her husband, watching them. She had known it would be difficult. In fact she had refused to marry him at first, not because she did not love him, but because she loved him too much. She had anticipated that he would face problems and prejudice when he returned home married to a German woman.

But then she had looked into his eyes and had known that he needed the special care and understanding that only she, who had watched him suffer, could give. Still she had hesitated, but he had taken her in his arms, smiling.

'*Bitte, Liebchen?*'

Please, darling? Ah, but he pleased her, this darling Scottish man with the charming smile! And so, with no thought for the future, she had cried eagerly, '*Ja, bitte, Liebling!*'

Standing quietly, Elise studied his people. She did not understand their language, but did they think she did not understand their emotions? Emotions are universal!

She had noted the mother's stunned shock and endured a weak handshake where a welcoming kiss and hug would have been appropriate. The father had accepted her, pleased to have his son restored to him at whatever cost. When it came to affairs of the heart, men were more understanding, though not necessarily more forgiving. His sister, Poppy, was just a pretty child, thrilled by an alliance that seemed romantic to a youngster.

The neighbours' reactions were predictable. They watched her warily, as if she might bite. Who could blame them? Perhaps they had lost loved ones in the war, as she had. Ah, but she could understand the unforgiving heartache of that!

But the young woman who has just come in, what am I to make of her? Elise wondered. She was very young and very beautiful. The room seemed lit by a joyful radiance as she flew across the floor to embrace James. And he had responded to that radiance. Elise accepted that this was something her husband could not help, although he'd pushed temptation away. What were these two to one another? she wondered.

Then she supposed he must have told her the situation,

because the young woman's radiance was snuffed out like a candle. Her expression was an open book to a nurse skilled in the study of human nature. So! She loves him, the poor rejected little one, thought Elise.

Jamie was speaking, and her quick ear picked up a word not unlike the German. *Freundin!* The dear foolish man was begging this broken-hearted girl to be her friend. But that is impossible! she thought. Can he not see it?

Jamie and his wife had been living in Agnes's house for barely a week and Agnes was driven nearly distracted. Not that Jamie was any bother, bless him. He disappeared into the mill with his father and spent most of the day there. That left his wife at a loose end, getting under Agnes's feet.

If only her companion this washday had been Kirsty or dear, lost Hannah! she thought as the foreign woman followed her around the wash-house.

It was 'Mistress Murdoch, what do you call this, please?' a hundred times a day in her eagerness to learn.

Agnes had counted on Jamie marrying Kirsty, and he'd married a foreigner. It was just a disaster, Agnes thought as she plunged her arms into a tub of soapy water.

'Mistress Murdoch, what do you call that clothing, please?' The German woman was standing at her shoulder, watching her wash Dougal's long johns.

'Breeks!' Agnes replied crossly.

'*Danke* . . . thank you.' The woman turned away quickly and began sorting coloureds and whites into two sensible heaps. Her face was averted and Agnes suspected she was crying. Agnes was immediately sorry. She longed to say a kind word to comfort the tearful woman, but what's the use? Jamie's wife wouldn't understand. She began scrubbing the collar and cuffs of Dougal's working shirt furiously on the washboard. She forgot that everyone in the world understands a friendly smile, and a hug can give more comfort than words.

Hannah Murdoch had stayed on at Le Havre hospital after the

armistice was signed. She stayed because for many soldiers the war had not ended on the eleventh of November 1918. Men still died from wounds and the effects of poison gas, not to mention the flu epidemic which had spread worldwide from its origins in Spain. But mostly she had stayed because of Captain Morris Winslow.

She had promised Morris that he would not lose his arm, but she and the medical team fought a desperate battle to keep it. Like the others, he had come from the trenches exhausted and undernourished, with little resistance to germs breeding in the poisoned soil. The morning Hannah noticed a red, puffy inflammation gathering round the wound had been the blackest moment of her life. Sister had immediately ordered irrigation, and for days and nights Hannah had hardly had an hour's rest. She had made up gallons of hypochlorous acid and boiled water and applied many dozens of dressings to draw out the deadly poison invading his body. She wept hopelessly in secret, but after many anxious days, dared to hope again.

Sitting in her cheerless cubicle one night after Morris had taken a turn for the better, Hannah studied her hollow-eyed reflection in the mirror. His arm was saved, the risk of blood poisoning gone. He would recover. The battle had formed a strong bond between nurse and patient, but there was much more to it than that. Today, when Sister wasn't present, Morris had put the wounded arm around her waist and pulled her close. 'Look, Hannah! Strength has returned!' His lips, his eyes had invited her kiss, and with all her heart she had longed to give it. But she dare not.

Staring in the mirror, Hannah faced the truth. I've fallen in love with him, she thought. That's why I care so much. I can't contemplate life without him, and I believe he feels the same way about me. Hannah was too tired to feel exalted. Instead, she rested her head on her arms and wept. This was an ill-omened love affair, and it was her fault. She had told Morris Winslow a pack of lies about her family background, but there was too much at stake to tell him the truth. What if she lost him for good when he found out who she was?

*　　*　　*

Though the war was over, a strong Territorial Army was necessary and so were keen schoolboys to train as cadets. Charles had been contemplating a gloomy future in farming and when offered the job of organizing training for young volunteers, he jumped at it. There was just one snag. He was expected to visit drill halls and schools all over Angus and Forfarshire using his own transport, and he couldn't drive. Where, oh where, is Mildred? he thought despairingly. He had contacted Mildred Holland's parents without success after her sudden disappearance. The elderly couple in turn had alerted their sons and families scattered the length and breadth of Britain, but none had heard from her. It was extremely worrying.

'Have you tried hospitals?' George suggested.

'Hospitals?' The thought was alarming. 'Are you suggesting she's met with an accident?'

'Not necessarily. She could be nursing. There's still heavy demand for nursing staff with many crocks like me on the scrapheap.' Charles eyed his son. George was slumped on the couch, unshaven, stained clothes shrugged on any old how. He was a slovenly mess, his expression bored and vacant. Understandably enough, he never went out. All he did was smoke endless cigarettes, eat large meals and put on weight.

Heaven knows how long he'll last like this, Charles thought. If only there was something George could do!

'Could you teach me to drive, George?' he suggested suddenly.

'For God's sake, Father, I'm blind!'

'But I'm not! You told me once that driving is going through the motions till it becomes automatic. Surely you remember how?'

'Of course I do, but . . .' George paused. A faint pulse of excitement stirred his weary apathy. Could it be done by using the network of private roads and tracks within the estate? He could remember every twist and turn. Once his father was proficient they might venture on to main thoroughfares to gain traffic experience. 'It's possible, Dad,' he said cannily.

'You'd have to be my eyes of course, but could I trust you to steer the car safely?'

'I'll give it a jolly good shot – without female distractions this time.'

George grinned. 'Don't worry. I'll make sure there're no back-seat drivers.'

'That's settled then. When do we start?'

George stood up. 'The sooner the better.'

It was an emotional moment. Charles took his son's arm and together they went outside. George paused for a moment and took a deep breath of fresh air. It felt mighty like a fresh start to living.

Peacetime problems were just beginning for the whole nation. Kirsty did not celebrate her nineteenth birthday. Like many women whose lives had been shattered by war, her dreams were over and she must face reality. It was difficult to see a way ahead.

Lloyd George had called a speedy General Election and the new Government took a long hard look at the country's economy. A gloomy prospect. Britain faced enormous debts and had lost her traditional markets abroad. The survivors of trench warfare were coming tramping home, confident that they had a secure place in Lloyd George's vision of a 'land fit for heroes'. The reality was not promising. Wages were low, prices high, and so was unemployment. The heroes were very soon disillusioned.

Samuel Rutherford was one of the lucky ones. He left the army quietly with a decoration for bravery, and was assured of a place at Glasgow Medical School next session. Meanwhile, he was gaining experience with a doctor tending victims of tuberculosis, raging unchecked in Glasgow's desperately overcrowded slums.

'Learning what real poverty is, Kirsty!' he had told her grimly. Kirsty admired her brother's dedication, but their father struggled to come to terms with it. Charles was proud of his son, but secretly hoped Samuel would change his mind and embark upon a military career. Sam would make an excellent army officer, but for his troublesome conscience. There was nobody to carry on the Rutherford army tradition, a sorry state of affairs! Charles thought. Kirsty had her own problems. Horse sickness had flared up amongst army horses brought back from France and the virulent infection wiped out nearly every horse in the Barry camp and spread to farmyards and stables. Carthorses and Clydesdales died in hundreds. Buchan and the Mearns were the most badly affected, but Angus estate did not escape.

'Only two Clydes left now, Maister,' Cunningham told Charles. He hesitated. 'And Thrawn Janet—'

'What about her?' the colonel demanded sharply.

'See for yoursel'.'

Charles strode into the stable. One look was enough. 'Oh, my God!' He met Cunningham's eyes. 'I'll stay with her, till—'

'Aye. She's lying peaceful now, sir, though she was a right ill-natur'd beast.'

Charles crouched and gently stroked the mare's brow. 'But she had spirit,' he said softly.

'There's many a Dundee tramcar will vouch for that, Colonel.' Cunningham closed the stable door softly and left them together. He had seen the tears, and knew better than most the bond that exists between a man and his faithful horse.

Kirsty was in terror in case the deadly sickness spread to Young Lochinvar and the mare Guinevere, but as the first tender green shoots appeared in surrounding woodland and hedgerows the disease petered out and it seemed they had escaped.

'We should make a start clearing the upper slopes now the weather's softer, Kirsty,' Charles observed as he prepared to set off in the car one April morning. He wore his bowler at a jaunty angle. Thanks to George's tuition he could drive confidently on the King's Highway, and the accomplishment had given his self-esteem a remarkable boost.

'We can't clear the ground without horses, Papa.'

'Ah, but we will have horsepower, my dear!' he laughed.

109

'I've ordered two Fordson tractors. They'll be delivered this week.' He swung the starting handle.

Kirsty looked at her father, horrified. She had balanced the books for that quarter and estimated that providing crops did not fail and there were no disasters they might just make ends meet, thanks to steady income from Murdoch's mill. 'Papa! A Fordson tractor costs £200. We can't possibly afford one, let alone two!'

'Yes, we can. Edward Merrilees has joined forces with us. I visited my solicitor last week and we drew up a partnership agreement. Edward gave me a blank cheque to go ahead and buy whatever's needed to improve the land.' The engine roared into life, and her father hopped smartly aboard.

'Why didn't you consult me?' she yelled furiously.

'Didn't have to, dear. You're under twenty-one.' He hastily released the brake, and shot off in a cloud of oily smoke.

Cunningham had been standing by at a distance. He approached. 'Trouble, miss?'

She blinked back tears. 'Would you believe it? He's found a wealthy idiot who's agreed to give him funds to buy two Fordson tractors!'

Cunningham groaned. 'He'll expect me and Geordie to drive the beasts.' He studied her sympathetically. She'd been looking downcast this wee while, her bonny face long as a wet weekend. 'Och well, here's something to cheer you,' he said. 'The young mare's in foal. I was keeping it to mysel' till I was sure.'

Charles Rutherford had his day planned. He'd been ordered to make a survey of Dundee Shell Factory and write a full report on disarmament. The manufacture of high explosive shells in the city had ceased, but with unrest seething in Ireland and civil war raging in Russia, military authorities were taking no chances.

A disused factory is a melancholy sight at the best of times, but the foundry looked even more depressing than Charles had imagined. He went inside and looked around. Machinery and steam compressors were still in place, as were driving shafts, dies and presses which had impressed former Prime Minister Asquith when he was made freeman of Dundee in wartime. 'Squiff' had been warm in his praises of munitions workers, whose output had far exceeded a target set by the Ministry of Munitions.

There was silence today, however, broken only by the occasional hollow clang of engineers dismantling machinery. The manager was supervising the safe disposal of dangerous materials, and he offered to accompany Charles on a tour of inspection.

'I wish you could have seen this place at the height of production in 1916, Colonel! Of course it was dangerous work with a deadly purpose. There were plenty in the city who condemned it, but the women who worked here never doubted they were helping to win the war.'

'Fancy recruiting women for a job like this. One does not associate the gentle sex with weaponry,' Charles remarked.

The manager smiled. 'The lasses are tougher than we think! Brave, too. Just imagine huddling beside tons of high explosive, knowing a Zeppelin bomber is prowling overhead. Yet they did it with a smile. One of them told me they felt honoured to share dangers our lads faced every day, God bless 'em. Two or three of my best workers stayed on to help us dispose of explosives. They know the risks involved, you see. Come, Colonel, let me show you where munitions were assembled.'

The manager ushered Charles into a section of the factory once devoted to ordnance assembly. There were two or three women working at benches in the background, but one worker seemed familiar, despite earth-coloured overalls from neck to ankles and a mob-cap pulled well down upon her brow.

'Excuse me a moment, Mr McManus,' he said. 'I'll have a word with this lady. I want to express my appreciation for the good work done here.'

'By all means, Colonel,' the manager beamed.

Charles strolled across. 'Good morning, Mildred!' he greeted his lost driver grimly.

Mildred Holland sighed. 'I might have known you'd track me down!'

His immense relief made him scowl. 'This is no job for a brainy woman!'

'On the contrary, if I hadn't used my brains I'd have been blown skyhigh months ago.'

'Thank God you weren't.'

'Well, yes.' She glanced up at him quickly, then looked away. Their last encounter still rankled. She wasn't sure she could forgive him for it, nor for turning up when she looked such a sight. The ravages of months of twelve-hour shifts were bound to show. She knew the nervous strain of ramming raw cordite paste into ammunition shells showed plainly in a thin, lined face. Mildred was suddenly aware of oily, dirty hands with broken, black-rimmed nails. Shamed, she stuffed them hastily into her pockets.

Charles saw signs of hard work and hardship and his emotion went so deep it hurt. 'Let me take you home, Mildred,' he said.

She looked at him. 'Where is home? I have no home.' That sounded bitter and she didn't care. She had kept on working here because she'd nowhere else to go. She dare not tell her pacifist father the work she'd been doing. He would find it hard to forgive. There was only a dreary room in a Dundee lodging house to look forward to and no job lined up after she was paid off.

'Your home is Angus House, Mildred. Come home with me,' he said.

But she had her pride, and she couldn't forget how he'd humiliated her. 'No thank you. I promised Mr McManus I'd stay and help.'

'But it's dirty, dangerous work!'

'Do you think I don't know?'

He gave her a dark look. The damage he'd done all those months ago nearly broke his heart. She was right, he had been miserably jealous of that charmer and womaniser, General Wilson. That's why he had lashed out at her. He was no charmer, just a dour military man who'd fought too many

112

battles and suffered too much grief to charm the woman that he . . . His thoughts teetered on the brink of a truth he couldn't face just yet, and he swallowed awkwardly. 'I'm sorry about the quarrel.'

She kept her eyes lowered. 'I'm sorry I ran away. It was childish.'

'It was. You should have stayed and made me suffer.'

'I would have enjoyed it.'

Charles thought he saw a hint of a smile. He decided this was as close to a truce as they could get. 'Right!' he went on briskly. 'Your job is to see this hazardous material is made safe and my job is to keep an eye on you. I'll make sure you don't bolt this time.'

'I can move fast, Colonel!'

'I can move faster, Miss Holland. I can drive.' Watching her jaw drop, Charles believed that this was possibly the most satisfying moment of his life.

Kirsty had deliberately avoided Jamie Murdoch since his homecoming. It had been easy, because he was making up for lost time in the mill. Under the agreement hammered out between the Rutherfords and Dougal, the mill buildings and surrounding land would belong to the Murdochs by the end of the year, and there were rumours of ambitious expansion planned. Kirsty realised that if Edward Merrilees had not stepped in when he did, the estate would have been in dire straits without that income. As it was, the two tractors had made short work of clearing and ploughing the south-facing hill slopes and seed potatoes were already planted in the furrows to clean the ground.

It was impossible to keep out of Jamie's life forever, though. She answered the doorbell one day in May, and there he was on the doorstep. He whipped off his bonnet. 'Kirsty, is your father in?'

'No. He's gone to meet Douglas Haig. The Fieldmarshal's sailing across the river on the Fifie today to be made a freeman of the city. I thought you'd be in Dundee cheering with the rest.' Her cool tone gave no hint of her emotion.

'Haig's welcome to a trip on the Dundee ferry, but I don't cheer generals. I've seen the damage they do.'

He hesitated, twisting his cap, the only sign of nervousness. 'May I come in? Maybe you could tell your father what I have in mind.'

She would rather not, but she stood aside and led the way into her father's study. She sat down at the desk and left him standing. 'Well, what's this all about?'

'I want to make your father an offer for the lodge now it's empty.'

'I see.' She let cool amusement show. 'Too many cooks spoiling the broth at the Milton?'

'We need a home of our own. Every couple does,' he answered. It had been a mistake to come in. He'd forgotten her father would be attending this carry-on in Dundee, or he would have postponed the visit. What had he expected from Kirsty? he wondered. Friendship? If so, he was disappointed. Her manner chilled him to the heart. The room was so charged with ice it made him shiver.

She made him wait while she pondered. The lodge was an attractive small house built of Aberdeen granite. It stood in quite a large garden a short distance from the rusting entrance gates. She wondered if she could stand the strain of passing Jamie's love-nest every day. She scribbled a note on the memo pad.

'I'll tell my father what you propose. We'll need a valuation done, then you can put in an offer.' She was surprised to find her heartbeat steady. Maybe when one's hopes die, love dies with them.

'Aye, well . . . I'll be on my way, then,' Jamie said lamely. He hesitated. His wife had shown a friendly interest in Kirsty. Maybe the two could be friends. 'By the by, Kirsty, Elise sends her regards.'

'Oh, does she?'

Jamie was angry. He muttered goodbye and headed for the door, stumbling in his haste to get away. He hadn't realised being alone with Kirsty in this devilish mood would pose such a threat to his peace of mind. She had grown so beautiful.

Quite stunning. Outside, he paused on the steps and took a calming breath. He was trembling. If only she hadn't grown so beautiful!

Charles was delighted at the prospect of selling the lodge. 'We could ask at least £170, Kirsty!'

'Papa, it's been empty for months!'

'He can well afford to make it habitable. That family's making money hand over fist. Calcutta mills have pinched Dundee's jute trade, but milling in Angus is still quite profitable. You don't see Murdoch's mill lying idle every second week like jute works, do you?'

'So you'll sell him the lodge?'

'Certainly! It's not as if the man's a stranger, he's almost one of the family,' said Charles tactlessly.

Kirsty distanced herself from the sale. She had persuaded George to teach her to drive, and was having lessons at weekends, while her father used the car during the week. She could still find time most days to head for the hills on Young Lochinvar, riding like the wind. Charles was pleased to have his son kept occupied. He had feared George might slip back into slovenly ways once he'd taught him to drive, but Kirsty took George in hand, guiding her brother around the estate, patiently explaining how it was run.

'The potato crop is coming away well, George,' she told him one day when they had climbed the hill as far as the new fields, and were resting their arms on the dyke.

'It's funny, Kirsty, you can smell turnips growing, but you can't smell tatties,' George remarked, sniffing. He stood upright suddenly, listening. 'What's that sound?'

She'd grown accustomed to George's hearing, sharper than her own. 'I don't hear anything.'

'Shh! There it is again!' He turned his head. 'There's an animal in distress. Quite close.'

'I hear it!' It was a whining sound, very weak and mournful. It led them to a clump of bushes and a tangle of fence wire carelessly abandoned by casual labourers hired last week to repair the deer fence. She parted the bushes and gave an involuntary cry. 'Oh, George, it's a poor dog!'

'Bring it here!'

'I can't. The poor thing's entangled in fence wire.' She felt sick. Kirsty recalled that one of the labourers had mentioned he'd lost a dog, but hadn't bothered to search for the stray. She was suddenly angry. Working on the tangle of wire, she freed first one trapped leg, then the others, unwinding coils of wire from the thin body. The dog made no sound though she knew she must hurt it. Its brown suffering eyes watched her efforts patiently.

'What's happening? Are you all right?' George called. She gathered the dog in her arms. It was a big dog, but so light she could carry it with ease to where George stood. He ran his hands over it. 'Oh, Kirsty, the poor thing!' he said as his fingers met the sharp ridge of spine, the corrugations of ribs. The big animal turned its head and gently licked his face.

With a struggle they made their way down the hillside, George carrying the dog, Kirsty guiding the pair of them.

'Take it to my room,' George ordered. He knew every inch of that room. He had coped with nightmares of guilt there and had paced the floor endlessly. Night and day meant nothing to him and he was sure he could care for a dog. He laid it down on the armchair close by his bed. He felt a warm, grateful tongue caress his hand. 'What does it look like, Kirsty?' he asked.

She had brought water and a bowl of light, nourishing food. Not too much, for the dog was half-starved. 'I'd say his mother was a labrador, his father a collie, and his grandparents greyhounds. Goodness knows what his great-grandparents were. He has a whiskery muzzle, and do you know, I believe he's smiling at you.'

George stroked the dog's rough head. 'I'm keeping this dog, Kirsty. He's had a rotten deal and now he's mine. Can you suggest a name?'

Kirsty studied the dog, now fed and watered and relaxing its injured limbs gingerly. Its jowls lifted in something remarkably like an Irish grin and its eyes smiled. 'Murphy!' she decided. 'Definitely Murphy, George.'

Once Murphy had recovered full use of his legs, he took

charge of George. The dog seemed to realise that his master was blind. He led George patiently around obstacles, pausing with a deep 'Wuff!' to warn him when there were stairs or steps to be negotiated. It was heart-warming to watch the blind man and the big dog finding their way around the estate together. Kirsty left them to it. She knew Murphy wouldn't let any harm befall his beloved master. George was in safe hands – or paws.

The sound of hammering had been echoing from the lodge for nearly a fortnight before Kirsty succumbed to temptation and went to take a look. She knew the carpenter working at the sawbench, and he was glad to pause for a moment to exchange a few words.

'There's central heating and a bathroom fitted wi' all sorts of foreign notions, Miss Kirsty, and a large extension round the back. It'll be a palace when it's done.'

Curiously, she walked round to the back, where stone masons had been at work. There was an empty, gaping doorway there, and to her horror, Jamie's wife stepped out of it.

'*Guten Morgen*, Kirsty. You are inspecting our new home?' Elise smiled. She had been hoping to meet this elusive girl. She had news for her.

'I can hardly recognize the lodge, you've made it so much bigger,' Kirsty remarked.

Elise nodded. 'It is for the *kind*. For the child. I am pregnant, you see.'

'No!' she breathed.

She should have been prepared for this. Jamie's children had been part of her dream, too. But how can I bear to watch this woman nurse his child, the baby that might have been mine? she wondered.

'Kirsty, you are so pale, are you all right?' Elise asked gently.

'I . . . I'm fine.' She managed to mumble congratulations, then excused herself and hurried away. Her mind was made up. She knew what she must do.

117

Nine

Kirsty had made up her mind to leave Angus estate. At least, till after Jamie and Elise's child was born. Afterwards, she would deal with heartache by avoiding the child and its parents.

She decided to seek refuge with her grandmother in Edinburgh. An open invitation to visit had been extended months ago, and it would cause no surprise if she were to accept it now. Though still hale and hearty, her grandmother Lizzie Robb was quite elderly and her only granddaughter had not seen her for some time. Kirsty first obtained her father's approval, then wrote to her grandmother and eagerly awaited a reply.

Although the colonel had installed telephone communications in Angus House some time ago, Lizzie scorned such new-fangled nonsense. It was a surprise to her son-in-law, therefore, when she came on the phone.

'Charles?' the familiar voice bellowed in his ear at full pitch.

He held the receiver at a distance. 'Mother-in-law, is that you?'

'Of course it is, Charles! I had Kirsty's letter this morning. I would welcome the dear child's visit, but what about this smallpox epidemic in Dundee? It's reported in the *Scotsman*.'

'Oh, that! There are only one or two cases, the first for eight years. They came from Portugal. I don't think you need worry.'

'One can't be too careful. Are you sure germs can't travel along phone lines?'

118

'Quite sure. Listen, if you're worried, I assure you Kirsty has been vaccinated.'

'But she will be travelling by train from Dundee, and railway coaches are to be avoided in epidemics, you know.'

Charles sighed. 'If it will set your mind at ease I'll drive Kirsty to Perth, which is smallpox free. She could pick up an Edinburgh connection from there.'

This suggestion met with approval, and Kirsty began packing. She chose her smartest outfits with skirts altered to the new shorter length. The June weather was warm and cloudy, with frequent showers. With an eye to staying in Edinburgh for some time, Kirsty packed warm jerseys, cardigans, and a raincoat which would deal equally well with summer showers and November chills.

She would miss her beloved horses and the birth of Guinevere's foal, but that couldn't be helped. Cunningham promised to look after the mare like his own bairn and exercise Young Lochinvar.

'But I'll no' ride him helter-skelter up the hill and loup dykes, like a certain young lady!' he said with a grin.

Though Kirsty longed to get away, leaving George was a worry. How would her blind brother cope without her? She was delighted to see George taking an interest in the running of the estate. He was out early with the dog Murphy, dogging Cunningham's footsteps. Fortunately, the grieve had endless patience with the blind man, and lent an attentive ear to George's suggestions.

'Could we grow strawberries in one of the lower fields next year, Cunningham?' George asked. He was sure it would be a good idea to sell selected berries to the Royal Hotel in Dundee. Orders from other high class establishments might follow.

'It's worth trying. There's one field that's been rough pasture for a while. Young Murdoch was after leasing it to sow malting barley, but I put him off. Cereals never did well there,' Cunningham said. 'By the by, did you know the man's bought himsel' a brand new motor?'

'No!' George was envious. 'What make?'

'Dinnae ask me. They say it's to drive his German wife around in.'

'What's she like?'

Cunningham shrugged. 'No beauty, but a decent enough woman.'

The blind man's hand fondled the dog, his expression grim. 'I pray I never meet her. I'd find conversation difficult.'

'You're no' the only one, Master George,' sighed the grieve.

Kirsty was waiting for her father on the front steps by noon on the day of her departure. She wore a tailored costume in a shade called 'Vieux Rose' and matching hat with sweeping white feather. The outfit had cost all of fifteen shillings in D.M. Brown's spring sale, but the expense was worth it.

George and Murphy were loitering in the sunshine to see her off.

'I'll miss you, old girl. Come back soon, won't you?' George said.

The sympathetic tone made her wonder. Her brother picked up on vibrations lost by sighted folk. Had he sensed her unhappiness? She kissed his cheek fondly. 'If you need me, George dear, I'll be back on the next train, I promise.'

He was listening intently. 'I say, that's not Dad's car!'

A strange motor swept round the corner and drew up at the steps. To Kirsty's dismay, Jamie Murdoch leaned out. 'Ready, Kirsty?' he called. 'Your father's been delayed in Dundee and he phoned the mill to ask if I'd drive you to Perth.' Jamie busied himself stowing her baggage on the back seat. He noted there was enough of it for a lengthy visit. But that's none o' my business! he thought. He'd already exchanged angry words with his mother about this trip.

Agnes had been at a loose end since the Women's War Relief Committee disbanded. Rather than be dependent upon her daughter-in-law's company, Agnes had offered to keep the books in the smart offices her husband and son now occupied in a new extension to the mill. She had an organized mind. Counting was no bother to her and she enjoyed office

120

work. She'd taken to the new telephone with the enthusiasm of a wee bairn to its dummy teat.

Dougal had been busy elsewhere that morning and it was Agnes who had taken the colonel's call, before passing the instrument across to Jamie. The man's request for assistance had begun a heated argument between mother and son.

'I'm surprised at you dancing to the laird's tune, James Murdoch! The mill's ours now and we're our own master.'

'The man's delayed and his daughter's waiting to catch the Perth train. I'm just doing a neighbour a good turn.'

'A daft turn, more like. A married man driving an unmarried girl? Folk will talk!'

'Och, away with you, Mother! The war changed all that.'

'Not in the Carse, it didn't!' Then her tone had changed. 'Jamie son, this is wee Kirsty we're talking about. I mind what you were to one another once and it worries me. She was single-minded when she was little and she's single-minded now. Is she still in love wi' you, and more important, are you in love with her?'

'For heaven's sake, I'm married!'

'You don't have to remind me,' she said drily. 'Just tell me this. Can you trust yourself alone with Kirsty Rutherford, and her looking so sweet and bonny?'

Then he'd stormed out in a foul temper.

Jamie said goodbye to George and helped Kirsty into the passenger seat. He held on to her elbow for a moment to steady her, the merest touch, but his heart raced. Badly shaken, he started the engine.

They drove in silence. Kirsty sat well away from him, but conscious of every move. He was a good driver and in different circumstances she would have enjoyed the drive. The new car smelled of expensive leather, and fresh scents of summer wafted in through lowered windows. She had an almost overwhelming urge to rest her head upon his shoulder. Instead, she remarked coldly, 'I believe congratulations are in order.'

His thoughts had been far away. 'What . . . ?'

'The baby, of course.'

121

'Who told you?' Jamie was stunned. Elise's pregnancy wasn't common knowledge.

'Your wife. I met her at the lodge.'

'Elise? She never told me!'

She gave a hollow laugh. 'She wouldn't. She hoped I'd suffer jealous pangs.'

'What nonsense! My wife is a kind person.'

'Is she?'

His hands had started shaking uncontrollably, a legacy of the terrible war. It took all his strength to hold the wheel steady. Did he really know Elise? She had made great strides with English, yet there was a lack of communication between them he was finding difficult to overcome.

He frowned. 'Why should Elise want you to suffer?'

'Maybe because she knows I was in love with you once upon a time.'

'But not any more?' The answer was suddenly vitally important.

'Of course not.' A lie, but a convincing one.

'That's fine then, Kirsty. No problem!' he said heartily. But when they reached the craggy, wooded outskirts of Perth he felt lost and miserable. He wished he'd listened to his mother. He couldn't trust his emotions when alone with Kirsty Rutherford, and her so sweet and bonny.

Elise was uneasy that afternoon, knowing her husband had volunteered to drive Kirsty to Perth. She trusted him of course, but had enough experience of life to know that even faithful husbands can be led astray. It had distressed Elise to hear Kirsty was leaving, although she wasn't surprised. She had hoped that if she could make the young woman face the inevitable they could become friends. Marriage had not brought Elise happiness. She had known life would be difficult, but had not expected loneliness and isolation.

She was a nurse and thrived on being needed, but even Jamie did not need her now. Her husband was involved with the mill and had ambitious plans for its future. He spent many hours in there. His health had improved and he had changed

122

out of all recognition from the sick, half-starved Scotsman who had won her heart. Sometimes she looked at the healthy, handsome man supping his mother's porridge laced with top of milk, and wondered if she had married a stranger.

Elise's refuge was the lodge Jamie had bought to be their future home. She loved the little house passionately and visited it every day, insisting the workmen build everything exactly as she wanted. Inevitably, her popularity suffered. The men muttered and swore under their breath. They did not understand that she demanded perfection not for herself, but for the unborn child. Already she adored this child. There would be no more loneliness when the baby was born here, in their charming little home.

Walking towards the lodge that day, she was so preoccupied with her thoughts that she paid little attention to a dog barking nearby. There were plenty of dogs on the estate, mostly working collies, but sheepdogs were too busy to run up and down hillsides and waste energy barking in such a frenzy.

Wuff! Wuff! Wuff!

There it was again, deep and urgent. She paused. Is this poor animal in a trap somewhere in the wood? she wondered. She left the driveway and followed the sound anxiously through the trees.

The dog came bounding at her from a gap in the trees. It was a large wild-looking dog and it seized her skirt in its strong jaws, tugging so hard it ripped the fabric. Elise was terrified, kicking and beating it with her feet and fists. The dog hung on grimly, dragging her towards the trees with all its strength.

'*Böse-Hund*! Wicked dog! Let me go!' she screamed, and then she saw the man lying where the ground fell away steeply in a tangle of rocks and heather into a deep gulley. The dog immediately released her and slithered down to him. Elise followed.

The man looked dazed and his head was bleeding. 'Where are you hurting?' she asked.

'Mostly my pride. I thought I could walk anywhere unaided.

Seems I can't. I've been blundering around trying to get out of this fix for ages, and driving poor Murphy daft.' He held a hand out, searching, and the dog moved within reach. He patted it. 'Good lad, Murphy. You brought help. Well done, old chap.'

Then Elise realized. 'You are blind!'

'Full marks!' he laughed. 'Let me introduce myself. George Rutherford, poison gas victim, blinded courtesy of Kaiser Bill.'

Tears blurred her own sight. '*Es betrübt Mich sehr . . .*' she whispered. 'I . . . I am so grieved!'

He looked startled. 'You must be James Murdoch's German wife!'

'*Ja*, I am Elise. The enemy woman,' she said bitterly. 'Why do you not say what everyone is thinking?'

George was silent, because he could think of nothing to say. Her voice was low and pleasant and did not jar upon his sensitive ears like some. He found he pitied her. She sounded unhappy. Expert fingers were probing his brow, which was wet with blood and she dabbed it off gently with a handkerchief. A scent of roses drifted up to his nostrils.

'You are lucky. You have only a small cut that will not need stitching.'

He stood up. 'Can you help me out of this pickle? I've no idea where I am down here.'

She took his arm, and after a struggle guided him on to the woodland path, the anxious dog at their heels. When they reached the driveway she paused, remembering the pride he valued. 'Shall I take you home, Mr Rutherford? I am a trained nurse, maybe I could attend to the wound.'

'I'll be fine now, thanks. Murphy knows the way and you've been too kind to me already. One of the maids will fix my head.'

He smiled, rested a hand on the big dog's collar and stepped out confidently. Once more she felt rejected. This brave blind man did not need her. It broke her heart to know it was her countrymen who had blinded him. Now he would not want to speak with an enemy woman, and his blind eyes would not see her longing to be his friend.

Charles Rutherford had very nearly forgotten the promise to drive his daughter to Perth. Thank heavens for that wonderful invention, the telephone! He replaced the receiver after phoning James Murdoch from the munitions factory to arrange alternative transport.

The foreman was passing the office as he came out. 'Did you find someone to drive your lassie to the train, Colonel?'

'Yes, thanks, but I've had no luck with the other matter. Nobody knows Miss Holland's address. Maybe if I could look at the personnel records—?'

'Sorry. They're locked away. You must bide your time till Mr McManus comes back frae Glesca.'

'That could be days! Surely you must know where Miss Holland lodges?'

'I'm a married man. I'd get my heid in my hands and my lugs to play with if I took an interest in women's lodgings!'

'You say she reported sick before handing in her notice three days ago?'

'Aye. She was poorly. Her work was done, so she just left.'

Charles cursed the pressure of work that had kept him busy this past week. He had arrived at the munitions factory early that morning to find Mildred had gone. He had spent fruitless hours trying to find out where she was, but she'd given him the slip again. He'd been so upset he'd forgotten all about Kirsty. He'd remembered Jamie Murdoch's new car in the nick of time.

Charles wandered into the main factory. Most of the machinery had been dismantled or returned to peacetime use and he went from there through to the ordnance assembly, where Mildred had worked. It was silent and completely bare. He stood in the chill gloom beside her bench and rested a hand on the dusty top. He was in such a state he did not hear the door open.

'Blasted brolly! I keep forgetting it!' Mildred said.

125

She was really there. Charles couldn't believe it. 'You don't look well!' he said.

'Thanks, that's a greeting guaranteed to make one feel worse, but yes, I've been ill, Colonel. Lochee water is suspect and the doctor feared typhoid. Fortunately, it's just mild fever.'

He snorted. 'Mild fever? You're white as a sheet and thin as a rake!'

'You know how to compliment a girl, don't you?'

'I'm sorry. I'm . . . I'm a dour devil.'

She sighed. 'At least you tell the truth. I thoroughly deserved the dressing down you gave me months ago. I was presumptuous.'

'No, you were right. I *was* jealous when General Wilson started sweet-talking you, and I lashed out at you in consequence. I . . . I lost the head, as they say.'

'Oh, the general's an old windbag. I never took him seriously.'

Encouraged, Charles took a step closer. 'Please, Mildred, come home with me?'

She had risen from her sickbed that morning hoping to see him one last time before walking out of his life forever. Her landlord did not encourage sick tenants. When he'd heard she'd lost her job he'd told her to pack her bags and go. Her parents would take her in, but what humiliation for a proud woman!

She longed to go with Charles Rutherford for deep and emotional reasons, but she hesitated. She knew he was a kind-hearted man beneath the stern exterior. Maybe he did not really want her, maybe he only pitied her, and she did not want his pity, she wanted . . . Oh, what was the use? She turned away, determined to go. 'No. You don't need me now, Colonel. You can drive yourself. Goodbye, and good luck . . .'

'Wait a minute! You forgot to look for your brolly!'

Mildred stopped, flustered. The umbrella was an excuse. It was lost, but she hadn't left it here. 'Silly me! I . . . I just remembered I left it somewhere else.'

'Where? Tell me!'

'At . . . at Angus House, when I did my moonlight flit,' she admitted.

'Then let's go get it, my dear one!' he cried triumphantly, offering her an arm. 'Come back with me to Angus House and stay to be my wife.'

Dazed by this odd twist of fate, Mildred went with him, without another word.

Poppy Murdoch harboured a secret. Two watercolours lay hidden in a cardboard portfolio in her room. She was proud of the paintings, the best she'd ever done, and destined for two young men she loved, Jamie, her brother and Samuel Rutherford, her friend. Poppy had not presented the paintings to her heroes yet, because she wanted them framed in gold. She'd priced gold frames at a Dundee art dealer's, and the price had made her gasp. Two and sixpence for plain, and seven and six for fancy! Poppy wouldn't dream of anything less than fancy, but fifteen bob for two! That would mean months of scrimping.

She'd left school at the turn of the year and gone to work at Jenny A'things in Invergowrie against her mother's wishes. Agnes had set her heart on her youngest daughter starting a sales apprenticeship in Draffen and Jarvie's, the high-class store in Dundee, but Poppy wouldn't hear of it. She cadged a lift to Invergowrie Main Street every morning on the milk cart, kept her strength up during the day with a jammy piece and a drink of water, and returned with Jamie in the new motor in the evenings. It was hard going, but by summer Poppy had saved enough from wages and running errands for customers to afford the fancy frames.

Filled with excitement, she caught the train to Dundee on her afternoon off, the portfolio under one arm. The city was booming again, after a few anxious months. The jute trade had picked up, and pavements vibrated to the thunder of mills working overtime. From the train she'd watched lorryloads of clay bricks heading from Errol brickworks to the council scheme of 250 houses soon to be built at Logie in Dundee's west end. It was rumoured that Mr Thomson the architect had ordered four million clay bricks from far and wide and the scheme would be a centrally-heated wonder.

But Poppy was not interested in bricks and mortar today, nor in the controversy raging over a site for Dundee's war memorial. The Nethergate outside the City Churches had been suggested, or beside the new City Hall gifted by Sir James Caird to replace the beloved Adam Town House, the Pillars. Neither site impressed Poppy. She hurried past chaotic scenes of demolition and headed for the art dealer's.

'What have we here, girlie?' the elderly man said kindly as Poppy opened the portfolio. He adjusted his specs and studied the paintings. 'Where did you find these?'

'Please sir, I did them myself,' she said shyly.

He gave her a surprised glance, then called to a young man who was loitering beside a stack of canvases. 'Joel! Come and take a look at this. Young lady says she painted them herself.'

He strolled over. 'Very pretty, if you like that sort of thing.'

'What do you mean?' Poppy demanded, indignantly.

'I mean they're competent, but not my idea of art.'

He was tall, thin, black-haired and not very good-looking, and she thought him extremely rude. 'I did my best!'

He laughed. 'My dear girl, the best is yet to come! At the moment you are a kitten with half-closed eyes. Come, let me show you something.' Swiftly, he produced canvas after canvas, ranging them along the back of the shop in a riot of brilliant colour. Poppy could see these were passionate paintings. At first glance they made no sense, but when she looked more closely, quick dabs of bright colour somehow captured exactly the restless beauty of land, sea and sky, the hardy spirit of working men and women.

The art dealer sighed. 'That's a right untidy mess you've made of my shop as usual with your blasted canvases, Joel D'Arcy!'

The young man was not perturbed. He left the paintings where they were and sauntered to the doorway. 'Don't worry, old man. They'll sell to the discerning.' He winked at Poppy. 'Goodbye, kitten. Did I open your eyes?'

The shop seemed dull after he'd gone. 'He's very good, isn't he?' Poppy said, awe-struck.

The art dealer shrugged. 'If you like that sort of thing.'

In England, Poppy's sister Hannah was also facing a thought-provoking experience. It had nothing to do with art, of course, and everything to do with falling head over heels in love with a patient.

Morris Winslow was recovering slowly from 'Pyrexia of Uncertain Origin', a diagnosis which covered a multitude of unknown horrors that had nearly cost him an arm. In the spring of 1919 he was still in hospital at Le Havre when at last the coveted BS label was attached to a jacket button and he was 'marked for Blighty'. Nursing staff began stripping the wards. They were soon on their way home to England with the wounded Tommies too ill to be moved at the end of the war.

Hannah travelled with the men to an officers' recuperation centre in rural Buckinghamshire. Like the others, Morris was in a weak state and still needed nursing. Not that it showed when he took Hannah in his arms one warm summer's day. She had wheeled the bathchair to their favourite spot, a grassy circle surrounded by laurel bushes and very secluded.

'When I get leave you'll come home with me, dear girl,' he told her. 'Mother and father are longing to meet you. They can't thank you enough for saving the son and heir. If I'd been snuffed out in France, lands and title you can trace back to the Doomsday Book would've gone forever.' Seated together on the rug she'd spread on the grass, he drew her close. 'I intend to make sure the Winslow line survives into the next century and beyond. I hope you like children, Hannah dear.' His eyes were teasing, but he was in earnest, she knew.

Hannah was speechless with happiness. This was as good as a proposal. She'd already had a friendly note from his mother Lady Margaret, thanking her for letters written on

Morris's behalf when he was ill, and ending with a sincere invitation to visit them.

Then Hannah came down to earth. Morris believed she came from a similar background. Hannah was convinced she'd lose him if he discovered she'd lied, yet the dilemma was that she wanted to be loved for herself, not the person he believed she was.

He was watching her. 'What is it, love? What's wrong?'

She took a deep breath. 'I've been telling lies, Morris.'

'I can't believe that, my darling,' he smiled. 'You're the most honest person I know.'

'No, I'm not.' She met his eyes and looked away. This was worse than she'd expected. He would never trust her again. 'I lied about my age,' she heard herself say. 'When I went to France I told the Red Cross I was 23, but I'm really only 19.'

'Is that all?' He laughed and pulled her over beside him on the rug.

'Sweetheart, I'd braced myself for a shattering revelation about your past!'

'No, no. Nothing like that.' They kissed, and her world steadied again. Oh, how I love him, she thought as they lay together on the grass. One day I'll tell him, she vowed. One day . . . but not yet.

Kirsty's grandmother was waiting to greet her at Waverley Station, dwarfed by a bustling crowd of travellers, and somehow less formidable than Kirsty remembered. Hugging the elderly lady, she was overcome by a rush of affection.

'Grandma, it's sweet of you to meet me. I would have managed on my own, you know.'

'Nonsense, my dear. I have a taxi waiting.' She briskly summoned a porter with a wave of her stick.

The two faithful servants who had tended Lizzie Robb for many years welcomed Kirsty in the hallway of the apartment in Royal Terrace. Bertha the cook and Ena the housemaid had long ago penetrated their mistress's disciplined exterior and discovered a kind heart beneath. The two of them twittered excitedly when they saw Kirsty.

'Bonnier than ever!' Bertha exclaimed. 'A wee bit pale an' peaky, but nothin' that good fare and a sniff o' Edinburgh air won't fix.'

'Tea, buttered scones and raspberry jelly waiting in the drawing room, ma'am,' beamed Ena proudly.

Kirsty relaxed in the beautiful room. The scent of roses in crystal bowls filled the air, the furnishings had faded to soft-toned colours over years of exposure to the sunlight flooding in. She smiled at her grandmother, who sat ramrod straight beside a silver teapot. She knew so little about this indomitable lady who had given birth to the mother Kirsty had never known.

'Tell me about my mother, Grandma,' she said. 'I don't even know where she was born.'

'In India, my dear. In a tent on the frontier with Afghanistan, to be exact.' Lizzie poured milk into the delicate cups. Milk in first.

'MIF, MIF!' The other memsahibs had cried in mocking chorus fifty years ago, when she was a young bride in Calcutta, new to the ways of army wives. She could still recall the humiliation of that social gaffe. Her careful mother had taught her to put milk in the cup first, so that boiling tea poured into precious porcelain would not crack the cup. That wasn't the 'done' thing in Indian circles!

'Anne, your mother, was born in a small village near Peshawar,' Lizzie went on. 'Your grandfather William was a major in the army at the time, you see, his troops patrolling the border with Afghanistan. I went with him.'

She paused. That also was not 'done'. Officers' wives remained in married quarters, their children were born in civilization, preferably in Britain, not in a poor goat-herder's dwelling and tended by caring strangers. 'There was trouble at the Khyber Pass, you see, and although the baby was due I wanted to be near William, in case . . .' She broke off. For a moment the fear for her husband's life and that of their unborn baby returned like a stab of pain in the heart. Such was the memory of the great love they'd shared. This intense emotion faded to the merciful ache she always carried with her for the two she had loved so dearly. She stared at the young woman who had inherited William's fearless blue eyes and bore such a likeness to their beloved only child. 'Can you imagine a love that would make one face such dangers, I wonder?' she said softly.

'Yes, I believe I can, Grandma.'

The misery on the young face startled Lizzie Robb. Aloud, she said, 'I think we'll arrange a little celebration this Friday evening, Kirsty. Nothing elaborate. Just a few friends, some music and dancing with handsome young gentlemen spared from the war. What do you think, dear?'

Her granddaughter smiled. 'I think you are a dear, scheming old matchmaker, Grandmama!'

'Well, there *is* that,' Lizzie nodded. She leaned across and added scalding hot tea to the milk in Kirsty's cup.

MIF indeed! she thought cheerfully.

Edward Merrilees cursed under his breath when he received an invitation for himself and partner to attend Mrs Robb's soirée in honour of her visiting granddaughter. He had almost recovered from his infatuation with Kirsty Rutherford. Only occasionally did she trouble his thoughts like an impossible dream. Recently, he had begun courting Patricia Lavelle, an attractive widow nearer his own age and a much more suitable candidate for marriage. In fact, he had been considering popping the important question when this invitation came in. He'd a good mind to refuse, but unfortunately Patricia was keen to accept.

'But of course we must go, Edward! It would be nice to be seen together as a couple, wouldn't it?' She gave him a roguish glance under her lashes. 'At least, I assume your intentions are honourable?'

'Oh, yes, absolutely!' Edward assured her. He wondered anxiously if that was tantamount to a proposal. Patricia seemed to think so. She kissed him with every appearance of joy and satisfaction.

*   *   *

On the night of the party, Kirsty was delighted to greet her friend Ruby Merrilees, but . . . she glanced around. 'Where's Pearl?'

'Married to a vet, would you believe? Pearl and I applied to the veterinary college to train as vets and they laughed us out the door. Women are not welcome. Pearl did the next best thing and married Peter. I work as kennel-maid and general dog-and-cats' body in my brother-in-law's veterinary practice, but I intend hammering on the blasted college gates till they let me in!' Ruby said grimly.

'Never mind. Guinevere is expecting!'

Her friend's eyes gleamed. 'When's the foal due?'

'Sometime in the autumn. Cunningham wasn't sure.'

'He should know a mare's pregnancy lasts on average 336 days!'

'Ruby dear, that stuffy old vet college doesn't know what it's missing!' Kirsty laughed.

Lizzie Robb had excelled herself. The carpet in the big room overlooking the garden had been removed for dancing, a pianist hired to play popular dance music in a romantic vein, and Bertha and Ena were supplying suppers in the conservatory. Kirsty made up her mind to flirt outrageously with the young men clustered around her and enjoy herself with abandon. Why shouldn't I? she thought with a momentary twinge of sadness. Who cares?

The pianist was striking up an old-fashioned waltz when Edward Merrilees approached her at last. He held out an arm. 'May I have the pleasure of this one, Kirsty?'

'Of course!' she smiled.

He took her in his arms. He'd swithered for some time whether to ask her to dance, and decided it would look rather odd if he didn't. Besides, it would be the acid test of his emotional state. He was convinced he was over the foolish episode. The girl was the same age as his daughters, for heaven's sake! I must've been daft! Edward thought.

But the moment he took her in his arms he felt his defences crumble. As they danced together he had the curious impression they floated on air. He was no longer aware of other dancers. Only the girl in his arms had any meaning for him. They danced together perfectly in tune to the beat of the music, or was it to the beat of his heart? He could not distinguish one from the other.

She smiled up at him. 'You dance awfully well.'

'Just the waltz, Kirsty. I haven't mastered the foxtrot.'

'Then I must teach you, Mr Merrilees!'

'Edward,' he said softly. 'Please, Kirsty. Call me Edward.'

Patricia Lavelle had seated herself beside Mrs Robb in the place of honour. Patricia watched the dancers, her own toes tapping. She was delighted with the way the evening was going. Edward looked very handsome and distinguished, and she had been accepted by everyone as his partner. Marriage was just around the corner, she was sure. She smiled complacently. 'Dear Edward! He can be relied upon to do his duty. See, Mrs Robb, how attentive he is to your dear little granddaughter, dancing with the child as if she were the only girl in the world! Her poor little head will be turned.'

'Yes, indeed!' Lizzie said thoughtfully.

Patricia Lavelle was a pleasant enough lady, but if there was one thing Lizzie could not stand it was a condescending woman. She could see that the widow had set her cap at Edward Merrilees and was convinced she'd got him. Perhaps one should not blame Patricia altogether, but Lizzie felt a lively spark of indignation. She was extremely fond of Edward. Surely he deserved better than this? Lizzie turned her attention to the couple on the dance floor. The man held the beautiful young woman tenderly in his arms. How well they moved together and what an extremely handsome couple they made. Kirsty and dear Edward Merrilees! Why didn't I think of that wonderful alliance before? Lizzie wondered . . .

Ten

When the waltz ended, Edward Merrilees was reluctant to surrender Kirsty to younger men clustered hopefully around. 'It's hot in here,' he said. 'Would you like a glass of lemonade, Kirsty? I believe it's made from a special Indian recipe of Mrs Robb's.'

'Really? I've never tasted it.' She accepted his arm and went into the conservatory.

Ena the housemaid was dispensing drinks at this strictly teetotal function. She added ice to tall, sugar-frosted glasses and filled them with a sparkling lemon drink. 'There you are, sir, nice an' cool. It's sweltering in there.'

Bertha the cook beamed and handed Edward a basket containing a selection of sandwiches and home-baked cream cakes. 'Away into the garden and give Miss Kirsty a breath o' good Edinburgh air, Mr Merrilees. It's a grand evening for it.'

He took her advice. The peaceful garden was brightly lit by oil lamps, the seating on the terrace in full view of those within. Lizzie Robb did not encourage dalliance in dark corners. Edward and Kirsty chose a wooden bench and table beneath a lantern casting a golden glow. They set the glasses on the table and placed the basket of food between. Edward could sense his elderly hostess's eagle eye fixed on him.

'I hear your young man came back safely from the war, Kirsty. I was happy for you,' he said sincerely. He didn't tell her that shortly after he'd heard he'd begun courting the widowed Patricia in an attempt to banish Kirsty from his thoughts.

'Jamie came home safely, Edward, but not to me. He'd

135

married a German woman who'd been his nurse in prison camp, you see.' She spoke so calmly she surprised herself.

'Oh, my dear! I'm so sorry.'

'It was my own fault. I was living in dreamland while Jamie was facing stark reality. One can hardly blame him for seeking comfort elsewhere.'

'But comfort isn't love, Kirsty.'

'For his sake I hope you're wrong!' She smiled, sipped the drink to steady herself, and purposefully changed the subject. 'Ruby tells me Pearl is married. I thought you disapproved of marrying young?'

'I do! But Peter is a good bit older, a qualified vet with a successful practice. He seems a decent chap with strong nerves to deal with one of my twins, so I gave them my blessing.'

'Poor Edward, I bet you'd no option!' she laughed. 'Never mind, you still have Ruby.'

He sighed. 'No, I don't. Ruby's wedded to the Vet College. Ruby will hammer on their doors till they let women in.'

'They never will,' she said seriously. 'Apart from the danger of contagious abortion in cattle causing miscarriages in pregnant women, you were there when we delivered the calf. That was dirty work requiring considerable strength, certainly no job for women.'

'You did it!'

She shrugged. 'I've worked on a farm all my life. I know my limitations.'

'But Ruby doesn't. That's her strength.'

'Well, good luck to her!'

Kirsty offered him the basket of food. 'Go on, choose a sandwich. We must finish this lot or Bertha will be deeply offended.'

'Let's see . . .' He studied the contents, then pulled a face. 'I can't abide cucumber!'

'I'll take cucumber if you'll take egg. I'm not keen on that. But I bags the chocolate eclair.'

'Done!'

They shared everything, laughing like children. Edward

136

felt the years slip away, and that was dangerous. He had to remind himself he was old enough to be this beautiful young woman's father.

Patricia watched Edward and the young granddaughter laughing together in the softly lit garden. Had it been any other couple she might have considered it charming, but it grated on her to watch these two carrying on like youngsters on their first date. She gave her elderly companion a veiled glance. Mrs Robb was a stickler for the proprieties, so why didn't the wretched woman take steps to break up that cosy tête-à-tête? The young hussy was flirting shamelessly with Edward, and – Patricia tightened her lips – the stupid man was enjoying it!

'Do you not feel a cold draught, Mrs Robb?' she asked.

'A draught? No, dear.'

'My Edward should not be sitting outside. Bad for his chest.'

'You show wifely concern,' Lizzie observed mildly.

'Perhaps I do!' Patricia smiled coyly.

'Oh? I heard no word of an engagement.'

'Let's just say that Edward and I have an understanding.'

'Ah, one of those!'

Patricia reddened with annoyance. 'What d'you mean? Edward Merrilees has been courting me for months and assures me his intentions are honourable. That's as good as a proposal!' she said crossly.

'As good as is rather a dangerous assumption where marriage is concerned, I would've thought, my dear.'

'Well, I trust Edward, even though he's making a perfect fool of himself with your brazen little granddaughter. Young people nowadays are quite shameless!' Patricia snapped.

Lizzie smiled sweetly and patted her hand. 'Attitudes have changed, dear. You and I belong to an older generation.'

Patricia was left speechless and fuming.

Lizzie felt a slight twinge of guilt which she speedily overcame. She'd been just a teeny bit catty, but she had plans for that charming couple which did not include this scheming middle-aged widow. She watched Edward examine the contents of a sandwich minutely. He passed it over to Kirsty, who seemed to be killing herself laughing.

Lizzie smiled contentedly. The situation presented obstacles of course, because of the age difference, but she relished the challenge. So what was the next move? Sightseeing! she thought with a flash of inspiration. Kirsty should explore Edinburgh, and handsome, obliging Edward would make a fascinating guide.

Elise Murdoch visited the doctor's surgery every month. She had done so ever since the pregnancy was confirmed, but now the birth was drawing close the monthly check was more important. All must be well for the adored child's sake.

Today, after the examination, the doctor asked her to remain seated. He studied his notes while she waited. He would not look at her. She was a nurse. She knew the signs!

'There is something wrong,' she said.

'Not exactly. Just an unforeseen problem.'

'You will tell me. I will understand.'

The doctor studied his patient. Her gaze met his, steadily. 'This will be a big baby at full term, Mrs Murdoch, and you are a very slender woman. I doubt if a natural birth will be possible. I could be wrong, of course.'

'But you are not often wrong?'

He hesitated. 'No, I'm not.'

'So,' she said quietly. 'It seems I will not welcome my baby to the world in the beautiful home I have prepared. My child will be born in hospital. Taken from me, and I will not know.'

She tried not to be afraid of the awful prospect. She had known dreadful hospitals, some cold and heartless as machines, others riddled with disease, dirt and danger. But of course she could not voice doubts that would insult this kind doctor's hospital. The fear for her baby's life was something she must suffer alone, she could not even tell her husband of the terrible risk. Jamie would be so terribly worried. More loneliness! she thought in despair.

The middle-aged doctor rose, came from behind the desk and patted her shoulder. 'Don't worry, my dear, you'll be fine.'

She shrugged off the friendly hand almost angrily. 'Do you think I worry for myself? I worry only for the child!'

To her surprise he laughed. 'I assure you this will be a wonderful child, Mrs Murdoch, every bit as strong, healthy and brave as his mother.'

'A boy, you think?' she said quickly, eyes shining.

'A veritable Julius Caesar . . . or maybe even a Juliet,' he promised.

Poppy Murdoch's painting, framed in gold, now hung in pride of place above Jamie's mantelpiece in the lodge. It looked splendid and Elise and Jamie had been delighted when she'd handed it over as they moved into their new home. Poppy should have been gratified by the praise, but she was not. A small voice kept mocking her: 'Quite pretty, if you like that sort of thing!'

Searching for the flaw, she remembered the effort she'd put into painting the scene, days of sketching, weeks of trial and error. That's why it looked laboured and lacking in spontaneity! she thought. She was so disheartened by the discovery that she had not given Samuel Rutherford his gift. He seldom visited Angus House anyway, and had probably forgotten all about her.

Recently, Poppy had found herself a new job that took her into Dundee six days a week. The art dealer had offered her a job in his shop and she'd jumped at the chance. Poor Agnes disapproved, but had given up any hope of guiding her rebellious daughter into respectable employment.

The pay was nothing special and the hours long, but Poppy was happy. She was learning to stretch canvases, restore damaged paintings, assemble frames and deal with fussy customers. More importantly, she was developing an eye for what was good, bad or indifferent. She decided she liked the work of Joel D'Arcy, the young man who had been so dismissive of her efforts. His canvases, however, remained unsold.

'Cluttering up the place!' her boss, Mr Archibald grumbled.

'Maybe if they were framed?' Poppy suggested.

'And maybe the man would pay for frames when pigs fly over Cox's lum!' he scoffed, referring to a landmark tall factory chimney in a city of tall chimneys.

'He hasn't been in since I started working here,' she remarked.

'He comes and goes, like all hard-up folk.'

'Could we maybe show two or three canvases in the window?'

Archibald shrugged. 'Please yoursel'.'

To her delight, she sold one. She waved the notes gleefully. 'Three pounds, Mr Archibald! Won't Mr D'Arcy be pleased!'

'Not once I've taken my commission!'

Archibald tucked the money in the till, but the canvases remained displayed prominently in the window.

Another two had gone by the time Joel D'Arcy strolled into the shop weeks later. His black brows lifted when he found Poppy behind the counter. 'Well, well! The kitten!'

'We sold three of your paintings,' she told him.

'Only three? The philistines!'

He had been in the shop for less than a minute and already she was furious. 'You should be jolly glad Dundee folk bought your blasted canvases. Most folk are working hard trying to scrape a living these days. Where have *you* been?'

'In Paris, painting a masterpiece.' He leaned across the counter, dark eyes smouldering. 'Paris would open your eyes, my darling kitten!'

'Oh, really?' Poppy said weakly.

Mr Archibald emerged from the back shop like a Jack-in-the-box. 'Will you stop filling the sensible wee lassie's head wi' nonsense, Joel?'

The young man was not offended. He laughed and pinched

140

Poppy's pink cheek. 'I am educating this child, Archibald. She's an investment for my future.'

'Not if I can help it, she's not!' grunted the art dealer grimly.

Kirsty had been delighted by the news that her father and dear Holly were to marry. 'It's a fairy story come true!' she remarked to Edward Merrilees as they walked round Leith docks one November day. He had wanted to show Kirsty the ship that brought raw materials from the rubber plantations he owned in Malaya. Malaya was a fascinating country, he'd told her. He wished he could take her there.

'I'm to be bridesmaid, Edward. Holly left the choice of dress to me, but it has to tone with dove grey and rose pink.'

'Sounds easy.'

She looked radiant today, he thought fondly. It was bitterly cold, but her young face glowed and her blue eyes sparkled. He longed to take her in his arms and hold her close. Just that, make no demands. That would be enough for him. Or would it? Edward kicked a loose stone moodily into the oily water. Jolly chums! That's what they still were after weeks of sightseeing. There was no hint of anything more than friendship in her candid gaze and easy manner. He'd taken her to the castle on its craggy hill, shown her Georgian splendour in the New Town and historic squalor in the Old. Patricia had been furious, and that had been a problem at first. Then Mrs Robb had introduced her to a retired Rear-Admiral, and Patricia's demands for attention had ceased. He never heard from her now. Rumour had it she'd flitted off to North Berwick to be nearer the Rear-Admiral.

'I'll go to Jenner's tomorrow and pick a really natty outfit,' Kirsty was planning happily.

'I'll be your chauffeur if you want.'

She linked arms. 'Would you? Oh, Edward, you are a darling! You can come and give your honest opinion.'

'No trouble.'

She would please him dressed in sackcloth, he was so madly in love, but of course he couldn't tell her so.

Mildred's invitation had placed Hannah Murdoch in a quandary. She'd been invited to meet Morris's parents for the first time on the weekend of the wedding, and couldn't cancel that important milestone without a pack of lies. Guiltily, Hannah took the easy way out and turned down Holly's request. The excuse sounded reasonable, but was false.

Guilt still bothered her as she and Morris drove along quiet country roads, bound for the Winslow mansion. Morris had borrowed a chirpy little Austin 7 for the long drive from the hospital to his home and their weekend bags were in the back. He was much better, and it was only a matter of time before he was discharged. He headed the little black car through an impressive wrought-iron gateway.

'Is this it?' Hannah asked.

'Yes. My little grey home in the west, my darling.'

She stared. Even at a distance the house looked huge. I can't go on with this charade, she thought frantically. I'm sure to make some ghastly faux pas and disgrace myself. How will Morris cope if I make him look a fool in front of his parents? No, he must be told right now! she decided nervously. There was still time to turn back.

'Morris, listen to me . . .'

'Why, there's dear old William, the gatekeeper!' He leaned out and waved. 'How are you, Bill?'

The old man whipped off his cap, beaming. 'Oh, welcome home, sir!'

Morris drove on. He reached for Hannah's hand. 'Sorry, love. What were you saying?'

She felt the strong grip of his hand. I did that! she thought. I gave him life and love and a perfect body. What does my accident of birth matter, if we love one another? 'Oh, nothing, my darling,' she said. 'I feel awfully nervous, that's all.'

He laughed. 'Buck up, sweetheart. They won't eat you!'

Margaret Winslow had been anxious to meet her son's new girlfriend. He'd had love affairs before, but mostly with young girls from their own set. Margaret sensed this one was quite different. A mother always knows! she thought. What if I don't like her? What if she's the brash, confident type I hate? She's a nurse, and nurses can be so bossy!

'They're here!' her husband called, throwing down *The Times* and rising eagerly. Dear man! There was no hint of apprehension in his expression, only happy anticipation. She followed him outside, their footsteps ringing on the mosaic tiles of the grand entrance.

The girl was younger than Margaret had expected, and she saw at once that the poor child was shaking with nerves. Margaret warmed to her. Her son had put an arm protectively around the girl, the arm he had very nearly lost. Margaret felt an emotional lurch of the heart. They owed this young girl such a great debt of gratitude!

Morris's voice rang out like wedding bells. 'Mum, Dad, this is Hannah!'

Margaret ran down the steps smiling. She took the girl's hand and kissed her cheek. 'Welcome, my dear!'

That night, after an exhausting day, Hannah knelt by a four-poster bed to say a prayer. Words would not come.

She'd managed wonderfully well that day, considering the splendour of the surroundings which Morris took for granted. She hadn't disgraced herself at dinner either. She'd noticed Lady Margaret watching to see if she could handle a baffling array of cutlery and crystal glasses. But all that was second nature to one who'd studied *Lady's Companion* and *Household Words*, not to mention *Etiquette of the Dinner Table*, and Hannah had managed beautifully.

Conversation in the drawing room had held pitfalls, however. Morris had regaled his parents with harrowing stories of battles leading up to his arrival in hospital. Lady Margaret had turned sympathetically to Hannah. 'You faced such danger looking after our poor Tommies, Hannah dear. How worried your mother must have been!'

Hannah hesitated. This was an opportunity to make a clean breast of everything, and they'd been so kind she'd decided she shouldn't keep up the pretence any longer, no matter what the outcome was. Unfortunately, Morris had misunderstood the reason for the hesitation.

'Hannah's mother died when she was a baby, Mum,' he said. 'Her father seems to have been overcome with grief and never leaves his remote Highland castle, and in my opinion takes very little interest in his lovely daughter!'

His parents had been all warm sympathy. 'Oh, my dear, what a terrible state of affairs!' Lady Margaret said.

Hannah's eyes filled with tears as she knelt by the bed. 'Mam, Mam! What have I done?' she whispered. These nice people believed dear Mam was dead and darling Dad was a sad old recluse. No wonder Hannah couldn't pray!

The instant Elise Murdoch opened her eyes, she knew the baby was coming. It was early morning and very dark. Jamie slept by her side and she did not wake him. She laid a comforting hand upon the stirring child. Don't be afraid, my darling, she thought soothingly. Maybe the thought reached the little unborn one. The discomfort eased a bit.

When Jamie stirred and yawned at six, she told him. He shot out of bed and groped for matches, a picture of alarm in the sudden glare of the lamp. 'You lie still, my darling. I'll tell my mother to come. She'll fetch the midwife when the time comes.'

She smiled fondly, he looked so anxious. She felt relaxed, exhilarated, ready to fight for their child. 'There is no hurry, *Liebling*. It will be a long day.'

'I know a first baby can take ages, sweetheart,' he said worriedly. He was struggling into trousers, hopping on one leg, buttoning his shirt all wrong. 'But I'll feel happier if Mam stays with you.'

'But not you?' She had assumed he would be with her.

'Me?' He looked surprised. 'Oh no. Husbands are not welcome!'

She said nothing, but felt sad. She had wanted him to be there. Not to watch an operation if it had to come to that, but she had hoped to open her eyes afterwards and find their baby safe in her husband's arms. It meant much to her.

144

He was bending over her. 'Lie still, dear. I'll bring you a cup of tea. Just fancy, it's the Colonel's wedding day!'

She laughed. 'That is a lucky day to be born.'

'So it is! Anything else I can do?'

She smiled and kissed him. 'Just phone the doctor, darling. He will want to know.'

Agnes was thrilled when she heard her first grandchild was on the way. 'I'll go round at once, Jamie. Don't worry, I'll see to her and the bairn when it comes.' He looked much more relaxed as he set off for work at the mill.

Agnes prepared broth and a piece of boiling beef to simmer on the hob for the men's dinner. There was no hurry, plenty time to spare with a first one. She took time to pack a basket with light, nourishing food for her daughter-in-law. It was a grand chance for them to become real friends during this ordeal. They'd been more like strangers since Elise and Jamie had moved to the lodge. With a last glance around the tidy kitchen, she set off.

Agnes knocked on the lodge door but didn't wait for an invitation to enter. 'Elise dear?' she called.

Elise answered from the bedroom. The house looked real bonny, Agnes noted, and lovely and warm from the tiled stove that heated the whole place. She went into the bedroom. Elise was fully dressed. She had the chest of drawers open, her arms full of nighties and baby things. Agnes smiled. 'My, you're well prepared, dear!'

'I have to be.' Elise packed the clothing into a small case.

Agnes was surprised. 'You're a cool one!' she joked. 'Are you planning a wee holiday afterwards?'

She went on packing items into the case. 'No. I go to hospital. A taxi is coming very soon.'

'Wha-at?' Agnes was badly shaken. She'd taken for granted the baby would be born at home as was natural. She'd hoped to ease her daughter-in-law's labour, help the midwife deliver the bairn and hold her wee grandchild in her arms when it was all over. She was bitterly disappointed. This woman with her foreign ways would deny her that wonderful

145

moment. They'd never got on from the start, and now they never would.

'None of my children was born in hospital. It's not natural. It's not done here!' she cried angrily.

Elise's hands gripped hard on the chairback, but she had schooled herself to hide pain. The kind doctor had been and examined her and said there was no hope of a natural birth. The pains were coming faster now. She could sense the child struggling to be born, the agitated little heart beating too fast, the threat of suffocation was growing by the hour. There was no time to lose. 'My baby will be born in hospital,' she said tersely, snapping the case shut.

'So you don't want me!'

Elise struggled to explain in a difficult language. 'It is not a question of wanting. You are not needed,' she said as gently as she could. And neither am I, my dear mother-in-law, she thought. My baby will be taken from me by surgeons. But the child must live. That is all that matters.

Not needed! Agnes had never been so hurt and furious. 'Very well, Elise. If that's the way it's to be, goodbye and guid luck to you both. You'll need it in thon sick place!' She stormed out and slammed the door. She could hardly see her way home to the Milton for tears.

At 3 o'clock that same Saturday afternoon, half the population of Invergowrie and the surrounding district turned out to see Colonel Rutherford wed his governess. Some said they'd seen it coming for years and a brainy wife would be the making of the dour man. Those who couldn't cram into the kirk alongside invited guests, waited outside in the chilly damp, stamping their feet in thawing slush. A cheer rose as the Colonel drove up with the best man, his son George. A big, shaggy dog with a huge red rose fastened to its collar guided the blind man, and the three disappeared into the vestry.

Kirsty arrived in the bridal car with Mildred and her elderly father. Cheers rose to a crescendo as they stepped out. It was like a dream, Kirsty thought. Mildred looked beautiful, smiling as she walked past crowds of well-wishers. At the doorway, Kirsty kissed her cheek and handed over a small posy of pink roses. They could hear the organ playing 'Here Comes The Bride'. Mildred smiled happily and hung on to her father's arm.

Walking slowly down the aisle behind them, Kirsty searched the sea of faces for Jamie. She spotted Dougal sitting with Agnes, who was looking grim, but Jamie and Elise were not there. He had not come! She felt keen disappointment. He had been on her mind when choosing the rose-coloured costume trimmed with dove-grey fur and the rose-trimmed hat which suited her so well. She wondered sometimes if she had set out deliberately to force Jamie Murdoch to realize what he had lost.

Seated beside Samuel, Edward caught her eye as they reached the altar. His warm smile settled her nerves, and she smiled at him before turning her attention to the moving ceremony which united dear Papa and her beloved Holly.

Mildred had arranged an informal reception afterwards at Angus House. The old house looked at its best when hosting large gatherings, with partition doors between dining and drawing room thrown wide open to make one huge space. Everyone mingled and chatted informally while sampling a magnificent buffet. Kirsty stood with Edward Merilees for the cutting of the wedding cake. She was glad now that Elise and Jamie hadn't come. She felt at ease, enjoying the occasion. Somebody was about to make a speech, and Edward handed her a glass of champagne for the toast.

'Ladies and gentlemen, may I—'

But a sudden commotion interrupted the speaker. Jamie Murdoch hurtled into the room, white mill dust still clinging to his shoulders. 'Listen everyone!' he shouted. 'My wife and I should have been with you to celebrate this happy occasion, but I have wonderful news. Elise has presented me with a fine son and mother and baby are doing well. Isn't this the happiest of days?'

A hearty cheer greeted the announcement and drowned the sound as Kirsty's glass slipped from her fingers and shattered. She turned and pushed her way through the crowd.

147

Jamie's son! The baby that might have been hers! Kirsty fled outside the house into darkness and stood weeping in the cold, quiet night.

Edward had followed, full of concern. 'Kirsty!'

She turned and buried her face against his chest. 'That should've been my baby, not hers! Oh, Edward. It hurts so much. Tell me what to do!' she sobbed.

He held her in his arms. All he wanted was her happiness, but there was only one solution he could think of to help rebuild her life. Would it be too much to ask, he wondered.

'Marry me, Kirsty?'

Her head lifted sharply and she stared at him with a shocked disbelief that cut him to the heart.

'Edward, you . . . you're a dear friend, but I don't love you!'

Eleven

Edward's proposal was an unexpected shock. She backed away, leaving a space of cold night air between them. 'Listen, Kirsty,' he said reasonably. 'I saw how Jamie Murdoch's announcement affected you. It was tragic. You can't go on like this. I'm offering you a safe haven.'

'You call a loveless marriage a safe haven?'

'Not loveless, I love you. D'you think I would ask you to marry me if I didn't?'

'No, I don't suppose you would.'

'Friendship and love. A recipe for a good marriage, Kirsty!'

'More like a recipe for one of Grandma's concoctions.' She frowned when he laughed. 'This is no laughing matter!'

'I'm not laughing! I fought hard not to fall in love with you. There's the age difference.'

'Nearly twenty years!'

'Thanks for reminding me.'

'I never gave it a thought till now.'

'I never intended to marry you till now.'

'So why did you ask?'

'You looked so damn miserable I had to do something. I know you don't love me, but I hoped you might care enough to accept.'

'Edward, I'm sorry.'

'Does that mean "no"?'

She hesitated. 'It means I'm sorry I don't love you.'

'So there's hope!' He reached for her hand and was heartened when her fingers curled round his. 'Think about it, my dear girl. There are advantages. I'd support you in whatever you aim to do with the rest of your life. You could marry me,

149

leave an intolerable situation behind and live in my house in Edinburgh close to your grandmother. If friendship is all you want, I'll settle for that.'

She believed him. His generosity was touching. Oh, if only I could love him! she thought. She was fond of him, but not with the depth of emotion she'd shared with Jamie. Dare she risk marrying this kind, caring man and making him unhappy?

'I'm so terribly sorry, Edward!' she said tearfully.

He sighed. 'Kirsty, stop apologizing, it's confusing.' He handed her a handkerchief and she mopped her eyes. 'That better?'

'Yes, thanks.'

'Then put on a brave face. We have a wedding to celebrate, remember? Though not an engagement . . . just yet.'

Elise had never been so happy. She was recovering after the caesarean section when a nurse brought her baby to her in the maternity ward. Elise greeted her son with a kiss. 'Is it permitted to hold my baby, please?'

The nurse handed him over. 'Just a wee cuddle then, dear.'

Elise studied the baby cradled in her arms. She touched one pink cheek fondly with a fingertip. He was big for a newborn baby and had an indignant look, as if he'd expected to fight for life and been denied the privilege. He frowned as he slept, small mouth working experimentally. One could not say he was beautiful, but beautiful is not a fitting adjective for a boy anyway, she thought. Handsome is better. Like his father, although their son did not have Jamie's dark hair.

Examining him more closely, she suddenly saw in the small face a remarkable resemblance. '*Vater!*' she breathed. The nose, brow, eyes and mouth could have been those of the dead father she had loved so dearly. Vividly, she recalled the carefree childhood spent in Berlin with her parents and brothers, before war took her loved ones from her. Now this little one would never know his kind German grandparents and two brave uncles. The likeness was so striking and the memories it evoked so painful, her eyes filled with tears that spilled over and dripped on to the child.

'Here, turn aff the waterworks, love. I already bathed this bairn!' The watchful nurse lifted the baby away. She was used to displays of emotion from new mothers, and one couldn't be too careful. With a comforting smile for the weeping mother, the nurse raised the little shawled bundle confidently to her shoulder and strode off down the corridor to the nursery.

Jamie visited the next day, waiting impatiently outside the ward for the doors to open on the stroke of three o'clock. He handed over his visitor's card and endured the sister's keen scrutiny as visitors filed past her.

Elise was waiting for him, looking pale, but happy. He kissed her tenderly and handed over a posy of flowers. 'It should've been red roses, darling, but choice is limited in November. You'll have to make do with chrysanths.'

'*Liebling*, they are lovely.' She watched as he put the flowers on the locker. The scene recaptured days in the prison hospital when their love was new, only this time the roles were reversed. The look in his eyes was the same and the wonderful loving smile.

Jamie looked around hopefully. 'Well, where's Junior?'

'In sterile nursery. Do you think Sister would allow precious baby to remain while visitors bring coughs and sneezes from outside?'

'The old dragon!' Jamie said, eyeing the stiffly-starched sister who kept strict watch over visiting hour.

'Oh yes, Sister is dragon! She breathes fire and has warm heart!' His wife smiled. 'If you behave and have clean hands, she may allow a visit to the nursery to see your son. He is very big and handsome.'

'That's my boy!' Jamie pulled up a chair and took his wife's hand.

'How are you, my darling? Was it very bad?' he asked quietly.

'I knew nothing, Jamie, but I feel sad because I was not awake to welcome my baby to the world.'

'You're recovering well and we have a healthy son. That's all that matters,' Jamie said. 'I wonder what we should call the handsome lad?'

151

'Jamie, I already know! Wait till you hear, it is *wunderbar*, a miracle!' she laughed delightedly.

'I can guess! You want to call him after the doctor. Well, Michael Murdoch sounds fine to me.'

'Michael is a fine name, but it is not that. When I held our baby I saw a most amazing likeness. I knew at once what the little one's name must be, Jamie. It is Jurgen!'

He was dismayed. 'But that's a German name!'

Elise's happy smile faded. 'My father's name. I will not change it. He is Jurgen!'

'No, darling! You can't do this.'

'It is done. You cannot forbid me!' she cried passionately.

'Elise, for heaven's sake!' Jamie had never seen his wife so determined, but he remembered hearing that women can take funny notions after giving birth. He tried reasoning with her. '*Liebchen*, think what will happen when the boy goes to school. Children can be cruel. Our lad's life will be a misery if he has an unusual German name!'

She began sobbing bitterly. 'You think I don't know? I know they will taunt my child at kindergarten. Your people have shunned me ever since I came, but your son had a German grandfather whether you like it or not. His name is Jurgen!' Her voice had risen and heads were turning.

'Elise—' Jamie began desperately.

'What is happening here?' Sister stood at the end of the bed. Her glance took in the distressed state of her patient and her lips tightened. Elise had collapsed against the pillows, weeping. 'Tell him my baby's name, Sister. It is Jurgen, the name of my dear, dead *Vati*,' she sobbed.

'Of course, my dear. That's a fine name. Go to sleep now,' Sister soothed. She gave Jamie an icy glare. 'You will come with me, Mr Murdoch!'

He followed the nurse sheepishly into the corridor. She faced him angrily. 'How dare you upset my patient like that! Don't you realize your wife is lucky to be alive? There were serious complications with this birth and you could have lost them both.'

'But she's chosen a daft name for the boy, Sister. She wants to call him Jurgen!'

'I've heard much worse!'

'It's a German name!' Jamie began to shiver. That damned legacy from the war! he thought. Jurgen. The name brought back scenes in the labour camp he would rather forget. There had been a guard with that name, he remembered. A merciless, sadistic individual . . .

The nurse was watching shrewdly. 'Did you fight in the war, Mr Murdoch?' she asked more kindly. 'Aye well, I can understand your misgivings, but you should let your wife have her way in this. Her father is dead and she wants his name to live on. It's a natural desire. It could hinder her recovery if you refuse, you know.'

He sighed. 'Maybe you're right. What's in a name, after all?' She smiled. 'That's the spirit! Now, I expect you'd like to see your bouncing boy . . .'

Later that day, Agnes added a second spoonful of sugar to her son's cup. He looked as if he needed it after the visit to Dundee Royal Infirmary, known locally with affection as the 'D.R.I.'

'I'm pleased Elise is recovering. How's the boy?' she asked.

His face lit up. 'Oh, Mam, he's braw! So big you'd think he was two months old, not newborn.'

'The wee lamb! I'm longing to see him!'

'It'll be a while before Elise is fit enough to come home.'

'I warned her against giving birth in that place, but oh no, she knew best!' Agnes said. 'Sure enough, there were complications.'

Jamie took a sip of strong tea to give himself strength for the next hurdle. 'Elise has decided to name the baby after his grandfather.'

His mother beamed. 'Dougal *will* be pleased!'

'No, Mam, I'm sorry. I meant his German grandfather.'

She sat down suddenly. 'I might've known! What's it to be?'

'He's to be called Jurgen.'

'Yoor-gen? I can't even spell it!' she wailed. 'It's a good

job my grandson's born big, Jamie. The wee soul will need his wits about him, saddled with a name like thon!'

Kirsty did not resume the visit to her grandmother's after the newly-weds had set off on honeymoon. Edward pleaded with her, but she insisted she needed time to consider. Reluctantly, he'd given in.

'Are you sure you won't come back with me, Kirsty?' he demanded worriedly at the moment of parting. 'Staying will be difficult for you, and leaving you will be sheer hell for me!'

'Cheer up, Edward, you'll survive!' She kissed him impulsively, and watched him drive off with his hat at a rakish angle. She wondered if the kiss had been wise.

In the meantime there was plenty going on to take her mind off matrimonial problems. Guinevere and Lochinvar's foal had been born and was now a promising colt with the stallion's dark colouring, his dam's good nature and Thrawn Janet's mischievous spirit.

'I left the naming o' the wee beast to you,' Cunningham told her.

'How about Merlin? He was a wizard by all accounts!' Kirsty suggested.

'Aye well, maybe young Merlin will bring a touch o' magic to bloodstock in the Carse. He's sturdy enough for a hunter, with plenty speed in those long limbs,' the grieve agreed.

Both Kirsty's brothers were at home for the festive season. Samuel had finished his first term at Glasgow medical school and was glad of a break. The three of them sat in front of a blazing fire one freezing December evening. Kirsty was on her knees with the toasting fork, making toast for supper. The dog Murphy was watching proceedings, a hungry drool of saliva dripping from his whiskery muzzle. Samuel lounged in one deep, shabby armchair, George relaxed contentedly in another.

'It was a first class wedding. I've never seen the Old Man so happy,' Samuel remarked.

154

'Nor dear Holly look so beautiful,' Kirsty added.

'I wish I could have seen them,' George said.

Samuel and Kirsty exchanged a worried glance. George was still subject to bouts of depression, though these were less frequent nowadays.

'Well, anyway,' Samuel continued, 'the two of them were determined nobody would know they were newly-weds, but they're in for a shock. They planned to do a bit of shopping and sight-seeing in London. I wonder if it's rained yet?'

'Why?' Kirsty asked.

'I charged the Old Man's brolly with confetti and rolled it up tight. It should make a sensational shower when opened!'

Charles's three offspring howled with glee as they pictured the scene.

'I'm glad we're four hundred miles away. Our dear father will be flaming. At least I bet his face will!' George laughed.

It was heart-warming to hear George laugh, Kirsty thought. Her brother worked hard on the estate and managed his disability well with Murphy's guidance, but he seldom laughed. She tossed a crust to the dog, who caught it expertly. 'There's to be a baker's strike this Christmas. Isn't it a shame?' she remarked. 'It says in the *Courier* people are hoarding bread.'

George looked concerned. 'A strike will affect Murdoch's mill, won't it? They depend upon bakery orders.'

'They can stand it!' Kirsty speared another slice on the trident and held it close to the firebars. The mill went from strength to strength while Angus estate struggled despite Edward's infusions of cash.

'What happened to the younger Murdoch girl?' Samuel asked idly. 'She was a wee pest! What was her name? Polly? No, Poppy!'

'I'm told she's a talented artist,' George volunteered. 'Elise Murdoch is enthusiastic about a watercolour Poppy painted for Jamie. Elise says it's quite brilliant.'

Kirsty twisted round, astonished. 'I didn't know you'd spoken to her!'

'Oh, yes. Before the bairn was born she invited me into the lodge to thaw out during the November cold snap. Elise makes a grand cup of coffee! I think she's lonely and needs friends. You should look in and see her, Kirsty.'

The acrid smell of burnt toast filled the room. 'Drat!' Kirsty cast the charred remains of the slice into the fire. 'I'll fetch more bread.'

After she'd made a hasty escape, George frowned. 'What's troubling little sister? Was it something I said?'

'Sensitive area, old man! It's no secret she was keen on Jamie Murdoch. It was a terrible blow to Kirsty when the man came home married to a German nurse.'

'I can imagine!' Poor Kirsty, George thought, and poor Elise too, a stranger in a foreign land. It was a wonder Jamie Murdoch could sleep at night, with two unhappy women on his conscience . . .

Agnes had decided to let bygones be bygones for her grandson's sake, and was at the lodge every day now that mother and baby were home. After all, one could hardly shun the wee one because of German connections and a name that Carse folk greeted with an incredulous '*Whut?*'

Elise was grateful for her mother-in-law's help as she recovered from surgery. She kissed her little son and told him how happy she was with the situation. 'You see, adored one, your *Grössmutter* loves you, and your *Mutti* adores you and will never be lonely again, now that you have come.' She spoke softly in the mother tongue which was natural to her, a language only she and her baby could share.

Agnes heard the foreign murmur and frowned. She hoped the bairn wasn't to be taught that gibberish. His unfortunate background was best forgotten. 'Time for a nappy change!' she said loudly.

She lifted the baby from the cradle. My, he's a heavyweight! she thought proudly. His mother had been warned not to lift him, and Agnes loved tending to her grandson. What with one thing and another, she was much too busy to keep an eye on her young daughter, which suited Poppy down to the ground. An excuse of first-footing a friend had been accepted without question and nobody thought to ask the friend's identity and sex. Which was just as well for everyone's peace of mind.

In Dundee, Joel D'Arcy was waiting on the platform. Gravely, he handed her a chocolate bar from the penny slot machine.

'Happy New Year!'

'There's a bite out of it!'

'I was hungry.' He took her arm and guided her through the crowd.

'Where are we going, Joel?' she asked eagerly. 'I put on warm clothes in case we climb the Law. Let's do that. You can see for miles from the top. It's pretty.'

His lip curled. 'Prettiness is banned for today.'

'Where then?' she demanded sulkily.

'We will view real life, my kitten!'

He led her down to the busy docks which were so much part of Dundee life that one was aware of the sea even when walking along the High Street. A smell of fish and seafaring mingled with the aroma of roasting coffee, Keiller's marmalade and Wallace's onion pies. Joel made her stand by the kerb and listen to the sound of seawater lapping, gulls mewing and ships creaking at anchor as boats lifted to an unusually high tide. They walked through the ornate Royal Arch, known locally as Pigeons' Palace, soot-blackened and streaked with white bird-droppings. He pointed out moody reflections on dark water in William IV dock, and dazzling silver sunlit ripples on the wide Tay estuary.

Afterwards, they wandered along the ancient Overgate, eating chips and peas bought from an enterprising stallholder. He showed her the subtle play of light and shade on weathered Dundee whinstone which magically transformed a smelly, squalid backyard.

'I don't know why you're showing me this,' Poppy grumbled, holding her nose.

'There is beauty in unpromising places if you have eyes to see it, my darling! In years to come you will remember words of wisdom from a master of the craft.'

'One with a big head!' she said rudely.

'You have sharp claws, my kitten!' He gave her a side-long glance.

'Would you care to see my paintings?'

'Oh, yes, please, Joel!' she cried eagerly.

He burst out laughing. 'Oh, my dear, innocent child!'

'I'm not a child!' she protested.

'No?' He raised his brows. 'Come along then.'

His room was in the attic of a tenement overlooking a whisky bond. It was untidy and not very clean. There were twisted tubes of oil paint littering shelves, discarded canvases, yellowed bottles of linseed oil, jars of turpentine and dirty jam jars everywhere stuffed with brushes of all shapes and sizes. But the room was flooded with clear, brilliant light from a dormer window facing east and a north-facing rooflight directly above a large wooden easel.

'Sit there,' he ordered, pointing to a rumpled, unmade bed. Then from a cupboard he produced picture after picture, displaying each one on the easel, shocking her with the many portraits of nude women, dazzling her with the brilliance of landscapes full of light and colour.

When the show was over, Poppy was humbled and tearful. She could never paint like this! 'Joel, you're a genius!'

He knelt, cupped her chin between his hands and stared intently into her eyes. 'You really mean that!' he said softly in wonder. He leaned forward and kissed her warmly and searchingly on the mouth. 'There, child. Now you are a woman.'

The lingering kiss awakened Poppy abruptly to the danger of the situation. She scrambled to her feet in panic. 'I'd better go!'

'Yes,' Joel agreed, darkly. 'You'd better.'

He escorted her to the station without touching her, hands plunged moodily into his pockets. It was bitterly cold, an early darkness had fallen, and they did not speak. The kiss had changed everything, Poppy thought unhappily. She wondered if he would kiss her goodbye on the public platform, or insist on seeing her home and kiss her as they walked on the lovers' path. But what would Mam and Dad say if she brought him home? They wouldn't like him. They wouldn't trust him. She wasn't sure if she trusted him herself. As for liking, the emotion he had awakened went deeper than that.

She turned to him shyly as the train steamed in. 'Thank you for a lovely day, Joel.' She wanted him to kiss her. She wanted it so much she was sure it showed.

'Don't mention it, dear girl!' He tipped his hat, raised a hand in casual farewell and strolled off, leaving her standing alone, choking back tears.

Hannah Murdoch came home at last towards the end of January, arriving one morning on the London sleeper, much to her mother's delight. Back home in the Milton, Agnes hugged her tall daughter then held her at arm's length. 'Let's look at you, love. My, but isn't she elegant, Dougal?'

'So she is,' he agreed. Privately, he thought his beautiful daughter looked tense and unhappy despite the smart costume that must have cost a packet.

Agnes was chattering on. 'You'll be home for good now, dear? Plenty of work for nurses in Dundee. There's typhoid in Lochee and you can get a dose o' the 'flu any time you step on the tram.'

Hannah hesitated. Should she tell them the truth? Maybe not yet. 'I've been offered a job abroad, Mam. I haven't made up my mind whether to accept or not,' she said glibly. That was near enough!

'You'd be daft to go abroad! Home's best, Hannah dear,' her mother said.

'I want to see the world, Mam.'

'I've seen enough of it looking out my own window.'

'There's the pay. I'd be well-off. I could send money home.'

'There's no need to do that, Hannah!' Dougal frowned.

Maybe there was little outward show of wealth in the house, only extra comforts and aids to make Agnes's life easier, but the Murdochs were wealthy. He and Jamie intended investing a large lump of capital in a new venture, but Dougal daren't let news of that leak into the Carse just yet.

Hannah laughed. 'Oh Daddy, don't be so stubborn and proud! Let me help you!'

Dougal was angered. 'If you want to help us, daughter, save your cash and stay independent!' he said brusquely. He found Hannah's lah-di-dah tone insulting. His elegant, perfumed daughter was more like a gentry lady than wee Kirsty Rutherford herself. It disgusted him to see her putting on such airs.

Hannah paid Kirsty a visit that afternoon. She needed to talk to the young woman she looked upon as a sister. Kirsty was level-headed and her advice could be trusted. Maybe that's why I want to be just like her, Hannah thought as they hugged emotionally. Hand in hand, the two women made for the schoolroom and settled down on the old, sagging sofa.

'You didn't marry Jamie!' Hannah remarked.

'No. He preferred a German nurse.'

'It can happen. Sick men are so vulnerable.' She thought about Morris, and their love for one another. Surely that was different?

Kirsty was studying her keenly. 'You don't look happy. What's wrong?'

Hannah hesitated. She couldn't possibly tell Kirsty about the lies she'd told. Kirsty was honest through and through and wouldn't understand. She couldn't tell her that Morris was heir to a knighthood and a vast estate and had begged her to marry him. He'd been offered a position in the Far East with the Diplomatic Service and wanted to marry Hannah and take her with him. She'd told him she must visit her reclusive father in his remote Highland lair to tell him what was intended, and had had a hard time persuading Morris not to come, too. *Oh, what a tangled web we weave . . .*

'I've been offered a job abroad, Kirsty,' she said aloud. 'It means travelling around, maybe not returning to Scotland for years. It's a difficult decision to take.'

'But you're longing to go!' her friend said. 'Well, I think you'll regret it if you don't.' She paused and her eyes twinkled. 'Besides, I suspect there's a man involved?'

'Yes, there is,' Hannah admitted. 'But not the type I should marry.'

160

Ahah! Kirsty thought. That explained much. A rough diamond, or a married man whose wife won't divorce him? Poor Hannah! Kirsty could understand the pain involved. 'Do you love one another?' she asked.

'Oh yes, dearly!'

'Then that's all that matters, Hannah. Go for it!' Kirsty smiled.

Charles Rutherford and his bride returned to Angus House a week or two after Hannah Murdoch left the Carse to follow her destiny. Samuel had returned to Glasgow for the new term and Kirsty was delighted to have Holly's company again. However, as the days passed she became aware of unusual goings-on in the house, quiet discussions taking place between George and her father behind closed doors. There was also a certain reticence in Holly's manner which made Kirsty uneasy. Matters came to a head at breakfast one April morning when the post arrived.

Charles slit open an official-looking envelope and scanned the contents. He glanced at Mildred. 'It's the solicitor's letter at last, my darling, the news we've been waiting for. We've accepted the offer. The sale's official!'

'What sale?' Kirsty sliced the top off George's boiled egg for him. She saw the glance that passed between husband and wife. 'What's going on?' she demanded.

'I'm selling Angus estate, Kirsty,' her father said quietly.

'You can't! That's a family decision. You know I would never agree!'

'I know, that's why I kept quiet. I'm sorry, Kirsty, but legally you're a minor. You have no say in the decision.'

'Edward won't let you!' she cried.

'On the contrary, Edward has serious problems with his business. He can't afford to put any more money in and was relieved when I suggested selling. He'll be glad of the cash. Times are hard for everyone.'

'Papa, why are you doing this?' she choked on a sob.

Mildred intervened. 'Kirsty dear, your father has accepted the job of curator in a military museum near Stirling castle. It

161

involves documenting exhibits and searching for other items of interest, which is right up my street!' Her eyes glowed with enthusiasm. 'The only drawback is we must live in Stirling, of course. We're in the process of buying a property at the moment, but we must sell Angus House first.'

'But what about us, Holly? What about George?' Kirsty asked tearfully.

Her father broke in. 'Don't worry, my dear, the estate will carry on as usual with George and Cunningham in charge, but the new owner will move into Angus House. You can either come to Stirling and live with us, or stay in the lodge with George.'

'But the lodge belongs to Jamie Murdoch!'

Charles laughed. 'It's James Murdoch who's buying the estate. He's agreed to give George a long assured tenancy of the lodge.'

'Suits me, Kirsty!' George said.

Jamie Murdoch and Elise, living in her beloved Angus House? What a cruel twist of fate! Kirsty stood up, the chair toppling. 'Well, it doesn't suit me at all!' she yelled furiously.

She stormed out of the house. At first she'd no clear idea where she was going, but anger directed her along the woodland path towards the Milton.

It was Jamie Murdoch's misfortune that he happened to be late that morning. Jurgen had colic and had kept his parents awake half the night. Jamie was tired and had missed breakfast. Kirsty accosted him on the way to work, attacking him like a small fury.

'How dare you steal our home!'

'You mean you weren't consulted for once?' he mocked.

'It's spite! You want to get at me!'

'Why should I want to do that?'

'Because . . . because . . .' She floundered. So many reasons, but mostly because she had loved him and would always love him.

He thrust his face close to hers. 'I'll tell you why I did it. You goaded me into fighting a ghastly war because your brother was a conchie. Maybe I would have volunteered anyway, but maybe I would have stayed for my father's sake.' He went on bitterly. 'And what happened to me, Kirsty? I rotted in a filthy prisoner-of-war camp while your precious brother won a medal!'

'That wasn't my fault, I couldn't help it!'

'Sure. Just as you couldn't help ruining that poor devil Merrilees!'

She stared. 'Edward? But I didn't!'

'Aye, you did!' he taunted her. 'You distracted the man at a crucial moment. While he was dancing attendance on you, he was being swindled out of valuable shipments. Don't blame me because I'm on the up and up and your family's on its uppers, Kirsty Rutherford. It's your own fault!'

Tears spilled down her cheeks. 'But why take my home away, Jamie? You know how much I love it!'

'I've had my eye on the house for years. I've an ambition to be the equal of a jute baron.'

Poignantly, he remembered that once upon a time when she'd seemed far beyond his reach he'd dreamed of buying her a mansion. Now he was rich and had set out deliberately to steal her home. Why? Was it revenge? And they said revenge was sweet! he thought. When he remembered what might have been, it nearly broke his heart.

She had started to cry softly. He couldn't bear that.

'Ah, Kirsty, don't cry! I'm sorry . . .' He took a step nearer, touched her shoulder. Perhaps that was his mistake. A moment later she was in his arms, her head pressed against him, her fragrance drifting headily to his nostrils. He'd forgotten how slender she felt in his arms. She raised her head. 'Jamie, we shouldn't . . . !'

'I know.' But how could they stop something that felt so right? He kissed her with the desperation of lost years, and she responded with the hunger of shattered dreams. When at last they drew apart, they stared at one another appalled. Forbidden love, broken trust, constant temptation if she stayed near him! Kirsty tore herself free and ran. She heard him shout after her and hesitated, then kept on running.

Agnes, the iron arrested in mid-air, had seen every moment of their meeting from her kitchen window. She thumped the cool iron on to the board with a wail. 'I knew it! I knew it! Oh, Jamie lad, where will it end?'

Kirsty knew what she must do. She was busily flinging items of clothing into a small case when Mildred looked in. 'Kirsty dear, where are you going?'

'To Edinburgh.'

Mildred was relieved. 'To your grandmother, of course! That's a good idea.' She could sympathize with the poor girl's distress, but Mrs Robb was a wise woman. She would know how to cope. 'Listen, Kirsty, you mustn't blame your father,' Mildred said. 'He's been at his wit's end making ends meet. He's not a young man, and the worry was making him ill. This job will suit him much better and I'm afraid I encouraged him to take it. Must you leave in such haste? Couldn't we discuss this calmly?'

Kirsty snapped the case shut. 'No, Holly. I'm sorry. I won't spend another night under this roof. I couldn't.'

'Very well, you know best, but let me drive you to the station.'

'Thanks, but I need to be alone. I'll catch the Perth bus on the main road.'

'But it's raining!'

Kirsty kissed her. 'Don't worry, Holly dear, I won't melt.'

But Kirsty was drenched walking to the bus stop and thoroughly chilled before the bus arrived some time later. It was a slow journey by bus and train to Edinburgh, with long periods of waiting in between, but Kirsty welcomed the tedium. She couldn't remember when she'd eaten last, but food didn't seem important any more. Another torrential downpour greeted her at the top of Waverley Steps as she squelched her way wearily towards Royal Terrace. When she reached her grandmother's door she walked past without a glance.

Exhausted and barely conscious, Kirsty stumbled towards Edward Merrilees' doorway. He had offered her a safe haven, and that's what she needed now.

164

Twelve

E dward Merrilees came running downstairs when an agitated housemaid found Kirsty slumped on the doorstep. She was soaked to the skin and blue with cold. He gathered her in his arms and carried her to the drawing room and laid her on the sofa. He couldn't imagine what had possessed her to travel to Edinburgh on a rotten day like this, nor why she'd suddenly turned up in such a state. But those questions could wait. Edward glanced at the housemaid, who had followed him anxiously.

'Minnie, phone Dr Guthrie and ask him to call. You'll find the doctor's number on the pad. Then fetch a warm blanket while I get the young lady out of these wet clothes.'

Minnie looked shocked. 'Oh, but sir—!'

'Hurry now!' He was already unfastening buttons and easing Kirsty's arms out of the jacket. The housemaid scuttled off. What a story for Cook!

The warmth from a blazing fire revived Kirsty. Edward began chafing her numb hands and feet and she murmured 'Edward!' She realized that only a petticoat preserved her modesty, and covered herself hastily with her arms. 'I'm so cold. Terribly cold!'

That was a bad sign. He whipped off his jacket and wrapped it round her then hurried to the drinks cabinet and examined its contents. He poured a seafarer's tot of rum and supported her while she drank.

'It tastes like Christmas pudding,' she murmured. 'I like it.'

'Well, don't tell your grandma for Pete's sake.'

Minnie returned at that moment. 'The doctor'll be here in half an hour . . . oh, michty!' She covered the patient with the blanket. 'It's no' quite the thing for a gentleman to tend to the young leddy, sir.'

He paid no attention. 'Light the gas fire in my room and put a couple of hot-water bottles in the bed, Minnie. I'll carry Miss Rutherford up there.'

'To your bedroom, sir?' The housemaid's brows shot up. She could hardly wait to tell Cook. She gathered Kirsty's discarded clothing. 'Just give me five minutes till the kettle biles,' she said and headed for the kitchen at a trot.

Edward tucked the blanket tenderly around his patient. It seemed like a dream come true, but why had she come? He watched as she snuggled into the warmth and closed her eyes with a contented sigh. He could not resist the temptation. He kissed her, and to his delight she smiled.

Kirsty escaped pneumonia, although she had a severe chill and painfully sore throat. Edward slept fitfully in the spare room with the door ajar, alert to her faintest cry.

Lizzie Robb arrived the next day. 'So!' she said severely. 'You have seriously compromised my granddaughter, Edward Merrilees. It's the talk of the terrace.'

'Already?'

'Yes indeed.' She looked smug as she drew off her gloves. 'One wonders why Kirsty chose your doorway in which to collapse.'

'I intend to ask her when she gets her voice back. At the moment she can barely whisper.'

'And is occupying your bed, rumour has it!' his visitor added.

He sighed. 'Mrs Robb, twins with measles have occupied my bed, not to mention chickenpox, whooping cough, flu and tummy upsets. It's anyone's bed in an emergency. I, of course, retire to the spare room.'

'You realize you must marry the girl. I shall insist!'

'You can insist till you're blue in the face, ma'am. Much as I love Kirsty, I'll only marry her if she'll consent to have me.'

She grinned wickedly. 'My dear Edward. How romantic!'

*   *   *

A week passed before Kirsty felt fit enough to take more than a passing interest in her surroundings, but at last her throat was less painful and she could appreciate the sacrifices Edward Merrilees had made for her. His own bedroom, for instance. There was a lingering fragrance of the hair dressing he used.

'You shouldn't have given up your bed for me, Edward,' she said.

'You're right,' he agreed. 'It's the talk of the terrace.'

'Oh, Edward, I'm sorry! Now I've ruined your reputation as well as your business.'

He sat on the edge of the bed. 'Who told you you'd ruined my business?'

She repeated what Jamie had said and he laughed. 'It's true a couple of shipments went missing while you and I were getting to know one another, but the ships had been delayed. They turned up eventually.'

'But my father said your firm was in trouble and that's why you agreed to sell the estate.'

'My dear, every firm is having difficulties after the ghastly war, but that's not the reason. It was the estate's only hope. Your father isn't interested in farming. George could run it despite the blindness, but he needs working capital. Murdoch showed us the books and explained his plans and frankly I was impressed with him. I would have warned you what was in the wind, but the Colonel insisted on total secrecy. It must've been a shock.'

'It was. I'd no say in the sale, and now I've lost my home!'

'Is that why you came to me?'

She hesitated. 'You offered me a safe haven once.'

'Oh, my darling!' he said softly. 'Does that mean you'll marry me?'

'Yes. If you still want me.'

'Want you?' He swept her into his arms. 'Kirsty, I'm the happiest man in Scotland!'

'I'll try to make you happy, Edward.'

'Of course you will, my sweetheart!'

He was confident, but she felt like crying. He deserved her wholehearted love, and she loved him only as a dear and trusted friend. Was that enough, could it ever be enough to make Edward happy?

Once the engagement became common knowledge, Lizzie Robb removed her granddaughter from Edward's care and wedding preparations began. The elderly lady had warned him the ceremony would be quick and quiet. He'd been delighted to hear it.

Charles Rutherford was not so pleased. When he heard the news, he caught the early morning train from Stirling the very next day and came knocking on his mother-in-law's door as breakfast was served. He was invited to share the meal.

'Listen, Mrs Robb—' he began, pulling in a chair.

'Prices have risen frightfully since the war, Charles,' she said, piling bacon rashers and fried eggs on to a hot plate. 'Two and fourpence a pound for bacon and fifteen pennies for half a dozen eggs. Imagine!'

'Yes, it's scandalous but—'

'And one and sixpence for half a pound of Melrose tea, Papa!' chimed in Kirsty, pouring a cup.

'This marriage,' he persisted grimly. 'I'm against it.'

Lizzie stared. 'I can't imagine why. Edward Merrilees is a fine man.'

'I'm not denying it, but he's twenty years older than my daughter.'

'A *young* twenty years older, Charles,' his mother-in-law pointed out.

'Edward will be a reliable, well-off and devoted husband, just what Kirsty needs.'

He turned to her. 'Is that true? Is that what you want?'

'Yes, Papa. I believe it is.'

He stared in surprise. His daughter had changed in some way he couldn't fathom. She seemed in full control, while he'd come prepared to rescue a vulnerable girl from a domineering older man. He'd even intended to forbid the match. Now, after studying this surprising transformation, he wasn't sure if he could.

'I just want you to be happy, Kirsty,' he said lamely. 'That's all that matters to me.'

'I know, dearest Papa.' She kissed his cheek fondly.

'That's all right, then,' he grunted. 'Just wanted to be sure before giving my blessing, y'know.'

Lizzie Robb quietly slid a loaded plate towards her son-in-law.

Charles turned his attention hungrily to bacon rashers and perfectly cooked fried eggs. Sunny side up, as it happened.

Kirsty soon discovered that her grandmother's idea of a quiet wedding consisted of a gathering of around one hundred and fifty relatives, neighbours and friends, preferably in St Giles Cathedral. There was no use arguing over the guest list, but Kirsty doggedly rejected the cathedral in favour of her grandmother's own kirk. St Andrew's in George Street boasted eight fixed bells which made a joyful sound not unlike the famous Edinburgh fisher song *Caller Herring*. They were both agreed that the Royal Terrace apartment would host the reception and some modern dancing. After all, as Lizzie pointed out, the ballroom was where the romance had begun.

Wedding preparations were well under way when the elderly lady produced a battered cardboard box. 'Kirsty dear, I wonder if you'd be interested in this?'

She produced a wedding gown and veil in perfect condition, all lovingly wrapped in butter muslin. Marvelling, Kirsty touched the delicate fabric with a fingertip. 'Whose was it?'

'Your mother's. I just wondered if maybe . . .' she looked at her granddaughter hopefully.

'It's beautiful, Grandma,' Kirsty said. 'But I can't wear it.'

'Why not? I'm sure it would fit.'

'My mother and father were married in St Giles with a guard of honour of hussars. We agreed my wedding was to be a quiet affair. I shall wear a blue gown and fresh flowers in my hair. Don't you think that's more fitting?' She did not mention she was marrying Edward for the wrong reasons, and felt she had no right to wear her mother's gown.

'I suppose so,' the old lady sighed. She laid the garments

169

back in the box and closed the lid. She looked so dejected that Kirsty hugged her.

'It's a wonderful family heirloom, Grandma. One day another bride will be proud to wear it, I'm sure.'

There were sunshine and showers on Kirsty's wedding day. A little like life, her father remarked as they walked arm in arm through a crowd of onlookers. Grandma's kindly old minister met them at the church door and led them in, with Edward's delighted twins bringing up the rear. The organ pealed as they entered the packed church.

There was a much larger congregation than Kirsty had expected and she suspected her grandmother had been very liberal with verbal invitations. What did it matter? Everyone she loved was there. Grandma Robb, elegant and determinedly dry-eyed as befitted a brigadier's widow. Dear Holly dabbing her eyes and sobbing like any proud mother. George also stood in the front pew, one hand resting lightly upon Murphy's collar. At the sight of the wedding party the dog's tail began wagging, sending hymnsheets flying. Samuel gave Kirsty a grin as he gathered them up. A group of emotional servants dressed in Sunday best occupied the second pew and Kirsty gave them a warm smile. They had a busy day ahead with Grandma's planned reception and hosts of extra guests. It was noble of them to turn out for her.

Then she caught sight of Edward standing at the altar. She met his loving glance and smiled, before moving confidently to join him. Perhaps this was not the wedding of her dreams to the man of her dreams, but she was done with dreaming and was marrying Edward, her dearest friend. Love and friendship, she thought. A recipe for a happy marriage?

Jamie Murdoch stood on the dusty, bare floorboards of Angus House that particular day. He knew it was Kirsty Rutherford's wedding day, though he hadn't mentioned the fact to a soul. Some perverse instinct had driven him here today. Murdochs owned her house now and that was comfort. If he needed it.

Elise was with him, the baby in her arms. Their hollow

footsteps echoed through silent corridors and empty rooms. Elise longed to go home to the lodge, but knew better than to say so. She was wise in her husband's ways and knew how to avoid annoying him. Elise found his ambition almost frightening. She could get her own way only in small matters, which were nevertheless important where Jurgen was concerned. Then she could fight fiercely and win. She kissed the top of their son's fair, downy head.

The huge kitchen had been left dirty and unscrubbed when the Rutherfords' servants walked out for the last time. Ashes lay grey and cold on the fender, spilling from an old black range. The servants' quarters were up a narrow uncarpeted stair and were still furnished.

'Good,' said Jamie, looking round the spartan rooms. 'We'll live here while builders and decorators are busy in the rest of the house.'

'We stay here?' Elise could not believe her ears. The rooms were cold, dark and ugly.

'Aye. We can keep an eye on the work and make sure it's done properly.'

'But the lodge, Jamie. What about our home?'

'Home no longer, my dear!' he said cheerfully. 'We're going up in the world, Elise. One of these days you'll be mistress of the grandest house in the Carse, and then maybe in a while we'll move on to a jute baron's mansion in the city.'

Unhappily, she hugged the sleeping baby. His weight lay heavily on her heart. 'But the lodge is the home I prepared for the child. I love it and so does he.'

His expression hardened. 'Nonsense! How can he? He's only a baby. He'll love this house when he grows. It's a gentleman's residence, and my son will be a gentleman. He'll learn to ride and fish and shoot grouse and pheasants, just like the gentry.'

'No, no! I do not want my son to kill. Not even birds!'

'What rubbish!' he laughed. 'You're a town sparrow and don't understand country ways, Elise. My mother will help with the flitting and George Rutherford's been given a long

171

lease on the lodge, providing he helps Cunningham run the estate. The small house will suit a blind man, besides being easier to manage on the wages I'll pay.'

'And more humiliation, I imagine,' she said scathingly.

Jamie was irritated. Couldn't she understand he was doing this for their son, who would be their only child after his difficult birth? 'The Rutherfords are broke. They can't afford to feel humiliated,' he said.

There had been no sign of George Rutherford during their tour, although his room in this house was still furnished and occupied.

'Where is George anyway?' she asked. 'We have not seen him today.'

He hesitated. 'He's in Edinburgh attending his sister's wedding.'

She looked up sharply. 'Kirsty married? I did not know, Jamie. Why did you not tell me?'

He shrugged. 'Why should I? It wasn't important.'

She rocked the baby in silence. Her muscles were still weak and she ached inside, but not only with Jurgen's weight. Nobody had mentioned to her that Kirsty Rutherford was getting married. Not even Agnes her mother-in-law, who loved weddings. Elise felt a helpless anger. Did they think she was a fool? Did they think she could not see that Kirsty's marriage was very important indeed to Jamie, who had once loved the girl?

Although trade had boomed in Dundee for a short spell following the war, a slump soon followed. By the early 1920s, in the city there were more than ten thousand men out of work, not counting those disabled from the war. A great wave of resentment rose, levelled at Lloyd George's government which had promised much and delivered little. It was hardly surprising that the appeal for public funds to raise a War Memorial on the Law met with apathy.

A halfpenny on the price of a loaf was the last straw for families living on the dole and riots broke out. Windows were smashed and food shops looted. Police reinforcements

172

were called in to help Dundee's amazingly tall bobbies keep the peace.

Poppy Murdoch considered herself fortunate to keep her job with the art dealer. The contents of Mr Archibald's shop did not attract looters, but wealthy gentlemen in large houses still demanded paintings to line their walls. Mr Archibald made a respectable living and even gave Poppy a modest rise.

But Agnes was not pleased to have a daughter in trade now that the Murdochs were well off. 'There's no need for you to be working in a shop,' she grumbled.

'You think I should stay home and work?' Poppy said. Dougal lowered the newspaper. 'Mind your lip, young woman!'

Poppy had learned diplomacy, dealing with awkward customers. 'Och, Dad, you can see Mam runs the house so beautifully I'd be twiddling my thumbs.'

Agnes beamed. 'That's true. Still, you could be a lady of leisure and look out for a rich husband with a thousand a year.'

'Aye,' Dougal nodded. 'A bonny lassie like you could take your pick of the young swells in the Carse.'

'Maybe I could, but . . .' Poppy paused. Joel D'Arcy hadn't been near Archibald's shop since he'd kissed her and strolled out of her life three years ago. She never doubted that he'd return one day and she wanted to be there when he did. Of course, she couldn't tell her parents that. This required cunning.

'If I'm to marry a swell and be mistress of a big house, I'll need to know about pictures, won't I? There's always hundreds of pictures in swanky houses,' she said innocently.

They hadn't thought about that. Agnes turned to her husband. 'She's right, Dougal. Pictures is respectable. I went off the notion of Poppy working in Draffen's after the dressmakers went on strike, and of course I'd draw the line at her working behind Willie Millar, the grocer's counter, though it's a high-class shop. But advising wealthy folk which picture to buy does seem more refined and ladylike.'

'Righto, just as long as it keeps her out of mischief,' Dougal said, returning thankfully to the newspaper.

So Poppy went on working for Mr Archibald with her parents' blessing, and also began painting in her spare time. Her studio was the old wash-house, abandoned now that Agnes had new sinks and piping hot water on tap. She painted in oils and from memory, using her imagination. Working like that gave Poppy's landscapes a vivid, dreamlike quality that was startling and unusual. She became so engrossed she would be at her easel until daylight failed and be up at the crack of dawn to start again.

Diffidently, she showed Mr Archibald one of the finished canvases. He narrowed his eyes, cocked his head to the side and pursed his lips.

'Get that framed, Poppy.'

'But it's so big it'll cost pounds, Mr Archibald. I'd an awful struggle bringing it on the train.'

'Do it at my expense, lass. Then put it in the window.'

It didn't sell right away, though it attracted attention because of the astounding twenty-five pound price tag the dealer put on it. Poppy was staggered. That was enough for a down payment on a semi-detached bungalow. It sold at last to a rich mill-owner from Broughty Ferry whose daughter was interested in modern art. Mr Archibald pocketed ten per cent and replaced the painting with another of Poppy's, even pricier.

She was studying lists of recent purchases one September afternoon months later when a shadow fell across the counter. She looked up and her heart quickened. 'Oh, it's you!'

Joel D'Arcy smiled. 'Thanks for the enthusiastic reception.'

'What d'you expect? Where have you been?'

'Here and there.' He glanced around and curled his lip. 'I see Archibald is still living in the past. But who's responsible for the *art nouveau* in the window?'

'I am.'

'You mean you painted that?' He crossed to the window and stared at the painting for a full minute before turning and staring at Poppy. There was a strange gleam in his eyes. 'Your brushwork could be better, but it's good, and there's no doubt it will sell. It would appeal to those who like pretty pictures, and more importantly to those who know.' He came round the back of the counter and kissed her lightly. 'Congratulations, top cat.'

'Oh, Joel, I've missed you!' Her knees had gone weak with his praise. She leaned against him and he took her in his arms and kissed her properly, a skilled and practised kiss that left her dazed and helpless. Fortunately, Mr Archibald was attending an auction sale and they had the shop to themselves.

'Listen, Poppy,' Joel said. 'You'll get nowhere if you stay in Dundee. You'll marry some dull oaf and have a football team of kids. I won't let that happen to you. You must come to Paris with me and let this talent flower.'

'Joel, I can't!'

'Why not?' He ran an appreciative eye over her. 'You're a woman now, my darling. A sleek beautiful cat, not a weak pretty kitten.'

She lowered her eyes. It wouldn't do for him to see how he had excited her. Paris! She longed to go there with him, but knew her parents would not hear of it. Unless perhaps . . .

Over the last few months she had struck up a friendship with the daughter of the mill-owner who'd bought her first painting. Ursula Proudfoot was a year or two older than Poppy and one of a new generation of well-off, independent young women. Ursula was busy persuading her parents to let her enrol at the Sorbonne in Paris to study French. What if I were to go with Ursula to university? Poppy schemed. Both sets of parents might be persuaded that two young women setting off to study together was safe enough. Money would be no problem now the Murdochs had plenty, and she could stress the advantages of hobnobbing with toffs.

But once I reach Paris with Ursula, what then? Poppy wondered. She wouldn't dwell on that just yet. 'Can you give me time to arrange everything, Joel?' she asked.

'Sure. I can wait.' He gave her a sidelong glance. 'I've

rented the same attic room in the Seagate. You know where to find me if you want me.'

'Yes, I know,' she said, blushing. She wondered if she could trust herself to go there alone – or trust him not to take advantage, if she did.

James Murdoch was instrumental in his parents' decision to allow his young sister to accompany Ursula Proudfoot to Paris. There were wheels within wheels, of course. Jamie had plans for processing linseed oil and had his eye on Proudfoot Ltd as an influential customer.

'But what use is French to our Poppy, Jamie? There's not a single Frenchmen in the Carse,' Agnes argued.

He smiled. 'Mother, the world's growing smaller by the minute. There'll be French tourists all over the place and it'll be handy if Poppy can speak the language. Besides, living in Paris will be an education for the two lasses, Mr Proudfoot says, like a posh Swiss finishing school, only cheaper. Ursula Proudfoot will give our Poppy useful hints on how to behave in society and I wouldn't be surprised if Poppy clicked with a wealthy count and did very well for herself.'

Agnes was swayed by her son's arguments, but remained secretly apprehensive. She had already lost one daughter to foreign lands and had a premonition that Poppy's departure into a dangerous world lurking outside the Carse could lead to a similar disaster. Still, she'd given the project her blessing and taken a most superior afternoon tea with the Proudfoots in their Broughty mansion and could hardly back out now. Poppy packed and went off merrily on her travels. Agnes had insisted her daughter must have the finest outfits Draffen's could provide. This was to keep upsides with wealthy Miss Proudfoot, who, had Agnes only known, didn't care tuppence what she wore.

Agnes bravely dried her eyes and stifled misgivings after Poppy had gone. She devoted her considerable energy to voluntary work relieving the sad lot of the unemployed, a charity quite suitable for a woman of substance.

It took Jamie nearly four years to refurbish Angus House to his

176

satisfaction, but it was done eventually. Already he'd hosted important dinner parties in the dining room, wining and dining men who could be helpful to him. During the General Election a couple of years ago Jamie had hoped to have Winston Churchill, Dundee's MP, to dine. Winston was in the city standing as a Liberal candidate, but was recovering from an appendicitis operation and lacked the usual fire. Despite the best efforts of his wife Clementine, Churchill lost his seat to Neddy Scrymgeour, the Prohibitionist, and left the city in a depressed and angry state with the chant of Dundee urchins ringing in his ears, '*Vote, vote, vote, for Neddy Scrymgeour, he's the man to gie wis ham an' eggs.*'

Jamie made do at the election dinner with another unsuccessful candidate, a 37-year-old Independent Liberal called Garnet Wilson. Jamie's unerring instinct told him that this young man, nurtured in the local drapery trade, would go far.

Rather to her husband's surprise, Elise had proved to be an excellent hostess popular with his guests. She had never taken to the house and Jamie had feared she would put a damper on entertainment. He still couldn't understand why she charmed distinguished visitors so, for she had little to say, preferring to listen with genuine interest to even the dullest and most boring guest. Jamie and his wife had run out of conversation long ago, except on matters relating to their son, although those usually provoked fierce argument.

Jurgen was nearly five years old, a strikingly handsome, fair-haired, blue-eyed child. As Jamie had predicted, the little boy loved the big house and the freedom it offered. He rode an unpredictable Shetland pony with fearless ease, showed a keen interest when Cunningham caught seatrout in the Gowrie burn, but strangely enough shared his mother's abhorrence of guns and killing. It worried Jamie.

'He cried like a baby when Cunningham shot the vixen. I wouldn't want my son to grow up to be a pansy, Elise,' he remarked.

'He will not be pansy. He is kind-hearted, that is all. He cried for little motherless foxes.'

'All the same, he needs to be toughened up. I'll see about a boys' boarding school for him.'

Her heart lurched. 'But he's only four! I thought he will go to kindergarten in Invergowrie, and then to fine academy in Dundee to finish education.'

He laughed. 'He's a gentleman's son, my dear. He'll go to the best boarding school in Edinburgh. In fact there's such competition for places it's high time his name was on a waiting list. They'll take him when he's seven.'

'That is too young. I will not allow it,' she cried vehemently.

His expression grew cold. 'You're thinking of yourself, not the boy. You're selfish and possessive because he's the only one.'

'I could not help that!' she said defensively. Her barren state had been a bone of contention for years. He would have liked the big house filled with handsome children. Well, so would she, but it was not to be. She paused. Selfish, possessive? Am I these horrible things? she wondered. She loved the boy so much it could well be true, and that was not good for him either.

'Very well,' she said quietly. 'When he is seven I will let him go.' She lifted her head and stared at her husband defiantly. 'But till then, Jurgen is mine.'

Jamie contacted the Edinburgh school and received a cordial invitation to meet the headmaster and be shown around. The invitation included Elise, but she declined. When the time came to surrender her son into this school's care, Elise would make her own thorough inspection.

Jamie could have driven to Edinburgh, but had found the Forth ferry such a scutter on previous occasions he decided to take the train and travel in the comfort of first class. He landed at Waverley station just before eleven with plenty of time to spare before summoning a taxicab to keep the appointment. Sauntering past rose-scented gardens, he crossed busy Princes Street and cast an eye over the wide variety of goods displayed in shop windows.

He was staring fascinated at a clockwork train set he was

tempted to buy for Jurgen – and himself! – when he felt a light touch on his arm and spun round.

'Kirsty!'

She had haunted his thoughts as he travelled to Edinburgh, but he hadn't expected to see her and didn't even know where she lived. He hadn't seen her since they'd met in anger on the lovers' path and kissed with passion before they parted. Aye, a lot of water had flowed under the Tay bridge since then! She wore a loose, fur-trimmed jacket which did not hide an advanced pregnancy. Ah, but she was beautiful, he thought. More beautiful than ever!

'I can hardly believe it's you,' he said softly.

She laughed. 'I was about to say the same. What are you doing in Edinburgh?'

'Inspecting an Edinburgh boarding school for my son's education.'

She was surprised. 'Is he that age now?'

'He soon will be. He's going there when he's seven.'

She very nearly cried – poor wee soul! – but instead remarked lightly, 'Are Dundee schools not good enough for you?'

'It'll do the boy good to get away from home,' he answered. 'Being an only child he spends too much time with his mother. His grandmother spoils him shamefully, of course.'

'That's a grandmother's privilege,' she smiled.

Kirsty had mixed feelings about this unexpected meeting. Her life was peaceful and settled and she had grown to love her husband in a quiet way. When her thoughts happened to turn to her life before marriage she tended to shy away from Jamie Murdoch's memory like a startled horse.

The shock had been so great when she came upon him today that even the unborn baby stirred. She almost hurried on by, but somehow she could not. She had to speak to him.

Studying him more closely, Kirsty saw he had changed greatly from the country lad she'd known. He was a commanding figure, expensively dressed, but that was not where the difference lay. The hard set of mouth and chin gave his expression an unfamiliar cast. From time to time she'd heard

Edward mention James Murdoch's business methods with disapproval. The man was hugely successful, Edward said, but had a reputation for ruthlessness. Some said he had no heart.

No heart! Had he really changed so much? Kirsty wondered.

'Tell me about Angus House, Jamie,' she said. 'Have you made it beautiful?'

'Aye, it's grand, just the way you wanted it.' His expression softened, eyes warm with memories, and for a fleeting moment she glimpsed the man she'd loved. 'The lawns are trimmed and the rose garden flourishes.' He met her eyes steadily. 'And the trees along the lovers' path are taller and shadier now.'

She looked away. Shared memories, dangerous memories! 'And the horses?' How she missed the horses!

'The horses are improving bloodstock in the Carse, just as you wished. I bought the mare from Miss Ruby, as you know, and another two foals were sired by Young Lochinvar. Merlin is a wicked beast like your father's old mare, but he goes like the wind.'

'I'm glad everything turned out so happily for you, Jamie.'

'Well, yes . . .' He looked away across the street where tramcars rumbled by and car horns blared at plodding horse-drawn carts. The peace of the gardens beyond was disrupted by a train passing through the cleft overshadowed by the castle rock. He didn't look happy.

'When's the baby due?' he demanded abruptly.

'Any time.'

He took her hands and held them tightly. 'How different our lives might have been, Kirsty! I envy your man.'

Then he was gone without saying goodbye, pushing his way roughly past crowds of idle window shoppers. She stared after him, badly shaken.

She lay awake that night while Edward slept peacefully. Edward had been worried when she'd confessed she'd gone walking on her own in town that day.

'Darling, you took a risk. I begged you not to go out alone when the baby's due.'

'It was too nice to stay in and I couldn't wait till you came home, love. I didn't go far, Edward.' Significantly, she hadn't told her husband she'd met Jamie. This reticence troubled her, nagging at her conscience with a persistance that gradually developed into pain. Rousing suddenly, she realized what was happening. She wakened her husband.

'Edward, the baby's coming!'

He was awake in an instant, snapping on the bedside lamp. She sat up, glad of his supporting arm. Edward had made sure that the doctor and midwife were the best to be had for a home confinement, and the doctor had been reassuring on her last visit to the surgery. She was young and fit and he didn't foresee problems, he'd told her.

Everything was just fine, but now that the time had come Kirsty was frightened. She couldn't forget that her own birth had cost her mother's life. What if history were to be repeated? She began to panic.

'Edward! What if something goes wrong?'

'Don't worry, it won't. I'll be with you all the way.' He was as good as his word despite the midwife's disapproval. At one stage in the labour he was ordered to leave. 'I'm damned if I will!'

Kirsty was forced to laugh, despite everything. 'Oh, Edward, you're a brave man! I wouldn't dare disobey Nurse Finnigan!'

The midwife relented and said he could stay if he behaved himself, and Edward was present some time later, holding Kirsty's hand as their baby was born.

'A perfect little lass as bonnie as her mother!' the doctor announced.

Another girl for Edward!

Kirsty felt a crushing sense of disappointment as she remembered that Jamie Murdoch's wife had presented Jamie with a son and heir.

In tears, she couldn't face her husband. 'I'm sorry, my darling, I wanted so much to give you a son!'

Thirteen

E dward looked exhausted, but he kissed her, smiling. 'You're both well, my love. That's all that matters.'

Proudly, the midwife presented the baby to the new parents. Kirsty held her daughter, waiting for motherly love to flow. Nothing happened. Has meeting Jamie Murdoch done this? she wondered. Elise presented Jamie with a son. Is that why I feel I've failed Edward? Surely every man longs for a son?

'She's beautiful,' he said emotionally.

'Yes.' Kirsty closed her eyes. She could hardly bear to look at her daughter. The midwife hurriedly removed the baby.

'Let her sleep. She's tired out,' she heard the doctor say, but it wasn't exhaustion that bothered Kirsty, it was a baffling host of conflicting emotions.

Edward was sitting by the bedside when Kirsty awoke next morning after a good night's rest. He greeted her with a kiss. 'Hullo, you clever girl. How does it feel to be a mum?'

'Strange,' she admitted. She propped herself on an elbow to peep into the cot. Edward lifted the baby out and settled her in Kirsty's arms. Eagerly, she folded back a corner of the shawl to study her daughter. The baby's eyes were open. Of course she was much too young to recognize her mother, but bright eyes in a tiny snub-nosed face looked up at Kirsty.

'Lovely, isn't she?' Edward said proudly.

Kirsty laughed. 'Oh, Edward, hardly! She's more like a wee elf in a story book.' She cuddled her daughter with heartfelt relief. It's all right, she thought. I really do love my wee elf!

'What'll we call her?' he said. 'Of course, Ruby and Pearl are gems, but I don't think Amethyst or Diamond would suit this one, do you?'

Kirsty had considered names before the birth, but none seemed suitable for this small individual. 'What was your mother's name, Edward?' she asked.

He hesitated. 'Er . . . Sophie.'

'Sophie? Why, that would be perfect!'

He wasn't sure he agreed. His mother had been a somewhat flamboyant character, who'd taken great delight in teasing her very conservative husband and son. Cautiously, he studied his tiny daughter and fancied he detected quite a resemblance. Edward sighed. 'Sophie it is!' and sealed the brave decision with a kiss.

By the time Jurgen Murdoch was six he had earned a bad reputation. This puzzled him, because he tried very hard to be good.

This Sunday, Miss Pringle, the Sunday School teacher, had told the class that badness started inside you. An apple can look good on the outside, yet be rotten at the core, she said, and so can people. You should never judge anyone by good looks alone, she'd said, glaring meaningfully at Jurgen.

Ugh! He'd pulled a dreadful face at the thought of his insides being mushy and rotten and Miss Pringle had been furious. She'd dragged him out of class and stood him in a corner for the rest of the bible lesson. He wasn't given a biblical picture to colour, and that was always the best part of the morning. Jurgen considered this treatment unfair, and told Mutti so when they met after church. Usually he could make her smile, but not this time. She looked sad, as if he'd been involved in another fight at his primary school.

If someone at school took up the chant 'Yoor-gen's a Je-rry, Yoor-gen's a Je-rry!' he would wade in with fists flying. Jurgen's reputation was deplorable with parents of damaged little boys, but he'd earned respect and admiration from many schoolmates. Especially little girls.

Today his mother defended Miss Pringle. 'She cannot be blamed, Jurgen. Her loved one was killed in the war and in her sorrow she punishes an innocent little boy because his mother is German.'

So, it is this German thing again! Jurgen thought. 'Oh, Mutti, I wish you weren't a stuck-up German Frau!' he sighed.

She grabbed him furiously. 'Who call me that, Jurgen? You will tell me!' He was very frightened. He had never seen his mother anything but gentle and kind, and this wild, wounded creature was someone he did not recognize. He could see that her hurt and anger went much deeper than his own childish griefs.

'J-Jimmy Jamieson told me his mother said it to his father.'

She let him go and swore in her German tongue. 'That woman! And she so nice as ninepence to my face!' Her fists clenched as if she might punch the portly Mrs Jamieson if they chanced to meet.

The little boy flung his arms round his mother, willing the murderous rage to stop. Her blue velvet Sunday jacket was trimmed with beautiful silver fur, rich and soft under his clutching little hands. She was taller and better dressed than other mothers and she drove her own car to collect him after school. Is that stuck-up? he wondered anxiously. If so, he didn't understand why other mothers should hate her. She was polite and friendly to everyone and generous with many offers of lifts. He was so proud of her, always so proud!

'Mutti, Mutti! Listen!' he gulped desperately. 'I did tit-for-tat. I told Jimmy Jamieson his mum was a fat Angus cow.'

She stared at him blankly for a minute, then burst out laughing. It was not her usual laughter, it was high-pitched and harsh, and tears coursed down her cheeks. Still, Jurgen thought, it was better than anger.

She hugged him. 'That was very rude, *Liebling*. But maybe this one time we will excuse rudeness to a cruel lady.' She stared at him for a minute, her thoughts far away. Her sad, abstracted look distressed him.

He tugged her hand. 'What is it? Have I done wrong?'

She sighed. 'No, no, my darling. I was thinking that you should go to a new school soon, Jurgen. Your father wishes it, and maybe he is wise. It is a boarding school in Edinburgh where our family background is not known.'

He wailed. 'I don' want to leave you an' Daddy!'

She knelt unheeding in the dust to look in his face. 'I know. It breaks my heart to send you, but it is for the best. The school will seem strange at first, but soon you will make friends. There will be interesting work and good games to play. You will be happy. In a very short time you will not miss your daddy and mummy at all.'

'Honest? Cross your heart?' Jurgen wiped away tears. A new school would be an adventure. He liked adventures.

'Yes, honest, cross my heart!' Elise promised, smiling. But I shall miss you desperately, my beloved little son, she thought bleakly. Without you, how will I fill the empty days?

It was baking hot on the Left Bank of the Seine that August. The south side of Paris sweltered, despite deep shade cast by the learned facade of the ancient Sorbonne, and the cool green chestnut trees in surrounding parks and gardens. From a high vantage point, Poppy Murdoch looked down on a maze of narrow cobbled streets and wondered if the north bank of the river, the posh side, would be cooler. Streets of the Latin Quarter below were lined with seedy, rundown dwellings similar to this one. The area had been frequented long ago by Latin-speaking students and was now a magnet for struggling writers, artists and various oddities lumped together under the uneasy heading of 'Bohemians'.

Poppy Murdoch sat cross-legged on a rooftop, or more accurately on a narrow duckboard running behind a flaking stone balustrade which edged a sagging old red-tiled roof. Joel D'Arcy rented the sparsely furnished attic apartment aired by the open window on her left. Joel rented it in theory, that is. It was Poppy who paid the rent out of her earnings as a waitress in a nearby cafe.

She rested her back against a stone chimney which boasted an amazing cluster of sooty chimney pots. It offered shade, but not coolness. Her friend Ursula Proudfoot was perched languidly on the window sill.

'So what'll you do now I'm going home?' Ursula asked. 'I mean, you can't come with me in your condition, can you?

You haven't told your parents you're pregnant. They'll have a fit if you turn up looking like this.'

'I shall wait three or four months till after the baby's born, then break the news gently.'

Ursula laughed. 'Like . . . hey, Mum and Dad, meet your grandchild . . . sorry about the wedding, my dears, but there wasn't one?'

'Something like that,' Poppy yawned.

Dark, industrial Dundee belonged to another world, far removed from this city of light. Maybe I'm Bohemian through and through now, she thought. Certainly she had adopted a Bohemian way of life and was dressed oddly by Dundee standards in a pink, ankle-length cotton shift, a grubby white blouse, scarlet bandeau tied low round the forehead clasping a wild mane of golden hair. Her neck was festooned with strings of cheap necklaces, arms and fingers loaded with clinking bangles and gaudy rings which Joel had brought back from heaven knows where.

When he returned from these journeys his paintings became even more fantastically coloured and difficult to understand. Poppy had developed an eye for what was good or bad, but she didn't know what to think about Joel's paintings. They could either be the inspired work of genius or the ravings of lunacy. She wasn't experienced enough to know for sure. Her own canvases sold quickly when displayed in the open air in the Place du Tertre, but Joel's were difficult to move.

'When's Don Juan due back?' Ursula asked idly. She did not like Joel and made no bones about it.

Poppy shrugged. 'Soon, I suppose.'

'If my darling Gilbert carried on like that I would ditch him. I don't know what you see in that awful man.'

'Neither do I. There's love for you!'

'And look where it's landed you. In the soup!' Ursula smoothed her dark shining hair. She'd taken enthusiastically to the Eton crop. 'I was wanting you to be my bridesmaid when Gilbert and I marry in September, and now I can't ask you, Pops. You'll be the size of an airship by then.'

Poppy giggled. 'You seem certain your parents will approve

of Gilbert when you take him home. He's as lovable as a spaniel pup, of course, but not bright. He scraped through his finals by the enamel on his nice white teeth.'

'That's so,' she agreed. 'But Gilbert is titled and his family can boast generations of dim aristocrats going way back. Daddy and Mummy will welcome Sir Gilbert with open arms. You mark my words.'

Poppy sighed. 'If only life were so simple!'

Her friend looked concerned. 'Listen, Poppy dear, Gilbert and I will be leaving for Scotland next week when term ends. Why not come home with us and face the music? Once your mother and father recover from the shock they'll rally round. I bet your mother will help to look after the baby and eventually you could marry someone really nice. Please forget about that scoundrel D'Arcy, Poppy?'

Poppy closed her eyes and leaned wearily against the hot stone. 'That's the problem, Sula dear. I can't.'

Joel returned a month later, appearing in the midst of a violent thunderstorm, black hair slicked wetly across his brow. He bent to kiss her, dripping raindrops. 'How's my queen?'

'Fed up and miserable. Where've you been?' she demanded petulantly. He hated to be questioned, but she was tired, the baby weighed heavily and the oppressive atmosphere made her body feel heavier still. Only a few sous remained in her purse. She'd been too dispirited to paint and too ungainly to work. The larder was bare apart from stale bread and hard cheese.

'I'm hungry, top cat,' he said pathetically. And indeed he did look very thin. She hardened her heart.

'Too bad. If you want to eat, work. I can't any more.'

He straightened slowly and stared at her. 'Very well then, I will.' He was as good as his word. From morning till night he slaved at the easel in the freezing north-facing attic. At weekends he hawked the paintings around dealers, markets, anywhere he thought he might pick up a few francs. Sometimes he was successful and they feasted, more often he wasn't and they lived on bread and broth. Still Joel went on painting, despite an autumn cold which he picked up in September and couldn't shake off.

In late October, Poppy gave birth to a baby girl. She lay on old newspapers on the floor of the dusty apartment, tended by the kind old woman on the stair below and a medical student who'd taken pity on her. Joel made himself scarce. He drank most of the proceeds from his latest picture in the Lapin Agile, a favourite haunt of writers and artists, and judged his return when he was certain the birth would be over. He was delighted with the baby.

'A little beauty!' he said, cradling her in his arms.

'Marie, I thought,' Poppy said.

He grimaced. 'Much too ordinary for my daughter. Celeste sounds better.'

Poppy giggled. '*Bien*! Marie Celeste it is!'

Poppy's youthful vigour was restored after the baby's birth. As she fed and tended the little black-haired baby Poppy was filled with such love her fingers itched to express powerful emotion in the only way she knew, on canvas. She waited till Joel had set off on a journey into the freezing countryside with a batch of paintings on his back to try his luck, then set eagerly to work.

Maybe enforced idleness had developed fresh insight, perhaps the joy of motherhood inspired a more vivid imagination, but for whatever reason Poppy painted as she'd never painted before. When after several ecstatic, creative days the picture was finished, she didn't know what to do with it. She dreaded Joel's return in case he was scathing. The work was so personal, springing from the very depth of her soul, she knew she couldn't accept criticism. Fortunately as days passed, there was no sign of him. There was no money left in the kitty either. In desperation, Poppy dressed Celeste warmly, tied the baby to her back with a shawl and carried the painting in trepidation to a dealer she knew in Montmartre.

Joel came home a few days later, thin, gaunt and discouraged, with few pictures sold and only a franc or two in his pocket. 'Charlatans. Idiots. Fools!' He flung down the canvases, sat down and put his head in his hands. 'The rent's due and we can't pay, Poppy. What if we're thrown out?'

She hugged him. 'Darling, we won't be. I've started painting again, and Monsieur Jacques bought my picture.'

He looked up, startled. 'Jacques? How much?'

Her face glowed. 'A hundred francs, Joel. Imagine!' She waited for him to cheer, but instead he sat motionless. He looked ghastly, grey-faced.

Poppy cried out. 'Joel! What's wrong?'

He didn't answer, but got to his feet and began feverishly collecting discarded canvases. He bound the bundle with rope and slung it on his back then headed for the stairway, bent double under the load. Poppy followed, scared and bewildered. 'Joel, stop it, please stop! Where are you going?'

But he acted as if he didn't hear her, staggering down the stairs into the alleyway and out on to patchy grass that served as a drying green. There he piled the pictures high, fumbling in his pockets for the cigarette lighter.

Poppy screamed, suddenly realizing his intention. 'No, Joel, don't!' But already his thumb had flicked the lighter and he'd set light to the pile. Flames licked greedily at the paint and leaped high with a hungry crackle. The wooden stretchers blazed and sparked, paint bubbled, canvas blackened, twisted, then burned bright scarlet, fanned white hot by the night wind. Joel stood watching, head thrown back. Smoke, sparks and hot white ash spiralled upwards into the black November night.

Sobbing, Poppy flung her arms round him. 'Joel, Joel, why did you do it?'

He held her close, stroked her hair. 'You're the success, my queen. This world doesn't want my paintings.'

That hundred francs! she thought tearfully. Oh, how tactless of me! I should never have told him. 'Oh, Joel, I'm sorry!'

He laughed. 'Don't be sorry. Now we can eat.'

The laugh ended in a fit of coughing that went on and on, racking his thin body. Frightened, Poppy thought it would never end, but at last the spasm passed and he leaned weakly against her. A slow trickle of blood ran down his chin.

Poppy's heart lurched with dread. 'Oh, Joel!' Gently, she wiped his clammy face, wiping the blood away.

He sighed. 'So now we know what the future holds, Poppy.' He glanced at the dying flames. 'How symbolic, my dear. An artist's funeral pyre.'

'Don't say that!' she cried. 'Maybe—'

He smiled. 'No maybes, kitten.'

She choked back tears. 'I'll never leave you, Joel! Celeste and I will be with you till—'

He checked her with a finger on her lips. 'Shh . . . my love. Don't say it! It's too final.' He held her in his arms as together they watched the flames die and darkness creep back. He laughed softly as the final embers glowed and black ash stirred and floated in the wind.

She looked at him through a mist of tears. 'How can you laugh?'

'I was thinking, Poppy,' he said. 'Now the world will never know whether Joel D'Arcy was a genius or not.'

'You make the best coffee in Scotland, Elise,' George Rutherford said.

She smiled. 'You say that because tea is Scotland's national drink next to whisky. You have nothing to compare with, George.' She turned to look at him. He could not see her looking, but she liked to do it.

'I wish I could take you to Draffen's tearoom,' he said. 'The coffee is almost as good as yours, served with little silver pots of cream.'

'Which Murphy would lick with one scoop of the long tongue and disgrace us,' Elise smiled, patting the dog, who wagged agreement.

'They wouldn't let Murphy across the threshold. It's a high-class establishment. Scruffy mongrels are out.'

'If Murphy may not go, then I will not go, George!' She poured coffee into a cup and left it close by the sensitive fingertips where he could feel the heat.

He lifted it and drank. 'That's what I lov – er like about you.' George went on hurriedly. 'Your husband's a wealthy

190

man, you live in a beautiful mansion, yet you haven't changed. You're still the lovely kind person you always were.'

She sat and stared. She could stare openly, because he could not see the emotion. Ah, if only he knew how much she had changed! If only he knew how wealth had alienated husband and wife, how the loss of her son to boarding school had broken her heart! If only she could tell him that the only place she felt at home was in this little lodge with him, a man whose blind eyes did not see the imperfections her husband pounced on mercilessly. Jamie grumbled that she was too tall, too thin, her hair too long. She spent too much time with unimportant guests and not enough with those who mattered – to him.

The silence had gone on too long. 'I'm sorry. I've offended you,' George said awkwardly.

'No, you have not,' she said softly. 'Those are the nicest words anyone ever say to me.'

'Well, it's true. You won't get flattery from a blind man.'

'It is strange, George,' Elise said thoughtfully. 'I nurse many men blinded in the war and they find loss of sight difficult to accept. I have this strange feeling that you welcome it.'

He was silent. 'How very perceptive of you, my dear!' he said quietly. 'I do welcome it in a way, Elise. It's God's revenge for what I did. Rough justice. It makes me feel better.'

She sat on the footstool and held his hand. 'Tell me, my dear. Perhaps it will help.'

He hesitated only for a minute. 'It . . . it happened at the battle of the Somme. We'd been ordered to check a German outpost for snipers, and as we approached one of my men flung down his rifle and ran away. Of course there's only one sentence and punishment for cowardice in face of the enemy, and that's death.' He paused, his fingers gripping her hand, then went on doggedly. 'I was officer in charge of the firing squad that morning. I didn't discover till it was too late that the soldier we'd just executed was a boy of 15. He was big for his age, you see. He'd written the number 18 on a slip of paper which he kept hidden in his boots, so that he could truthfully swear he was "over 18". He was just a poor, deluded country boy who'd joined the army for a lark, and we shot him because he was afraid.' Tears dripped on to her hand. Elise held him in her arms and let him weep against her shoulder.

It is time this great guilt was cleansed, she thought. Such a tragedy is a wound festering in the mind. She waited patiently for the tears to stop, then she said, 'I am glad you tell me.'

He mopped his eyes. 'I'm sorry. I . . . I don't know what you must think of me!'

She kissed his cheek gently. 'This is what I think. That you are a man of great conscience. That you are the kindest man I know, and that I love you.'

His hands reached for her blindly. 'Do . . . do you know what you are saying?'

'Yes, I do know. I am telling you I love you.' It is forbidden and nothing can come of it, Elise thought. But now he knows I love him. And I am glad!

Agnes sat knitting at her usual vantage point in the Milton overlooking the pathway between the big house and the lodge. The sock needles clicked fast as she glanced at the clock. Three hours Elise has been in the lodge this afternoon! Three whole hours alone together and no sign of leaving yet. And this wasn't the first time, oh, dearie me, no! Far from it. Heaven knows what was going on between them.

The question was, what to do about it? Warn Jamie? There'd be the devil to pay! He'd fling the blind man out. Aye, and the wife, too. Oh, the scandal! A word in Elise's ear maybe, friendly-like? Well, that made more sense. Her daughter-in-law wasn't daft, though she was acting like it. Elise knew better than most the power of gossip.

Agnes paused. Was this her now? But no, there was someone else on the woodland path. Land's sake! she thought, it's a tinker woman. There was a tinkers' winter camp of hump-backed dwellings down by the river and the women often came around the doors begging, while their menfolk stood by to pick up anything useful lying around. She stood up, peering through the screens. The tink was heading this way with a bundle of useless rubbish in one hand, a bairn on her back and a hard-luck story, but I'm fly to all that, Agnes thought. The tink had the effrontery to rattle the doorknob trying to get in. Fortunately, Agnes kept the door locked nowadays, with valuable stuff lying around and fine furniture decorating the place. This was a determined wee besom, though. She stopped rattling the knob and began beating on the door panel with a fist. The cheek of her! Agnes wouldn't put up with that. She strode into the lobby and flung open the door.

'Be off wi' you! I can't be doing with beggars.'

The tink was a dirty, down-at-heel wee creature with a white, pinched face and the wee bairn on her back was whimpering forlornly. It was a sight calculated to rouse your pity, Agnes thought. She hardened her heart. 'Go on, get away, I've nothing for you.'

'Oh, Mam, don't you know me?' the woman sobbed.

Agnes put a hand to her heart, which had stopped for a moment. 'Oh, Poppy!'

Her daughter's black-haired child of shame peeped at Agnes from the tattered shawl. The bairn's eyes were very dark. Heaven alone knew who the father was! But that was forgotten in Agnes's vast relief. Poppy was home and safe, after many, many months with no word and constant worry. Agnes opened her arms with a great shout of joy, enveloping mother and child in a loving hug. 'Poppy, my wee lamb, thank God you're home!'

Sophie Merrilees was four when she found out she was a disappointment. She always remembered the moment, because it was the day her wee brother, Peter, was born. She'd overheard Minnie and Cook talking in the kitchen.

'They're over the moon it's a wee laddie this time,' Minnie said, polishing the silver. 'The master had two lassies already when Sophie was born, and the midwife told me afterwards they were dead set on a boy. Sophie was a terrible let-down.'

'They never said,' Cook frowned.

'Well, they wouldn't, would they?' Minnie breathed on a spoon, and polished it to a shine.

Sophie waylaid her half-sister Ruby. 'What's a let-down?'

'I suppose . . . a disappointment.' Ruby eyed her thoughtfully. 'Why d'you want to know, dear?'

'Cause Minnie says I was a terrible one when I was born.'

Ah yes, Ruby could guess how that conversation went, and it made her wild! She'd sometimes wished she could be a suffragette, but even flappers were to have the vote in 1929 and it was too late. She wagged a finger at the little girl. 'No, darling, you will never be a disappointment. You will grow up to be as good as any man if not a damn sight better. And don't you forget it, my darling!'

'No, Ruby,' Sophie promised dutifully. Mummy said Ruby was banging her head against the Vet School door but they still wouldn't let her in. Sophie had looked, but there were never any bruises.

The next significant incident in Sophie's childhood occurred when she was nearly six. Daddy had bought a family house near Inverleith park, because Sophie's greatgrandma Mrs Robb had moved to Stirling and everyone said Royal Terrace was going downhill. Sophie was glad they'd got out before the stately terrace slid downhill into the Forth. By then, Peter was sitting up in his pram taking notice, and they were out for a walk in the park with Nanny, feeding ducks and watching grown-up men sail model yachts.

'Big bairns!' Nanny remarked.

There were lots of boys from the famous school whose turrets you could see nearby, standing watching the boats race one another. They were all dressed in school uniform, though it was a Saturday afternoon. Sophie wandered away from Nanny, who was blethering to a friend. The yachts were tacking, and she stood at the pond's edge fascinated, watching them come towards her. Unfortunately, a crowd of excited schoolboys came running towards her, following the boats. Frightened, Sophie took a hurried step backwards and fell bottom first into the pond. Fortunately it was not deep, though she yelled and threshed around helplessly.

'Dobson, that's your fault. In you go and save her!' shouted one of the boys, bigger than the rest.

'No fear! These are my Sunday breeks. Matron'll murder me!'

'Oh blast!' muttered the big one under his breath and jumped into the pond, scooped up the wet, floundering child and dumped her on the flagstones. His schoolmates cheered.

White-faced, Nanny came running up and hugged the embarrassed lad. 'Well done! The wee lass could've drowned if you hadn't been so quick.'

'It's nothing. The pond isn't deep,' he said, blushing scarlet.

'Modest too!' Nanny beamed. 'What's your name, sonny?'

'It's Murdoch. Jurgen Murdoch.'

Nanny rummaged in her purse and brought out half a crown, which she pressed into the youngster's palm. 'There, Jurgen. That's for you.'

'Yoor-gen,' Sophie repeated to herself, and tucked the strange name carefully away in her childish memory.

Kirsty was content with life, once having reached the early 30s. Turbulent years were over and she led a busy life as wife and mother. Of course, she and Edward had had their problems like everyone else during the hungry 20s. In 1926 the General Strike had hit Edward's business hard at home and he'd been forced to shoulder a heavier workload to avoid crippling losses. His hair was silver now, his shoulders a little stooped, but the business had survived. Kirsty's bookkeeping and accountancy skills were invaluable, and between them they'd weathered the storm and hung on to vital Far Eastern contracts for cargoes of latex and teak.

On Monday 6th May 1935, Britain was on holiday celebrating the Silver Jubilee of King George and Queen Mary. In a light-hearted mood, Kirsty and the two children left the family house overlooking the Botanic Gardens. Sophie and Peter were in a high state of excited anticipation, bound for town to view celebrations in Princes Street. The tram was jam-packed with adults and school children but they found seats upstairs, most of them occupied by senior boys in school uniform. One of them, a handsome lad seated beside a pretty schoolgirl, gave Sophie a wave.

Kirsty was intrigued to see her eleven-year-old daughter turn beetroot red.

'Who's that, dear?' she asked.

'Shh, Mum, he'll hear! It's Jurgen. Jurgen Murdoch.'

It can't be! Kirsty thought, shocked. Yet it must be. 'I never heard you mention him before,' she said. That in itself was unusual with Sophie, who was a chatterbox.

'Jurgen doesn't bother about me, Mum.'

Which didn't answer the question, Kirsty noted. The wistful tone was illuminating though.

'She's soppy about him,' Peter remarked casually.

'Shut up, you little creep!' his sister hissed furiously.

Why is it that incidents from an unhappy past have the power to ruin your peace of mind? Kirsty wondered in the months following that chance meeting. Sophie put on a spurt and grew tall, obviously taking after Edward's side of the family. With pride and trepidation Kirsty watched her little girl turn into an attractive youngster, not pretty by film star standards, but with striking looks which promised to be memorable. One or two bashful schoolboy suitors lounged at the gate after school. The Murdoch boy was never mentioned, but Kirsty was sure she'd spotted them chatting in the park. It bothered her. Why was Sophie so reticent, would history repeat itself? Oh, she prayed her beloved daughter wasn't heading for a broken heart!

1936 started badly with the death of good King George so soon after the Jubilee. Events looked set to continue unhappily as the popular Prince of Wales took over as Edward VIII amidst dark rumours surrounding the romance of the new king and the divorcee, Wallis Simpson.

However, the Merrilees had more to concern themselves with than rumours of royal scandal and reports that German troops had marched unopposed into the Rhineland. Edward

196

received a disturbing letter from Malaya Shipping Enterprises, his agents in the Far East.

The letter reported serious delays and shortages in the orders from Johore, laying blame squarely upon bad management in the plantations belonging to Edward's firm. If matters did not improve, the contract would be terminated, they warned. This was a disasterous threat. News spread quickly and if it were true nobody would touch the firm's goods. Edward could be ruined. He was plagued with guilt. He should have gone to Johore long before this to check up on things. He said as much to Kirsty.

'I must go out there right away, darling,' he decided. 'Frankly, I wasn't impressed by the new manager the board appointed when old Charlie Ainslie retired. The new man's obviously not competent.'

Kirsty studied her husband. He looked tired and drawn. 'How long will you be away?' she asked anxiously.

He shrugged. 'It could take a year or more to sort things out. It depends what I find when I get there.'

She knew he would not spare himself. He was not a young man, and the workload involved could be the death of him. Someone must be on hand to make sure he didn't overdo it.

'I'm coming with you,' she said.

'You can't! What about the children?' But he couldn't hide the hope in his eyes. They hadn't been parted for a single day since they were married.

'Sophie's at an important stage in her education and it would be a shame to interrupt that, but I believe she'd settle down happily as a boarder at her school,' Kirsty said thoughtfully. 'I'm sure Mildred and Papa would be delighted to take her for school holidays. We should take Peter with us, though, he's a bit young to leave behind. I'll ask his teacher for a list of schoolbooks so he won't miss too much schooling.'

'I believe that could work, dear!' Edward agreed. He smiled for the first time. 'I've always wanted to take you to Johore, Kirsty, and maybe now I can.'

'That's settled then. We'll tell Sophie when she comes home from school and hear what she thinks.' She paused suddenly as she thought about her sensitive daughter. How would she take it? 'Edward, I'm afraid this will come as a bit of a shock to the poor darling!' she predicted anxiously. And so it did, but not in the way Kirsty anticipated.

Sophie slung her schoolbag on the sofa and stood with her back to the sitting-room wall while her parents outlined their plans. Every word smote her like a blow, whilst they just smiled.

They're pathetic! Sophie thought. They wanted her to agree, but it wouldn't matter to them if she didn't. They would go anyway. They would leave her and take Peter.

She forgave Daddy, because she understood he must go to deal with money problems, but she could not forgive her mother for going with him and leaving her behind. Why abandon me? Sophie wondered. Then it dawned. She remembered a chance remark overheard years ago. She was a let-down when she was born. A disappointment because her mother had wanted a boy.

'You do understand, don't you, darling?' her mother was saying.

'Oh, yes,' Sophie said bitterly. 'I understand! You don't love me like you love Peter. You never have. You didn't want me when I was born, did you? You wanted a boy and I was a big disappointment.'

'Who told you?' Kirsty cried in astonishment, caught off guard.

Sophie had hoped for a denial, hugs, kisses, reassurances that she had been wanted and welcomed as joyfully as Peter. Instead she heard an admission of guilt she knew she could never forget.

'Oh, Mum!' she wailed, and fled from the room.

Fourteen

K irsty was in tears. 'Oh, Edward, Sophie will never forgive me.'

'Of course she will!'

'But I *was* disappointed at first when she was born. I'd hoped the baby would be a boy because you had two daughters already, but darling, who could have told her?'

'Whoever it was should have had more sense!' he said angrily. 'Shall I have a word with Sophie to set the record straight?'

'Would you, dear?' she said. 'She might listen to you. I doubt if she'll believe a word I say now.' Children need to know they're wanted and welcomed into the world, she thought, and even quite small children can be surprisingly perceptive. She remembered overhearing whispers when she was a tiny girl in her foster-mother's care. In that way she'd learned her birth was responsible for her mother's death and her father's grief. Sometimes she'd felt so guilty she'd wished she'd never been born. Ah yes, you should be careful what you say when a small child is around!

'Edward, maybe I should stay home with the children,' she said worriedly.

He hesitated. He wanted to do what was best for them all, but he needed her with him. Edward doubted if he would survive the heavy load of work and worry awaiting him in Johore without his wife by his side. 'No. Kirsty. Changing your mind now will only complicate matters,' he decided honestly.

'But if I go with Peter, won't it seem we're favouring him?'

'That's the dilemma, but that's where tact comes in. Wish me luck with Sophie, darling!'

Later that evening it seemed Edward had worked the miracle. He and Sophie withdrew to her room after supper, and soon after emerged smiling. 'I'm pleased to announce we've reached an agreement,' he told Kirsty.

Sophie eyed her brother. Resentment lingered miserably, but had eased after a talk with Daddy, who'd tried to explain everything. 'I'm to get a bank account, Peter, and I'm going to boarding school. I'll stay with Grandad and Grandma Mildred in Stirling for the holidays. And Daddy will give me an allowance so's I can buy anything I want.'

'Anything you *need*, Sophie love,' Edward smiled. 'There *is* a difference!'

'I want a lowance too!' Peter grumbled.

His sister looked smug. 'You can't have one till you're old as me. You're going with Mum and Dad to a hot place swarming with snakes and creepy-crawlies, dangerous ones.' That was a nightmarish thought to Sophie, one reason she was jolly glad she wasn't going.

Unfortunately, her brother took a different view. 'Wizard!' he cheered. 'There's nothing dangerous in Scotland 'cept wasps, bees an' adders, an' those aren't kill-you-stone-dead dangerous, are they?'

'N – no.' Sophie wished she hadn't broached the subject. She should have remembered Peter trapped beetles and horrid flying things in jam jars for observation in his bedroom then set them free in the back garden. By that time the vile beasts were house-trained and made a beeline for her room. Boys! Sophie wondered in disgust why her mum and dad had ever wanted one.

Sophie was still resentful next week, despite a successful visit to the bank with her father. She'd met the bank manager, who'd made a gratifying fuss of her. No wonder, with all that money in her new account and a monthly allowance. She was wealthier than her school friends, who could only average one shilling a week pocket money. Unfortunately, Grandad Rutherford had power of attorney, which meant he acted as a brake on reckless spending. Worse luck.

Because Sophie's spirits were low, her best friend Buffy Anderson suggested attending a cricket match that Saturday. Cricket was a terrible bore, but their hero Jurgen Murdoch was captain of the school cricket eleven and they could cheer as he strode on to the pitch in white shirt and flannels. It was a warm summer day, and the girls sat round the edge of the playing field with other spectators. Jurgen was no mean bowler, and his opponents' wickets were falling like skittles.

'Isn't he wonderful?' Buffy breathed. 'I dunno how we'll endure the school holidays, Sophie. He's going to Berlin in August.'

'How d'you know?'

'He told me at church last Sunday. He's been chosen to lead a group of Boy Scouts at the Olympic Games because he speaks fluent German. He's a keen Scout, you know.'

'Everyone knows why you were keen to join the Guides!'

'Jurgen's promised to send me a postcard,' Buffy said.

Another wicket fell while Sophie sulked. Why should Buffy be favoured with a postcard? Favouritism was a sensitive issue at the moment. She studied her friend enviously. What's she got that I haven't? she wondered. Buffy had metal braces on nice white teeth, but she had lovely eyes, curly hair and no spots. Sophie had one on her chin she was trying to hide with calamine lotion.

'Jurgen probably pities you, Buffy,' she said.

'Why should he?'

'Because you look a sight with braces on your teeth.'

Her friend gazed at her with an odd expression, then she said quietly, 'Sophie, don't!'

'Don't what?'

'Don't be catty. It doesn't suit you. I know what's biting you. Your mother and father are going abroad and leaving you behind and you feel hurt. But don't try to hurt me to make yourself feel better. It won't work.'

Sophie's lip quivered, tears welled up from a deep pool of

misery and dripped down her cheeks. 'Oh, I'm sorry, Buff,
but they're t-taking Peter. They must love him better'n me
'cause he's a boy.'

'Nonsense!' Buffy grinned. 'Nobody in their right mind
would love boys better'n girls. Are you keen to go to
Malaya?'

'Not really,' she admitted. 'I hate creepy-crawlies and
there's hundreds there. Peter doesn't mind them, he's a
budding enema – entyma – oh you know what I mean!'

'Bug-hunter,' her friend nodded wisely. 'If you ask me,
your mum and dad want you to stay safely at home 'cause
they love you. Anyway, you're top of the class and they
must feel awfully proud of you. You can't pass any more
school exams if you're stuck out in Malaya, can you?'

'N-no.'

A great cheer went up. Jurgen's over had ended in victory
and the man of the match was striding towards the pavilion.
Buffy pulled Sophie to her feet. 'Come on!'

The pair raced after the tall young man and caught up
with him. Jurgen smiled down kindly at the two eager young
faces. 'This is most flattering, ladies! Is it an autograph
you're after?'

'Please, Jurgen, could you send Sophie Merrilees a postcard from the Olympics?' Buffy begged.

'Sophie? Of course I could!' He remembered he'd once
hauled the little Merrilees girl out of Inverleith pond, and
he laughed. 'Didn't know you were interested in athletics,
Sophie. Maybe in pond events, eh?'

The two girls stared adoringly after him as he sauntered
on his way, smiling. Gosh! He actually remembers hauling
me out of Inverleith pond! Sophie thought happily.

Buffy linked arms. 'Feeling better?'

Sophie smiled gratefully at her own special friend. 'Ever
so much better, thanks, Buffy!'

Agnes Murdoch had Poppy home again and had been down
on her knees thanking the Good Lord. All the same, Agnes
found her daughter's return was a mixed blessing.

There were those in Invergowrie who passed by with averted faces when confronted by Poppy and her bairn in the street. Agnes herself had endured sly digs and hurtful snubs at meetings of the Mothers' Union.

Honestly! she thought. There were plenty tales she could tell about some who were pillars o' the kirk if she cared to reveal goings-on she'd witnessed on the lovers' path! Agnes was sorry for her daughter. She had no doubt her pure, innocent lassie had been led astray by a scoundrel who'd enticed her into a life of sin. She'd questioned Poppy, but Poppy remained tight-lipped. All she'd say was she'd nursed the man devotedly during his last illness and had held him in her arms and kissed him as he died. Which was more than the wretch deserved, Agnes thought grimly.

She studied Joel D'Arcy's little daughter anxiously for signs of the TB that had carried off the father, but could detect none. Marie Celeste was black-haired, dark-eyed, olive-skinned and foreign-looking, but otherwise glowed with health and had abundant energy.

Heaven help us! Agnes thought as her small granddaughter darted about the house, as difficult to catch as a buzzing bluebottle on a windowpane.

'Come here, Marie Celeste!' Agnes shuddered as she made a dive for the quicksilver child. Fancy calling a bairn after an abandoned ship! One shouldn't tempt fate!

Months of dedicated feeding soon restored the undernourished pair to rounded health, but by the spring of 1936 Poppy showed signs of restlessness. 'I thought I might have a word with Mr Archibald to see if he'd give me a job, Mam. I don't expect you and Dad to support us forever,' she said tentatively while helping her mother in the kitchen.

'We can afford it! We're well off now, lovie. There's no call for you to work for money. There's plenty charities screaming for well-heeled women to do good works if you're interested, Poppy dear.'

'No. I want to earn a living. I have to be independent.' Agnes was hurt. 'Me and your dad are just a pair of interfering busybodies, is that it? We were only trying to help!'

Poppy hugged her. 'Don't go into a huff, Mam! You and Dad have been wonderful, but I can't go on taking without giving something back. You couldn't either, could you?'

Her mother didn't deny it. She sighed. 'Well, Poppy, if you're dead set on working, at least let me look after the bairn.'

Poppy hesitated. Celeste did pose a problem. Poppy adored her beloved little daughter, but how could she work and care for Celeste properly at the same time? Her mother's offer did make sense.

'All right, Mam, thank you for offering,' she agreed. 'But on one condition! You'll tell me at once if the wee monkey becomes too much for you to handle!'

On cue, the dark-eyed winsome rascal climbed on to Agnes's knee, twined her arms around her grandma's neck and kissed her. Agnes's heart filled as she hugged the child. 'Don't worry, Poppy,' she smiled. 'The day I'm too old to look after my own grandchild there'll be such a stir in this house everybody in the Carse will know!'

Kirsty spent a frantic summer preparing for their voyage. There were suitable tenants to be found for the family house, and a round of goodbyes to relatives and friends. After some heart-searching, she and Edward thought it wiser to settle Sophie in Stirling with her grandparents at the start of the school summer holidays. Sophie had raised no objection, and Charles and Mildred had been eager to have her.

'It'll be nice to have young company, Kirsty dear. It'll remind me of the happy times I spent with you and Hannah. By the way, what news of her?' Mildred asked.

'Hannah's still nursing abroad in outlandish places and finds it too tricky to come home. Her mother gets letters from exotic places but sends her own mail to a post office box number. Hannah doesn't seem to be married, though I could have sworn there was a man in the picture last time we met.'

'Maybe it didn't work out.' She gave Kirsty a keen glance. 'But you've married well. You're very happy with the man you love, aren't you?'

'Oh, Edward is a wonderful husband, Holly!'

Which, Mildred noted, did not quite answer the question.

Kirsty's brother Samuel Rutherford was now a busy GP working in Glasgow's appalling slums, but he managed a quick farewell visit to his sister and brother-in-law before returning to his duties in a TB clinic.

'Still engaged to that nice nursing sister, Sam? When do you plan to get married?' Edward asked.

'We're too busy to arrange a wedding at the moment. Besides, my room and kitchen in the Gorbals and my unsociable working hours are enough to make a saint think twice!' he smiled.

More excuses! Kirsty thought. Poor Sam. This engagement had dragged on for years, always with some plausible excuse to postpone tying the knot. Could Sam be another victim of the terrible war? she wondered. Did he lack confidence to live a normal family life, only happy when tending to the poor and sick? It was possible. A sensitive man like Sam would find it hard to forget that society had labelled him a coward.

Later in the year, Kirsty and Edward drove through the tranquil Carse of Gowrie to say goodbye to her brother George. Though she spoke frequently to her blind brother on the phone, Kirsty hadn't visited the estate since leaving home years ago. It would be a painful experience for her to see the dear old house under Jamie Murdoch's ownership, and she wouldn't risk meeting him and his wife. However, George had mentioned on the phone that Jamie and Elise were attending a business convention in Aberdeen which would last all week, and had suggested Thursday for the visit. Kirsty had agreed. Thursday should be safe!

'Oh, George, you do look well!' Kirsty exclaimed as she kissed her brother at the lodge door. And so happy! she almost added. The haunted look had gone, even the sightless eyes, once dull and lifeless, seemed brighter as he turned a smiling face towards them. He shook Edward's hand. 'Come in. Come away in!' He led the way confidently. A large shaggy dog greeted them with a deep, friendly bark and

George laughed. 'Meet O'Ryan, dear old Murphy's son and as devoted as his dad, with the same mischievous streak. Likes to drag me through puddles when he has the chance.'

It was a cheerful visit filled with laughter, but there was something about the comfortable room which Kirsty found odd. At first she couldn't place the oddness, then she noticed a bowl filled with flowers sitting on the window ledge, an arrangement of pink roses, white lilies, trails of speckled ivy and blue campanula. No blind person could possibly blend the colours so skilfully. Looking round the room, she fancied she detected more evidences of a woman's deft touch. So who cares for George? she wondered. It was intriguing!

At that moment, the dog barked, the back door opened and a woman's voice called out. 'Darling, I'm back!'

The woman came quickly into the room but stopped abruptly when she saw George's visitors. She had no time to hide the eager happiness and telltale love in her eyes. 'Oh – Kirsty!' Elise Murdoch faltered. 'I – I did not know . . . !'

Their eyes met for a significant moment before Jamie's wife regained composure. It was smoothly done and Kirsty doubted if Edward had even noticed anything. But *she* had. Now she understood the reason for her brother's happiness. He and Elise had fallen in love. Kirsty didn't know whether to be shocked or delighted.

Jamie Murdoch was angry. The anger was controlled and no trace of it showed on his handsome features as he and his wife dined in the big dining room that evening. He laid fork and knife neatly side by side. 'There's mildew on the wheat in the lower fields, Elise. The crop's ruined,' he remarked. 'Rutherford's not up to the job. Serves me right for employing a blind man out of charity.'

He sat back and watched her. He'd been watching the pair of them secretly for months now, suspicion hardening to certainty.

Her distress was so clear! 'All wheat is blighted with mildew this year, Jamie. You cannot blame a man for a damp season because he is blind.'

'Well, maybe not,' he agreed pleasantly, and watched her transparent relief. He could read her mind so easily.

Elise had filled out over the past year. Love had softened the unhappy contours of her face and rounded the tall, slender figure. She's a bonnie woman now, he thought, but it's not love for her husband that's worked the transformation. Oh no!

Hidden from view, he'd watched her today after they'd returned early from the Aberdeen conference. He'd told her he was going to the mill, but instead he'd hidden in the shady summerhouse. He'd seen her hasten eagerly down the lovers' path. Eager to be with the blind man.

Jamie clenched a fist, crushing the starched napkin and letting it slip to the floor. A blind man! What an insult to a husband, not to mention the scandal there would be if it got out. As it would!

Elise was nervously eyeing the discarded napkin. 'D – do you not want dessert, Jamie? It – it is gooseberry fool.'

How apt, my dear! he thought. I may be playing gooseberry, but I am no fool. He was restless and anguished this evening, but not because he knew his wife was unfaithful. Today he had seen Kirsty. Sitting hidden in the summerhouse he had watched her walk along the driveway with her silver-haired husband. It was so unexpected. He was in deep shock as he sat amidst the ruins of a disastrous marriage and watched the woman who should have been his wife walk past. If only he'd had the sense to wait! If only there hadn't been a war! If only he hadn't been wounded and vulnerable and close to death! If only . . .

He stood up abruptly. 'I don't want dessert. I've work to do.' He couldn't blame Elise. His only real emotion at the moment was extreme irritation because she'd been so indiscreet in her search for happiness. He was terrified in case his good name would be dragged through the mud in the divorce court.

Jamie headed for his study and closed the door. He reached for the phone and dialled his solicitor, who was a personal friend. He had to put a stop to this dangerous affair between

Elise and George Rutherford, and the plan he had in mind should finish it. For good.

Sunday 16th August 1936 saw the end of the Berlin Olympic Games and Jurgen Murdoch knew he would never forget the experience. He had thrilled to the sound of vast, disciplined crowds shouting in unison beneath hundreds of fluttering red flags adorned with a black crooked cross, a swastika, the symbol of a new German regime, the Third Reich, his friend Volker had informed him.

Jurgen had watched top athletes perform. He'd relished speaking German as freely and fluently as English. But most of all, he would always remember meeting Ernestine. Ah, sweet Ernestine!

She wasn't what Jurgen would have called pretty. He'd fancied other girls who were prettier by far, but when British Scouts had paraded in the arena alongside Hitler Youth on the first day of the Games, she'd smiled at him shyly. His heart had given an almighty lurch and hadn't steadied since.

He'd discovered she was one of a party of girls from Volker's school enlisted to keep the ground free of litter and her name was Ernestine Brecht. They had exchanged a few hurried words during track events, a clasp of the hands that had raced through his body like an electric shock, but it wasn't till rain threatened one evening towards the end that there came a chance to shelter together in an empty grandstand, and talk freely.

She glanced round to make sure they were not overheard, then declared gleefully, 'Jurgen, I'm so pleased that Jesse Owens and the other black men won so many gold medals! Did you see our Führer sneak away with a face like thunder when Jesse won the 200 metres and broke the record? Oh, I couldn't help laughing and clapping!'

'You were the only one in your party who did,' he observed. He looked at her curiously. 'The others looked petrified. Why?'

She hesitated. 'If you have to ask, you won't understand. You're British, Jurgen. You wouldn't believe me.'

'I'll always believe you!'

She clutched his hand. 'Oh, how I wish you loved me, Jurgen! We could run away to your country and live happily ever after!'

'Hey . . . not so fast!' He laughed, but he was shocked all the same. He had not gone as far as lasting love and commitment and he was alarmed and disappointed. Up till now she had not seemed a pushy sort of girl. That had been part of her charm.

She dropped his hand. 'I've shocked you, and I'm sorry, but – but I need a friend badly. Once I had many, but now they're too scared to be seen with me because my father is quite a famous scientist.'

'Oh, Ernestine, that's no reason at all!' he laughed.

She sighed. 'How can I expect you to understand? My *Vati* is an outspoken man. He doesn't trust Adolf Hitler and his followers. Often he refuses to do what they want because it's against his principles. He is openly critical of the regime and doesn't care who knows it. Mutti and I have begged him to be discreet, but he says someone must speak before it is too late.' She gave a helpless little shrug. 'Oh, they've left us alone so far because my father's research is vital to them, but what will happen when it's completed? They watch us all the time.' She was suddenly struck by a terrifying thought. 'Oh, Jurgen, they'll have noticed I laughed when the black man won gold and the Führer sulked!'

'Silly girl! They' can't punish you for laughing!' He hugged her, amused by such foolishness.

She rested her head wearily against his breast. 'I knew you wouldn't understand.'

'Listen, Ernestine, let's write to one another,' he said. 'You can tell me everything that's going on and I'll visit you in Berlin whenever I can. How about it?'

Her eyes shone. 'That's wonderful! I'll feel safer if you know what's happening to me.'

'Nothing will happen!' He would have given in to temptation and kissed her then, but she pushed him away.

'No, Jurgen, you shouldn't be seen with me.' She glanced

209

over her shoulder in terror. 'Someone's coming!' She turned and ran, darting frantically along deserted tiers of seating towards the exit. He yelled after her, but she didn't stop.

The intruder was his friend, Volker. He vaulted over the rail and looked around suspiciously. 'Has that girl gone?'

'Thanks to you!'

'Yes, you should thank me. Leave that one alone, Jurgen!'

'Why? Is she your girlfriend?'

'No fear!'

'Then why shouldn't I enjoy her company?'

He shrugged. 'Let's just say she's a rebel with doubtful antecedents, but you'll be leaving Berlin soon so I don't suppose it matters. Chances are in a few weeks you'll have forgotten Ernestine Brecht ever existed.'

'You think so?' Jurgen said mildly. He begged to differ, but had no intention of starting an argument.

'I know so, my friend!' the Hitler Youth leader said, his eyes a cold, icy blue. Then he laughed and flung an arm across Jurgen's shoulders. 'Come on, Jurgen my friend, why not take a beer with me and forget this foolish little flirtation?'

When Kirsty and Edward Merrilees left Edinburgh with Peter, a chill early mist hid their last glimpse of the river and the first smoky hint of autumn was in the air. They left from Waverley station bound for the southern outskirts of Glasgow. There was nobody on the platform to see them off. Their beloved little daughter had shown no desire to kiss her parents and brother goodbye and Kirsty was taking the heartache of her daughter's rejection with her to the Far East.

By economical packing, the baggage was limited to two cabin trunks and a smaller one containing bits and pieces Peter swore he couldn't live without. Peter had been subdued since Sophie left to live with her grandparents. In fact, it was a dejected little group that sat in a First Class compartment surveying the passing countryside. Kirsty closed her eyes. This last sight of Scotland was almost too much to bear.

The train pulled into a station and stopped with much

clanking and hissing of steam. Peter gave a rousing yell. 'Mum, look!'

She blinked her eyes open and thought she must be dreaming. Sophie was on Stirling platform jigging with excitement. Beside her stood Charles and Mildred, escorting a ninety-five-year-old lady. Kirsty shot to her feet.

'Dear Grandma Robb!' Edward was already fumbling eagerly with the carriage door.

'Hurry, Dad, hurry!' Sophie yelled. 'We're coming to Glasgow to see you off!'

'It was Sophie's idea, Kirsty,' Charles and Mildred Rutherford explained after they had all climbed aboard and settled themselves.

'You know, I did wonder about those empty reserved seats,' she laughed. She put an arm thankfully round her daughter.

Sophie hugged her. 'Great-grandma thought it a wizard plan, Mum.'

'Absolutely wizard,' nodded the old lady.

Peter was beaming happily as the train set off once more. He whispered in his sister's ear. 'I'll send you a picture postcard of dangerous bugs, if you like, Sophie. That'll be safer than the real thing.'

'Brilliant, thanks, Pete.' She suppressed a shudder and hugged him. 'I'll miss you terribly, you wee terror!'

'I wish you were coming,' the little boy said, tearfully.

'Oh, one of us has to stay behind to look after the old folks, Pete.'

Mildred burst out laughing. 'Why do I suddenly feel ancient?'

When the train steamed into Greenock, Sophie pointed to the white superstructure of a ship visible in the dockyard. 'I say, Dad, is that yours? It's huge!'

Edward laughed. 'Not as big as the *Queen Mary*, and not likely to receive the Blue Riband, but yes, love, that's the P&O liner *Strathmore*. I thought the name would remind us of Scotland. We don't intend to be seasick *and* homesick.'

The liner was due to sail on the evening tide, which gave

plenty of time for a leisurely goodbye. Time for them all to climb the gangway and set foot on deck. Time to explore cabins, and sample afternoon tea in the lounge. Time for a very old lady to remember another voyage in a different age.

The years slipped away for a moment and Lizzie Robb felt she was a young bride on honeymoon with her soldier husband, heading for India and unknown dangers. 'I expect the ship will call at Bombay, Kirsty,' she said. 'Will you cast a flower into the water for me when you reach your grandfather's beloved India?'

'Of course I will, Grandma.' Fondly, she hugged the indomitable lady who'd had such an influence upon her life. She wondered if without her grandmother's prompting she would have married Edward, or even met him. Maybe not, yet it had been a wise decision to marry him. She loved him quietly, contentedly and believed she had made Edward happy.

Time and tide wait for nobody, however. Soon street lamps made shimmering reflections in the darkening water and the liner blazed with light. Edward, Kirsty and Peter walked the promenade deck with Sophie for the last time. The others had already said goodbye and gone ashore, leaving the little family together.

Sophie held her mother and father's hands. She could feel her mother's wedding ring and the strength of her father's fingers. Peter stumped along in front, whistling to keep his spirits up. He loathed goodbyes.

She glanced curiously at her parents. You can tell a lot from expressions, she thought, and theirs were certainly expressive. Dad was hiding his emotion behind a shaky smile, but poor Mum looked shattered. That's because they're leaving me behind! Sophie thought.

She watched the pitiful struggle they were making to be cheerful for her sake, when she knew they felt awful. She could see they really loved her and wanted her to be with them, it all became quite clear when you looked into their eyes and felt the strong grip of their hands. Gently, she eased her hands away, for it was time to go.

At that moment, Sophie felt she'd grown up quite suddenly and was wiser in the ways of adults who, unlike children, were afraid to show emotion. She reached up and kissed them both, and even managed to laugh reassuringly, though it took effort. 'I'm glad we have a boy in the family, you know. Take care of Pete for me, will you?'

'Darling, darling, this parting is breaking my heart . . .' Kirsty wept.

'I know.' Sophie looked up into her mother's brimming eyes and was satisfied. It's OK, she thought. Everything's fine between us now. 'I love you,' she told them and knew instinctively that was the right thing to say. She paused for a moment to smile at her mother, so smart and defiantly colourful in a strawberry-red costume and hat, her silver-haired father with an arm thrown protectively around his wife and son. Then Sophie turned and ran back down the gangway to the crowded quay.

Edward watched her go, deeply troubled. Was it wise to leave Sophie behind? He'd been keeping a close eye on the situation in Europe and what he'd heard on the wireless and read in the press had only served to increase anxiety. But most worrying of all had been a small item in the financial press about a substantial increase in demand for latex. The British government had quietly ordered the manufacture of enough gas masks for every man, woman and child in the British Isles.

Gas! Edward's blood ran cold at the thought. Was it safe to leave Sophie at home to face the danger of bombs and gas attacks if there was another war? Well, he thought, it's too late now, but at the first hint of trouble we'll send for her. I've plenty of business colleagues I could ask to take care of her on the voyage. Edward was confident that whatever happened Britain would protect her interests in the Far East. Rubber and tin were important commodities should there be war in Europe.

'Dad, why's Mum crying?' Poor Peter couldn't recall it ever happening before and even the big, exciting luxury liner felt suddenly strange and menacing in consequence.

213

'It's because Mum wants Sophie to be with us, Pete, but that's not possible at the moment.'

'Why not? Is it 'cause it's dangerous?' the little boy asked, remembering the insects.

Edward smiled. 'No, Pete. There's no danger where we're going. The island's defended by big guns and the seas are patrolled by battleships. Singapore is probably the safest place on earth.'

Fifteen

The travellers gained their sea legs as the *Strathmore* sailed the choppy waters between Ireland and Scotland, but after a week at sea the liner's decks grew warm and the sun rose high and hot in a blue sky. Edward had planned a long, leisurely sea voyage. The ship would be visiting many ports of call which had connections with his firm's extensive trading, and he wanted Kirsty to be familiar with all aspects of the business.

Between ports, Peter ran freely round the decks, clad only in shorts and sandals, but at times the heat became too much, even for him.

'Phew, I'm baked!' he said, flopping in the shade beside his parents' deckchairs. Perfectly at home on the liner by now, the little boy was growing bored with travel and longing to reach Singapore. Peter hadn't realized their destination would be so many wearisome thousands of miles from home, and said so.

'Never mind, Pete. We're due to stay in Bombay for a few days. We'll do some exploring ashore then,' Edward promised.

'I hope it's cooler!' Kirsty fanned herself with a magazine.

'I wouldn't count on it, love!' Edward tipped a panama hat over his eyes and relaxed for a snooze. Kirsty smiled to herself. She could see the long, restful sea voyage had done Edward a power of good.

India was an incredible shock to her. She had never experienced such intense dry heat, dazzling colour and deep, dusty shade, nor seen such confusion of carts, sacred cows, motor cars and animated people. Edward hired a horse-drawn ghari and an obliging Indian syce to show them the sights. Their driver decided the foreigners should harbour no illusions and though they were shown Bombay's beauty spots they were also introduced to the darker side. They were impressed by palaces set in gardens shaded by sacred trees, and sickened by scenes of abject poverty.

Kirsty was glad to return to the *Strathmore* at dusk. The ship felt like home to her now.

That evening after dinner she went on deck and cast a garland of sweet-scented hibiscus into the water, shedding a tear or two. 'That's for you and the soldier you loved, dear Grandma Robb,' she whispered as the bright garland floated from the floodlit liner along a rippling track of golden light and was lost in darkness.

They said goodbye to friends they'd made on the journey from Britain to India, and welcomed newcomers joining the ship for the remainder of the voyage. There was quite a buzz of excitement in the coffee lounge on the day the ship was due to sail, when news spread that a member of the British ambassador's staff had arrived on board.

'Titled, good-looking and definitely uppercrust, Kirsty,' her friend whispered.

'Married?'

'Yes, worse luck,' sighed the spinster. 'Look! Here he comes . . . with his wife!'

Kirsty looked, and received such a shock she cried out loudly. 'Hannah! Hannah Murdoch!'

The elegant lady she'd addressed turned pale. 'Oh, my God! Kirsty!'

Lady Hannah Winslow's worst nightmare was a meeting with Kirsty Rutherford, the woman whose lifestyle she had adopted. Hannah had woven a rich fantasy around her own humble beginnings, but now the game was up, she thought in panic. Unless . . . ?

Hannah changed a horrified expression into a beam of incredulous joy and hugged her foster-sister. 'My dear, how

216

wonderful to see you again!' In a whisper she hissed in Kirsty's ear, 'For heavens sake play along with me, Kirsty! I'll explain later.' Hannah turned to her husband. 'Morris darling, this is such an amazing coincidence! Kirsty and I were great friends when we were children. Our fathers were officers in the same regiment during the Boer War and I used to leave Papa's gloomy old castle and spend lovely summer holidays with Kirsty on her father's estate. We rode ponies and shared a governess, didn't we, dear?' She gave her dazed friend a sharp dig with an elbow.

'Y – yes, we did.'

'You were good at maths, Kirsty, I was good at English.'

'Very good at making up stories, you were!'

'. . . Er . . . yes.' She patted Kirsty's arm. 'My dear, we'll catch up with all the news later!'

'I can hardly wait,' Kirsty said grimly.

Kirsty had retired to her cabin that night when there was a quick tap on the door and Hannah entered furtively. 'Our menfolk are enjoying a *chota peg* in the bar, Kirsty. They're engrossed setting the world to rights, so we shouldn't be disturbed.' She flopped down on a nearby chair. 'Oh, Kirsty, I'm so sorry!'

'You're sorry? I'm confused!'

'Well, you see . . .' Hannah took a deep breath and confessed the whole complex sequence of events, while Kirsty listened with growing amazement.

'Why on earth did you do it?' she asked.

Hannah sighed. 'It started when I was a VAD in the Carse. I was mixing with toffs and thanks to you and dear Holly I spoke their language. Everyone assumed I was out of the top drawer and being so tall added to the illusion. Then I met Morris and we fell in love, and after that I couldn't admit what I'd done in case I lost him. It would've broken my heart, Kirsty, and his too. I couldn't risk it.'

Kirsty was sorry for her. 'Well, you got what you wanted in the end, my dear, you're a toff in your own right. But doesn't Morris think it odd you can't produce a grumpy old recluse and a remote Highland castle?'

217

'Oh, I put an end to that myth years ago,' Hannah said with a hint of pride. 'Morris was working in a remote area of Turkey at the time while I stayed in England nursing our babies. When he came home I told him my father had died in the interim and hadn't left a bean because the estate had been sold to cover the old soak's debts. Mind you, I wept buckets for the dear old soul. I'd grown fond of him.'

Kirsty couldn't help laughing, but then a more serious thought struck her. 'What about your own mother and father?'

Hannah's eyes brimmed. 'Oh, Kirsty, it's awful! I daren't tell them the truth in letters home. They think I'm still unmarried, a dedicated nurse living abroad in out-of-the-way places. Mam and Dad don't even know they have two lovely grandchildren at boarding school in England.'

'How sad! Mam would love grandchildren!'

'Don't rub it in!' she wailed. 'That's not all. Morris thinks Mam's letters come from a dotty old nanny of mine who won't accept I'm grown up and married. What else could I do, Kirsty?' she sobbed. 'Her letters come in the diplomatic bag and have to be explained away somehow. But oh, Kirsty, I feel so mean!'

Kirsty did her best to comfort Hannah, but what a tangled web she'd woven! She shuddered to think what would happen if the truth ever came out.

Despite Hannah's problems, Kirsty was delighted to have her company after the ship left Bombay. Hannah in her role as ambassador's wife was a lively and captivating companion who charmed passengers and crew alike and was obviously devoted to her handsome husband. Kirsty decided to stop worrying about Hannah and enjoy the remainder of the voyage.

There was much excitement on board towards the end of December as the *Strathmore* came in sight of green hills clothed from shore to summit with jungle growth. Very soon, the ship had entered a strait edged with palm trees and tropical vegetation and the passengers crowded on deck to view the scene.

'The Malacca Straits,' Edward said. 'We'll dock in Keppel harbour quite soon.'

'Will there be dangerous bugs there, Dad?' Peter asked eagerly.

'There's no danger here, son!' Edward smiled. 'Keppel harbour's on the south of Singapore Island, guarded by big guns.'

Hannah gave Kirsty more information as the liner sailed on. 'Wives in the Diplomatic Corps pray for a posting to Singapore, Kirsty. They say the social life's good.'

'I can believe it.' Kirsty said. The air was warm and scented, though the evening breeze was cool. I would be perfectly happy if only Sophie could be with us, she thought. Maybe they should send for her. The worsening situation in Europe worried Edward and he believed their daughter would be safer in Singapore with them. Maybe he was right. How wonderful if the family could be reunited. Kirsty decided she would write to Sophie and suggest the possibility.

Dougal Murdoch sat in the panelled boardroom of Murdoch and Son (Milling) Ltd and stared at his son. 'You've sold Angus House?' he said incredulously.

'It's mine to sell, Dad. I don't need shareholders' permission. Or yours, for that matter.'

'I'm not denying it. I'm just wondering why the devil you're selling when you've spent good money fixing it the way you wanted.'

He shrugged. 'I have my reasons. The estate stays under family control, of course. I've no claim on that, only the house.'

Father and son were alone in the boardroom of the modernized mill complex. The auditors and shareholders who'd invested capital in Murdoch's had just left after the annual general meeting. They seemed well satisfied with profits, dividends and targets set for expansion.

'I'm surprised Elise agreed to the sale,' Dougal remarked.

Jamie glanced at him sharply. How much does the old man guess? he wondered. Aloud he said, 'She knows we've bought a mill in Dock Street that's more handy for harbour shipments and railway deliveries, and she agrees with me that it makes sense to move to Dundee.'

'It makes sense, but it'll break her heart. Elise had found happiness here.'

'What do you mean by that?'

'I'm no' blind, like some!'

'Then you'll understand why I'm selling the place!' his son said.

'Aye, son, I understand.'

It's tragic when a man marries the wrong woman, Dougal thought. But Jamie was tackling trouble head-on and maybe that was best. All the same, it was a great pity Angus House was to be a victim.

A thought occurred to him. 'What about Jurgen? He loves that house.'

Jamie's expression hardened. 'Why doesn't he live in it then? I wanted him to start an engineering course in Dundee, but oh no. He's gone off to Germany instead.'

'You can hardly blame him. He's curious to see his mother's country.'

'Curious my foot! He fell for a German lass he met at the Olympics; they've been writing to one another for months. I've seen the letters,' Jamie said disapprovingly.

'Love letters?'

'How would I know? They're in German.'

Although Marie Celeste D'Arcy loved Grandma Murdoch, she missed her mother. There was nobody to speak French with while Maman was working, and Celeste was terrified in case she forgot the precious words. Her Maman had told her that her dead Papa had spoken nothing but French to her when she was tiny, and so she never wanted to forget a syllable of it. She lived in terror in case the few memories she had of his dear, shadowy presence faded away completely. If only I'd been a big girl when Papa was alive, I would remember so much more! she thought. I would remember the colour of his eyes and the funny things he said as I sat on his knee.

That Sunday morning, Celeste had made a beeline for the

rhododendron bushes before church. She'd hidden in her favourite hiding place, hugging her knees and polishing precious memories of Papa till they shone. Grandma Murdoch was roaring angrily in the distance. 'Celeste, you wee monkey! Where are you? Come and get your hair done. It's nearly time to get ready for Sunday School!'

Celeste sighed. There was no escape from church these days. Grandma said everyone had to go and pray there wouldn't be another war. Celeste believed it was up to God to stop it, and a great babble of prayer would only annoy Him. Anyway, she'd rather see the crocodile. Grandma said that was what you called St Agnes schoolgirls walking two by two. The girls were assorted sizes and walked down the driveway every Sunday from their boarding school in Agnes House to the sheds where their bikes were stored. Then they rode two by two to church in Invergowrie, a teacher in front and one behind.

Crocodile? Oh yes! It had nasty teeth. She'd been very curious about the school and its pupils when it started. A board of governors had bought Uncle Jamie's house and turned Angus House into St Agnes' School for Girls. They'd made the front lawn into a hockey pitch and the rose garden into tennis courts, and the smaller girls played rounders and netball in the stable yard. One day Celeste had plucked up courage and confronted the crocodile. She had reasoned that educated schoolgirls would be sure to speak French.

'Bonjour, mesdemoiselles!' she'd greeted it, smiling as she appeared from the bushes.

The crocodile had halted in confusion, its faces quite blank. The teacher had shouted, 'Come along, girls! Never mind her. Keep in line!'

'Get out the way, you wee show-off!' someone said crossly as the crocodile regrouped.

'Smarty-pants!' somebody hissed at her as it marched past. Hurt, Celeste had never approached the unfriendly beast again.

This Sunday she was just about to abandon the crocodile and obey Gran's summons when she noticed the blind man coming. Celeste cowered down. Oh, but she was afraid of *l'aveugle*! She sensed a darkness in him that had nothing to do with blindness. His eyes were blank and his expression lifeless, as if he bore a great weight of sadness. Celeste had no idea what to say to him and his big dog. So she hid. But the terrifying thing was, though the man was blind, he could tell where she was. The dog would whine softly and the blind man's empty eyes would swing towards her hiding place. Celeste would shiver in her shoes till he'd passed safely. Fortunately, he never stopped or spoke. But today, to her horror, he did.

'Celeste?' he called softly. 'I know you're there. Won't you please talk to me?'

'Why should I?' she said in a small, scared voice.

'Because I'm lonely. Maybe you're lonely, too?'

She considered this for a full minute. She could understand loneliness. 'Can you speak French?' she asked.

'A little. I speak German better.'

Peeping through the leaves she watched him and wondered. She couldn't understand blindness, it was too terrible to contemplate.

'Maybe you could teach me French, Celeste?' the blind man said.

'M-maybe.'

He seemed satisfied. He smiled, surprising her. She hadn't known he could. She watched the dog tow him away on his rounds of the estate.

'Celeste, will you come here this minute, or else . . . !'

She sighed. Gran sounded wild. Celeste crawled out from under the bushes and went skipping on her way.

The very next day, Celeste's mother received an extraordinary proposition. Poppy had been working for Mr Archibald the art dealer for many months, but when the old man sat her down in the office that Monday morning to explain what he had in mind, it almost took her breath away.

'You want me to take over the business and run the shop? Mr Archibald, you're joking!' Poppy gasped.

'You should know by now I never joke where money's

222

concerned, Poppy,' he said. 'I should've retired years ago, but I'm loathe to see a fine business ruined by strangers. I'm a widower as you know, and me and Effie weren't blessed wi' bairns. You're the nearest I have to a daughter, my lass. To tell the truth it nearly broke my heart when you went off with that rascal D'Arcy. I don't intend losing sight o' you again.'

'Joel taught me everything I know about modern art, Mr Archibald.'

He nodded. 'The works the man left behind fetch high prices today. Pity artists have to die afore folk'll buy.'

'If only he had known!' Poppy murmured. 'But do you really think I could run the business?'

'Yes, you could. I've watched you since you came back, Poppy. There's nobody can pull wool over your eyes. You're smart, and there's a sharp edge to your tongue when it's needed.'

Poppy glowed with pride for Archibald did not hand out praise lightly.

The old man patted her shoulder. 'That's settled then. Mind you, Poppy, I'll still attend auctions fishing for bargains, when I'm not fishing for brown trout in season. I'll instruct my lawyer to draw up a contract so that the salary and profit-sharing side is legal and binding. All you have to do is find an honest assistant.'

'I know the very person!' she cried delightedly.

Her friend Ursula Proudfoot had married Sir Gilbert Bosanquet some years ago, but the couple remained childless. Gilbert had shown a surprising aptitude for his father-in-law's troubled jute trade and had been absorbed into the family business. Ursula was kicking her heels in frustration in a Broughty Ferry mansion not far from another large property owned by Poppy's brother, Jamie. Poppy was confident Ursula would jump at the chance of work. Apart from being bored stiff, Lady Ursula Bosanquet loved pictures and had a sure eye for what was good.

Britain celebrated the coronation of King George VI and Queen Elizabeth in May 1937, but Jurgen did not join in the festivities. He was on his way to Germany after a shouting match with his father.

'I forbid you to go!' Jamie had stormed. 'For heaven's sake, Jurgen, you've only been working in the mill a month. You're the boss's son. What will the workers think? Germany of all places! Haven't you read the papers recently?'

'I'm not interested in politics.'

'Herr Hitler's gone far beyond politics, my lad. It's downright aggression!'

'I'm sorry, but I'm going. It's important.' He'd walked out and his father had yelled after him.

'Why the hell won't you admit it's a lass you're after?'

Dad was right of course.

Jurgen was wedged into a corner seat in a packed compartment on the Berlin train. Conversation had died since he'd entered the compartment. His travelling companions kept giving him odd looks. He guessed that a fair-haired young man wearing expensive British clothes and speaking faultless German would be an object of suspicion. Jurgen was too worried to care.

He and Ernestine Brecht had corresponded regularly since the Olympics, and he'd visited her parents' home in Potsdam on two happy occasions. He had liked Professor and Frau Brecht, Ernestine's father and mother, but for Ernestine herself the emotion went far deeper.

They'd kissed for the first time as they'd walked hand-in-hand in a deserted snow-covered park on his last visit. It had been a tender, loving kiss that had moved him deeply. When it ended he'd held her close. 'Do you kiss all your boyfriends like that?'

'No. Only you. There is only you for me.'

'You're kidding! There must be others, a bonny lass like you!'

She'd teased him, eyes alight with mischief. 'We-ell, Volker has been very attentive. You remember Volker of the Hitler Youth group?'

'Oh, yes, I remember!' He'd frowned uneasily. What was going on? Volker had been less than friendly to Ernestine at the Olympics. 'I wouldn't trust Volker if I were you!' he'd warned.

Laughing, she'd kissed him. 'Volker's harmless, silly! There's no need to be jealous. You're the only man I will love, for ever and ever . . .'

So much for undying love! Jurgen thought bitterly. Ernestine Brecht had not written to him since they parted months ago. Memories of that last meeting still haunted him as the train reached its destination. The crowds spilled out on to the platform and Jurgen followed. Outside the station he hailed a taxi and gave the address of her parents' house. Her silence had driven Jurgen crazy with worry. As weeks and months passed without a single reply to his more and more frantic letters, he'd grown bitter and morose. He'd tried to forget her, without success. He'd even asked Grandma Murdoch's advice, but she'd only warned that young lasses could be fickle. Knowing Ernestine he had found that hard to believe, but it was possible.

In the end he'd just had to travel to Germany to find out what had happened and hear from her own lips why she'd stopped loving him.

Jurgen ordered the driver to drop him off nearby and walked the rest of the way. Rounding the corner of their street, he paused in amazement. Professor Brecht's house was dark and abandoned. The lower windows were boarded up roughly and the upper ones were gaping wide and broken, as if with stones. Jurgen walked into the neglected garden and waded knee deep in weeds. His eyes filled with anguished tears.

What has happened to them? Where have they gone? And why hadn't Ernestine written to tell me?

Kirsty Merrilees had found Singapura, City of the Lion, a fascinating mix of ancient and modern. There were elaborate colonial buildings, like the famous Raffles Hotel which fronted the shore, then there were air-conditioned restaurants, well patronized dance-halls and theatres, all mingled with alleyways leading to more traditional Malayan dwellings. Main streets policed by Punjabis and Sikhs in white turbans

225

and military uniform were also an odd jumble of gleaming limousines, buses packed with extrovert Chinese, lumbering oxcarts, rickshaws, bicycles and porters balancing loads on the ends of long bamboo poles. Edward had rented a white-walled villa on the outskirts of Singapore city with three smiling Malay servants to wait upon them. Kirsty led a leisurely life in the languid heat.

Her husband was often away from home, visiting rubber plantations which lay across a wide white causeway that ran straight as an arrow across Johore Strait to Johore and the Malayan peninsula. Peter attended a school for expatriate British children and had settled down well.

Kirsty might have felt lonely if Hannah Winslow had not introduced her to friendly embassy wives who invited her to a round of coffee mornings and light entertainments. She learned to play bridge and whist when summer heat or monsoon downpours made it impossible to venture out, and joined Hannah in the embassy pool, polishing swimming strokes learned in the Gowrie burn. Then, of course, there were the joys of golf, played at the Ladies' Golf Club. Life was easy and pleasant, and time passed easily and pleasantly. Troubled Europe seemed far away, yet cast uneasy shadows.

Edward and Kirsty had decided Sophie should travel to Singapore, but their daughter proved stubborn and refused to budge.

'She's scared of bugs, Mum!' Peter said wisely.

'No, Pete.' Kirsty frowned over her daughter's passionate reply to another letter begging her to reconsider. 'She says that now she's in fourth form she wants to study hard. She hopes to take a degree course at St Andrews University. Her heart's set on going there when she leaves school.'

'Why St Andrews?' Edward frowned. 'Last time we heard, she wanted to go to Edinburgh.'

Kirsty was suspicious. St Andrews wasn't far from Dundee, where Jurgen Murdoch was working in his father's business, Hannah told her.

'Anyway,' she said aloud, 'the news is better since Mr

Chamberlain and the German Chancellor signed a non-aggression pact in Munich. The Prime Minister says it means peace in our time.'

Edward looked doubtful. 'I hope he's right.'

Kirsty folded her daughter's letter and tucked it into the envelope. 'Well, let's wait and see what 1939 brings, shall we?' she said.

The year began happily enough with the embassy party, followed a month later by a whist drive for charity. Kirsty seized the opportunity to quiz officers' wives about the island's defences in the event of war. She was assured they were first-class. Gun emplacements guarded shipping lanes to east, west and south. To the north, the Malayan peninsula consisted mainly of 400 miles of impenetrable jungle, deep rivers and tangled vegetation infested with snakes, wild animals and mosquitoes. 'Not the place one would go for a holiday!' she was told.

'But safe from attack?'

'Oh, perfectly safe, dear!' a colonel's wife smiled. 'Besides, far eastern countries have been warring for years and are too weak to try anything. No need to worry. Shall we get on with the game? Hearts are trumps!'

As the year wore on, Kirsty found the hot, humid atmosphere unusually trying, and when yet another spell of dizziness and nausea sent her to the doctor, he confirmed her suspicions. She went home to Edward in a daze. 'Darling, we're going to have a baby!'

He greeted the news with mixed emotions. 'I'm delighted, of course, Kirsty love, but by the time this one's twenty, I'll be ancient!'

Kirsty hugged him. 'Think of the wisdom you can pass on to the child.'

'The poor kid will find me a terrible bore!' He studied her anxiously. 'But will you be all right, my darling? Maybe you should go home to have this baby. You could bring Sophie to Singapore with you after the baby's born,' he suggested in a flash of inspiration.

'No fear! You'll work too hard if I'm not here to keep an

eye on you,' she smiled, kissing his furrowed brow. 'Don't look so worried, darling! The doctor says everything's fine and I'll be well looked after. Once the baby arrives there'll be plenty of time to persuade Sophie to join us and meet her new brother or sister.'

Edward gave in at that point, reassured.

William Charles Merrilees was born seven months later, after an uneventful pregnancy. He weighed a respectable seven pounds and eight ounces and came into the world on a day that was to prove memorable ever after: 3rd September 1939. Hitler's armies had marched into Poland and Britain was at war with Germany.

Kirsty cried when the news broke. She hugged the tiny infant. 'Edward, why was our baby born on this particular day? It seems ominous. What does it mean?'

'A ray of hope for the future, my love.' He kissed them both. To tell the truth, Edward was scared. His three daughters were far away, facing the threat of air raids and gas attacks, and now he and Kirsty had a vulnerable infant to consider as well as a ten-year-old son. Still, his father-in-law's letter before this happened had been full of quiet courage. The old soldier had prepared for the worst. He wrote that he and Mildred had criss-crossed window-panes with anti-shatter tape and laid in a stock of blackout material.

> Not that we expect much enemy action here if war is declared. This is considered a safe area. The plan is to evacuate Edinburgh children to homes in Stirlingshire if war comes. I'm relieved Kirsty and Peter didn't attempt the journey home, Edward. You will be safer in Singapore. It is the jewel in Britain's eastern crown and will be well defended.

Peter, bless him, had greeted his new brother with delight. He hung proudly over the cot, fondly studying the dark-haired baby and holding one-sided conversations with him. 'I'm glad you're a boy, William. You can play with my toys when

228

you're older, though maybe not the penknife with the metal thing that takes stones out of horses' hooves.'

That made Kirsty smile. As she watched over her two fine sons, the future did not seem so black.

Not that war news became more encouraging as time went on. The Netherlands were over-run and Heinkell bombers swooped upon shipping in the Forth and Tay. Later, word came from France that a disastrous retreat had turned into something resembling victory on the beaches of Dunkirk. That was followed by a real threat of invasion as the rescued army desperately regrouped. But it didn't happen. The Battle of Britain was fought and won in the air and in the bombed and battered cities, but eventually the enemy lost patience, and turned their attention elsewhere.

Life in Singapore had gone on much as usual during these troubled years. The wives of soldiers and officials played whist and bridge at embassy parties and took coffee and cake in the Raffles Hotel. There were more soldiers on the streets and a greater concentration of naval ships berthed in Keppel harbour, but these were the only signs of war. On Edward's visits to the plantations, he reported that British, Indian and Australian troops were guarding strategic points in Malaya. 'I find that reassuring, Kirsty,' he said.

She frowned. 'But I thought it was mostly jungle.'

'Oh no, there are railways and roads, too. They're needed to transport latex and rice to the ports. Didn't you know?'

Of course, she should have thought of that! Touched by sudden fear, she glanced anxiously to the verandah, where Lia the Malayan nurse played with William. Their son was now a sturdy two-year-old. Thanks to Lia, who adored him, William's vocabulary was an amusing mixture of English and Malay. The wee boy's laughter echoed through the warm air as he and the little nursemaid played peek-a-boo.

Always sensitive to his wife's moods, Edward put an arm around her. 'Don't worry, love. At the first sign of trouble, we'll get out,' he promised.

But trouble came swiftly and unexpectedly and by mid-December 1941 Malaya was under attack, the important garrison of Penang had been evacuated and Japanese forces were advancing rapidly towards Johore, outflanking the defenders.

'How can they move so fast?' Kirsty asked Edward.

'Bicycles, my dear. Then artillery and tanks bring up the rear.' Edward had much on his mind. Air raids on Singapore city were much more frequent. That morning Morris Winslow had told him on the quiet to get his wife and family out. He'd offered them transport on an embassy vessel bound for Australia, but warned it was leaving Keppel that evening. Morris and Hannah would be on it, since he'd been entrusted with maps and documents which must not fall into enemy hands. Edward heard a rumble of gunfire quite close. It did not come from Singapore's meagre air-raid batteries or the gun batteries pointing uselessly out to sea. 'Pack some essentials quick as you can, Kirsty. We're leaving.' he said.

Hannah had been pacing the deck of the *Pandora,* looking out for them. She breathed a huge sigh of relief when she spotted the little family approach just as dusk fell. They had abandoned the car and were battling their way to the quayside through a milling crowd of desperate Chinese and Malayan refugees and panic-stricken British families.

Hannah shivered. Even safe on deck she could sense their fear. Gunfire lit the northern sky with firework patterns, strangely beautiful in their own deadly way.

Kirsty and Hannah embraced emotionally on a deck packed with embassy staff. William clung to his mother's skirts, whimpering. Peter stayed close to his father. The little boy hadn't said much, but his pallor was ample evidence of terror.

A great weight seemed to lift from Kirsty's shoulders as she heard the ship's engines throbbing. The crew cast off the mooring hawsers and she hugged her two sons. 'We're safe now, darlings!'

Morris appeared on deck, carrying lifejackets. 'Here, put these on!'

Edward drew him aside. 'This will frighten everyone, Morris. Is it necessary?'

'I'm afraid so. There are Jap submarines out there.' As he spoke he glanced uneasily towards the dark sea, waiting beyond the dimmed lights of the besieged harbour.

Sixteen

The lifejackets were clumsy and cumbersome. Kirsty helped Peter don his, but William lay down on deck and threw a tantrum when she approached. Though Kirsty struggled to calm the little boy, William was bewildered and exhausted and refused to co-operate.

Watching this distressing scene, Edward decided what his small son needed was peace and quiet. Kirsty, too, could do with a break after all she'd been through, and he saw with gratitude that Hannah was acting nobly by taking the tired wee lad off her hands. Fortunately the two women had picked quite a secluded corner of the deck. They'll come to no harm here in the meantime, he thought. He turned to Peter. 'Let's go round to the starboard side, Pete, and I'll show you the ship's guns,' he suggested, and father and son went off together along the crowded deck.

'There, there, darling.' Hannah crooned. She lifted William off the deck and settled him in her lap. She rummaged in the bag Kirsty provided and unearthed a clean nappy and bottle of orange juice. Soon William was comfortable again, contentedly drinking juice. By a stroke of good fortune, Hannah was wearing a blue satin jacket that day. Fleeing from the embassy, she'd had no time to change into something more practical and William's sleepy fingers fastened content-edly upon satin softness that was familiar. His lids drooped immediately and he fell fast asleep. Hannah rested her back against the metal superstructure and stoically prepared to endure discomfort.

'Let me take him now,' Kirsty offered.

'No, no. Don't waken the wee soul.'

Kirsty kissed her friend's cheek. 'You're a dear. I'll find some blankets to make you more comfortable.'

Kirsty searched, but there were no blankets to be had on deck. Impatiently she discarded her lifejacket at the head of a companionway and made her way below. It was hot down there, and she found the main saloon packed with embassy families and staff, mostly women and children and older men. There were no blankets to spare, but they told her that the *Pandora* was scheduled to rendezvous with a much larger ship waiting to uplift the refugees and take them to safety in Australia.

Meanwhile, the ship had cleared the damaged sea wall and picked up speed. There were smiles of relief as she pulled away from the island and even some joking and laughter.

A series of dull explosions reached them and portholes turned lurid for an instant as the northern sky was lit up with flames. Laughter faded as they stared at one another, appalled by this fresh horror. Most had left relatives, friends and faithful servants behind, and the rumbling explosions sounded deep-seated and ominous.

Kirsty ran into the passageway to investigate and met Morris Winslow emerging from his cabin. He carried a briefcase secured to a wrist by a short chain. 'What was that noise?' she asked.

'I suspect sappers will have destroyed the causeway over the Johore Strait to stop the Japanese crossing. It's the island's only link with the mainland.'

'Oh, Morris! Does that mean there's no hope?'

'Precious little if our forces have retreated to Singapore, Kirsty. Nobody expected an attack across land from the north! What are you doing down here anyway?' he frowned. 'We should be transferred to the *Iolanthe* soon.'

Briefly she explained her mission, and he took her to the crew's quarters, where blankets were available. They were returning down the passageway when a thunderous explosion rocked the vessel. The *Pandora*'s engines stopped abruptly with a hiss of escaping steam. A klaxon broke the eerie silence harshly and feet pounded above them as crew ran to action stations.

'Too late!' Morris muttered. 'Oh, my God, much too late!'

Kirsty took a few hurried steps, lost her balance and fell. To her consternation she found a trickle of water had soaked the blankets. She abandoned them as Morris hauled her to her feet.

'The ship's listing already. Let's get out of here.'

They hurried unsteadily towards the companionway as smoke drifted after them. An acrid stench of burning and high explosives hung in the air. Reaching the saloon doorway, they found the occupants awake to their danger and on their feet milling about in panic. Frightened children screamed and clung to their mothers, adding to pandemonium.

Morris stopped. 'We must get them out of there, Kirsty.'

'I can't help you!' she cried. 'I left William with Hannah and I don't know where Edward and Peter are.'

He grabbed her arm. 'Look, it won't take long, but these people are terrified. If there's a sudden scramble for the door those kids will be trampled underfoot.'

She turned and followed him. At least her family were on deck, but these poor souls wouldn't stand a chance if the ship went down. Fortunately, Morris's presence had a calming effect and the evacuation was accomplished smoothly, even with a touch of humour. When she'd helped to carry the last child up the companionway, Kirsty paused to glance back. To her horror, water was now knee deep in the passageway and lapping the bottom steps. Even as she paused, an urgent message blared out across the decks.

'Abandon ship! Abandon ship!'

Up on deck, they were confronted by a chaotic scene. An undisciplined mob of frightened people crammed every inch of space.

She turned to Morris frantically. 'You didn't tell me there would be chaos! How can I find my family in this?' she yelled at him.

'Listen, Kirsty, it's important we stay together . . .' Morris made a grab for her, but she'd already dived into the crowd. 'Wait! Your lifejacket!' Desperately, he tried to struggle after her.

Hannah had been dozing when the torpedo struck amidships. William stirred and whimpered. Struggling to her feet she soothed the little boy, settled him on her hip and stared around her dazedly. She was alone. Where's Morris? And where have Kirsty and Edward gone? Hannah wondered in a panic. Everyone aboard ship was on the move, pushing, shoving, milling around. Someone began screaming, a high-pitched, frantic sound that mingled with a tremendous hiss of escaping steam. Hannah pressed herself and William back against the superstructure and waited, confident Kirsty would appear soon. A klaxon was making a hideous din now, but presently it stopped. Several minutes later came a command that electrified Hannah.

'Abandon ship! Abandon ship!'

But how can I? she thought, staring round desperately and hugging Kirsty's child. Morris had only left her to go to their cabin, but he'd been gone ages. Where were they all? A massive surge of terrified people suddenly rushed for the boats and despite Hannah's protests she and William were carried with them. She came face to face with a burly sailor heaving women and children unceremoniously into a small boat. She hung back. 'No, no. I'm not going. I won't leave without my husband.'

'Orders, ma'am. Women an' children first.'

She resisted strongly. 'I refuse to go. You don't understand. You see, this child isn't—!'

'No time to argue, lady!' He pinioned her arms, heaved Hannah and William in and immediately cast the boat adrift.

Hannah fell heavily while trying to protect the child. William howled and there was a chorus of screams as the little craft rocked dangerously. Hannah pulled herself upright and hugged William, who seemed struck dumb with terror, but unscathed. The argument with the crewman had made Hannah unpopular. The other women glared and muttered resentfully.

'Man the oars!' she screamed at them. The boat was drifting helplessly, broadside to the choppy seas.

The oars were light, more like paddles, but at least they kept the boat moving head on to the waves with two women rowing. Hannah heard someone yell her name and glanced over her shoulder. She was shocked to find how low in the water the ship lay. To her horror, Kirsty was leaning desperately over the rail.

Her frenzied cries came echoing across the water. 'Hannah, Hannah! Please, please look after my baby!'

Hannah groaned and cuddled the silent little boy. 'Kirsty, Kirsty! Why didn't you come?'

Kirsty gripped the rail. She was too late, the boat was already carried away on a strong rip of tide. Morris had battled his way through the crowd to reach her. Taking in the situation with one horrified glance, he took her in his arms and she buried her face against his shoulder.

'Oh, Morris, I couldn't find Edward and Peter anywhere, and Hannah and William are gone!'

Hannah sighed with relief when she saw her husband at Kirsty's side. She'd feared the worst, but at least he was alive.

Aboard ship, Morris hustled Kirsty away. 'Come on! Get to the boats.'

She struggled wildly. 'No! I have to find Edward and Peter.'

'There isn't time!'

Morris spoke brusquely. He was a strong swimmer and his instinct was to take a header into the water and go after Hannah's boat. But he had no choice. Chained to his wrist were important documents relating to the defence of India. Those must be delivered to the War Office in London and at all costs must not fall into enemy hands.

And of course, there was Kirsty. Morris picked up the struggling woman and carried her screaming and kicking to the last lifeboat.

Brawny arms hauled her into the boat and Morris clambered in after her clutching the precious briefcase. Released hurriedly into the water, the boat bobbed in darkness on a black sea littered with the flotsam of disaster, then the sailors pulled away from the sinking ship.

Morris touched Kirsty's arm. 'The *Iolanthe* is bound to have seen what happened, Kirsty. Don't worry, she'll pick everyone up.'

She turned on him furiously. 'I could have gone back to Hannah and William and found Edward and Peter. I'll never forgive you for this, Morris Winslow!'

She huddled miserably, shivering in her thin jacket, but deep down she knew he'd only done what he could to save her, and when the huge bulk of the *Iolanthe* loomed out of the mist she knew they were saved.

A very lucky mist, the captain assured his rescued passengers, for it reduced the risk of submarine attack. He also declared he would not hang about searching for survivors till it cleared and low-flying planes spotted them. Although, he added gloomily, no doubt the Japanese pilots were back at base drinking sake and toasting the Emperor after the shattering news that had just reached him over the radio. The Singapore garrison had just surrendered on the evening of 15th February 1942.

He told them that he'd combed the area for survivors and picked up a few and now planned to slip away from Singapore island and set course for Australia. When they reached Sydney, they would proceed homewards to Britain by devious routes avoiding U-boats and picking up essential cargoes en route. Eventually they would head for the port of Liverpool and arrive in dear old blitzed and battered Blighty.

Kirsty walked the decks, but the search only confirmed what she dreaded. None of her loved ones was aboard. She stood at the stern and gazed at the ship's white wake stretching back into the mist as the captain made good their escape. They were out there somewhere, but mist clouded her eyes and shrouded her thoughts. She had never known such fear and loneliness. She knew Morris Winslow watched from a distance. She sensed his sadness and despair, as deep as her own. They were both heartbroken, this was no time for bitterness and blame. Useless, frustrated anger had cooled long ago.

'Morris?' she called tentatively. He crossed the deck and stood beside her.

'I'm sorry, Morris,' she said. 'I shouldn't have said what I did. It wasn't your fault.'

'Forget it. I understand.' Impulsively, he reached for her hand.

She stared into the darkness and voiced her greatest fear. 'Are they still alive?'

'Yes,' he answered confidently. 'I trust Edward's resilience to save Peter and Hannah's courage to bring William back to you one day. We must have faith in them, Kirsty. That's our only hope.'

Hannah's boatload of women and children had glided through a night of thick mist and scraped ashore next morning on a shingle beach goodness knows where. When the *Pandora* sank, they had tried to set a course for the *Iolanthe*, but the mist came down on their floundering efforts and a strong tidal race had carried the boat northwards into the Malacca Strait.

After they had scrambled from the small boat and lifted the children ashore, the women walked across the shingle and took stock of their surroundings. Someone spotted the roofs of military-style buildings and reported signs of life beyond the palm trees and thick vegetation that fringed the shore. The women cheered up and there were sighs of relief and a move towards the habitation. Hannah did not join the jubilation. Some sixth sense urged her to be cautious.

'The Japanese have reached Singapore and I expect they'll have occupied this place. We should get back in the boat and steer clear of it.'

Her companions stood in a united group. They were all wives of embassy employees of one sort or another and knew Hannah well, though not socially. She was already unpopular because of her argumentative arrival on their boat, behaviour which they had privately considered high-handed. Now they were all equal in adversity and she no longer held status as an embassy official's wife.

They dismissed her warning scornfully. 'Good heavens, Lady Winslow!' said one. 'If the Japanese capture Singapore no doubt we'll be escorted back there. Women and children are of no use to them, so they'll probably ship us home. The worst that could happen is we'll be detained.'

'Exactly!' Hannah had no intention of sampling the hospitality if she could possibly help it.

The others stood scowling resentfully, and she guessed they were thinking she considered herself too fine to mix with the wives of clerks and cooks. If they only knew!

'So you won't join us?' the leader said coldly. 'Then at least give us the boy.' She reached out to grab William.

Hannah hesitated. Maybe that would be the safest option for him. William eyed the stranger and howled, hanging on to Hannah's skirt, and Kirsty's pleading face swam momentarily before Hannah's eyes. She snatched the little boy away from the woman. 'Leave him! William and I will stick together.'

'Very well, Lady Winslow. I just hope you can live with your conscience,' their leader snapped. Without more ado the small group filed past her and headed for the enemy camp.

Left alone, Hannah rummaged in Kirsty's bag and discovered bottles of juice, packets of rusks, plenty of small cans of fish and meat and, thankfully, a can opener. She fed William and allowed herself a drink of juice and a rusk, then hesitated over nappies. They seemed a pointless encumbrance.

'Okay, William. You're a big boy now,' she told him.

'Okay, Ha-na,' he replied. In his newfound freedom he toddled happily at Hannah's side along a well-defined path leading off northwards.

Hannah went cautiously. She had no idea where they were and no clear plan of where they were going, except that India and comparative safety lay far, far away to the north. They met nobody, though she noted the jungle track was fairly well used, probably by Malay fishermen scared

239

off by recent fighting. The path did not stray far from the shore, which was fortunate when evening came. She decided a sandy strip of beach was preferable to dangers lurking in the undergrowth.

William approved the site and they bathed delightfully in the sea. Afterwards the sturdy little boy scampered naked along the sands with Hannah following, a warm wind drying her thin clothing. Seawater soothed her bare, blistered feet. She'd discarded high-heeled sandals long ago.

Before the quick darkness fell, Hannah had found a sandy cleft between two sheltering rocks and settled down, William cuddled in her arms clutching a corner of the satin jacket between finger and thumb. Exhausted, they both slept soundly, till strange voices and a sense of imminent danger wakened Hannah with a start.

She looked over the rock. There were soldiers everywhere, some resting on the sand, others moving like shadows in the dawn light. Hannah shrank back in her hiding place, but the slight movement had attracted attention. A face peered in and someone standing further back growled a question.

'It is a woman and baba, *Havildar*,' the soldier replied.

Hannah sat up. *Havildar* – Sergeant! She realised with relief that they were not Japanese, but were speaking a North Indian dialect with which she was quite familiar. She and Morris had lived outside Delhi for five years when Morris was on the Indian embassy staff there. With a quick ear for languages, Hannah had picked up enough of the local dialect to hold a reasonable conversation.

'Greetings, my friends!' she cried in the same language, which caused a mild sensation. More soldiers crowded round, but one, obviously the leader, came to the fore. Hannah rose, sleepy William clutching her skirts. She placed her fingertips together and salaamed to the sergeant. 'Greetings!'

He was studying her with surprise. 'You are a *pukka memsahib!*'

'Not so proper, *Havildar*,' she smiled. 'The baba and I are fugitives.'

'And I and my men are all that's left of the Indian

17th Division in this area,' he said heavily. 'One of our number, Mohan Singh, went over to the enemy and agreed our withdrawal and now we are prisoners without guards. They took our weapons, and ordered us to march north to Kuala Lumpur under a white flag with a safe conduct pass. They are diplomatic with the Indian army, you see, because they hope perhaps for an Indian alliance.' He shook his head sadly. 'It is a shameful situation for brave soldiers.'

'It is a wise man who lives to fight another day,' she said reassuringly. An idea struck her. 'Could we travel with you, *Havildar*? Would it be *pukka*?'

He studied her gravely. 'You are dark-haired and so is the child. You could pass for Pathans, but we will see about a *chuddur* to clothe and cover you and a shirt for the boy. If the Japanese notice, we will say you are the Jemadar's widow and child. There is an element of truth. Our lieutenant and his family were killed. I am leader now.'

Hannah glanced doubtfully at the little boy. There was a very long journey ahead for William, but maybe they had trucks. 'What is our transport, *Havildar*?' she asked.

His dark eyes glinted amusement. 'Our feet, *memsahib*!'

The fall of Singapore was a crippling blow to Britain and marked the end of British power in the area, although at least events in the Far East had brought America into the war.

Nearer home, the surrender had meant more worry and anxiety for the Murdoch family. Agnes celebrated her seventieth birthday in a sombre mood that spring. 'There hasn't been a cheep from Hannah since the Japanese captured Singapore, yet she was out there last time we heard,' she said worriedly.

'Communications are hopeless these days, love,' Dougal said.

'Only soldiers' mail gets through.' He was enjoying a birthday cake made with fresh eggs and a whole week's ration of butter and sugar. Much nicer than the cakes Agnes made with marge and dried egg powder.

'And wee Kirsty and her man were out there too, Dougal!'

his wife went on. 'To think I was pleased when Hannah told me. I thought Kirsty would bring our lass home.' Abstractedly, she carved another slice of the birthday treat.

'Please may I have another slice, Grandma?' Celeste asked politely, though her stomach grumbled impatiently. She hadn't tasted anything so nice in ages.

'Just a wee piece, then. I'm saving some for your mum.' Agnes slipped the bairn a generous hunk. She was proud of the good manners instilled into Celeste at St Agnes's school. Poppy had been set against sending her daughter as a day girl to the posh girls' school because Dougal had insisted on paying the substantial fees, but he and Agnes had won the day. The school situated in the former Angus House was so convenient Poppy hadn't a leg to stand on.

The cake had risen like a dream, she thought. It was sandwiched with her own strawberry jam and had a wee skim of pink icing decorated with hundreds and thousands, which were off ration – if you could get them. Agnes now wished she hadn't disposed of the hens when she became well-to-do. To make the birthday cake she'd had to grovel for half a dozen tiny bantam eggs from her neighbour, who happened to be the old flame Jamie had dumped in favour of wee Kirsty when that affair was going strong. The woman had control of black-market eggs, and made sure Agnes went down on her knees begging.

'We should count our blessings,' she said aloud. 'At least Jamie won't be called up. He's too important.'

'Too old, you mean.' Dougal grunted. He resented his son taking over the business and making decisions without consultation. You'd think I was old, he thought sulkily, and not a spry chap of seventy-four who's a valued member of Winston Churchill's Home Guard.

Like many Dundee businesses, Jamie Murdoch had welcomed an upsurge in trade since war broke out. The city had suffered such grievous losses in the Great War, Dundonians could hardly believe they were to be involved in another.

242

Even the town council was blinkered where war was concerned and half-hearted about providing air-raid shelters till a sudden rain of bombs caused deaths in the city and concentrated minds. Very early in the war, Dundee bairns had been evacuated to Edzell, Alyth, Forfar and other country havens, but most hated the foreign environment and were back playing on city streets within six months.

However, jute mills were working full-time to keep up with a demand for sandbags. Over four million had been churned out already by a mainly female workforce. Shipping and submarines in the harbour kept the shipyard busy with repairs, and conscription took care of aimless crowds of unemployed men hanging around corners in Hilltown, the narrow flavoursome Overgate and other Dundee howffs. Jamie Murdoch was pondering this upswing in the city's fortunes as he patrolled the wet, pitch-black streets of Blackscroft. In his role as Air Raid Warden, he was checking blackouts for chinks of light. A cheery crowd of female spinners coming out of a back shift at the mill gave him a rousing goodnight. He responded and grinned. Dundee was always a woman's town, Jamie thought. The men are going to war and their wives are the breadwinners. Nothing's changed.

He was glad to reach the civil defence post when the tour of duty ended that wet night. The entrance to the post was heavily protected by a wall of sandbags, although there had been no enemy action to speak of since the tenement in Rosefield street had been demolished with loss of life. A bad business!

It was lamp-lit and warm inside the disused storeroom. A kettle steamed on the primus stove and some of the lads sat around on benches hugging tin mugs of tea. Jamie's wife was dispensing it from the tea-urn. Elise looked up and smiled when he came in. 'Can I do you now, sir?'

The men laughed. 'Proper comedian your missus. She has Tommy Handley and ITMA off to a T, Jamie,' remarked one.

'To a cup of tea, Bert!' Elise said merrily, pouring out a cup for her husband. She added milk and a liberal spoonful of precious sugar.

Elise wore a Red Cross uniform and he thought admiringly how well it suited her slenderness.

'Look at this, Jamie!' Her eyes sparkled as she held out a paper bag. 'Buns! They were under the counter in Andrew G. Kidd's, but I am in nurse's uniform, so they slip them to me. If you search, you may find currants.'

Hot, sweet tea and a currant bun, what bliss! Jamie sat down beside his wife with a sigh of contentment. He suspected she'd kept none for herself, and was touched. He smiled. 'So how many broken legs in casualty tonight, my darling?'

'None, thank goodness. Only two sprained ankles, and what you call a "keeker", for a poor man who walk into a lamp post and now has one black eye. This blackout is very dangerous even though they paint the edges of the pavement white.'

'Well, at least Jerry can't see where he's going either,' somebody said.

Elise laughed. It didn't hurt to hear them talk about Jerry. They spoke openly in front of her, and that was good. Maybe they have forgotten I was once Jerry too, she thought.

It had been terrible for Elise just before the war, when the woman Jessie Jordan was unmasked in Dundee as a German spy. Jessie Jordan had opened a hairdresser's shop in Hilltown. She offered Vienna perms for ten shillings, and all the time was secretly sketching airfields and drawing maps and passing on information to *Abwehr*, the German secret service. Elise had to endure a wave of spite and nastiness after the woman was caught.

But I endured it, she thought, and I proved at Rosefield Street that I was British. I helped men dig out dead and wounded with my bare hands. Now, they have forgotten I was Jerry.

'Ready, Elise?' Jamie had drained the mug and was on his feet. They left the post to a chorus of cheery goodnights. Hand in hand, husband and wife picked their way along Blackscroft to Broughty Ferry Road. 'Sorry I couldn't bring the car, Elise. I've used all my petrol ration,' he said.

'No matter. This is good, walking hand in hand in the rain when nobody is awake but us two.'

'Yes, it's good,' he agreed. It had taken war to bring them together at the beginning, and another war to give him back the woman he had loved and married.

'I worry about Jurgen,' she said.

'So do I, love, now he's in the RAF.'

'No, Jamie, I worry not only because he flies on dangerous missions, I worry because he is seeing Kirsty's daughter.'

He wished she hadn't mentioned that name. Not now when they were so happy, working together. 'He's sorry for the girl, that's all. Goodness knows what's happened to Kirsty and her family in Singapore.'

'There is more than sympathy,' she said. 'Sophie followed him to Tealing aerodrome, close to Dundee. She is working on a farm nearby, so that they can meet.'

He shrugged. 'Why are you bothered? Sophie's a nice lass, darling.' Privately, he thought fate had taken a hand in the affair.

Elise paused. A late vehicle crawled past, masked headlamps casting dim reflections on the wet road. 'But what about the German girl he loved? What about Ernestine?'

'That was over long before the war!'

'I wonder. I have read her letters and also those he wrote to her. You remember they were returned undelivered?' She sensed disapproval. 'Oh, I know I should not do it, Jamie, but Jurgen was so sad. I had to know the reason and he would not tell me. Her letters were innocent, full of love, and so unaware of the dangers she faced living in Nazi Germany. I was terrified for her. I do not know what happened to Ernestine, but I do know Jurgen loved her. Maybe he still does, and that is why I worry for Sophie and Jurgen.'

He laughed. 'No need to worry about calf love, *Liebchen*. Jurgen has got over that.' Jamie put an arm round his wife to protect her. The night wind was cold and gusty on the open road beside the river.

Despite the horrible weather, Elise felt warm. The love

245

affair with George Rutherford was now a tender memory that haunted her sometimes. Jamie's forgiveness had never been put into words, but husband and wife were happy at last, united in war work.

It is wonderful to love a man faithfully and without guilt, Elise thought. She knew the anguish of living with the ghost of a lost love, and she would not wish that fate to fall upon her beloved son.

Kirsty Merilees had tired of blazing sunshine. She remembered the humid heat of Singapore and the burning heat of Australia like a continuation of purgatory. She was tired of poverty, although Morris had arranged a small handout of cash from the British Consulate in Sydney. The Australians were kind to the refugees. Her own sea-stained clothes were replaced and she now had a canvas kitbag stuffed with odd, ill-fitting garments that she donned every day without much thought of what she looked like.

Endless months had passed since she and Morris had escaped from Singapore. What she would have done without him, she couldn't imagine. Probably plumbed the depths and given in to despair long ago as the ship passed from icy gales in the South Atlantic to parching heat in Australia, from calm seas to tropical storms as the *Iolanthe* made slow and tortuous progress across dangerous oceans.

Often the ship lay inexplicably idle in foreign ports for weeks, then moved on fast, picking up cargo here, passengers there, flirting with danger everywhere.

Kirsty had grown tired of searching every port of call, hoping against hope she might find her lost husband and sons waiting there. Morris always accompanied her, but she sensed he walked beside her without hope of success. At first that had annoyed her, but as azure tropical seas gave way to cold Atlantic grey late in 1943, she too was tired of hopes raised, only to be dashed.

At last the *Iolanthe* made an approach to Liverpool, creeping cautiously through the Irish Channel where U-boats had claimed so many others. Morris and Kirsty stood on deck well wrapped-up against the cold, hardly able to credit they were nearing the end of their long journey.

'You know, Morris,' she remarked with a sigh, 'once I might have hoped Edward and Peter, Hannah and William would be waiting on the quay, but now I don't. I'm tired of hope, I have no energy left to hope with.'

'I know,' he nodded soberly. The cold, dark, November afternoon was not welcoming. There were no lights visible ashore, only misshapen silhouettes of bombed buildings against dark clouds. He shivered. 'So what are your plans?' he asked her.

'I don't have any. I don't know what to expect. My father is an old man. Is he still alive? I don't know. My daughter was just a girl when we left, now she's a young woman. I don't know what she looks like now and what her interests are. Oh, Morris!' she cried as a dreadful thought occurred. 'I could meet my own daughter in the street and not know her.'

'I know. I'll be a stranger to my two children. But it'll be all right, Kirsty. Trust me.'

She squeezed his hand. Trust him? He'd been her anchor and comfort! Her thoughts turned to William, her lost little boy, and to Hannah. There had been no word of them at any embassy in any port. She sighed. 'I hate bringing bad news to people I love, Morris. To Sophie, my father and Holly, and my friends at the Milton of Angus.'

Morris nodded gravely. 'You mean Hannah's mother and father, of course.'

She stared at him, speechless for a moment. 'You know?'

He smiled faintly. 'My dear girl, when I was recruited into Intelligence, my background was thoroughly vetted and so was Hannah's. I've known for years.'

'But you never said a word!'

'Why should I?' he shrugged. 'Hannah would have felt guilty and ashamed, and I didn't want that. Besides, there are secrets I keep and lies I tell in connection with my work. I'm no better than dear Hannah.'

'All those fibs, all that make-believe, and all for nothing!' Kirsty said.

He looked at her. 'She envied your background and your personality. She wanted to be just like you, and now I've met you I can understand why.'

'Oh, Morris . . . !' she said brokenly. The wind was icy cold against her skin. He leaned forward and kissed her gently on the mouth.

Seventeen

Morris's kiss had unnerved Kirsty. Their arrival in wartime Britain under a bleak November sky was a daunting experience, and she had persuaded herself it was no wonder emotions were running high. The port was unfamiliar, they had no means of identification and barely the price of a meal between them. Surely it was natural two weary travellers should find comfort in one another's arms?

After all, the two friends had turned to one another many times for comfort and reassurance during the uncertain months spent in Australia after escaping from Singapore. They'd discussed every topic under the sun while the *Iolanthe* underwent essential repairs in preparation for the lengthy journey home. They'd clung together in terrifying storms and howling gales, staggered hand in hand along heaving decks in terrible weather and donned lifejackets in mid-ocean when threatened by U-boat attack.

They'd been constant companions and friends for many months, but Morris's kiss had changed everything. Somehow, the friendship was damaged and both were uncomfortably aware of it. They had no idea whether Edward, Hannah and the two boys were alive, but the lost loved ones stood between them like a living presence.

Their friend the captain suggested they should contact the Salvation Army for help and lodgings while their official interrogation and documentation took place. Later, they were grateful for this sound advice and the warm clothing distributed in the Salvation Army hostel.

'So what now, Kirsty?' Morris asked, after all the red tape had been seen to and it was time to move on.

249

'I've written to my family in Stirling. They'll be expecting me any day. What about you?'

'I have documents to deliver in London first,' he said. 'After that I'll go to see my children. Mark and Deborah will be waiting at my parents' house. But what am I going to say to them, Kirsty? I don't know yet what happened to their mother.'

'I can't pretend it's going to be easy,' she sympathized. 'But I do know exactly how you feel. I have to find words to tell Sophie I don't know where her father and brothers are. I've written to her of course, but actually talking face to face will be awful. She'll be so upset. Then I must visit Hannah's parents with the same dreadful news about their daughter.'

'I wish I could come with you to the Murdochs, but the poor old souls don't even know I exist. The shock would be too much, I feel.'

He looked so troubled, she hugged him. 'Never mind, Morris. It seems a terrible mess right now, but maybe one day everything Hannah did will make sense.'

'You think so? I wish I could be sure, my dear,' he said sadly.

Sophie Merrilees had spent a week of precious leave as a land girl on the lookout for her mother, nose pressed against the windowpanes of Charles's house in Stirling. By Saturday morning she'd given up hope, and was slumped dejectedly in a chair. 'Why hasn't Mum turned up? I thought she'd be desperate to see us.'

Mildred looked up from a wartime breakfast of dried egg on toast. Dried egg wasn't too bad scrambled, but even when toasted the 'national loaf' tasted like doughy cardboard, in her opinion. 'Darling, she'll be asked endless questions and have to fill in masses of forms before they let her go. For one thing, she'll have no identity card or ration book.'

'And no family!' Sophie added tearfully. 'What's happened to them? Where are Dad and Peter and William? Oh, why is Mum all alone?'

Charles lowered the morning paper. 'That's the tragedy of

war, my dear. It separates husbands and wives and breaks up families. When your mother comes home I'm sure she'll have more news.'

If Mum ever does come home! Sophie thought, her patience almost exhausted. She'd intended to meet the train that morning and had decided against it. She just couldn't face another disappointment. Just as well too! she thought, her eyes on the clock. The train must have arrived by now and nobody had turned up. Sophie glanced up and down the street. It was nearly empty, apart from two or three men and one dowdy wee woman.

Mildred stood up suddenly. 'Can that be Kirsty . . . ?'

Charles stared. 'Oh, dear heaven, Mildred!' he said softly. 'It is!'

'That's Mum?' Sophie echoed incredulously. The stranger had paused uncertainly outside, obviously missing an iron gate and railings which had been sacrificed to the war effort, but now she was coming up the path. Sophie saw a middle-aged woman in an old overcoat, shabby even by wartime standards, fair hair showing strands of silver beneath a dark-coloured beret. Her only luggage was a small battered case and her face looked pinched and tired-looking, drained of colour by a bitter January wind. She bore little resemblance to the pretty, fashionably-dressed mother Sophie remembered, and yet there was something about the small figure which Sophie recognized instantly and could never forget.

In that telling moment, as she watched her mother wearily negotiate the path, she saw how much she must have suffered, and could only guess at the anguish she'd known. Sophie ran to the front door and flung it open, then stood motionless, not knowing what to say or how she should be feeling now. Then her mother smiled and held out her arms, and everything was miraculously all right.

'Sophie my darling, how tall you are!' Kirsty marvelled.

'Mum! Oh, Mum!' The two women fell into each other's arms, smiling, laughing and crying.

'You smell of Lifebuoy soap!' Sophie laughed, wiping her eyes.

251

'Salvation Army carbolic, darling! I haven't had a decent bath for ages!'

'We're only allowed five-inches of hot water, Mum. Coal's in awfully short supply,' Sophie explained happily. 'Grandpa painted a black line on the bath to make sure we don't take more than our share, but you can have ten inches, Mum darling, you can have a whole foot if you like!'

'Two feet!' beamed Charles, coming into the hallway with Mildred hard on his heels. His beloved daughter had come home, and there had been times in the darkest hours when he'd believed he might never see her again. Well, things are looking up! Charles thought optimistically. There was victory in the Middle East, mostly due to that excellent chap, Montgomery, and there was hope of a Second Front in Europe one day. Mr Churchill said they'd reached the end of the beginning, but Charles felt sure it must be the beginning of the end.

Charles studied his daughter with concern. He noted tell-tale signs of grief and knew she would go on suffering till she knew for certain what had happened to her husband and children. How helpless he felt in the presence of such sorrow, and how he pitied her!

'Welcome home, Kirsty dear,' the old man said gently, kissing her cheek. Then he took her cold hand and led her inside to the warmth.

Kirsty soon became used to life in wartime Britain. She'd been issued with an identity card, ration book and clothing coupons and had been fitted with a gas mask. She luxuriated in five-inch bathwater and precious Lux soap. Her silver-fair hair was trimmed in a neat pageboy and she went on an Edinburgh shopping expedition with Sophie which used up almost all the clothing coupons. Still, the results were worth it.

'Three cheers for the President of the Board of Trade, Mum!' Sophie enthused as Kirsty paraded for her in the dress shop. 'Mr Dalton ruled skirts must be two inches shorter to save material, and you have super legs!'

Kirsty had to agree that austerity suited her. Studying her reflection in the shop mirror, she decided a plain, tailored look made her seem years younger. Smiling happily, she thought with a sudden pang of sorrow, if only darling Edward could see me now! Closing her eyes, for a moment she could imagine he was watching approvingly. He wore the good humoured, quirky smile she loved and her spirits lifted as she opened them again. The sensation of his presence had been so vivid, surely that was a good omen? She smiled at her new younger image, but it suddenly blurred with tears and she turned quickly away.

While in the city, they seized the chance to visit Edward's twin daughters, but found only Pearl at home. She was now a busy wife and mother helping her husband in his veterinary practice.

'Ruby?' Pearl smiled in answer to Sophie's eager question. 'Oh, she's still hammering on the Vet College door, Sophie dear, but they refuse to let her in. She's never married, as you know. In fact, she's somewhere down south at the moment, helping to patch up poor animals and pets badly injured in the blitz. Such wonderful work she does! Can you imagine it, Kirsty?'

'Yes, knowing Ruby, I can.' Kirsty nodded. She knew Ruby Merrilees would be completely absorbed in her dedicated, heart-rending task.

'Did you know Daddy's business was forced to close down shortly after your grandmother Robb died at the ripe old age of ninety-eight?' Pearl went on. 'When trade with the Far East stopped there was no option but to go into liquidation. It does seem a shame, because Dad will have no business to come back to now, and I'm afraid there's more bad news, Kirsty. The Army requisitioned your house as its HQ and built bomb shelters and antitank defences all over the grounds when there was an invasion scare. They insist it's in a strategic position. Oh, Kirsty, isn't war awful?' She dabbed her eyes. 'We keep praying Dad and the boys are safe. Have you had any more news?'

'No, Pearl, nothing!' Kirsty admitted sadly.

*   *   *

253

Edward Merrilees had plenty of time to reflect on past events as he lay sick and exhausted in a safe hiding place on the island of Sumatra. He thought how odd it was that trivial decisions could have such disastrous consequences. Today, in between recurring bouts of fever and delirium, he whiled away time recalling events that had taken place before the *Pandora* sank. He marvelled at small decisions he'd made which had assumed enormous importance.

When William had thrown his spectacular tantrum, Edward and Peter had gone round to the starboard side of the vessel. There was not much to be seen on that area of the deck. It was damp and unpleasant and therefore less crowded. Peter was interested in the guns, but Edward was not impressed by the ship's fire power. He'd been about to suggest returning to Kirsty and William when one of the engineers came up on deck for a breath of air. The exciting beat of powerful engines echoed from an open doorway behind him.

'Oh, Dad, I wish I could go and see the engines!' Peter said.

The man overheard and smiled. 'So you can, son, if your dad agrees.'

'Please, Dad?'

Edward hesitated, then smiled, 'Oh, very well, Pete!' A small decision of incredible significance!

Edward and Peter had spent an interesting twenty minutes in the engine room and had just climbed the metal stairway leading to the upper deck when the torpedo struck. Edward was flung forwards with knockout force and Peter landed close by, dazed but unhurt. Peter told him afterwards he'd been faced with a terrible scene of injury and panic, while his father lay unconscious. The injured were screaming in agony and terrified people were scrambling away from a large hole blown in the deck.

A young man was crawling around nearby, groaning and muttering, 'Broken! Oh no! Please not broken!'

Peter had been panic-stricken. He needed help with his injured father and had called out to the young man. 'Are – are you badly hurt? Could – could you help us?'

He'd looked up. 'Just a tick. Lost my specs. Hopeless without them,' the young man answered. He pounced suddenly. 'Ah! Not broken, thank heavens!' He'd put on a pair of horn-rimmed glasses and took in the situation. 'Your dad?'

Peter had nodded tearfully. 'He's hurt. Please help me get him to my mum. She'll know what to do.'

Frowning, the young man had studied the destruction. 'Sorry. Can't be done. There's no way across that gap, and the companionway below us is blown to smithereens.'

Peter had begun to cry. 'What are we going to do?'

'First, turn off the waterworks, there's enough water in the sea, thanks!' the stranger had smiled cheerfully, then looked around more carefully. 'I say, we're in luck. If the ship does happen to sink we can use that life raft. It's big enough to hold three of us. We can just step aboard and head off into the sunset.'

'But what about my dad?'

'He's OK. He's coming round.'

Edward could hazily remember the escape from the sinking ship. He had regained full consciousness in the life raft. It was dark, but he could see Peter on one side, a stranger on the other. The stranger smiled, a glimmer of light glinting on horn-rimmed glasses. He was smartly dressed with suit, white shirt and old school tie, all very much the worse for wear.

'Good evening, sir,' the young man beamed politely.

'Oh, Dad, you're better!' Peter cried. 'This is Dobbie. He's an embassy clerk, he says. The ship sank, but he saved our lives, Dad.'

Memory had returned at that point, and with it the horror of their situation. 'Pete! Your mother and William!' He'd stuggled up and the raft rocked dangerously.

Dobbie put a hand on his chest and pressed him back down. 'They'll be okay, sir. Women and children were taken off first. There was a larger ship waiting close by to pick everyone up. Looks like she missed us in the fog, though.'

'So what now?' Edward demanded. He could see the

situation was precarious. The sea was calm at the moment, but if the weather worsened they could easily overturn.

Dobbie had his head on one side, listening. 'Don't worry, help is at hand . . . er . . . maybe!'

He'd started shouting, and presently a shadowy craft loomed out of the mist. Seen close to, it looked strange. It had a tall mast and huge angled sail which was furled on a long boom at the moment. A clattering engine propelled the high-sided vessel in a cloud of blue, evil-smelling exhaust. Dobbie changed from shouting in English to a torrent of fluent Malay and a row of curious faces appeared, staring down at them. The engine stopped in a gust of oily smoke and the junk wallowed and settled.

Dobbie had turned to Edward, grinning. 'We're in luck! It's Koti Tamah and his crew of ruffians. I recognized the sound of his junk's ghastly engine, but I feared the Japanese might have commandeered it. The game would've been up for us then.'

Peter's nostrils twitched. 'This boat smells awful, Dobbie!'

'Of course it smells awful! It's a fishing boat. It was my job to issue licences to fishing boats in these waters, which in Koti's case legalized profitable smuggling to which we turned a blind eye. In return, he did some useful spying for the embassy. A resourceful chap, old Koti Tamah!'

A rope ladder was flung over the side and willing hands had helped them aboard. They were safe for the moment. But that was months ago . . .

The tiny, malarial village where Edward now lay was not the healthiest spot. They'd arrived there eventually after many months spent fishing, cruising along the straits and spying upon the enemy. Koti Tamah had a brisk trade going with the Japanese army. Edward had been angered by this at first, till he discovered that the fishy delicacies Koti sold to high-ranking officers came from a toxic source. There had been an increase in food poisoning in military camps recently.

Still, the stress and danger involved in avoiding capture had not improved Edward's health. He went down with malaria and, although he had recovered after a fashion, was left with a troublesome pain in his chest.

Perhaps the eagle-eyed old Malayan had noticed his passenger's discomfort, or maybe the hurricane season was approaching, but whatever the reason, they had come ashore. 'In a safe place, *Tuan!*' Koti had assured him, grinning.

Koti was sitting cross-legged beside Edward's day-bed at that moment, fanning the invalid with leaves and seeing off flies with a flywhisk.

The malaria had returned, more difficult to fight this time. Edward lay sweating and shivering with alternate fevers and chills. There was no quinine, no Glauber's salt, nothing to combat the illness. His chest ached.

'It is fortunate indeed we brought you to this very safe place,' the old man said gravely.

Edward stirred. 'What makes you think it's all that safe? Our battleships are at the bottom of the sea, Rangoon has gone, the British army captured and humiliated and the Japanese are everywhere.'

'But they will not come here, *Tuan*,' he said confidently. 'They believe this is very dangerous leper colony. They came once and saw for themselves some bad cases and women and children heavily bandaged. All very ill and infectious.'

Resourceful chap! Edward thought. His mind felt clearer. The herbal concoction Koti's wife had given him must have reduced the fever. Koti Tamah kept the palm leaf moving gently. Koti had his own grave opinion concerning the *tuan*'s health, but prayed he would be proved wrong.

Edward watched the young man and the boy appear from the river bank where the boats were safely hidden. Dobbie had long ago cut the legs off his trousers, making ragged shorts which were tied round his waist with the old school tie. With escape from Sumatra in mind he'd traded the Austin Reed jacket for drums of diesel. The once white shirt was dirty-grey and smeared with oil-stains which blended nicely with a jungle background. He wore native sandals and was deeply tanned. Only the spectacles were recognizable.

257

Peter had become Dobbie's constant shadow. The boy had stretched during the last few dangerous months. He was tall for his age now and showed promise of being a handsome man one day. But will I ever see that day? Edward wondered with a lurch of the heart.

'The boat's ready, sir. We'll leave whenever you're fit,' Dobbie said.

The boat in question was an old naval whaler which Koti had produced from somewhere, no questions asked. It was twenty-five feet by eight feet beam with three feet of freeboard, powered by an ancient two-stroke engine, which Dobbie reckoned should be capable of seven knots on a good day. He'd told Edward he'd calculated it would take about six weeks to travel the 2,500 miles to India. Allowing for travelling cautiously by night till they'd cleared Sumatra, though more time could be lost dodging Japanese planes and transport ships en route.

Half a dozen Malayan saboteurs with a price on their heads had volunteered to come with them as crew. Edward knew perfectly well it was a hazardous, desperate journey, but their only hope of escape. If they stayed in hiding, sooner or later the Japanese would be back and they would be captured, and then he shuddered to think what would happen to the courageous people who had concealed them.

He knew he wasn't fit enough to make the journey. He knew he would be a hindrance and might ruin their chance of escape. Edward summoned a smile. 'I've been thinking. You and Peter must leave right away, Dobbie. I'll follow later when I'm stronger.'

'But, sir . . . !' The young man met Edward's eyes. He paused. They both knew caring for a frail elderly man would endanger them all. Dobbie nodded.

'I – if you're sure, sir.'

'Very sure, Dobbie.'

Peter was dismayed. 'You must come with us, Dad. Everything's ready. The boat's loaded with rice and fresh water, fruit and dried bananas and four drums of diesel. We can catch fish on the way, too. Dad, you've got to come!'

258

'Later, Pete. When I'm better.' He searched in a pocket. 'Here, son, you'll need this.'

Peter's eyes widened. 'Your compass!' He had coveted it, but never expected to own one of his father's most prized possessions. He hugged Edward emotionally. 'Gosh, thanks, Dad!'

Edward held his son in his arms one last time, then gently let him go. 'When you find your mum, kiss her for me, and Sophie and wee William, too. Look after them till I come home, will you, son?'

'Okay, Dad. I will,' he promised, struggling not to shame himself and cry.

'Goodbye, sir,' Dobbie said in a voice gruff with emotion.

'Look after him, Dobbie. Take him safely home,' Edward said quietly as the men shook hands.

'Don't worry, I will.' He paused a moment as if he might say more, then straightened his shoulders. 'Come on then, Pete.'

Edward watched them go. They turned and waved, and he smiled and waved back cheerfully, though the effort was almost too much. The fever was returning, but Edward closed his eyes and felt at peace. Kirsty, my dearest love! he thought. He was so sure she was alive and had survived the shipwreck with William. He could see her smile, he could hold her hand and kiss her smiling mouth, she felt so near, so close . . .

'Next time I go out in the blackout I'll take you with me, George. You're wizard in the dark, being blind,' said Celeste, Poppy Murdoch's young daughter. Celeste had grown in beauty and grace over the past few years, but had taken a tumble outside the lodge, running through the pitch dark at full pelt with news for George that wouldn't keep. Both knees were skinned and there were two large holes in the long black school stockings, which would make her granny weep.

George had provided a first-aid kit and Celeste was busy patching her knees with sticking plaster. 'I'll have to take my stockings off. Good job you're blind, George,' she said cheerily.

259

'It has its advantages,' he agreed.

George Rutherford was a different person from the morose man Elise had left behind when Angus House was sold. That was mostly due to this eleven-year-old bundle of mischief. Celeste had taught him to speak French, not very well it had to be said, but he'd persevered because he sensed it was important to this fatherless child. They spoke English more often nowadays and that gave George a quiet sense of satisfaction. Gradually, despite the blindness and without intending to, he had become her father-figure. Not quite the blameless, saintly father crowned in glory that Joel D'Arcy remained in his daughter's imagination, but still, an easy-going, reliable dad who could dry tears, enjoy schoolgirl jokes, provide additional sweetie coupons and first aid when needed. Oh yes, and more frequently these days, share confidences about boys. He dished out good advice in that direction, which George suspected was seldom heeded.

'Gran's had a letter from that Kirsty woman,' Celeste said.

'I had one, too. She's coming to stay with me.'

'Just invited herself here? What cheek!'

'Make allowances, Celeste. Kirsty's my sister and we haven't seen one another for years,' he said mildly.

Her bare legs patched, Celeste slid off the seat on to the rug beside the dog. Biddy, George's present guide dog, was a favourite of Celeste's, being female. 'I wish I had a sister. Or even a brother,' she sighed. 'Everyone in my class has one. Even Biddy has two dog brothers and a bitch sister, and I'll never have any.'

'I wouldn't give up hope. Your mum may marry.'

'No, she's ancient, she's nearly forty.' She hugged her knees. 'But I will have dozens of children. You just wait till you see my beautiful children, George!'

'I only wish I could, my dear,' he said gently.

Kirsty was nervous when she stepped off the train at Invergowrie station. Looking round, little had changed, yet she knew that beneath the surface everything had. She herself had changed into quite a different person.

'Kirsty!' A man stepped forward to greet her, and she stared for a moment before recognition dawned.

'Sam!' She hugged her brother emotionally. 'They told me you were a very busy Glasgow surgeon. I didn't expect to see you here, Sammy!'

'The bush telegraph told me you were staying with brother George for a spell, and I had a free weekend. It's time we Rutherfords got together, Kirsty!'

Sam was right. It was a heart-warming experience to meet her two brothers again. Sitting round a cosy fire in the lodge, Kirsty noted that it was a very masculine dwelling now, apart from a few bedraggled ox-eye daisies in a jam jar, sitting prominently on the mantelpiece. There were no signs of Elise's presence now.

'It makes me sad to see the state the old house is in,' she remarked. 'Why on earth did the Murdochs sell Angus House to a school? They should have known that would mean hockey pitches and tennis courts in the grounds and extra classrooms and kitchens built on. Heaven only knows what it's like inside!'

'My friend Celeste tells me the gymnasium is wizard,' George said.

'Yes, of course. Poppy Murdoch's child is a pupil there,' Sam said thoughtfully. He studied his older brother with a doctor's observant eye. George seemed content with his lot, which some might consider a sadly unfair one. There had been rumours of an unhappy love affair a while ago, but if rumours were true he'd recovered well and seemed happy now. Sam glanced at the jar of wilting daisies obviously arranged by a childish hand just above George's head. They somehow radiated a possessive air. Eyeing the flowers, he wondered about this fatherless child who'd befriended George. Poppy Murdoch's daughter! How strange. He could remember Poppy when she was not much older than Celeste.

Elise Murdoch had never been happier, despite the war and shortages and concern about her dear son in the RAF. By

261

April 1944 Jurgen's squadron of Hurricanes had been transferred south, much to the distress of Sophie, his sweetheart.
Sophie had joined the Land Army when women over eighteen
were called up for National Service and had managed to
follow Jurgen to Tealing aerodrome just outside Dundee.
But she could not follow this time.

There was something in the wind. Polish soldiers had
guarded the Angus coastline since Dunkirk, regrouping and
training, but were suddenly not to be found. Free French and
Norwegian submarines based in Dundee Harbour were in a
state of readiness. Home Guard, ARP wardens and all other
voluntary services were quietly preparing to take over more
onerous duties.

'But nobody says anything, Jamie, because careless talk
costs lives,' Elise said seriously as she walked along Dundee
High Street with her husband. 'That is why "Salute the
Soldier" week is a good idea. It will raise money to win
the war.'

The April morning was mild and sunny. They were heading
for City Square to organize 'Salute the Soldier' displays. They
were both in uniform, Jamie as ARP warden and Elise as Red
Cross nurse.

Oh, I am so happy when we work together! she thought.
She reached for her husband's hand and squeezed it to assure
him of her love. He returned the pressure, smiling. So happy!

And then, quite unexpectedly outside Burton's 'fifty-
shilling' Tailor, they met Kirsty Merrilees. The place, time,
and date were in Elise's memory forever after, because that
was when happiness ended.

'Kirsty! Mam told me you'd arrived safely in this country,'
Jamie exclaimed delightedly. Then his expression sobered. 'I
heard about the loss of your husband and the boys. I was
so very sorry, my dear.' He had dropped Elise's hand to
clasp Kirsty's. Maybe it was just a spontaneous gesture of
sympathy, but oh, how it hurt!

As Elise stood watching, her heart was sinking. You are a
fool, Elise! she thought. Fool to think he could forget. Fool
to think he would stop loving her.

Kirsty caught sight of Elise's expression and withdrew her hand. She had seen Jamie and Elise approaching before they had noticed her, and they had looked so happy together she hadn't wanted to intrude. Looking around desperately for some means of avoiding them, she could find none, and now as she'd feared, meeting Jamie and his wife had reopened all the old wounds.

'I'm so sorry about Hannah, Jamie,' she said awkwardly. 'It's been two years since I last saw her and I've heard nothing since. I keep telling myself she's a survivor. She has to be! My little boy was with her, you know.'

Elise was sad for her. She touched her arm with genuine sorrow. 'Kirsty, I am so sorry. You must miss him so much.' It is a terrible thing to lose one's child, she thought, remembering how she had cried when Jurgen went to boarding school, how empty life had seemed for a while. But that was nothing to this!

She could see the shine of tears in Kirsty's shadowed blue eyes, but grief only enhanced her beauty. Who could compete with such charm? Elise turned to Jamie, suddenly desperate to get away. 'Jamie, I'm sorry, but we should go now. We are late and they will be expecting us.'

He said goodbye, but Elise sensed his reluctance to leave. She knew it was wrong to feel jealous of Kirsty Merrilees, but could not fight it. That was when Elise realised that her brief spell of happiness was over, and she could do nothing about it . . .

Kirsty went on her way, her eyes filling with tears after the encounter. Meeting Jamie and his wife, so happy in one another's company, had been a very emotional experience for her. The sight had accentuated her own loneliness and made her long for Edward's comforting presence. The touch of Jamie's hand had roused emotions she'd believed long dead, and all the time she'd been aware of Elise standing silent and watchful.

As she walked away, she recalled a telephone conversation she'd had with Sophie recently. Her daughter had been close to tears because Jurgen Murdoch's squadron was leaving Scotland. 'I don't know how I can bear it, Mum!'

'Do you love him so much?' she'd asked gently.

'Yes, I do. We hope to get married once this wretched war ends.'

'Then you must be patient and wait, Sophie. That's all you can do . . .'

But as she'd replaced the receiver Kirsty's heart had been heavy. She'd wondered how she would cope if her daughter married Jamie Murdoch's son. Now she'd met Jamie again, Kirsty was seriously concerned. She was shaking and tearful after the meeting and found the din of traffic and tramcars unnerving. Turning on her heel she headed quickly for the bus station, and a bus that would carry her out of the city's noise and grime into clean country air.

Next day, Kirsty decided she couldn't put off the visit to her foster-parents. Agnes saw her coming, and was standing with arms outstretched in the Milton doorway, beaming. 'Kirsty, my wee lamb!'

'More of a sheep now, Mam dear!' she laughed tearfully, hugging the kind woman who'd saved her life when she was a tiny baby and had been a mother to her ever since. Dougal Murdoch was next to greet her with a kiss. He was in Home Guard uniform and it was an emotional homecoming.

It would have been a happy one, if Kirsty had brought good news. All she could do was tell how they'd all become separated after leaving Singapore. She successfully avoided any mention of Morris Winslow, Hannah's husband.

When she'd finished, Agnes sighed. 'Well, they say no news is good news, Kirsty. It's some comfort to know our lass got away safely in a lifeboat with your wee bairn. We'll just have to hope and pray Hannah and wee William are safe.'

Dougal agreed. 'If only the ship that rescued you had seen them! But still. I'm hopeful they'll turn up one day, aye, and your man and young Peter, too.'

Agnes was on her feet, heading for the kitchen. 'On that cheerier note, let's have a cup o' tea.' Passing the window, she paused. 'Dougal, there's a man coming down the path, heading for our door.'

'Och, he'll be selling something. I'll soon get rid o' him.' He stumped off to answer the doorbell.

Left alone, Agnes put a hand on Kirsty's shoulder. 'It's grand to have you back, lovie, just grand. You know, I've always wished that you and Jamie—' She broke off as Dougal came hurrying back, looking flustered. 'It's someone for you, Kirsty.'

Her eyes widened when she recognized the visitor Dougal brought with him. 'Morris! What on earth are you doing here?'

'I had to come,' Morris Winslow said breathlessly. 'I had to tell you Hannah and William have reached India safely. There was a letter waiting when I arrived home. Hannah's exhausted and footsore, but ecstatic because she found our names listed with those who escaped to Britain on the *Iolanthe*. She says to tell you, Kirsty, that William is just wonderful.'

She hugged him. 'Oh, Morris, Morris! Thank God!'

Agnes collapsed in a chair. 'Hannah's safe and the wee one! I can hardly believe it.'

But Dougal frowned. 'If you don't mind me asking, who are you? Why would our daughter write to you?' He looked suspiciously at Morris.

Hannah and William were safe, that was all that mattered now, and Morris had had enough of charades and deception. Hannah's parents had been through enough; they deserved to hear the truth.

'I'm sorry, I should've introduced myself, Mr Murdoch,' he said gently.

'I'm Morris Winslow, Hannah's husband.'

Agnes stared. 'But Hannah isn't married!'

'It's true, Mam,' Kirsty broke in. 'Morris and Hannah have been married for quite a while.'

Agnes was bewildered. 'I don't understand, Kirsty. Why didn't Hannah tell us? Why keep us in the dark?'

Dougal Murdoch hadn't liked the way their lass had behaved the last time she came, and this latest development

265

had not surprised him. 'She's ashamed to own us, of course, that's why,' he said flatly. 'I saw this coming long ago. We should never have agreed to let her be educated in the big house. It gave the poor lass grand notions far above her status. Worst of all, it made her ashamed of her roots.'

'You mean she's ashamed of her mam and dad?' Agnes was deeply shocked. 'Oh, Dougal!'

Morris watched their distress helplessly. He should never have allowed things to go so far, and hurt these good people. He felt just as much to blame as Hannah. The past can't be undone, he thought with sudden inspiration, but there's always the future! He reached for his wallet. 'Look, Mrs Murdoch, look.' He pressed two photographs into Agnes's hand. She fumbled for her specs and peered at the images. 'They're lovely children. Who are they?'

'They're your grandchildren, ma'am,' he told her quietly. 'Mark and Deborah Winslow.'

'Hannah's bairns!' Agnes cried, a catch in her voice. Two grandchildren she hadn't known she had, two lovely children who had never known their Scottish grandpa and grandma! She hadn't cuddled them as babies, told them stories, sung them the old songs. She and Dougal had missed so much, and maybe, so had they. Her eyes ached with tears. She would find it hard to forgive Hannah for those lost years, gone forever . . .

Eighteen

Silently, Agnes handed the photographs to Dougal. She refused to meet Kirsty's eye, though the younger woman was watching anxiously. He studied the snaps intently, then glanced at Morris. 'You must be proud of them,' he said stiffly. Dougal too, was hurting.

'Yes, I am,' Morris agreed. 'They're a credit to their mother. Please keep the photos, Mr Murdoch.'

'No.' He handed them back. 'They're not ours to keep. I'll leave Hannah to decide that issue when she comes.'

The old man's dignity shamed Morris. He tucked the photos away. 'I'm sorry. I've upset you. Maybe I shouldn't have come.'

'It was a brave thing to do,' Dougal conceded. 'I can't pretend it hasn't been a shock to both of us. Still, I appreciate your honesty. It's high time this affair saw the light o' day.'

'Would you like a cup of tea?' Agnes offered tentatively.

'It's a very kind offer, Mrs Murdoch,' Morris said gratefully. 'But I'm afraid I can't stay.' He turned to Kirsty. 'I have to catch the London train this evening.'

Agnes looked concerned. 'London's dangerous! Those buzz-bombs are inhuman. They don't care where they land. Poor Londoners! When will it end?'

'Very soon now, we hope, Mrs Murdoch,' Morris said.

Kirsty followed him to the door after he'd said his goodbyes, hoping for a word in private. They stood in the shelter of the porch. Morris said, 'I like your hair. You look so young it's alarming.'

'A shampoo and set and shorter skirts can work wonders,'

she said lightly. His admiration was inappropriate but warming. She reached up impulsively and kissed him. 'Thank you for bringing me such wonderful news, Morris, and for the way you handled things with Agnes and Dougal. And thank you for loving and understanding dear Hannah.'

'Kirsty, about you and me—' he began.

'We clung together for comfort when it was needed, that's all,' she said.

Then she smiled. 'But I'll always be glad it was you, Morris!'

He took Kirsty's hands and kissed her. 'Goodbye, Kirsty my dear. I promise to keep in touch and badger the War Office to find Edward and Peter.'

Her eyes filled with tears. 'Oh, Morris, would you? It means so much!'

He turned away from the sight of her sorrow. It upset him. He took a deep calming breath of fresh air. 'It's so beautiful here!' he said.

'Yes. It's where I want to be, always,' Kirsty murmured.

The statement took her by surprise. She hadn't known she felt like that, till this moment.

The winter of 1944–45 was cold and hard. Allied troops fought their way across Europe through flood, ice and snow. Battles were fierce and success was not always guaranteed, but when the first hint of spring thawed the ice it was clear the war was won.

It was freezing in Poppy's shop too, despite a small electric fire at her feet. She was alone in the shop one particular day, towards the end of March. She had sent Ursula home with a sore throat that she had caught in the overcrowded tramcars and which Poppy had no wish to share. She wore a red shawl over a blue jersey, a faded green velvet skirt from her Bohemian days reaching from her waist to the tops of black boots large enough to accommodate a pair of her father's socks. Her long hair was bundled into a thick black hairnet, into which she'd absentmindedly stuck two paintbrushes. She was using a third to restore a modest blush to a Victorian maiden's faded cheek.

'Yes?' she said vaguely when the shop door opened.

There was no response and she painted on for a minute or two before looking up. The customer was a middle-aged man. He was studying cheap framed prints, which were all she risked on display in the front shop since a lone raider had strafed High Street during 'Salute the Soldier' week, cheered on by the crowds gathered in City Square, who had believed it was all part of the entertainment. Nobody was hurt, but windows had suffered.

'If you don't see what you want, sir, there's more in the back shop.'

'The front will do fine, thanks. I came to see you, Poppy.'

'Me? I don't know you, do I?'

He held out a hand, smiling. 'Samuel Rutherford.'

'Sam!' She came forward, hand outstretched. 'Fancy you remembering. I was a wee pest, wasn't I?'

'Yes, but a charming one.' He made no attempt to let go her hand. She took his breath away. It wasn't that she was pretty, or had made any attempt to be. Unusual garb gave her an old-fashioned look, unlike any other woman he'd ever met. And her hair! He smothered a grin.

'I like the paintbrushes – very oriental!'

She laughed. 'I say, isn't it wonderful that Hannah has escaped from Singapore with Kirsty's little boy?'

'Yes, wonderful news!' He let go her hand, which he realized he'd held far longer than was strictly necessary.

'What about you, Sam? Last I heard you were engaged. Are you married now?'

'No. Fate intervened. My intended met someone much more suitable during the Clydebank blitz. I gave them my blessing and soothed wounded pride by studying neuro-surgery. That's what I do now.'

'Neurosurgery? Gosh, that needs brains!'

They laughed together. Sam remembered suddenly how as a child she'd always made him laugh. There hadn't been much laughter in his life recently. 'Will you have dinner with me tonight, Poppy?' he said impulsively.

She paused, wondering what she was letting herself in for. His eyes hinted at much more than a simple invitation to dine. Then Poppy knew exactly what Joel would have advised. She imagined she could hear him whispering. *Go on, Kitten! Never turn down the offer of a free meal!*

She laughed and Sam smiled. 'Does that mean you will?'

'Yes, it does,' Poppy said happily.

It was 8th May 1945 and the whole of Britain was celebrating the end of war in Europe. Cheering crowds had gathered on London's battered streets, but the mood in the lodge of the former Angus House was very far from festive that memorable day. George Rutherford was suffering the stormy blast of Marie Celeste D'Arcy's anger.

'Why does she have to marry him, George? Him, of all people!' Celeste stormed, punching a fist into a cushion.

'Sam's a nice chap. Maybe your mum loves him,' George ventured.

'Who could love a man that studies brains?'

'Maybe if I had one I could—'

'Be serious, George! Why can't Mum marry you? I'd like to have *you* as my dad, George.'

'I'm very honoured, but a trifle old for your mum. Even Sam is stretching it a bit.'

'He's ancient!' Celeste looked disgusted. She flung the pummelled cushion at the wall. Biddy, George's guide dog, considered a retrieve, then thought better of it. 'I've had a father! I don't want another. Anyway, I've no intention of going to live with them in horrible, smelly Glasgow.'

'You may have to. Your grandma's not so young as she was.'

'Then I'll board at St Agnes's, and he can pay the fees.'

'We-ell, I suppose that might work,' George agreed, fighting down a small, unworthy glow of relief that she wouldn't be leaving after all.

*   *   *

Kirsty felt almost unbearably nervous as she waited at Stirling railway station. The London Express was due any minute and on it would be Hannah and William. It was three years since she'd last seen her son. He was five years old now and would almost certainly have forgotten his mother. He would not even recognize her.

She walked restlessly up and down. There were election posters pasted over faded wartime ones. When the war ended the Government lost no time calling a general election. She supposed they had to. The country was exhausted, everything was run-down, broke and nearly bankrupted.

The train was coming, a great steaming monster whose vibration shook her to the core as it rumbled in. She was still shaking after it had stopped.

Hannah appeared briskly. Oh, she was so thin and pale! Kirsty thought. She had forgotten how tall Hannah was, too. Hannah lifted down a little boy who could easily have been Hannah's son. He stood on the platform beside a small brown suitcase, looking apprehensive. Hannah took his hand and spoke a few comforting words.

Kirsty's mouth had gone dry. She waved. 'Hannah!'

Hannah's thin face lit up. She picked up the case and hurried towards her, holding William's hand. 'Kirsty dear!' They hugged tearfully. The boy stood aside, watching silently.

Kirsty turned to William. Her instinct was to hug him joyfully, but something in the wary little face warned against it. She smiled, touching his dark hair with a light caress. 'Welcome home, William.'

Suddenly shy, he turned to Hannah and whispered in a strange language. She laughed, noting Kirsty's baffled expression. 'William speaks fluent Hindi. He's heard nothing else for years. In fact, he prefers it to English. Anyway, he thinks you look golden and shining, like *ghee*. That's butter!'

'What a lovely compliment – I think!' Kirsty laughed.

She picked up the suitcase and took William's small hand. Hannah held the other, and the two women walked out into the sunshine, the silent child walking between them.

271

Hannah insisted she should stay only one night with Charles and Mildred. 'No longer, Kirsty,' she said, as they lingered by the fireside long after the rest of the household had gone to bed. 'It's kind of the Colonel to ask me to stay, and it's a terrible wrench leaving William, but the sooner I'm gone the sooner he'll adjust to his new surroundings.'

'I'm frightened, Hannah,' Kirsty confessed. 'How will I cope when you've gone? You and William have been through so much together, how can I possibly measure up to you? You saved his life.'

'No, I didn't!' she protested. 'It was those wonderful Indian soldiers who saved us both, because the Japanese were allowing them to trek northwards under a flag of surrender. Those men carried William when he was tired, though they were exhausted themselves. They went short of food so that we could eat and hid us from danger at great risk to themselves. They helped us cross the mountains to safety in India. Please don't think I'm brave, Kirsty, because I'm anything but. I couldn't even face the truth about myself and my own background.' She covered her face with her hands and broke down, weeping bitterly.

Kirsty put an arm round her shoulders. 'Hannah dear, it's all right, don't cry. Morris made everything all right.'

'I know. He told me.' She lifted a tear-stained face. 'But oh, Kirsty! How can I face Mam and Dad after what I did to them?'

'Why don't you take Morris and the children with you when you visit? That would be a good place to start,' Kirsty suggested.

Hannah smoothed her skirt with thin, nervous fingers. 'Morris admires you, you know, Kirsty, but I'm too tired to pretend to be you any more. I'm afraid the poor darling's stuck with Hannah from the Milton.'

She laughed. 'I shouldn't worry, my dear. Admiration's flattering, but it's Hannah from the Milton that Morris loves.'

Kirsty couldn't tell how William felt when Hannah said goodbye, because he didn't even cry. The small, serious face with its fading tan remained quite impassive as Hannah hugged him tearfully then climbed aboard the train.

Hannah had been at pains to explain to him that she was not his real mother and had only taken care of him till he reached home. She had assured Kirsty that the little boy had seemed to understand perfectly. Even so, tears would have seemed natural as the train pulled out of the station taking his beloved companion of the past three years from him. He remained dry-eyed and didn't object when Kirsty took his hand and led him gently outside.

'Let's buy some sweets, William!' Kirsty suggested brightly, the jovial tone sounding artificial even to her own ears. She'd saved sweet coupons for him, but sweets were in short supply and a long queue waited outside the sweetie shop. She hesitated. 'Oh dear, William, I'm afraid we don't have time to wait,' she told him, walking on.

If William was disappointed he didn't show it. She only wished he would. She would have welcomed tears and protests, anything rather than this dull, unnatural apathy.

When they stepped into the hallway they were greeted by a rattling clackety-clack which startled William out of his silence. 'What's that?'

'Your grandpa's typewriter.' She gave him a gentle push towards the study. 'Why don't you go and see?'

Charles stopped typing to smile at the solemn child. 'Hullo, William.'

'What are you doing?' William asked in careful English.

'Writing my memoirs.'

'They are very noisy.'

'Oh, they are! You should read 'em!' Charles laughed.

'I only read small words in big writing.'

'That's jolly good for five. One day when this is finished, you can read all about the days of my life. I'm writing this for you young ones, so you don't go and do the daft things I did.'

William didn't quite understand the sentiment, but the old man sounded kind. For the first time, William smiled. 'Grandpa,' he said, experimentally.

More than anything Kirsty had been dreading bedtime. Hannah had tended William last night, but now it was her turn, and she felt inadequate and close to tears as she gently washed the scarred little body. 'Ulcers better now,' he said matter-of-factly.

The small suitcase was pitifully empty, just a few items of warm clothing Hannah had bought. No toys. Kirsty helped him into pyjamas and tucked him into bed. He lay looking at her with huge eyes. 'I hate the dark,' he said in a small voice. 'It gives me bad dreams.'

'Then I'll leave this little light on till morning,' Kirsty promised.

'Will you sit beside me?'

'For as long as you want, my darling.' She sat down, smoothing a lock of tousled hair out of his eyes. Her love was so deep it was beyond the power of words, but surely he must feel it? He lay quietly watching her till his eyelids drooped and his small clenched fists gradually relaxed their grip. Kirsty picked up the tattered scrap of faded blue satin he'd dropped.

William smiled in his sleep. 'Home now, Mum,' he said quite clearly.

Soldiers and civilians had had enough of the old establishment. They'd even had enough of the man who'd led them through the darkest of days. People were weary, shabby and hungry, and wanted no reminders of the war. After the general election, Winston Churchill was out and Clement Attlee was the new Prime Minister.

There were also changes coming in Kirsty's own life. Not long after the end of the war in the Far East, she received a letter from Morris. He wrote that her beloved Edward had died peacefully in Sumatra in 1943. She'd been a widow for many months, and hadn't even known.

Reading Morris's kind words offering sympathy and support, she couldn't hold back tears. Her heart ached for Edward, dying alone and so far from home. She'd never known such desolation, grieving for Peter, too. There was no word of his whereabouts, though Morris urged her not to be too despondent. Information about survivors was still extremely scrappy and confused. She took no comfort from it. How could a young boy possibly survive all on his own?

She had to deal with her grief and find strength to comfort Edward's distraught daughters. It was fortunate for Sophie that Jurgen Murdoch had been demobbed from the RAF and was back home in Dundee. They turned up in Stirling a few weeks later with news that helped to cheer everyone.

'We're getting married, Mum!' Sophie announced happily.

'Darling, that's wonderful!' Kirsty hugged her daughter, then the tall young man. 'Congratulations, Jurgen.'

Charles beamed. 'A wedding is just what's needed. Get the champagne glasses out, Mildred.'

'No point, dear. There's no champagne.'

'Yes, there is. I buried a bottle under the Anderson shelter. Where's my spade?'

'Wait! I'll give you a hand, sir!' Jurgen offered eagerly. It was a relief to laugh at the eager pair. Even William joined in the laughter, though he didn't know what all the hilarity was about. Sophie hugged him. 'You'll be my pageboy, dear wee brother. You'll wear the kilt.'

'The quilt?' he squeaked in alarm.

There was more laughter at that and Grandma Mildred, who had consideration for a boy's feelings, took him on her knee and showed him pictures of brave kilted warriors.

Kirsty's thoughts turned to wedding plans. 'Sophie, I wonder if my mother's wedding dress would fit you?'

'It's stored in a drawer in the spare room,' Mildred added. 'Dear Mrs Robb made me custodian of the family treasures.'

'Sorry, Mum. It's much too small and the veil's too long.'

Sophie was secretly thankful the old-fashioned dress didn't fit. She had her own plans. Jurgen had given her an RAF parachute and one of her friends had offered to make a wedding gown from its silky white folds. Kirsty swallowed her disappointment. She herself had refused to wear that lovely dress. Now she could sympathize with Grandma Robb!

After the two men had returned in triumph with an earth-encrusted bottle, Jurgen turned to Kirsty. 'Did you know that my father has sold the old mill on Angus estate and transferred the machinery to our Dundee works, Mrs Merrilees?'

'No, I didn't, Jurgen,' she frowned. This was not welcome news. 'How are your grandparents taking it?'

'Not well, I'm afraid. Grandpa's resigned as company chairman. I guess it was his form of protest.'

'Angus House gone, and now the mill!' she said sadly. Where would it end?

In the following weeks Kirsty tried to adjust to a future without Edward. How she missed him! The Territorial Army wanted to buy their Edinburgh house, and she let it go with few regrets. Once the sale was accomplished she took stock of her finances. She saw that in order to make ends meet and educate William she must find a job and somewhere to live that wouldn't cost the earth.

'Why not make your home with us, my dear?' her father suggested.

'We'd love to have you and wee William,' Mildred added.

'It's tempting, but . . .'

Kirsty studied the elderly pair thoughtfully. Her father sat at the typewriter drafting another chapter of the memoirs. His wife was helping, dipping into a heap of reference books. They looked happy and self-sufficient. If they had needed her she would have accepted her father's offer without hesitation, but they were in excellent health and well looked after by Florence, their faithful housekeeper. Their happiness only served to heighten Kirsty's loneliness and isolation. Yet William needed a home. William must have a settled place to live after all he'd been through.

'First of all I'll take William to meet his Uncle George, Dad. We can stay in the lodge,' she said. 'Maybe after that I'll be able to make up my mind what to do.'

'Uncle George, is it dark in there?' William asked curiously, perched on George's knee, peering into his uncle's blind eyes.

'Very.'

'Aren't you scared?'

'I was at first. Not now.'

'Maybe no shadows in there,' nodded William wisely.

'Right. No shadows in there and Biddy to guide me along.' His hand reached for the dog, who snuffled lovingly against his fingers. He turned to Kirsty. 'Actually, I'm glad you came, Kirsty. There have been big changes here and I'm leaving the lodge. Biddy and I are going to Forfar.'

'Oh, George!' She was dismayed. 'Whatever for?'

'That's what I said,' Celeste butted in sulkily. Celeste had been unable to resist George's visitors. She found she liked Kirsty on better acquaintance and William was everything she'd longed for in a small brother. Her mother and Sam's marriage had not produced babies, although they were obviously so happy together. Sam was working in a Glasgow hospital and Poppy was a dedicated career woman who'd just opened an art showroom in Glasgow. They were hopeless! Celeste thought in disgust.

'The Murdochs have sold the mill and the estate,' George explained. 'My tenancy's secure because the lodge is a separate entity, but I'm leaving anyway. There's a venture which has started in Forfar to train guide dogs for the blind and they could use my experience with my dogs to help other blind people to adapt. It's worthwhile work, Kirsty.'

'It sounds perfect for you, dear,' she agreed warmly. She glanced out of the window at the old house. The school had cut down more trees to erect an ugly Nissen hut. Poor dear, shabby house! The sight brought tears to her eyes.

'What about me, Kirsty? George never even considered me!' Celeste grumbled as she accompanied Kirsty and William on their visit to the Milton.

'Forfar isn't far, dear. You can hop on a bus and visit him anytime.' She glanced down at the despondent girl. 'It'll be good for George to get away from here, Celeste. In your heart of hearts, you must know it.'

'I s'pose.' She kicked moodily at the muddy path, and swallowed horrid, lonely tears.

Agnes was waiting at the door, arms outstretched for William. 'The wee lamb! The bonny pet!' He suffered kissing and hugging with good grace. The fuss was rather nice, if confusing. Was this yet another grandma? William wondered. He was intrigued to find this grandma's room was in chaos, chairs stacked on a table, their footsteps hollow on uncarpeted floors.

'Goodness, Mam! What's going on?' Kirsty asked in astonishment.

'We're flitting!' Agnes replied. 'Me an' Dougal are flitting to Buckingham to be near Hannah and the grandchildren now the mill's gone and there's nothing to hold us here. There's been time wasted and precious years lost, Kirsty love, and we intend to make up for it.'

'Of course you do, love.' Kirsty hugged her. 'I think you're very brave.'

'Oh, michty me, Kirsty, so do I!' Agnes said grimly.

They turned at the sound of footsteps behind them. 'It *is* you, Kirsty! I was sure I heard your voice, but I thought I must be dreaming!' Jamie smiled. His shirtsleeves were rolled up and he wore an old pair of dusty dungarees. Apart from flecks of silver at the temples, he looked scarcely a day older than the young man she'd once loved and lost.

Kirsty pushed her small son in front of her to hide her confusion. 'This is William,' she said awkwardly.

'He's sweet, Uncle Jim,' Celeste added. 'I'm adopting him as a brother.'

Jamie shook William's hand solemnly. 'In that case, welcome to the family, William.'

He met Kirsty's eye. 'I'm delighted Jurgen and Sophie are to be married, Kirsty. Aren't you?'

She hesitated. Of course she was pleased her daughter was getting married, but she wished it had been to anyone but Jamie's son.

'I'm pleased Sophie is happy,' she answered carefully.

'Which doesn't answer my question,' he noted grimly.

Tactfully, Agnes removed William and Celeste upstairs to examine old toys and bits and pieces, leaving the two of them to sort out old scores.

However, Jamie didn't purse the matter. He smiled lightly. 'I gather from Sophie this wedding is to be the grandest affair Stirling has ever seen.' He paused a moment, then went on a little awkwardly, 'Forgive me, Kirsty, but I know Edward's business failed and you're not well off. Will you let me foot the bill?'

Her eyes flashed with temper. How dare he! The offer was insulting. How could she hand over plans for her daughter's wedding to Elise Murdoch? It was unthinkable! She forced a smile to hide her anger. 'Thank you, but I'll manage.'

He shrugged and turned away. 'OK. Let me know if you change your mind. Now, on with the flitting!' And he lifted a cardboard box and marched outside.

Kirsty was still undecided about the future when she returned to Stirling, but at least she had plenty to occupy her mind. 'We have a wedding to plan!'

'Oh, what fun!' Mildred beamed. 'You know, I always thought Sam and Poppy let us down with that quiet little wedding in a Glasgow registrar's.'

'Well, I intend to have a wonderful white wedding with all the trimmings!' Sophie declared. She had been demobbed from the Women's Land Army and was back in her old room in her grandparents' house, much to Kirsty and William's delight.

'I must admit, the parachute wedding gown is gorgeous,' Kirsty said.

'Yes, isn't it? The veil was a problem till I remembered the muslin screen in your bedroom window, Mum.'

'I wondered where it'd gone!'

'It's perfect with Great-grandma Robb's tiara,' Sophie went on. 'Buffy's demobbed from the ATS and I've asked her to be bridesmaid. She says she could take her mum's evening gown to bits to make a bridesmaid's dress, so I said OK, go ahead. Then there's William's outfit. A green velvet doublet with the kilt, I think.'

'I wanna soldier kilt, not a sissy one,' William protested.

'And a soldier kilt you shall have, dearest!' Sophie laughed, kissing him.

Jurgen Murdoch had settled down to civilian life. He enjoyed working in his father's mill and looked forward to marrying Sophie. His future was predictable and settled, and he told himself he was a lucky man. But still . . .

'Why are you always staring out to sea?' Sophie asked curiously one afternoon as they were strolling hand in hand by the river.

'Am I?' He was surprised. It was a few days before the wedding and the two were enjoying a peaceful break in Dundee after a hectic spell of preparation and wedding rehearsals in Stirling. This was their favourite walk, not far from the Murdochs' house. Jurgen came here often by himself if he wakened early. He would stand looking eastwards, watching the sunrise turn the grey estuary to gold. He didn't know why the dark eastern sea oppressed and fascinated him, nor why sunrise gave him hope. He smiled and drew Sophie close, an arm around her waist. 'Oh, I'm just looking at ships.'

'I see no ships.'

'Only hardships!' he grinned.

'You big joker!' She punched him gently, her eyes full of love. Marrying Jurgen was the fulfilment of all Sophie's dreams. Sometimes she could hardly believe it was happening. 'There'll be no hardships for us, darling,' she said confidently.

'None whatsoever.' He kissed her, with a dull twinge of regret. But that was natural enough in a pilot who'd taken part in the dangerous excitement of dog fights, wasn't it?

Elise Murdoch was selecting flowers from her garden. The mansion house had been prepared for a few guests staying on after the wedding and Sophie the bride had returned to Stirling for the great day. Only the big Chinese vases in the hallway stood empty, waiting for Elise's flower arrangements. She snipped some perfect white roses and glanced towards the gate again. The woman was still there. It was strange. She'd been loitering by the gate for at least ten minutes now. Elise called to her. 'Can I help you?'

'No. Yes . . . I'm sorry!' She was obviously nervous. She consulted a slip of paper. 'You are Mrs Murdoch, perhaps?'

'Yes.' Elise came to the gate, looking through. This was a young woman, slim and dark-haired, very plainly dressed. Hearing the unmistakable accent in her voice, Elise was suddenly uneasy. 'Who are you?'

'I am Ernestine Brecht. I am . . . I was . . . Jurgen's . . . friend,' the woman said in halting English.

'Of course!' Elise said. It had seemed inevitable that this girl would turn up sometime. But not now, so close to the wedding! Unfortunately, both her husband and son were at home, though Elise was confident they were safely out of the way at the back of the house. She hesitated, then opened the gate and beckoned her in. 'We will speak German, Ernestine, that would be best.' For one thing, that meant they could speak freely. 'What are you doing here, my dear?'

'When the British freed us from the labour camp they asked all displaced persons if they'd any relatives or friends to go to. I thought of Jurgen. He . . . he is the only one. After a time I was granted a visa. First I went to Angus House. They sent me here.'

'But what happened to your parents?'

'Forced labour is very hard for older people. They died in the labour camp. I survived because I'm young and strong, but even then . . .' She broke off, biting her lip.

'Come into the conservatory. Tell me about it,' Elise said impulsively. It is a risk, she thought, but this poor girl has been through so much. She deserves just a little kindness, then I will send her away. The large conservatory seemed the safest place to talk. She made Ernestine sit down while she put the flowers in water.

'Jurgen's home is very beautiful,' Ernestine said.

'We spruced up the paintwork for the wedding. Jurgen and Sophie are getting married very soon, you see.' Elise told her. This girl had a right to know the truth.

281

'He is getting married?' Ernestine said quietly. 'Then I'm glad he's found someone to love. I'm glad he's happy. Now that I know this, I will make a new life for myself.'

'My dear, what will you do?'

She shrugged. 'Berlin is in ruins. Maybe I will go there and help.' She stood up. 'You've been kind, Mrs Murdoch, but I'll leave now.'

'Yes, that might be best.'

'Oh, no, you won't, Ernestine!' Jurgen rushed into the conservatory. 'Would you leave without seeing me? And as for you—' he turned angrily to his mother. 'You'd let her go without a word?'

'Jurgen, I thought it would be better if—'

'I'll be the judge of that, Mother!'

Raised voices in angry, fluent German had alerted Jamie to trouble. He came out of the drawing room and stood in the doorway. 'What's going on?' He stared at the stranger. 'Who's this?'

'Her name is Ernestine Brecht, Father. We met years ago, before the war,' Jurgen told him.

'It's that girl you met at Hitler's Olympic Games!' Jamie cried in horror. 'For heaven's sake, Jurgen, get rid of her!'

He flushed. 'No, I will not!'

'All right!' Jamie shouted. 'Go ahead and upset poor Sophie if you must, but what a way to start married life!'

Ernestine broke down in tears. 'No, no! I do not wish to make any unhappiness for Jurgen and his love. I will go at once.' She made a dive for the door, but Jurgen was quicker. He grabbed her.

'Oh no you don't. You'll stay, Ernestine!' He gave his scowling father a mutinous glare. 'We'll talk this over, quietly and sensibly.'

'Oh, Sophie, you look absolutely beautiful!' Kirsty said on her daughter's wedding day. She dabbed her eyes. 'And I daren't cry. It'll spoil my make-up.'

'No need for tears, Mum. It's a perfect day and everything will be perfect,' Sophie said happily. They stood downstairs in the empty house waiting for the last two cars to arrive. Kirsty's first, so that the mother of the bride could make an entrance in solitary state, then the bridal limousine for Sophie and Charles, who was giving his granddaughter away. After all the hard work and excitement, Sophie felt serenely calm. She was confident not a single detail had been overlooked. She caught sight of her veiled reflection in the mirror above the mantelpiece and couldn't resist a smile. Was this vision of loveliness really her?

The doorbell rang urgently.

'Ah, there's my taxi!' Kirsty gathered gloves and handbag and hurried to answer the summons. She opened the door, smiling, but the smile froze on her lips when she saw who it was. 'Jurgen dear! What—?'

'Sophie. I have to speak to Sophie,' he said.

He looked so grim she stood aside without a word. He walked past her, and she heard her daughter scream. 'Jurgen, you mustn't see me before the ceremony. Oh, darling, it's bad luck!'

'Yes. I know.'

Jurgen looked at his beautiful bride. It was the worst, most wretched moment of his life, but he had to speak. 'I'm sorry, Sophie, I can't marry you.'

'What?' Sophie dropped the sweet-scented bouquet. 'I don't understand! What's wrong?' Was Jurgen taken suddenly ill? She hurried to him, crushing the flowers beneath her feet. She would have hugged him but he pushed her away.

'No, please don't! I've spoken with the minister and explained why I can't go through with it. He agrees I need more time to think this over. He'll tell the guests the wedding's off.' He looked at her abjectly. 'I'm so sorry, Sophie dear!'

Wildly, she wrenched off the veil. 'You're sorry! Is that all you can say?'

'I know it's hard, but it's miles better than enduring an unhappy marriage,' he said.

'But I thought you loved me! You told me . . .' she cried.

'I do, Sophie, I do, but –' he shrugged helplessly – 'not enough.'

Nineteen

'The Murdochs have brought nothing but shame and sorrow to our family!' Kirsty said bitterly. It was only now, a week after the calamity that should have been Sophie's happiest day, that she could bear to talk about the whole sorry episode at all.

Mildred raised an eyebrow, but said nothing. She decided not to mention that Agnes Murdoch had saved Kirsty's life as a baby and Hannah had brought William safely home from the Far East. It was better to let Kirsty get everything off her chest, she thought. She carried on unravelling an old woolly jumper, destined to become socks for Charles.

'Do you know why Jurgen changed his mind?' Mildred asked gently.

'No. Sophie won't even talk about it,' Kirsty said. Thinking about her broken-hearted daughter only increased the sadness. She tried to look on the bright side. 'Anyway, I'm glad she's gone to Edinburgh with Buffy. Leaving Stirling is the best thing she could do.'

'We'll miss her. Still, we have you and William,' Mildred said comfortably, ripping out more crinkly wool.

But for how long? Kirsty wondered. She hated idleness and there was nothing for her to do in this well-run household.

Unexpectedly, it was her brother George who suggested a solution when he phoned one evening. 'Celeste is taking this move of mine to Forfar pretty badly, and that worries me now her grandparents have gone to live in England. You wouldn't consider taking over the tenancy of the lodge and keeping an eye on Celeste for me, would you?'

'I'd love to, George! But William is supposed to start

285

school this autumn. I was thinking of finding a job after I decide which one to send him to.'

'That shouldn't be a problem. St Agnes's primary department takes boys too, and I know the headmistress is looking for a secretary. You've had office experience helping Edward. Why don't you apply?'

'It does sound ideal,' she agreed. She felt a stirring of excitement. It would be fun working at a school William attended, and in her beloved Angus House of all places! Maybe the lodge could provide a home for herself and William and a refuge for Celeste.

'Okay, I'll have a word with Miss Cameron the headmistress tomorrow,' George promised. 'By the way, dear, about the lodge. I should remind you that Jamie Murdoch is the landlord.'

There was a long pause, then Kirsty sighed. 'Oh well, George, I suppose beggars can't be choosers. The question is, will Jamie Murdoch want *me* as a tenant?'

Raised voices and arguments between father and son had disrupted the peace of the Murdochs' beautiful mansion overlooking the river ever since Jurgen had jilted Sophie Merrilees.

These days, Jamie Murdoch spent as much time as he could at the mill in a bid to escape. Jurgen did not accompany his father. What was the use? The pair would only argue bitterly. At least when occupied in the mill Jamie could forget all his problems.

In a way, war had been good for business. Vegetable oil had taken over from fishy-smelling whale oil years ago in the softening of jute fibres, and Murdoch's mill had been in the forefront of crushing linseed for oil and using the residue to make linseed cake for cattle. This was very popular with cattle breeders because it 'put a shine upon the beasts' backs'. Production of cattle for the home market had become vitally important during the war because of the U-boat blockade and Jamie had experimented with various feeds, to great success.

286

Jamie loved the Dundee mill with an intensity which sometimes surprised him. It was his own creation of course, unlike the mill on the Angus estate he'd once run with his father. Normally, Jamie enjoyed doing the rounds of the mill, breathing in the mealy scents of all the different cereals, and watching his men at work in their smart green company overalls. But today Jamie was having difficulty concentrating. George Rutherford had phoned to give notice that he was moving out of the lodge. That, Jamie thought, was a relief, though he knew Elise's love affair with George had ended long ago. But the new tenant George had suggested was even more unwelcome. Kirsty Merrilees!

Should I let her have the tenancy? Jamie pondered. And if I do, could I bear to have her living so close amidst all the memories of a love we once shared?

One Sunday several weeks later, Sophie Merrilees steeled herself to travel to Dundee to confront Jurgen. She hadn't spoken to him since the dreadful day they should have been married, but now her anger had cooled a little there were things that had to be said. The bus that took her, tense and apprehensive, along Broughty Ferry Road towards the Murdochs' house was a wartime relic with wooden seats, supremely uncomfortable, which suited her mood.

She hadn't told Jurgen she would be calling, but she was fairly confident she'd find him at home as she walked up the path and pressed the doorbell.

Elise looked shocked to see her. 'Why, Sophie, my dear . . . !'

She ushered her visitor in, calling to Jamie, who came hurrying from the study. Jurgen appeared on the upstairs landing and a young woman followed him. She was dark-haired and pale, and nothing special to look at, Sophie thought incredulously. How could he prefer her to me? She turned pointedly to Jurgen. 'I came to talk . . .'

'I thought we'd talked enough, Sophie. I thought you understood,' he said wearily. 'Ernestine and I fell in love before the war. But then her father criticised the Nazi regime

287

and he and his family were sentenced to years of forced labour. When I heard no word from Ernestine I assumed she'd stopped loving me. It broke my heart, but I tried to put it behind me and forget about her. Then Ernestine came looking for me after the war, and we realized our feelings for one another were just as strong as ever. It wouldn't have been right for me to marry you.'

'You lied to me! You told me you loved me!'

He sighed. 'I did love you. When news came that your father had died and you were so sad . . .'

'You asked me to marry you because you pitied me! That's all it was. How humiliating!'

'I'm . . .'

'Don't dare say you're sorry!' she warned fiercely, fighting back tears.

Nobody spoke. In the distance a wireless played restrained Sunday music.

'So what are you going to do now?' Sophie asked more quietly.

'I'm going back to Germany with Ernestine. I helped to bomb the country to ruins. It's only right I should lend a hand with rebuilding.'

'I see.' So he'd already moved on, away from her. There was no hope of rekindling their love affair. It was over, past mending.

She stared jealously at Ernestine. She'd expected to find her gloating triumphantly, but instead to her surprise she saw in the German girl's expression a sympathetic understanding which was somehow shaming. It threw a fresh, disquieting light upon Sophie's own past behaviour.

She had, Sophie realized, worshipped Jurgen for years and dreamed about a fairy-tale wedding and living happily ever after. But it had been her fairy tale, not his. Jurgen lived in the real world. He had humoured her because he was a sympathetic, kindly person at heart. She remembered how often he'd stared out to sea with a longing, faraway look in his eyes. Now she understood why.

Sophie summoned up all her courage and managed a smile

for her rival. 'I wish you luck with this man, Ernestine. I think he's too kind-hearted for his own good.'

'Thank you, Sophie, but I already know this good fault,' Ernestine smiled.

Impulsively, Elise Murdoch hugged the lovable girl who might have been her daughter-in-law, then gently let her go. Sophie walked out of the house without a backward glance.

Kirsty returned to the Carse to find the Angus House she knew in her youth no longer existed. In its place was a school with bare floorboards echoing to the beat of young feet, and corridors that smelled of cabbage and coffee. The high ceilings rang with youthful voices, peals of laughter and shouted orders from teachers to stop shouting, to stop whistling, not to run in the corridors. The working day was regulated by bells to tell children when to sleep and when to rise, when to work and when to play.

The downstairs rooms that had once been filled with antique furniture now held desks and blackboards and smelled of chalk-dust. Upstairs rooms were devoted to dormitories lined with rows of iron beds and lockers. Smaller apartments housed Matron, housekeeper and live-in members of staff. Baths and hair-washing were on a strict rota because of inadequate hot water and a temperamental boiler.

Right from the start Kirsty had liked Miss Cameron the headmistress, a cheerful lady with a bush of grey hair and a wide knowledge of the wily ways of children. Miss Cameron occupied a suite of two rooms on the ground floor, a small room for rest and sleep she called the 'boudoir' which led off the former library, now the headmistress's study which she shared with her secretary. The large room was crammed with books and plants and the organized muddle of Miss Cameron's papers and accounts.

'Don't tidy too much, Kirsty dear,' she warned, 'or I'll never find anything.'

'Beats me how you find anything as it is.'

'Oh, I may lose things for a bit, but they always turn up.'

She broke off automatically to yell through the open door. 'Stop that whistling, whoever you are!'

Kirsty loved working in the school. She found the orderly discipline and rules soothing after the chaos of escape from Singapore. She welcomed clanging bells that split the days into routine periods of work and play. She enjoyed checking invoices to the sound of a hockey match in progress outside on the pitch or a choir of fresh young voices singing in the music room, but most of all, she enjoyed being with the children.

William had settled down well in a pre-fab built to accommodate the little ones as St Agnes school expanded after the war to take both boys and girls in primary classes. The concrete-coloured structure offended Kirsty's eye, but William liked it.

'We got a Muriel in our classroom today, Mum,' he announced one afternoon when he and Kirsty had brought Celeste home to tea after school.

'That's nice, dear,' Kirsty said, amused. Obviously some new little girl had taken her son's fancy.

Celeste looked up. 'He means a mural. Sixth Form art class painted an animal ABC round their room.'

'A Muriel! That's what I said.' William was indignant. Fortunately the doorbell rang before he started arguing. Kirsty answered the summons, still smiling, but the smile soon faded. 'You! What are you doing here?'

Jamie Murdoch ruefully reminded himself that he had not really expected a smiling welcome. 'I've come to collect the rent. I'm your landlord, remember?'

'Could I ever forget? I didn't think you'd come in person. I didn't think you'd have the nerve. Why not send an invoice which I could then pay by cheque?'

'This is the way your brother handled it, Mrs Merrilees. I see no reason to change.' If that was the way she wanted to speak to him, Jamie thought grimly, then so be it.

'George's case was quite different.'

'Not so very. George had a rent book which he made sure I signed and dated after payment. I presume you have it handy?'

'Well . . . yes.'

'Then I'll come in, if I may. You can pay cash or cheque for a month's rent, whichever you prefer. I'll sign the book and go away. What could be simpler?'

She stood aside without a word.

Celeste was delighted to see her uncle. 'Come for the rent, Uncle Jamie? You're in luck. Kirsty got paid yesterday,' she said cheerfully.

'Glad to hear it.' He smiled fondly at the girl. 'So they let you out of custody to visit?'

'Miss Cameron says it's all right, if I'm back in time for prep.'

'Sensible woman,' Jamie commented.

He watched as Kirsty counted notes and coins in her purse, then worriedly consult a bank statement before finally writing a cheque. So she is hard up! he thought. He felt a twinge of pity which he hastily pushed aside. The less emotion he felt for Kirsty Merrilees, the better. It had brought him nothing but heartache in the past. 'Thanks,' he said brusquely, signing and dating the rent book with a flourish.

He gave nothing away till he had returned to his car and was safely behind the wheel. He sat there recovering his composure, alarmed to find his hands gripping the steering wheel, nerves badly shaken by the encounter. And I'll be forced to repeat that process, month after month, year after year, for as long as she stays, he thought.

But the obvious solution, sending out invoices instead, didn't even occur to him.

The weather was terrible that winter, and blizzards raged. Phone and electricity lines came down under a weight of snow, trains and buses were cancelled due to snowdrifts. The pupils of St Agnes's delighted in the disruption. Central heating struggled to cope and lessons were taken in overcoats and mitts or abandoned altogether. Miss Cameron ordered snow-clearing duty for her pupils and turned a blind eye to snowmen, snowfights and sledging.

'I'm glad Celeste's decided which subjects to take for her

Highers, Kirsty,' Miss Cameron said. She wore a red pixie hood and two or three jumpers and warmed her hands round a mug of cocoa. 'Languages, of course,' she went on. 'English, Maths, Science. She's a clever lass. She tells me she wants to be a teacher.'

'Yes, she's certainly keen to teach,' Kirsty smiled.

Miss Cameron suddenly put down her mug with a frown. 'Who's that whistling out there? Honestly, Kirsty, how many times do I have to tell them?' She crossed to the window and yelled furiously.

The whistling ceased abruptly. Miss Cameron looked abashed. 'Ooops! It's a visitor! Nip outside, aplogize profusely and see what he wants, will you, Kirsty dear?'

Kirsty went out into a glorious crisp morning, skies a clear icy blue after snow. Shading her eyes against the white glare, she called to a tall young man who stood at the bottom of the steps. 'Sorry about that. Our headmistress objects to the girls whistling, you see. Can I help you?'

He mounted the steps hesitantly. 'D – don't you know me?'

'I don't think so . . .' Then she paused. There was something about the youthful features that bore a strong resemblance to . . . oh! . . . she hardly dared hope . . . 'P-Peter?' she ventured.

'In person, Mum!' Peter grinned, hugging her fiercely. His dear mum seemed smaller than he'd remembered, he thought emotionally – and older, too. But he'd have known her anywhere.

And of course he himself had shot up since his fourteenth birthday. Like a beanpole! Dobbie had remarked as they'd trekked along the baking trails. Dobbie had been forced to look up at him, instead of down.

'Oh Peter, I can hardly believe it's you, after all these years . . .' Kirsty's eyes had filled with tears. 'And look at you! You were just a little boy last time I saw you, now you're grown up. And oh, Peter . . .' Her voice broke, 'You look so like your father.'

'Don't cry.' He put an arm round her shoulder. 'I'm home,

Mum. Everything's OK. I tried to phone from Grandpa's, but the lines are down so I just got on the next train. It took hours to get here!'

'And oh, how happy I am to see you, love!' Kirsty tucked a hand under her son's elbow. 'Come on, Pete darling. You can meet Miss Cameron and we'll ask if I can have the afternoon off. You and I have years of catching up to do.'

'What I don't understand, Peter,' Celeste said, much later, 'is where you got to? The war ended ages ago, so why didn't you just come home?' There was no hockey practice that afternoon because of the conditions and she'd headed for the lodge to meet Kirsty's son. She tossed another log on the fire in the lodge's cosy front room and settled down to listen.

'After Burma, my friend Dobbie and I returned to Sumatra to look for my dad. We had to leave him behind when we escaped in a small boat during the war. We meant to go to India, but were blown off course and landed in Burma, half-dead,' he explained.

'And did you find your dad?' Celeste asked curiously.

'No. He . . . he'd died.' Talking brought back painful memories. He remembered the shrine the villagers had raised around Edward Merrilees' last resting place. Women and children brought fresh flowers there every day in the cool of evening. It had made him terribly sad, yet fiercely proud to find these people had loved and respected his dad so much. He wished his mother could have seen it. He looked across to where she sat with one arm round William his brother, a schoolboy he remembered as a two-year-old.

'It . . . it was so peaceful there, Mum. People were so kind, they . . . they'd cared for him,' he said in a voice that quavered.

Kirsty didn't say anything, only nodded gently as if she understood what he was trying to tell her, and was comforted.

'What'll you do now? Will you go to school?' Celeste asked.

'There's not much point. I've missed too much,' Peter shrugged, There were huge gaps in his education it would take years to fill. He was well-versed in survival skills,

293

though. He could ride out a typhoon in a small boat and walk for miles enduring hunger and thirst while dodging cruel enemies. But what use was that in post-war Britain?

Sophie had found a job in Edinburgh's Botanic Gardens, thanks to her Women's Land Army experience. It was mostly digging, raking and mulching, but she enjoyed working outdoors. She shied away from any emotional involvement, though she'd made a few new friends since moving to the city.

Her sole concession to her past life was a visit to nearby Inverleith pond whenever she felt really down in the dumps. Leaving the Botanics, she would take her lunch down to the boating pond, throw crusts to the ducks and wallow in memories. After all, this was where the disastrous romance had begun.

Sitting on a chilly bench moodily munching a sandwich, Sophie noticed the young man had appeared again. She'd seen him on several occasions at the pond, without paying him much attention. He usually fed the ducks, hovered around on the opposite bank, then went away again.

Today was different. It was cold and grey and the park was deserted except for Sophie. The young man was studying a few dispirited ducks who'd lost interest when they saw he was empty-handed. He edged closer to the bench.

'It's cold. It might rain,' he called.

'It might.' She looked away pointedly. That usually deterred advances, but she was surprised to find him suddenly standing beside her. She was even more startled when he spoke.

'You're Sophie Merrilees, aren't you?'

'How did you know?' She studied him suspiciously.

He held out a hand. 'Harold Dobson. We met here once.'

She ignored the hand. 'I don't remember you.'

'Well, you wouldn't. People don't, usually.'

She looked at him more closely. He wasn't tall or handsome, though it was a pleasant enough face and the eyes, magnified behind horn-rimmed specs, were clear and kind.

He didn't seem to mind her not remembering. He glanced at the rejected hand as if it belonged to someone else and put it away again.

'I must apologize,' he said. 'I pushed you into the pond when you were a wee girl. Accidentally, of course. My friend Jurgen pulled you out. I was afraid to get my new trousers muddy.'

A vague memory stirred. A small boy with specs hovering apologetically in the admiring crowd around Jurgen. Growing up, he'd often been there, always in Jurgen's shadow. She smiled. 'I remember you now, Harold Dobson!'

'You do?' His face beamed his pleasure. 'My friends, and your brother Peter's one of them, I'm proud to say, call me Dobbie. I'd be honoured if you'd—'

She stared, so surprised she dropped the sandwich, much to the delight of the watchful ducks. 'You're not . . . not the Dobbie who saved Peter? That . . . that wonderful man?'

'Well, Pete's the wonder, really,' Dobbie said modestly. 'Not a word of complaint from the boy all those years, even when we missed India and landed in hot water in Burma.'

'Dobbie . . . oh, Dobbie!' she cried. 'You saved Pete . . . and . . . and my poor darling dad . . . Oh . . . oh . . . I'm going to cry . . .' she wailed miserably.

'Go ahead. You can have my shoulder.' He sat down beside her.

She hadn't cried since Jurgen. She'd been frozen inside, but once the thaw started it wouldn't stop. She cried humiliated tears for the ending of a fairy tale and all those hurt in the process, including herself. She cried on Dobbie's shoulder with his undemanding arm gently around her, and when she'd finished crying, spent and weak, she accepted the hanky he offered and mopped her red, swollen eyes.

'Better?' he said.

'Yes.' And she did feel better, as if she'd been cleansed somehow. Her head still rested on Dobbie's shoulder and she made no move to shift from that comforting position. 'Thanks, Dobbie.'

'You're welcome.' They sat close together, watching ducks

295

gobble the muddy remains of Sophie's sandwich. They didn't say much, both aware of magic abroad.

'Those blasted new trousers! I wish it'd been me who'd fished you out,' he said wistfully.

She turned her head and smiled at him. 'Shall I fall in again, so you can save me?'

'Not necessary, my dear.' The look in her eyes and the joy in his heart told Dobbie they were falling in love, which was much more pleasant and lasting than a plunge in the muddy pond.

Jamie Murdoch's house had been echoingly empty since Jurgen married Ernestine Brecht and took her back to Germany to make a home there. Elise felt the loss of her son keenly. It was as if the heart had gone out of the house. Recently, her husband had made matters worse and done something Elise could never forgive.

'How could you give Kirsty Merrilees's son a job in the mill? He's working where our own son ought to be.'

'Jurgen had his chance and didn't take it,' Jamie answered brusquely. 'Peter Merrilees is grateful for the work, interested in the job and a good worker.'

'That is not the point. He is not our son, he is hers!'

'That's just jealousy, Elise.'

'Yes, I am jealous! Do you blame me?' she cried wildly. 'Every month you go to the lodge to see that woman.'

'Of course I do. I collect her rent,' he said coldly.

'Rent? It is a pittance you take from her. I have seen receipts and it is less rent than George ever paid. That pretty house is worth much more. I – I was so happy there once.'

'Yes. We know why, don't we?' he said, goaded into indiscretion.

She stared at him. 'That . . . that is unkind,' she said quietly. She had tried so hard to make amends for the love affair. She had fought against loving George, if indeed it's possible to fight love like an enemy. For a while, she and her husband were reconciled, but peace had only lasted till Kirsty

296

Merrilees returned. There will be no peace for us now, Elise thought in despair. Never!

'Now I know what I must do.' She stood up resolutely. 'I shall go to Germany to Jurgen and Ernestine. Make sure they are all right. I've been meaning to do so for some time.'

'And afterwards?' he demanded.

She didn't answer. Instead, she dropped a light kiss on his forehead and left the room. He heard her footstep on the stairs and the bedroom door close softly behind her. Was she packing already? Jamie wondered uneasily as heavy silence settled once more upon the quiet house.

'You and I should get married, Pete,' Celeste announced unexpectedly one evening, as they strolled companionably along the woodland path through the old Angus house estate.

'What?' Peter's thoughts had been far away. Murdoch's mill was facing increased competition these days and he was trying to think of a way of halting the decline.

Her words took him totally by surprise. He was fond of Celeste in a platonic sort of way. He envied the brains that had taken her to university, and admired her striking looks and boundless energy – but Celeste as a *wife*?

'Marry you?' he said doubtfully.

'Yes. It's perfect. We'd make a wonderful couple. You know how I'd love to open my own special school one day for children with learning difficulties? Well, you could help.' She turned to him eagerly, her face aglow, and Peter realized she was serious.

'Professor Polanski thinks it's a great idea!'

'Oh, him!' Peter said glumly. He was fed up hearing about her wonderful professor.

'Don't be like that! He's really enthusiastic, about my plans, except he didn't seem to be so keen on us marrying – at least, not yet.' She looked doubtful for a moment.

He hid his relief. 'Wise chap. After all, your mum is married to my uncle. That's a bit too close for comfort, isn't it?'

'Sam's my stepfather, Pete. Professor Polanski says that's OK,' Celeste persisted.

'Never trust a bearded professor. What's he hiding?' Peter joked, feeling flustered.

'You're impossible! He only grew a beard to look older,' she said sulkily, flouncing off towards the lodge. 'Anyway, I'm jolly glad I don't have to marry you just yet, Peter Merrilees. I'll wait till you've matured,' she called over her shoulder.

He grinned after her, then set off along the overgrown path towards the deserted mill that had once been both home and livelihood to the Murdoch family. It seemed wise to give Celeste time to cool down before he returned home.

He hadn't been to the Milton for ages, and to his surprise there were signs of activity in the old buildings. New wooden doors had been fitted to the warehouses and strange noises came from inside – clattering and hissing and the lowing of cattle.

Peter glanced inside and saw that the place had been fitted up as a milking parlour. A line of cows stood in the stalls, awaiting the attention of a slight young woman in white overalls.

'Well, what d' you know? A modern milkmaid!' Peter said.

She glanced up, but didn't stop working with a cluster of cups attached to the milking apparatus. One wise old cow turned its head and eyed Peter reprovingly. So did the girl. 'She don't like to be disturbed when milking. Neither do I,' she said tartly.

'Sorry. I'm just an ignorant townie.'

'I might have known!' She was studying the gush of milk coursing through glass pipes.

Looking around, Peter saw the whole area had been tiled and was spotlessly clean. He was impressed. 'I didn't know this even existed,' he said admiringly.

'My dad bought this place six months ago. We have the farm next door, but he bought Angus mill for sentimental reasons. My grandpa used to work on the estate. His name was Cunningham,' she explained without looking up from her work.

'I've heard my mother mention Mr Cunningham and the horses,' he recalled.

She glanced up. 'You're a Rutherford?'

'My mother is.' He liked the way this girl spoke. There was no nonsense about her.

'Get out o' here!' she yelled suddenly and he jumped. She laughed at this reaction. 'Not you! Lucas, my dog. He sneaks in and wolfs the cattle feed when he thinks I'm not looking.' She patted the sheepish collie. Lucas the dog inspected Peter with an innocent air, his muzzle still covered in crumbs, while the girl went back to work. 'I'm Maggie Cunningham, by the way,' she called.

'Peter Merrilees.' Peter's thoughts were far away. He'd had an idea, and could hardly wait to start working on it. When Maggie Cunningham turned round he'd gone.

Townies! she thought, scornfully.

As the years had passed, the building that had once been Angus House grew shabbier and the gardens more unkempt, but under Miss Cameron's kindly guidance the school had prospered.

Miss Cameron was now nearing retirement age, and Kirsty herself was well into her fifties. There were bound to be changes soon, she realized. There would be a new headmistress, and new brooms sweep clean. It was a worrying thought. Kirsty loved her job and was keen to keep working till William finished senior school in a couple of years. William was now a pupil at the academy in Dundee, and had reached an important stage in his education, soon to take the Highers. He was a big, handsome lad, growing out of clothes and shoes as fast as his mother could buy them. Kirsty had to keep working just to clothe her son in expensive school uniform. There was nothing else for it. Thankfully, rent for the lodge was reasonable. There was only William at home now, although Celeste turned up at weekends. She was teaching in Edinburgh and lodged with Sophie and Dobbie since their marriage, in that happy household containing Kirsty's little granddaughter.

Peter had accepted rooms in Jamie Murdoch's house, an arrangement of which Kirsty disapproved, but was helpless to prevent. Jamie lived there on his own apart from a housekeeper. Elise spent her time in Germany looking after two grandchildren while Ernestine helped Jurgen in the construction firm he'd started. Maybe Jamie Murdoch had got what he deserved, Kirsty thought, but she couldn't help feeling sorry for the lonely man. She gave him tea when he called for the rent, and often they sat for a while and chatted, reminiscing.

Winter that year was bitter, and an icy north-west wind swept down the Carse on New Year's Day. Another birthday! Kirsty thought. She'd long since stopped celebrating her New Year birthday, though her family never forgot. She wished term would start. She missed the children. That night, wind rattled the lodge windows and found its way under Kirsty's bedroom door with disturbing little sighs and whispers. It was a creepy sound, making sleep difficult. She was already half awake when William burst into her bedroom.

'Mum, you'd better come!'

'What is it?' She tumbled out of bed, shrugging on a dressing gown.

'Fire!' He dragged the curtains aside. 'Look!'

The black night was turning red. Through the trees she could see windows lit with flames, and a howling wind carried the smell of burning wood towards them. She clutched her son's arm in terror.

'William! The school . . . the school's on fire!'

Twenty

As the first weak rays of sunshine filtered across the dawn sky, Kirsty and William became aware of the full extent of the damage. The fire brigade had managed to extinguish the blaze, but the building was little more than a shell. Most of the interior had been completely destroyed. They stood in silence on the lawn, gazing in disbelief at the blackened, smoking ruins of the once-proud house.

'Thank goodness the children are on holiday and nobody was hurt,' Miss Cameron said, coming across to join them. She stared at the ruin and sighed. 'You know, I can't help feeling somehow responsible for this. I've warned the board time and again the electrical wiring should be checked and the central heating boiler replaced, but nothing was done. I should've insisted the work was carried out, Kirsty.'

'It's not your fault. Nobody can blame you,' Kirsty said.

'Oh, can't they?' Miss Cameron looked sad. 'When I rang the chairman of the board earlier to tell him what had happened, he said their only option now was to go ahead with plans to merge St Agnes's with Ochterblane School. In other words,' she finished dolefully, 'they intend to give me the sack, take the insurance settlement and wash their hands of the place.'

'So we're both jobless,' Kirsty said, dismayed.

'Exactly. I was planning to retire at the end of next term anyway, but it's much worse for you. You're younger than me for a start, and you have a fifteen-year-old son to feed and clothe. In my experience fifteen-year-old boys eat like horses and grow like beanstalks.'

The two women stared sadly at the ruined house. The wind

had dropped and a few last wisps of smoke and steam drifted lazily skywards from gaunt black spars. I've just witnessed the total destruction of my family home, Kirsty thought, the pain suddenly almost too much to bear. I'll remember the dear old house with love and gratitude all the days of my life. She turned away with an effort.

'Mum!' William called, appearing at that moment from behind a fire engine. 'I've some good news, the prefab's OK – it hasn't been damaged at all. That's something, isn't it? I looked inside, and guess what? There was my Muriel on the wall, fresh as the day it was painted!'

'That's encouraging,' Miss Cameron said thoughtfully. 'It may be possible to salvage something from this sorry mess. I wonder . . . How about starting a nursery school for four- and five-year-olds? Kirsty, you'd be the ideal person to run it!'

'That's not a bad idea,' Kirsty agreed slowly. She frowned. 'But I wouldn't know where to start. I couldn't do it on my own.'

'Don't look at me, dear!' Miss Cameron said hastily. 'Like I said, I'm on the brink of retiring. Starting a new venture's not for me.'

Kirsty was alone in the lodge when Jamie Murdoch called round the day after the fire. She sat, staring dejectedly into space, as the full impact of the disaster sank in. No job, no money. She almost wept when she opened the door and found Jamie standing there.

'Surely the rent's not due yet?' she asked despairingly.

'Och, Kirsty! Give me credit for some decency!' he said. 'I came to make sure you and William were all right.'

'William's at school. He's quite well, thanks.'

'And you?'

'I'm fine.'

But she wasn't, he realized, alarmed by how shaken and miserable she looked. 'Must we stand on the doorstep?' he said. 'I've been up to the house to assess the damage and I'm frozen. I could do with a cup of tea.'

To be sure, he did look cold, Kirsty thought. She stood aside silently. Jamie took stock of the room while she boiled the kettle. It felt chilly, and he was glad he'd kept his overcoat on. Maybe she couldn't afford to heat the place or maybe she was too upset to bother. Either way, the situation worried him.

'There you are, Mr Murdoch. Milk and no sugar,' Kirsty announced briskly, coming back in.

He accepted the tea and nibbled a biscuit, wondering how he could possibly offer to help without offending her. He didn't know what her plans were now the school was unlikely to reopen. Would she leave the lodge? He had to admit he didn't want her to.

'Did you notice the prefab wasn't damaged in the fire?' she asked abruptly.

'I didn't, to be honest. But it's quite separate from the house so I suppose it would escape.' He gave her a shrewd glance. 'Why?'

'I've had several parents of pre-school children on the phone, wondering if nursery classes in the prefab would continue. I told them I'd be willing to keep it going if I could find financial backing.'

'And if you can't?'

'I'll give you a month's notice and move on.'

'That's blackmail,' he protested.

She glared at him indignantly. 'No, it isn't! I haven't asked for your help. In any case, why should you care what happens to me?'

'Because I was there when your father brought you to the Milton with scarcely a flicker of life in you,' he answered frankly. 'My mother believed you were worth saving and she fought hard for you, Kirsty Merrilees. That's why I care.'

She looked at him in silence for a minute. 'So you do have a conscience, Jamie. I've often wondered.'

'Aye, well . . .' He looked uncomfortable. 'Now about this prefab. It's self-contained, isn't it?'

'Yes, it is,' Kirsty told him. 'It has its own water, light and heating. But it belongs to St Agnes's. They'll want rent for use of the building.'

'Once they've collected the insurance they'll probably sell

the place, but we'll face that if it happens.' He finished the tea and stood up.

'We?' Kirsty repeated, frowning.

'You didn't think I'd leave you to face this disaster on your own, did you? I'll finance the project. It can be a loan or an investment, whatever your conscience will allow you to agree to. Besides, I don't want to lose a careful tenant, they're hard to come by.'

'Wait a minute!' She grabbed his arm. 'Jamie, think about it! I'm not a trained teacher, I'll need help.'

'You brought up a family, didn't you?'

'No, I didn't.' Two bright tears gathered and slid down her cheeks.

'Other people brought up my children. I lost them all for so many precious years – and now you've taken Peter away from me.'

'I . . . oh Kirsty, I'm sorry.' He simply hadn't realized how she must be feeling. He looked down at the hand on his arm, fighting a sudden urge to lift her hand to his lips and kiss it. 'Loneliness is a terrible affliction,' he said quietly. 'Oh, I know it's my own fault, Kirsty, but I have more in common with your son than I ever did with my own boy.'

He knew why, of course. There was so much of Kirsty in Peter, while Jurgen was Elise's son and always had been. He looked at her. 'If you want me to send Peter home, just say the word.'

She hesitated. There were rumours that Jamie's wife had left him and he'd quarrelled bitterly with his son. He must miss his family dreadfully. 'No, don't do that. Peter loves his job and enjoys having his independence too, especially now he's courting Maggie Cunningham. He took her to the pictures last weekend, you know.'

'The chummy seats, I bet,' Jamie grinned. 'That's serious courting.'

'I'm happy for them,' Kirsty said. 'Cunningham was a fine man.'

'Aye, so he was,' Jamie agreed fondly.

The room had lost its chill. As he turned to leave, he felt happier. Comforted, somehow.

'I'm home!' Celeste announced cheerfully a week later, barging into the lodge. She dumped a large suitcase on the living-room floor and lifted a startled Kirsty off her feet in a huge hug.

'What are you doing here? What about your job in Edinburgh?' Celeste made a face. 'It was only supply teaching! That's no job at all, Kirsty. I handed in my resignation and packed a bag the moment Uncle Jamie told me.'

'Told you what?

'About the school in the prefab, of course. Honestly, Kirsty!' Kirsty stared at the vivid young woman before her. 'You mean you really want to help me start this school?'

'Of course I do! It's like a dream come true for me. If all goes well we'll be able to teach little ones during the day and adults with learning difficulties in the evenings. It's what I've always wanted to do.'

Matters moved swiftly once Celeste took charge. The prefab was altered and extended and brought up to Celeste's exacting specifications, with Jamie picking up the bill. The finished building was then approved by the local authority and registered as a nursery school and adult learning unit. Celeste and Kirsty could hardly wait to get started. Everything had fallen neatly into place by the time the school was ready to open that September. Kirsty was to be Celeste's classroom assistant, and she'd taken on another helper too. Maggie Cunningham's widowed Aunt Doris lived nearby, was reputed to have a wonderful way with children and the tact and patience required to cope with over thirty small pupils.

The very first day of school is a traumatic experience for any parent and child, and Kirsty's new venture was no exception. Some children left their parent without a backward glance and dived into the toy cupboard, others clung to their mothers and had to be gently prised off and coaxed inside.

'Bedlam!' Kirsty laughed.

'Aye, so it is,' beamed Doris, enjoying every minute of it.

Celeste soon proved herself an excellent teacher. She was unfailingly cheerful, firm, and scrupulously fair, with a bellow loud enough to command instant silence. In no time at all she had her small pupils organized, coats hung neatly on pegs, and their red pinnies on. The homesick and shy were left in Kirsty and Doris's tender care in a quiet area, while the more sturdily independent were grouped round small tables, busily drawing and scribbling with chunky crayons.

Peter Merrilees usually called in to see his mother at the weekend, and on this particular Sunday after the school had opened, he brought Maggie Cunningham with him. Kirsty was at the prefab to make sure everything was ready for Monday morning, but Celeste was at home, working. Professor Polanski, her former university lecturer, had sent her some information on a condition she'd never even heard of. It was called dyslexia, or word-blindness, he explained, and could account for many instances of difficulty in reading and writing. It was fascinating! Celeste thought.

She glanced up when Peter arrived, and jumped to her feet. 'Peter darling!' She hugged him with delight. 'I hadn't forgotten you, I promise. I've been frantically busy, but now I'm back we can start where we left off.'

'And where was that?' Maggie asked, stepping into the room.

Celeste stared at her. 'Who's this?'

Peter took a deep breath. 'Celeste, this is Maggie, the girl I hope to marry.' The statement took him rather by surprise and left Maggie dumbfounded, but it was, Peter realized, exactly how he felt. He took Maggie's hand and drew her close. 'You will marry me, won't you, Maggie?' It was hardly the ideal time or place for a proposal, but she didn't seem to mind.

'Oh Peter, I thought you'd never ask,' Maggie cried ecstatically. 'Of course I will!'

He pulled her into his arms and they kissed, forgetting all about Celeste for one joyful moment.

She let out a furious yell. 'Stop it, you two! Stop!' They paused and stared at her in astonishment. 'Stop fooling around, Peter. Don't you remember? You're going to marry me!'

He shook his head. 'I'm sorry, Celeste, but that was never going to happen. It was all your idea, not mine. It's Maggie I love, and Maggie I'm going to marry.' He stared at the girl in his arms and couldn't stop smiling.

'We've been courting for months,' Maggie added.

'I don't believe this!' Celeste stormed. 'Professor Polanski warned me I shouldn't marry you, Peter Merrilees!'

'Oh, be quiet, Celeste!' Peter was sick and tired of this argument. 'If he's so clever, why don't you marry your know-it-all professor?'

'Maybe I will!' she retorted wrathfully. 'He's nice to me. We can talk and argue for hours, and never—' She paused in mid-sentence. It felt as if light had suddenly illuminated her thoughts. Professor Polanski! She'd never thought of him like that before, but now . . . She wondered how he felt about her. He'd often held her hand and gazed into her eyes with wistful tenderness, she realized, but she'd thought it just part of his academic aura. Why hadn't she noticed before? Dazed, she looked at Peter and Maggie. Their engagement seemed unimportant to her now. 'Yes. Maybe I will,' she murmured again, dreamily.

Kirsty rang her daughter with the exciting news that they had two weddings to look forward to.

'Great news, Mum! Surely Grandma's wedding gown will fit one of the brides?' Sophie asked, highly delighted.

'I'm afraid not. Maggie has a family gown of her own to wear, and Celeste is planning to dress in traditional Polish style in honour of her professor – who is a darling, by the way.'

'Poor Mum! We're a wayward lot, aren't we?'

'I live in hope. Maybe it'll fit your little Catriona one day.'

'I doubt it. She's growing like a weed. It's my two boys who are neat and wiry like my darling Dobbie.'

What a season of weddings! On top of the two happy occasions in Kirsty's own family, the nation celebrated when Princess Margaret married Lord Snowdon. Then, just as Kirsty was settling down thankfully to a peaceful spell at school, along came William with a new girlfriend.

William had left school and was now a handsome third-year medical student, sporting a varsity scarf wound dashingly round his throat. He ushered his girlfriend into the lodge one Saturday morning.

'Mum, meet Muriel!'

Kirsty couldn't help laughing. 'Muriel! Oh, William, I might have known!'

The poor girl looked baffled. 'It's odd, Mrs Merrilees, but William laughed too, the first time we met. Please tell me, what's the joke?'

'Oh, my dear, I'm so sorry.' Kirsty wiped her eyes. 'Maybe William will explain.'

'I'll do better than that.' He grabbed her hand. 'Come on, Muriel, I'll show you!'

Kirsty watched as the young couple ran laughing, hand in hand, up the driveway towards the little school. They paused to kiss, then went on their way more slowly, arms entwined, to have the mystery of William's mural explained to his Muriel.

Kirsty turned to Jamie, who'd called round for a cup of coffee and a chat. 'What a lovely girl! That's another wedding in the air, I suppose. This is costing me a fortune in wedding presents.'

'At least they'll have a good start in life, thanks to your father,' Jamie remarked. 'Colonel Rutherford knew what he was doing when he left William the royalties from his memoirs in his will. That book is a classic.'

'Yes, William and his grandpa were always very close,' Kirsty recalled fondly.

Jamie looked thoughtful as he took a sip of coffee. He'd gradually slipped into the habit of dropping in for a chat now and then, and Kirsty made him welcome. She knew he was a lonely man.

Today, Jamie had something on his mind. She knew all the signs by now. Pouring herself another cup, she sat down and waited.

'About Angus House . . .' he began.

'Oh yes?' Kirsty sat up, interested. Jamie had bought the overgrown, deserted ruins some years ago, but they remained untouched.

'Kirsty, you know I always intended restoring the old house to its former glory,' he explained awkwardly. 'But I just can't afford it now I've retired. Building costs have risen and it cost much more than I expected to split my own house into flats when Peter got married.' He smiled suddenly. 'Not that I grudge it, mind! It's good having Peter and Maggie and their brood living downstairs, and the other owners are nice friendly folk.'

'It was a good idea for your sake, Jamie,' she said gently. 'I know you appreciate the company.'

Elise had never returned, and the rift with Jurgen had not been healed.

'Aye . . . well,' he said uncomfortably. 'All the firm's capital is tied up in developing Peter's range of dog food – Lucas, he calls it. It's catching on grand, Kirsty! We've switched production from farm feeds to dog food to keep up with demand.'

'So I heard,' Kirsty smiled. 'Peter and Ruby Merilees spent weeks getting the formulation just right. Ruby's an expert in animal nutrition, as you know.'

In 1947 the Vet College had opened its doors to women at last, and Ruby had been awarded an honorary fellowship right away, in recognition of the dedicated work she'd done with animals wounded or made homeless during the war.

But Kirsty's smile faded as Jamie went on. 'There's something else, Kirsty. I'm going to Germany. Elise is ill.'

'Oh, Jamie! I'm so sorry.' It was a blow, for all sorts of reasons. 'Is . . . is she bad?'

'I won't know till I get there, but Jurgen sounded worried on the phone. I said I'd leave right away.' He stared at her, unspoken thoughts passing silently between them. 'I'm sorry, Kirsty,' he said quietly.

She pressed his hand. 'Yes, my dear. I know.'

In the year or so that followed, the school kept Kirsty busy from morning till night, and she welcomed the hard work. She had no time to spare to miss Jamie's visits, or to feel lonely.

The school had grown and prospered over the years under Celeste and Professor Polanski's guidance and was renowned for the patient work and research done there to help children and adults afflicted with word-blindness.

Kirsty and Doris served as honorary grannies to both children and adults, dispensing orange juice and biscuits to one age group and cups of tea and comfort to the other. Apart from a few terse notes, Kirsty seldom heard from Jamie Murdoch, which didn't surprise her. His strengths did not include letter-writing. He'd explained that Elise's illness was a debilitating one and recovery, if it happened, would be painfully slow. Soon after, Peter told her that Jamie's flat in the converted mansion was up for sale.

Kirsty felt both hurt and saddened. So Jamie didn't intend to return to Dundee. Well, why should he?

She was surprised one mild spring morning when walking to school to find lorries parked beside the old house and workmen busy inside the gutted shell. She approached the foreman, an Invergowrie man she knew.

'What's going on here, Mac?'

'Rebuilding the old place, Mrs Merrilees,' he said.

'Who is? Is it James Murdoch?' she asked curiously.

He shook his head. 'No. Mr Murdoch sold it a while back. All I know is that the new owner put the job out to tender and our firm won the contract. The old house is to be made into flats for retired folk.' He grinned at her. 'You'll have new neighbours soon!'

She smiled, gave the gaping windows a wistful glance and walked on. Though she'd no hope of living there, it did Kirsty's heart good to watch Angus House slowly being restored to its former splendour. Mac assured her that no expense was being spared. The interior featured every comfort and labour-saving device imaginable, with a flat for a resident warden.

She was passing the house one afternoon when a well-to-do stranger appeared round the corner, studying the building critically. He was middle-aged, silver-haired and very handsome. Kirsty frowned. Hadn't she seen him somewhere before?

At that moment he caught sight of her and hesitated, then approached. 'Mrs Merrilees?'

'Jurgen Murdoch!' she cried, recognizing him with a shock. For an instant all the anguish she'd felt when he'd jilted Sophie came flooding back, then she pushed the bad memories aside. That was all in the past.

The same thoughts had obviously been going through Jurgen's head. 'How is Sophie, ma'am? Is she happy?'

'Yes, very. She married your old school friend Harold Dobson, you know. They have three lovely children now.'

'What a wise girl!' Jurgen laughed delightedly. 'Dobbie's a wonderful chap.'

Kirsty laid a hand on his arm. 'Jurgen, how's your mother?'

His expression changed. 'Mum died very suddenly a year ago.' He glanced up at the house. 'That's why I wanted to rebuild Angus House.'

'So you're the mystery owner!'

He laughed. 'I thought Angus House would be a sound business venture. Besides –' he glanced affectionately at the old stone walls – 'I've always loved this house.'

'Was that why you bought it?'

'Well, there is another reason, the main one, in fact—' Jurgen paused to wave to a figure who'd just appeared in the doorway. 'Over here, Dad!' he called.

Kirsty looked across, and her heart lurched. 'Jamie!' she whispered incredulously. He was a little stooped, much thinner, but it was undoubtedly him.

Jurgen turned to her. 'Dad cared for my mother devotedly

during her long illness. He couldn't have done more for her, and I believe he made her very happy in the end. The strain took its toll though, and he's been ill for months. That's why I wanted Angus House made ready for him. He always longed to come back to Scotland, but he really needs care. Converting the house into retirement flats seemed the best way to do it tactfully.'

Jurgen smiled, and so did she. They knew how proud James Murdoch could be.

Kirsty held out both hands to the elderly man. 'Welcome home, Jamie.'

He beamed. 'It's a real welcome, seeing you, Kirsty my dear!' He waved a hand at the house. 'What d'you think of my son's brainwave? Apartments for the elderly retired, like his auld dad. Trust a Murdoch to spot a niche in the market!' He patted Jurgen's shoulder.

'Never mind the flattery, Dad,' Jurgen laughed. 'Don't worry, I'll see you get the best apartment.'

It did Kirsty's heart good to see father and son so happy together. She took Jamie's arm and smiled at Jurgen. 'Now, how about a guided tour of my dear old house, you two?'

Several months later, when summer was ripening into autumn, Kirsty and Jamie walked slowly up the hillside above Angus House towards the spot where her brother George had found an abandoned dog and with it a fresh purpose in life. She leaned on the old gate, glad to rest for a moment, and gazed across the rounded hills. 'This is where I used to ride Young Lochinvar,' she said dreamily.

'You were a wild wee devil on horseback,' Jamie said. He laid a hand on hers, resting on the gate. 'But I loved to watch you.'

'I didn't know you did,' she said, surprised.

'Oh, you'd be amazed what I saw!' he teased.

'You cheeky rascal!' But she laughed, turning her head archly like the young lass he'd once known.

'Kirsty,' he said quietly, 'I'm lonely.'

'How can you be lonely, you daft man? The house is bursting at the seams with active retired folk!' she laughed.

'I'm lonely because the woman I love lives two hundred yards away from me in the lodge,' he said. He took both her hands in his. 'Would you consider flitting two hundred yards, my darling? Come into my home, and into my heart, where you've rested this long, long while?'

She reached up and kissed him softly on the lips. 'Only if you make it legal and marry me in the kirk, James Murdoch. We're much too old these days to face another scandal in the Carse . . .'

Epilogue

Kirsty wakened with a start, confused for a moment. Then she realized she'd been asleep and dreaming.

That was one of the perks of extreme old age, she supposed, although even on the brink of her hundredth birthday she didn't feel old. Still, Sophie and Celeste had ordered her to rest in bed that Hogmanay afternoon and you didn't disobey those formidable two lightly! There was a long, tiring, wonderful night ahead, they'd reminded her, and an amazing New Year's Day in store for Kirsty tomorrow, on her birthday.

It was the end of one thousand years, and in a very few hours I'll have lived for one hundred of them, she thought with amazement.

With a grin, Kirsty propped herself up on one elbow and switched on the bedside light. It was already dark, and she must have been asleep for quite a while. She was a little stiff after lying for so long, recalling her whole life, remembering all the loved ones, the joys and sorrows that had made up its rich pattern. I wouldn't change a single thread of it though, now I can see the purpose behind it all, she thought. No. Not even if I could.

The midnight-blue gown studded with black jet stars that she was to wear tonight hung from the wardrobe door. It was very posh! Celeste had taken her to Dundee to choose it. There had been so many changes in the old city, and all for the better, Kirsty thought. The cold concrete of the sixties had been swept away and a new Overgate was rising behind the ancient steeple church. It had pleased her to see old factory

314

chimneys gone and the air clean and clear, some fine old jute mills converted into flats, bringing new life and energy to the centre of the beloved old city.

Celeste had stopped the car by the riverside before driving home to Angus House, and they'd sat quietly looking across at the Fife hills, the wide, glorious river shining before them. No words had been needed. She had seen the river in all its changing moods throughout her long life, but I could never forget this one peaceful scene, Kirsty had thought.

Her flat in the dear old house was packed with members of Kirsty's large family, all gathering to celebrate the millennium and her birthday. She wished dear Jamie could have been there to share the special festivities, and her beloved Edward too, father of her children. Well, they would be with her in spirit, always in her thoughts and in her bright, loving memories.

Kirsty rose in leisurely fashion and put on the beautiful dress. She was determined to be ready well before celebrations began, so that she wouldn't miss a single minute of the fun. She wouldn't let her great-granddaughters loose on her face with creams and blusher and eye-liner, though! She was proud of the lines put there by laughter, tears and the passing years. Why hide the honourable trophies of life?

She smiled at her image in the glass, still small, dainty and deceptively fragile. She liked the way Celeste had set her shining white hair. It made her look younger. Not a day over ninety-eight, she thought with a giggle.

'Mum, you're up!' Sophie glanced in cautiously with Celeste at her elbow and a crowd of young ones clustered behind. No doubt they'd all been waiting impatiently for an old woman to waken, Kirsty thought with amusement. An air of expectancy rushed into the room like a stirring breeze. So they were up to something!

Kirsty turned and smiled. 'Of course I'm up. What's up?'

'Behold!' Celeste cried dramatically, flinging the door wide.

Kirsty's hearing, still sharp, picked up the soft rustle of silk in the sudden hush. She waited, hardly breathing, watching the doorway. The young bride came shyly down the corridor. Her relatives fell back to let her pass, murmuring their admiration. She stood for a moment outlined in the doorway, a lovely vision in the white wedding gown and veil worn long ago by another girl, her great-great grandmother. She carried just one red rose plucked that morning from the wintry garden. She presented it to Kirsty, smiling.

'Oh, Great-gran, the dress fits perfectly and it's bang up to date! Isn't that amazing?' she cried.

Kirsty was so moved by this carefully kept surprise that she could hardly trust herself to speak. She held out her hands to Christine, Peter and Maggie's granddaughter. The girl had recently become engaged to a fine young man who had Kirsty's seal of approval.

Christine held the old lady's hands, felt their surprising strength and looked into eyes as softly blue as a December sky.

Kirsty smiled. 'Christine my dear, when you walk down the aisle in April wearing my mother's gown, I'll be so proud and happy I promise I'll dance at your wedding.'

Everyone laughed, and Christine hugged her. 'Dear Great-gran, you're a miracle!'

A miracle? Was she really?

Then Kirsty remembered a grieving, despairing father whose love would not let his tiny infant daughter die. She remembered a remarkable woman who'd fought against the odds to save the sickly baby's life. She looked at her large, extended family, old and young, gathered round her, looking forward to the dawn of a new century. All because of the courage, sacrifice and love of those others gone before.

A miracle? Yes, I'll settle for that, Kirsty decided contentedly.